BLOODY ROSE

"I should warn you," she said. "What we're going up against could be just as dangerous as the Horde. Worse, even."

To Tam, there was nothing worse than the prospect of never leaving home, of being cooped up in Ardburg until her dreams froze and her Wyld Heart withered in its cage. She glanced at her uncle, who gave her a reassuring nod, and was about to tell Freecloud that it didn't matter if they were facing the Horde, or something worse than the Horde, or if they were bound for the Frost Mother's hell itself. She would follow.

"One song," said Rose.

Branigan looked up. "Say what?"

"Take the stage." Rose set a halfpipe between her lips and rooted beneath her armour for something to light it with. Eventually she gave up, and settled for a candle off the table beside her. "Pick a song and play it. Convince me you're the right girl for the job. If I like what I hear, then congratulations: You're Fable's new bard. If I don't..." She exhaled slowly. "What did you say your name was again?"

"Tam."

"Well, in that case, it's been nice knowing you, Tam."

Praise for Nicholas Eames and
Kings of the Wyld

"George R. R. Martin meets Terry Pratchett"

Buzzfeed

"Nicholas Eames is the voice of modern fantasy"
Michael R. Fletcher, author of *Beyond Redemption*

"Fantastic, funny, ferocious. Hugely recommended. Read it now"
Sam Sykes, author of *The City Stained Red*

"A fantastic read, a rollicking, page-turning, edge-of-your-seat road-trip of a book. Great characters, loveable rogues that I genuinely cared about and all manner of fantastical monsters. All spiced with a sly sense of humour that had me smiling throughout. Wonderful"
John Gwynne, author of *Malice*

"Absolutely awesome. If the Beatles held a concert tomorrow (with all the necromancy required for that to happen), it still wouldn't be as good a 'getting the band back together' story as this. Full of heroes, humor, and heart"
Jon Hollins, author of
The Dragon Lords: Fool's Gold

"Nicholas Eames brings brazen fun and a rock & roll sensibility to the fantasy genre"
Sebastien de Castell, author of
The Traitor's Blade

"A fantastic epic fantasy! Just the right smidgen of tongue-in-cheek to work wonderfully. Go read"
Django Wexler, author of *The Thousand Names*

By Nicholas Eames

Kings of the Wyld

Bloody Rose

BLOODY ROSE

NICHOLAS EAMES

orbit

www.orbitbooks.net

ORBIT

First published in Great Britain in 2018 by Orbit

1 3 5 7 9 10 8 6 4 2

Copyright © 2018 by Nicholas Eames

Maps by Tim Paul Illustration

Excerpt from *Age of Assassins* by RJ Barker
Copyright © 2017 by RJ Barker

The moral right of the author has been asserted.

A CIP catalogue record for this book is available from the British Library.

ISBN 978-0-356-50904-4

Printed and bound by CPI Group (UK) Ltd, Croydon, CR0 4YY

Papers used by Orbit are from well-managed forests
and other responsible sources.

Orbit
An imprint of
Little, Brown Book Group
Carmelite House
50 Victoria Embankment
London EC4Y 0DZ

An Hachette UK Company
www.hachette.co.uk

www.orbitbooks.net

For my brother, Tyler.
If this book is worthy of you,
it's because you made it so.

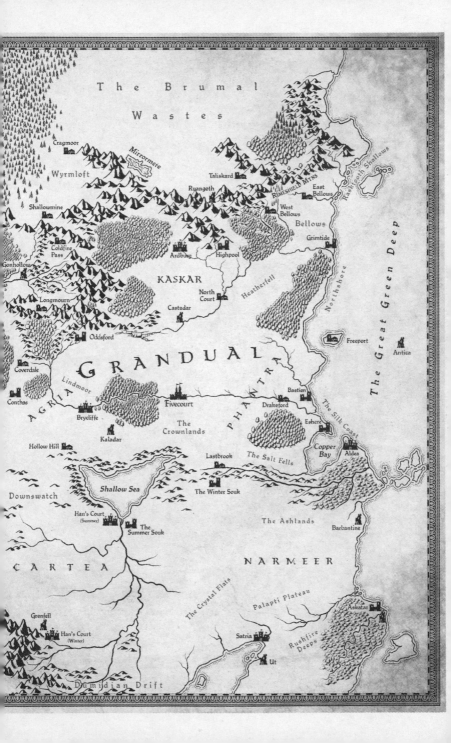

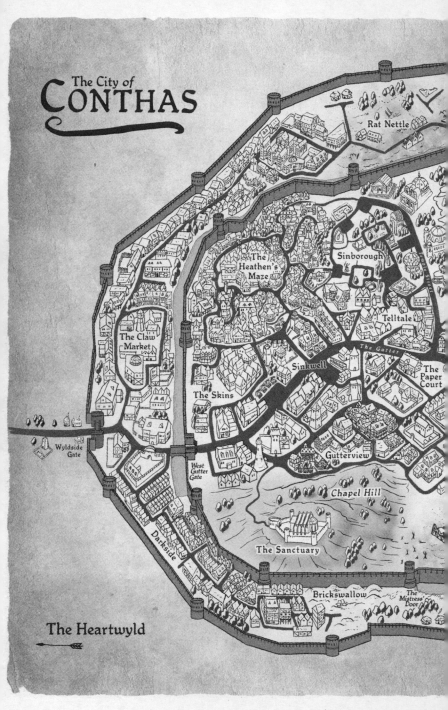

The City of
CONTHAS

Rat Nettle

Sinborough

The
Heathen's
Maze

Telltale

The Claw
Market

The Gutter

Sinkwell

The
Paper
Court

The Skins

Wyldside
Gate

West
Gutter
Gate

Gutterview

Chapel Hill

Darkside

The Sanctuary

Brickswallow

The
Mistress'
Door

The Heartwyld

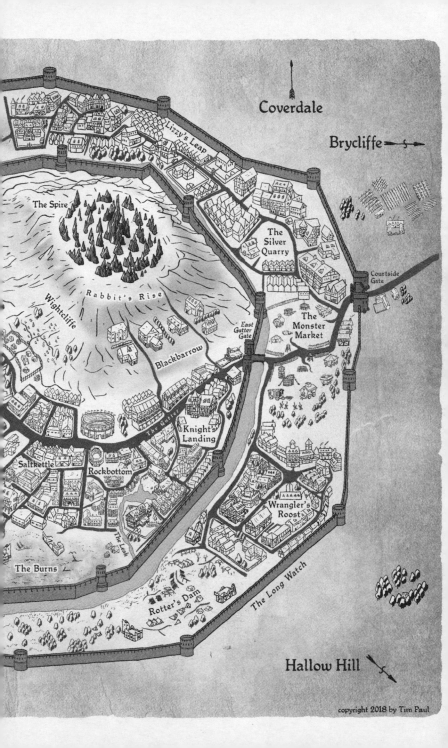

Chapter One

The Monster Market

Tam's mother used to say she had a Wyld Heart. "It means you're a dreamer," she'd told her daughter. "A wanderer, like me."

"It means you ought to be careful," her father had added. "A Wyld Heart needs a wise mind to temper it, and a strong arm to keep it safe."

Her mother had smiled at that. "You're my strong arm, Tuck. And Bran is my wise mind."

"Branigan? You know I love him, Lil, but your brother would eat yellow snow if you told him it tasted like whiskey."

Tam remembered her mother's laughter as a kind of music. Had her father laughed? Probably not. Tuck Hashford had never been much for laughing. Not before his wife's Wyld Heart got her killed, and never once after.

"Girl! Hey, girl!"

Tam blinked. A merchant with whiskered jowls and a fringe of yellowed hair was sizing her up.

"Little young for a wrangler, ain't ya?"

She straightened, as if being taller meant seeming older. "So?"

"So . . ." He scratched a scab on the bald crown of his head. "What brings you to the Monster Market? You in a band or something?"

Tam wasn't a mercenary. She couldn't fight to save her life. Oh, she could fire a bow with passing skill, but anyone with two arms and an arrow to spare could do the same. And besides, Tuck Hashford had a hard-and-fast rule when it came to his only daughter becoming a mercenary and joining a band: *"No fucking way."*

"Yeah," she lied. "I'm in a band."

The man cast a suspicious eye at the tall, skinny girl standing weaponless before him. "Oh yeah? What's it called?"

"Rat Salad."

"Rat Salad?" The man's face lit up like a brothel at dusk. "That's a bloody good name for a band! You fighting in the arena tomorrow?"

"Of course." Another lie. But lies, as her uncle Bran was fond of saying, were like a cup of Kaskar whiskey: If you're in for one, you're in for a dozen. "I'm here to decide what to fight."

"A hands-on sort of woman, eh? Most bands send their bookers to handle the finer details." The merchant nodded appreciatively. "I like your edge! Well, look no further! I've got a beast on hand that'll wow the crowd and have Rat Salad on the tongue of every bard between here and the Summer Souk!" The man shuffled over to a cloth-shrouded cage and tore its sheet off with a flourish. "Behold! The fearsome cockatrice!"

Tam had never seen a cockatrice, but she knew enough about them to know that the thing in the cage was not a cockatrice.

The thing in the cage was a chicken.

"A chicken!?" The merchant looked affronted when Tam told him so. "Girl, are you blind? Look at the size of that thing!"

It was a *big* chicken, no doubt. Its feathers had been daubed in black paint, and its beak was smeared with blood to make it look feral, but Tam wasn't convinced. "A cockatrice can turn flesh into stone with its gaze," she pointed out.

The merchant grinned, a hunter whose quarry had charged headlong into the trap. "Only when it wants to, lass! Any bee can sting, right? But they only sting when they're angry. A skunk always stinks, but it only sprays when you startle it! Ah, but look at this!" He reached into the chicken's cage and brandished a crude stone carving that vaguely resembled a squirrel. Tam decided not to point out the price written in chalk on the bottom. "It's already claimed one victim today! Beware, the—"

"*Bwok*," said the chicken, dismayed by the abduction of its only friend.

An awkward silence stretched between Tam and the merchant.

"I should go," she said.

"Glif's Grace to you," he replied curtly, already throwing the sheet back over the chicken's cage.

Tam wandered farther into the Monster Market, which had been called Bathstone Street before arenas started blooming like mushrooms all over the north and the scale-merchants arrived to set up shop. It was broad and straight, like almost every street in Ardburg, and hedged on either side by wooden pens, iron cages, and dugouts fenced by barbed wire. Most days it wasn't especially crowded, but there were fights in the arena tomorrow, and some of the biggest mercenary bands in Grandual were coming to town.

Tuck Hashford also had a rule about his only daughter going anywhere near the Monster Market, or the arena, or associating with mercenaries in general: "*No fucking way.*"

Despite that, Tam often took this route on her way to work—not because it was quicker, but because it *quickened* something inside of her. It scared her. Thrilled her. Reminded her of the stories her mother used to tell, of daring quests and wild adventure, of fearsome beasts and valiant heroes like her father and Uncle Bran.

Also, since Tam would likely spend her whole life slinging drinks and playing lute for coppers here in wintry Ardburg, a stroll through the Monster Market was the closest she'd ever come to adventure.

"Look here!" called a heavily tattooed Narmeeri woman as Tam passed by. "You want ogres? I've got ogres! Fresh from the hills of Westspring! Fierce as they come!"

"Manticooooooooore!" shouted a northerner with a shaved head and savage scars marring his face. "Manticooooooooore!" There was, indeed, a real live manticore behind him. Its bat-like wings were bound by chains, its barbed tail trapped inside a leather sack. A muzzle was clamped over its leonine jaw, but despite its captivity the creature still managed to look terrifying.

"Wargs of the Winter Forests!" another merchant announced above a chorus of deep growls. "Wyld born, farm raised!"

"Goblins!" an old lady hollered from atop an iron-barred wagon. "Get your goblins here! One courtmark apiece, or a dozen for ten!"

Tam peered into the cage upon which the old woman stood. It was crammed with the filthy little creatures, most of which looked scrawny and malnourished. She doubted even a dozen of them would give a band of half-decent mercenaries a run for their money.

"Hey!" the woman hollered down at her. "This ain't a dress shop, girl. Now buy a bloody goblin or get on with ya!"

Tam tried to imagine what her father would say if she came home with a pet goblin in tow, and couldn't help but grin. "No fucking way," she muttered.

She walked on, weaving through the throng of book-ers and local wranglers as they bartered and bargained with scale-merchants and rugged Kaskar huntsmen. She did her best not to gawk openly at the varied monsters or the merchants peddling them. There were gangly trolls whose severed limbs were capped with silver to prevent them regenerating, and a massive, muscled ettin that was missing one of its two heads. She passed a snake-headed gorgon chained by her neck to brackets in the wall behind her, and a black horse that breathed fire into the face of someone fool enough to inspect its teeth.

"Tam!"

"Willow!" She trotted over to her friend's stall. Willow was an islander from the Silk Coast, bronze-skinned and big for his kind. She'd remarked when they first met that Willow was a curious name for a guy his size, and he'd said it was because a willow tree provided shade to everything around it—which made a lot of sense when he put it that way.

Willow's black curls bounced as he shook his head. "Cutting through the Monster Market again? What would old Tuck say if he found out?"

"I think we both know the answer to that," she said with a grin. "How's business?"

"Booming!" He gestured to his wares, a variety of winged serpents in wicker cages behind him. "Before long every home in Ardburg will have their very own zanto! They make excellent pets, you know. Great with kids, provided those kids don't mind having corrosive acid spat in their faces from time to time. Also, they can't stand the cold up here and will very probably be dead inside a month. Next time I go home I'm bringing back lobsters instead. I could sell lobsters, easy."

Tam nodded, despite having no idea what sort of monster a lobster was.

Willow toyed idly with one of several shell necklaces he was wearing. "Hey, did you hear the news? There's another Horde, apparently. North of Cragmoor, in the Brumal Wastes. Fifty thousand monsters hell-bent on invading Grandual. They say the leader is a giant by the name of—"

"Brontide," Tam finished. "I know. I work in a tavern,

remember? If there's a rumour to be heard, I've heard it. Did you know the Sultana of Narmeer is actually a boy wearing a woman's mask?"

"That can't be true."

"Or that a seamstress who killed her husband down in Rutherford is claiming to be the Winter Queen herself?"

"I seriously doubt that."

"How about the one where—"

The sound of cheering interrupted her. Both of them turned to see a commotion at the nearest cross street, and a smile split Tam's face from ear to ear.

"Looks like the party's come to town," said Willow. Tam shot him a pleading glance and the islander sighed dramatically. "Go," he told her. "Say hi to Bloody Rose for me."

Tam spared her friend a smile before bolting away. She ducked around the bulk of a shaggy yethik, then slipped between a shouting huntsman and a barking wrangler an instant before the huntsman launched a punch that put the wrangler on his ass. She reached the next street as the first argosy was approaching and wormed her way to the front of the crowd.

"Hey, watch where—" A boy her age with a hawkish nose and limp blond hair turned his affronted scowl into what he probably thought was a charming smile. "Ah, sorry. A pretty girl like you can stand wherever she'd like, of course."

Ugh, she thought. "Thanks," she said, choosing a falsely bright smile over an exaggerated eye roll.

"You came to see the mercenaries?" he asked.

No, I came to watch the horses shit, dumbass. "I did," she answered.

"Me too," he said, and then tapped the lute slung over his shoulder. "I'm a bard."

"Oh? With what band?"

"Well, I don't have one yet," he said defensively. "But it's only matter of time."

She nodded distractedly as the lead argosy rolled up. The

massive war wagon was bigger than the house Tam shared with her father. It was draped in leather skins and drawn by a pair of woolly white mammoths with streamers tied to their tusks. The mercenaries to whom it belonged stood around a stout siege tower built on top, waving their weapons at the crowd massed along either side of the avenue.

"That's Giantsbane," said the boy next to her, as if the north's favoured sons required an introduction. The mercenaries—all of them big, bearded Kaskars—were regulars at the tavern where Tam worked, and their leader gave her a wave as the argosy went by. The self-styled bard glanced over, bewildered. "*You* know Alkain Tor?"

Tam did her best to ignore his tone and shrugged. "Sure."

The boy frowned, but said nothing further.

A hundred or so mercenaries on foot and horseback came next, and Tam picked out a few bands she recognized from the Cornerstone commons: the Locksmiths, the Black Puddings, the Boils, and Knightmare—though two of the latter's members were missing and an arachnian in steel plate armour had taken their place.

"Riffraff," sneered the boy. He paused, clearly wanting Tam to ask for clarification. When she didn't, he clarified anyway. "Most of these lesser-knowns will wrestle with trash imps in guildhalls and private arenas tonight. But the bigger bands—Giantsbane, for instance, or Fable—will fight in the Ravine tomorrow, in front of thousands."

"The Ravine?" Tam asked. She knew damn well what the Ravine was, but if this blowhard was gonna talk, then Tam figured she'd might as well choose the subject.

"It's Ardburg's arena," the boy droned on as a caravan of argosies rumbled past, "though it's not much to look at, really. Not a *real* arena, like the ones down south. I was in Fivecourt last summer, you know. Their new arena is the biggest in all the world. They call it—"

"Look!" someone shouted, saving Tam the trouble of

ramming her fist down her new friend's throat in an effort to shut him up. "It's them! It's Fable!"

Rolling up next was an argosy drawn by eight big draft horses in draconic bronze-scale barding. The war wagon was a fortress grinding over sixteen stone wheels, with iron slats on the windows and barbed chain screens hung over the side. The roof was ringed by crenellations of rusted iron, and crossbow turrets were mounted on all four corners.

In her periphery Tam saw the boy straighten and puff out his chest like a bullfrog about to bellow a mating call.

"That's the *Rebel's Redoubt*," Tam said, before this idiot could tell her something else she already knew. "It belongs to Fable, who've only been together for four and a half years but are arguably the most famous mercenary band in the world. You see," she went on, slathering every word in cloying condescension, "most bands only fight in arenas. They tour from town to town, and take on whatever the local wranglers have on hand. Which is great, because everyone, from the wranglers to the bookers to the arena managers—heck, sometimes even the mercs themselves—get paid, and the rest of us get a hell of a show. *Mercs* is short for mercenaries, by the way."

The boy gaped. "I know th—"

"But Fable," Tam cut him off, "well, they do things the old way. They still tour, obviously, but they also take on contracts that most other bands wouldn't dare. They've hunted giants and burned pirate fleets to cinders. They've killed sand maws in Dumidia, and once slew a firbolg king right here in Kaskar."

She pointed to a barrel-chested northerner sitting between two crenellations, his tangle of brown hair obscuring most of his face. "That's Brune. He's sort of a local legend. He's a vargyr."

"A vargyr...?"

"We call them shamans," Tam explained. "He can change at will into a great big bear. Now, the one in black with half her head shaved and tattoos all over? She's a sorceress. A summoner, actually. Her name's Cura, but people call her the Inkwitch. And see the druin, Freecloud? He's the tall one with green hair and ears like a rabbit? They say he's the very last of his kind, and that he's never made a wager he didn't win, and that his sword, *Madrigal*, can cut through steel like it was silk."

The boy's face had gone an extremely gratifying shade of scarlet. "Okay, listen," he said, except Tam was all done listening.

"And that"—she pointed to the woman standing with one boot on the battlement above them—"is Bloody Rose. She's the leader of Fable, the saviour of the city of Castia, and very probably the most dangerous woman this side of the Heartwyld."

Tam fell silent as the argosy's shadow enveloped them. She'd never actually seen Bloody Rose before, but she knew every story, had heard every song, and had seen the warrior's likeness on walls or sketched on posters around town, though chalk and charcoal hardly did the real thing justice.

Fable's frontwoman wore a piecemeal suit of dull black plate slashed with red—except her gauntlets, which gleamed like new steel. They were druin-forged (or so the songs alleged) and matched to the scimitars—*Thistle* and *Thorn*—she wore in scabbards on either hip. Her hair was dyed a bright, bloody red, and hacked off at the hard line of her chin.

Half the girls in town had the same cut, the same colour. Tam herself had gone so far as to buy a sack of hucknell beans, which bled their crimson coats when soaked in water, but her father had guessed her intent and demanded she eat them one by one in front of him. They'd tasted like lemons with a cinnamon rind, and had left her lips, tongue, and teeth so red it looked as if she'd torn the throat out of a deer. Her hair, for all the trouble she'd gone to, remained the unremarkable brown it had always been.

The argosy passed, leaving Tam to blink like a dreamer roused by the slanting afternoon light.

Beside her, the boy had finally found his voice, though he cleared his throat before trying it out. "Wow, you really know your stuff, huh? Do you want to, uh, grab a drink at the Cornerstone?"

"The Cornerstone..."

"Yeah, it's just—"

Tam was off, sprinting as fast as her legs would carry her. Not only was she hopelessly late for work, but her father, naturally, had yet another rule when it came to his daughter going for drinks with strange boys.

Which suited Tam just fine, since she was into girls, anyway.

Chapter Two

The Cornerstone

There were four people you could always find at the Cornerstone.

The first was Tera, who owned the place. She'd been a mercenary herself before losing her arm. "I didn't bloody lose it!" she'd say, whenever someone asked how it happened. "A bugbear tore it off and cooked it on a spit while I watched! I know exactly where it is—it's inside his damned dead body!" She was a big, broad woman, who used her remaining hand to rule her tavern with an iron fist. When she wasn't cussing out the kitchen or dressing down the serving staff, she spent her nights discouraging fights (often by threatening to start one) and swapping stories with some of the older mercs.

Her husband, Edwick, was always there as well. He'd been the bard for a band called Vanguard, but was now retired. He took the stage each night to recount the exploits of his former crew, and seemed to know every song and story ever told. Ed was the opposite of his wife: slight of frame, cheerful as a child on a pony's back. He'd been close friends with Tam's mother, and despite Tuck Hashford's rule concerning his daughter playing an instrument or consorting with musicians, the old bard often gave Tam lute lessons after work.

Next was Tiamax, who'd been a member of Vanguard as well. He was an arachnian, which meant he had eight eyes (two of which were missing, covered by crisscrossing patches) and six hands with which to shake, stir, and serve drinks. Consequently, he made for an excellent bartender. According to Edwick, he'd been one hell of a fighter, too.

The last permanent fixture in the Cornerstone was her uncle Bran. In his youth, Branigan had been an illustrious mercenary, a prodigious drinker, and a notorious scoundrel. But now, almost ten years after his sister's untimely death had brought about the dissolution of his old band, he was . . . Well, he was still a thief, still a drunk, and an even more notorious scoundrel, though he'd since added compulsive gambling to his list of vices.

He and Tam's father had spoken rarely over the past decade. One had lost a sister in Lily Hashford, the other a wife, and grief had led them each down very different paths.

"Tam!" her uncle shouted at her from the second-floor balcony directly above the bar. "Be a darling and fetch me a dram, will you?"

Tam set the stack of empty bowls she'd collected on the stained wooden bar. The tavern was busier than usual tonight. Mercenaries, and those come to rub shoulders with them, crowded the commons behind her. Three hearths were roaring, two fights were in progress, and a shirtless bard was beating a drum like it owed him money.

"Uncle Bran wants another whiskey," she said to Tiamax.

"Does he?" The arachnian snatched up the bowls and began rinsing them with four hands, while his remaining two cracked open a wooden shaker and poured something fragrant and rose-coloured into a long-stemmed glass.

"What is this?" asked the woman he'd made it for.

"Pink."

"Pink?" She sniffed it. "It smells like cat pee."

"Then order a fucking beer next time," said Tiamax. The mandibles sprouting from his white-bristled chin twitched in irritation. One of them had snapped in half, so the sound they made was a blunted click instead of the melodious scratching others of his kind produced. The woman sniffed and sauntered off, while the arachnian used a rag to dry three bowls at once. "And how will your uncle Bran be paying for that whiskey, I wonder?"

"Tell him to put it on my tab!" came Bran's voice from the balcony above.

She offered Tiamax a tight smile. "He says to put it on his tab."

"Ah, yes! The inexhaustible tab of Branigan Fay!" Tiamax threw up all six of his arms in exasperation. "Alas, I'm afraid that line of credit is completely and utterly exhausted."

"Says who?" demanded the disembodied voice of her uncle.

"Says who?" Tam repeated.

"Says Tera."

"Tell that bastard hatcher I'll handle Tera!" yelled Bran. "Besides, I'm about to sweep the board up here!"

Tam sighed. "Uncle Bran says—"

"Bastard hatcher?" The bartender's mandibles clacked again, and Tam caught a malicious glint in the manifold facets of his eyes. "One whiskey!" he exclaimed. "Coming right up!" He chose a cup off the counter behind him and reached up with one segmented arm to retrieve a bottle from the very top shelf. It was coated in mouldering grime and thick with cobwebs. When Tiamax pulled the stopper free it fairly disintegrated in his hand.

"What is that?" Tam asked.

"Oh, it's whiskey. Or near enough, anyway. We found six cases of this in the cellar of Turnstone Keep while the Ferals had us trapped inside."

Like every ex-mercenary Tam knew (except, of course, her dad), Tiamax rarely missed an opportunity to recount a story from his adventuring days.

"We tried drinking it," the arachnian was saying, "but

not even Matty could keep it down, so we turned them into bombs instead." The stuff trickled from the bottle's mouth like honey, except it looked and smelled like raw sewage. "Here. Tell your uncle it's on the house, courtesy of *that bastard hatcher*."

Tam eyed the cup skeptically. "You promise he won't die?"

"He almost certainly will not die." The bartender placed a spindly hand over his chest. "I swear on my cephalothorax."

"Your seffawha—"

Tera came bursting through the kitchen door wielding a sauce-stained wooden spoon as though it were a bloody cudgel.

"You!" She levelled her makeshift weapon at a pair of burly mercs wrestling on the rushes in front of a fireplace. "Can't you read the bloody sign?" Lacking another arm with which to point, Tera used the spoon to draw their attention to an etched wooded board above the bar, and even deigned to read it to them. "No fighting before midnight! This is a civilized establishment, not a godsdamned brawling pit."

She started toward them, patrons scrambling from her path like she was a boulder rolling downhill.

"Thanks, Max." Tam seized the cup and fell in behind the proprietress, using the swathe she cleared to cross half the commons before plunging back into the mob. Tera, meanwhile, had kicked one fighter into a curling ball and was thrashing the other's ass with the wooden spoon.

Tam slipped, slithered, and sidestepped her way toward the balcony stair, pilfering gossip like an urchin picking pockets in a market square. A trio of merchants were discussing the early frost that had wiped out most of Kaskar's harvest. They'd got rich importing provisions from Fivecourt. One of them made a jest about paying tribute to the Winter Queen, which drew a hearty laugh from the northerner on his right, while the Narmeeri on his left gasped and traced the Summer Lord's circle over his breast.

Many were discussing who would fight in the Ravine

tomorrow, and, perhaps more importantly, *what* they'd be squaring off against. Fable, she heard, had opted to let the local wranglers decide, and rumour was they had something special in store.

Most of the conversations swirled around the host of monsters assembling north of Cragmoor. *The Brumal Horde*, they dubbed it, and everyone—from fighters to farmers—had an opinion as to what its intentions were.

"Revenge!" said a merc with a mouthful of something black and gummy. "Obviously! They're still sore about getting their asses kicked at Castia six years ago! They'll try again next summer, mark my words!"

"They won't attack Castia," insisted a woman with a white spider tattoo covering most of her face. "It's too far away, and too well defended. If you ask me it's Ardburg needs to worry. The marchlords better keep their men sharp and their axes sharper!"

"This Brontide fellow..." mused Lufane, a skyship captain who made a living taking nobles on sightseeing tours above the Rimeshield Mountains. "Word is he's got a mighty grudge against us."

"Us?" asked spider-face.

"Everyone. Humans in general." The captain drained the last of his wine and handed his bowl off to Tam as she went by. "According to Brontide, *we're* the monsters. He led a raid over the mountains a few years back and smashed to rubble every arena he could find."

The first merc flashed a black-toothed sneer at that. "A giant calling *us* monsters? Well, it don't much matter what he thinks, does it? The day after tomorrow every band in the north'll be bound for Cragmoor, lusting for glory and looking to make a name for themselves. The Brumal Horde'll be nothing but bones in the muck come spring," he was saying as Tam moved on, "but the bards'll be crowing about it for the rest of their lives."

She skirted the stage. The drummer had finished up, and now Edwick sat perched on a stool with his lute in his lap. He spared her a wink before starting into *The Siege of Hollow Hill*, which drew a chorus of cheers from the commons crowd. They liked songs about battles, especially ones where the heroes were hopelessly outnumbered by their enemies.

Tam loved the old man's voice. It was weathered and warbly, comfortable as a pair of soft leather boots. Besides teaching her to play the lute, Edwick had been giving Tam singing lessons as well, and his assessment of her vocal prowess had ranged from "Careful, you'll break the glassware," to "At least they won't drag you offstage," before finally she'd garnered an approving smile and the murmured words, "Not bad. Not bad at all."

That had been a good night. Tam had returned home wishing she could share her joy with her dad, but Tuck Hashford would not have approved. He didn't want his daughter singing, or playing the lute, or listening to the lionised tales of retired bards. If not for the wage she brought home, and the fact that he'd had trouble holding down a job since his wife's death, Tam doubted she'd be allowed anywhere near the Cornerstone at all.

Bran glanced over as she approached. "Tam!" He thumped the table with an open palm, scattering coins and toppling the carved wooden figurines on the Tetrea board before him. His opponent—a hooded man with his back to Tam—sighed, and her uncle made a poor attempt at feigning innocence. "Oh, dear, I've accidentally upset the pieces. Let's call it a draw, Cloud, shall we?"

"Is a draw where one person is about to win and the other cheats to avoid losing?"

Bran shrugged. "Either one of us might have prevailed."

"I was *definitely* about to prevail," said his opponent. "Brune? Back me up here?"

Brune?

Tam stopped where she stood, gaping like a baby bird beneath a dangling worm. Sure enough, the man sitting to her uncle's left was Brune. As in *the* Brune. As in *Fable's fucking shaman*, Brune. Legend or no, the vargyr looked like most other northmen: He was big and broad-shouldered, with shaggy brown hair that did its damndest to hide the fact that Brune wasn't much to look at. His brows were wildly unkempt, his nose was crooked, and there was a finger-wide gap between his two front teeth.

"I wasn't paying attention," the shaman admitted. "Sorry."

Tam's mind was still reeling, struggling to make sense of what her eyes were telling it. *If that's Brune,* she reasoned, *then the man in the cloak . . . the one Bran called Cloud . . .*

The figure turned, drawing back his hood to reveal long ears pressed flat against green-gold hair. Tam's mind barely registered the ears, however, or the druin's pointed, predator smile. She was pinned by his gaze: half-moons hooked against a colour like candlelight glancing through the facets of an emerald.

"Hello, Tam."

He knows my name! How does he know my name? Had her uncle said it earlier? Probably. Definitely. Yes. Tam was shaking; ripples shuddered across the surface of the Turnstone whiskey in her trembling hand.

"Branigan here has been telling us all about you," said the druin. "He says you can sing, and that you're something of a prodigy with the lute."

"He drinks," said Tam.

The shaman laughed, splurting a mouthful of beer over the table and the Tetrea board. "He drinks." Brune chuckled. "Classic."

Freecloud produced a white moonstone coin and examined one side of it. "Brune and I are mercenaries. We're members of a band called Fable. You've heard of us, I assume?"

"I . . . uh . . ."

"She has," Bran came to her rescue. "Of course she has. Isn't that right, Tam?"

"Right," Tam managed. She felt as though she'd wandered out onto a frozen lake and suddenly the ice was groaning beneath her.

"Well," said Freecloud, "it so happens we're in the market for a bard. And according to Branigan you're just what we're looking for. Assuming, of course, you're willing to get a little mud on your boots."

"Mud on my boots?" Tam asked, watching cracks spider-web across the ice in her mind's eye. *Uncle Bran, what have you done?*

"He means travel," Bran told her. There was something thick in his voice, a sheen to his eyes that had nothing to do with being shitfaced drunk. At least she didn't think it did. "A real adventure, Tam."

"Ah." Freecloud's chair scraped as he stood. The coin in his hand disappeared as he gestured behind her. "Here's the boss herself. Tam," he said, as she turned to find a legend in the flesh just an arm's reach away, "this is Rose."

So that was it for Tam's knees.

As they buckled beneath her, Bran leapt from his chair. He reached her in time to pluck the cup from her hands before she collapsed. "That was close," she heard him say, as the floorboards rushed up to meet her.

"She's too young," someone said. A woman's voice. Harsh. "What is she, sixteen?"

"Seventeen." That was her uncle. "I think. The edge of seventeen, anyway."

"Not the sharp edge," grumbled the woman. Rose. It had to be.

Tam blinked, got an eyeful of glaring torchlight, and decided to lie still a moment longer.

"And how old were you when you picked up a sword?" asked Freecloud. She could *hear* the wryness in the druin's smile. "Or when you killed that cyclops?"

A sigh. "Well, what about this?" Armour clinking. "She fainted at the sight of me. What will she do when blood gets spilled?"

"She'll be fine," said her uncle. "She's Tuck and Lily's girl, remember."

"Tuck Hashford?" Brune sounded impressed. "They say he was fearless. And we've all got a bit of our fathers in us. The gods know I do."

"Our mothers, too," said a woman Tam didn't recognize. "Does she even want to go? Have you asked her?"

You do, said a voice in Tam's head.

"I do," she croaked. She sat up, instantly regretting it. The noise of the Cornerstone commons screeched in her skull like a boat full of cats. The four members of Fable stood around her. Bran was kneeling by her side. "I want to go," she insisted. "Where . . . uh . . . are we going?"

"Someplace cold," said the woman who wasn't Rose. It was the Inkwitch, Cura, who regarded Tam as if she'd found the girl squished on the bottom of her boot.

Where Rose was sturdy with lean muscle, Cura was waif-thin and wiry. She wore a long, low-slung tunic cut high on the hip, and black leather boots boasting more straps than a madman's jacket. Her fine black hair was long enough to tie back, but shaved to stubble on either side. There were bone rings in her ears, another through her left eyebrow, and a stud in her nose. Her skin was porcelain pale and crowded with tattoos. Tam's eye was drawn to a sea creature inked on Cura's thigh, its serpentine tentacles curling out from beneath the hem of her tunic.

The Inkwitch caught her staring and gave the cloth an inviting tug. "You ever see one up close?" Her impish tone implied that she wasn't referring to the creature tattooed on her leg.

Tam looked away, hoping her sudden flush was attributed to her fall. "You're going to fight the Brumal Horde?" she asked.

"We're not," said Rose. "We're finishing our tour first, and after that we have a contract in Diremarch."

"Our *final* contract," said Freecloud. He shared a meaningful look with his bandmates. "One last gig before we call it quits."

Branigan perked up at that, but before either he or Tam could ask anything further, Rose cut in. "I should warn you," she said. "What we're going up against could be just as dangerous as the Horde. Worse, even."

To Tam, there *was* nothing worse than the prospect of never leaving home, of being cooped up in Ardburg until her dreams froze and her Wyld Heart withered in its cage. She glanced at her uncle, who gave her a reassuring nod, and was about to tell Freecloud that it didn't matter if they were facing the Horde, or something worse than the Horde, or if they were bound for the Frost Mother's hell itself. She would follow.

"One song," said Rose.

Branigan looked up. "Say what?"

"Take the stage." Rose set a halfpipe between her lips and rooted beneath her armour for something to light it with. Eventually she gave up, and settled for a candle off the table beside her. "Pick a song and play it. Convince me you're the right girl for the job. If I like what I hear, then congratulations: You're Fable's new bard. If I don't..." She exhaled slowly. "What did you say your name was again?"

"Tam."

"Well, in that case, it's been nice knowing you, Tam."

Chapter Three

One Song

Around midnight a train of linked carriages hauled by sturdy Kaskar ponies clattered across Ardburg. It was free to ride, and spared drunks and those abroad late a long walk through often inclement weather. Tam flagged it out front of the Cornerstone and chose a carriage she thought was empty. It wasn't. There was a city watchman passed out on the opposite bench. His helmet was overturned in his lap, and from the reek Tam guessed it was filled with vomit. She pushed open the screens despite the cold, and once they were moving it didn't smell so bad.

The city was usually asleep this time of night, but since the fights were the next day, the streets were lively still. Light and noise spilled out of every inn, music from every tavern. The brothels, especially, were busier than usual, and from behind their drawn curtains Tam heard yelps of pleasure and pain, often mingling.

She saw a pair of black-robed priests cupping their hands to catch the falling snow. "The Winter Queen is coming!" cried one, a woman with her scalp shaved bare. This wasn't really news to anyone. According to her disciples, the Winter Queen (and the Eternal Winter said to accompany her return) was *always* coming. Tam figured those priests would be as surprised as everyone else if she actually decided to show up one day.

At last they left the chaos behind. Tam sat alone with her thoughts, and with the snoring soldier, of whom she asked the question that had been on her mind since leaving the Cornerstone earlier that evening.

"What the hell just happened?"

Tam approached the stage. She didn't even have an instrument. What sort of bard didn't own an instrument?

You're not a bard, she reminded herself. *You're a girl who's about to embarrass herself in front of two hundred people, including Bloody Rose herself.*

A glance toward the balcony told her Rose was watching, still dragging on the halfpipe she'd lit earlier. Freecloud was beside her, Brune and Cura farther along the rail. Word that Fable was auditioning a new bard had swept the room like a brushfire. Now that the racket was starting to dwindle, Tam would be expected to take the stage and sing a song that might or might not change the course of her life forever after.

Tera and Tiamax were watching from behind the bar. The arachnian offered her a three-handed wave and shouted, "You've got this!" over the din.

Bran was shooing patrons from the table closest to the stage, while Edwick—

"Here." The old bard thrust his lute into her hands. "This is yours now."

"No, I can't," she protested. The lute, which the bard referred to as *Red Thirteen*, was the instrument on which Tam had learned to play. It was Ed's pride and joy. He'd had it for as long as Tam could remember, and had never played another instrument that she knew of.

"Take her," he insisted. "Trust her. Do you know what song you'll play?"

Tam knew a hundred songs, but just now she couldn't recall even one of them. She shook her head.

"Well, good luck." Edwick retreated to a seat beside Bran, and the entire tavern suddenly hushed all at once.

Cradling her borrowed lute, Tam stepped onto the stage and crossed to the vacant stool. The boards squealed beneath her feet, impossibly loud. Her mind was racing, trying desperately to think of a song—any song—let alone one that would impress Rose.

And then she had it: *Castia*. It was rowdy and rousing, guaranteed to get the crowd on her side. It condensed the Battle of Castia, during which Grandual's mercenaries had overcome the Duke of Endland and his Heartwyld Horde, into seven verses and an instrumental solo Tam hoped to hell she was capable of pulling off.

Better still, it painted Rose's father, Golden Gabe, as the greatest hero in the five courts, without even mentioning that he'd crossed the entire breadth of the Heartwyld to rescue his daughter from almost certain death, or that Gabe and his bandmates, in the process of getting there, had cured the rot, killed a dragon, and destroyed half of Fivecourt. The last verse was dedicated to Rose herself, who'd led those besieged inside the city to victory at last.

Castia was perfect.

She took a breath. Waited for the silence to deepen, the way Edwick had taught her to, and then—

"Pfffft! The fuck is this!?" Branigan was standing, having sipped his whiskey before spewing it onto his lap. "What in the cold heart of hell did you put in here, Max? Lamp oil? Piss? Gods, is this hatcher piss?" He sniffed it, and went so far as to taste it again. "It's bloody awful!" Edwick dragged him down into his seat and hissed at him to shut up. "Sorry," he told the room. "Sorry, Tam. Go on, love."

Tam took another breath. Waited, again, for that utter silence to descend, and then plucked the opening chords of *Castia*.

A roar of approval went up from the commons. A great big smile broke across Branigan's face, and Edwick nodded approvingly. When Tam looked to the balcony, though, Rose seemed uninterested. She stamped her halfpipe out on the rail and said something under her breath to Freecloud. The shaman, Brune, pulled his long hair aside. He locked eyes with Tam and shook his head so slightly it was almost, *almost*, imperceptible.

She stopped. The song's opening notes were left shivering in the air. A confused murmur arose and left behind a bewildered hush.

"Can I start over?" she called up to Rose.

The mercenary's eyes narrowed. "If you'd like."

Tam closed her eyes, aware that her hands were trembling, that her foot was tapping nervously at the boards beneath her. She could hear her heart pounding, feel her blood rushing, see her dream of leaving Ardburg in Fable's company lingering by the door, already clenching its cloak against the cold outside.

Tam thought of her father, of how furious he'd be if he could see her now.

She thought of her mother, of how proud she'd be if she could see her now.

Before she knew it her fingers had picked out a melody, slow and soft and sad.

It was one of her mother's songs. Tam's favourite. Her father's, too, once upon a time. She was forbidden to play it, of course. She'd tried singing it to herself once, shortly after her mother's death, but grief had overwhelmed her, stifling her voice with sobs.

Now it spilled out of her. The lute sang beneath her fingertips and her words sailed toward the rafters like floating lanterns set loose on a summer night.

The song was called *Together*. It wasn't rowdy, or rousing. It didn't garner a cheer as she played it, and her uncle's expression (Edwick's, too) was mournful. As the song went on, though, the ghost of a smile haunted his lips. *Together* wasn't about a battle. There were no monsters in it. No one was slain and nothing at all was vanquished.

It was, instead, a love letter from a bard to her band. It was about the little moments, the quiet words, the unspoken bond shared by men and women who eat and sleep and fight alongside one another, day after day. It was about a band-mate's laughter, a bunkmate's snoring. Lily Hashford had dedicated a whole verse to describing her husband's sidelong smile, and another decrying the smell of Bran's socks when he pulled his boots off.

"They're my lucky socks," she heard her uncle confess to the old bard beside him. "I'm still wearin' 'em!"

Another unique aspect of *Together* was that the music ended before the words, so that Tam sang the last refrain with her lute in her lap. Her hands were motionless, her foot was still. Her aching heart beat a slow and steady cadence inside her.

The song ended, and you could hear the candles flicker in the silence that followed.

As one, two hundred heads turned to the balcony above. Brune and Cura were watching Rose. Freecloud was looking down at Tam. He was grinning, Tam saw, because he already knew.

"Welcome to Fable," said Rose.

And the crowd went wild.

Tam tugged the bell cord. When the carriage came to a stop she hopped out and called her thanks to the driver. Home was a short walk away, but she took her time. She bowed her head against the blowing snow and stepped carefully over cobbles slick with ice. Edwick's *Red Thirteen* was cradled in her arms like a suckling babe. The Cornerstone's bard had insisted she keep it, and when Tam refused—because she couldn't deprive him of his most cherished possession—he scurried into the back and returned with a near-identical instrument he dubbed *Red Fourteen*. So that was that.

Tam had never owned an instrument of her own before. As a girl, she'd assumed she would one day inherit her mother's lute, *Hiraeth*. But when her mother died, *Hiraeth* had disappeared as well. Likely, her father had destroyed it, or else sold it off so the sight of it wouldn't haunt him.

Uncle Bran had warned her against going home at all.

"Stay here tonight," he begged. "Or sleep in the argosy. I'll go by your place in the morning and sort things out with Tuck. I'll say it was me who asked Fable to take you on."

"It *was* you."

The old rogue considered that a moment. "Gods of Grandual, your old man's gonna kill me. My point is: If there's hell to pay, let me pay it."

There *would* be hell to pay—Tam was sure of it—but no matter how estranged she and Tuck had become these last few years, she couldn't leave without saying good-bye.

Bran regarded her sadly. "You've got a fire in you, Tam. I can see it in your eyes. I can feel it rollin' off you, hot as a hearth. I know Tuck, and if you take that fire home, he'll smother it. He'll snuff it out and stamp it to ash." When Tam only shrugged her uncle shook his head. "I'll drink to your valour, then," he said, and quaffed what remained of the horrid Turnstone whiskey. "You know, this stuff ain't so bad once you're used it."

Tam paused outside the door to her home, steeling herself for the ordeal ahead. She heard a meow from inside; Threnody, heralding her arrival. When she finally worked up the courage to enter, the cat threw herself against Tam's boot and purred contentedly.

Her father was sitting at the kitchen table, nursing a mug

of what she hoped was just beer. He was staring at nothing and toying absently with a strip of yellow ribbon.

"What did I tell you about putting bows on the cat?" he asked.

Tam shook off her cloak and hung it by the door, then knelt to scratch Threnody behind the ears. She was rewarded with another throaty purr. Thren was a long-haired Palapti, white as fresh snowfall. Tam's mother had brought her home from a tour down south. "But she looks so cute with it on there."

"She looks ridiculous. Don't—" He trailed off as she stood, his glare fastened to the instrument in Tam's arms.

"What's that for?" he asked.

"Playing music," Tam answered. *Great start*, she berated herself. *Way to butter him up.*

"Why do you have it?" he clarified.

"Ed gave it to me."

Tuck's perpetual frown deepened. "Well, you've no need of it. You'll return it tomorrow."

"I won't."

"You will—"

"I can't."

"Can't?" Her father looked suspicious. "Why *can't*?"

Outside, the wind picked up. It pummelled the walls and clawed at the windows with ice-cold fingers. Threnody finished circling Tam's foot and trotted over to her water bowl, oblivious to the tension in the room. Or maybe she just didn't care. Cats could be assholes sometimes, and Thren was no exception.

"Fable's in town," she said. "They were at the Cornerstone tonight. Uncle Bran—" She saw her father's knuckles go white, no doubt wishing the mug in his hands was Branigan's throat. "They mentioned they were looking for a bard, and Bran told them I could play . . ."

"Can you, now?" Her father's tone was breezy, conversational. That's when she knew he was *really angry*. "Self-taught, are you? A born natural? You haven't picked up a lute since . . . well, since you were little."

"Ed's been teaching me after work," she admitted. Boy, she was throwing everyone under the argosy's wheels tonight, wasn't she? She'd might as well confess that Tera had been giving her archery lessons twice a week, or that Tiamax poured her a beer at the end of every shift—that way her father could plot the murder of *everyone* in the Cornerstone.

"Is that so?" Tuck downed what remained in his mug and stood. "Then when you return his lute tomorrow you can let Ed know you're quitting. They need extra hands at the mill. You can start next week."

"I already quit," she told him, irritated by the dismissiveness in his tone. "I'm Fable's bard now."

"No you're not."

"Yes I am."

"Tam." His voice grew stern.

"Dad—"

His mug exploded against the far wall. Threnody bolted from the room as shards rained to the floor.

She said nothing, only waited for his rage to subside. He slumped back into his chair. "I'm sorry, Tam. I can't let you go. I can't risk losing you, too."

"So, what?" she asked. "I'm supposed to stay in Ardburg my whole life? Work at the mill for a few lousy courtmarks a week? Find some nice, boring girl to settle down with?"

"There's nothing—wait, *girl*?"

"Maiden's Mercy, Dad, are we really doing this now?"

"That doesn't matter," Tuck said. "Listen, this is our fault. I know that. Your mother and I told you too many stories. We made being a merc sound more glamorous than it is. It's a hard life, you know. Long roads, lonely nights. You're wet half the time, cold all the time, and then you fight some horrible thing in some awful place, and you're scared shitless it'll kill you before you kill it. It's not like in the songs, Tam. Mercenaries aren't heroes. They're killers."

Tam moved to join him at the table. She set the lute down and took her seat. The chair between them—her mother's chair—remained empty as a chasm.

"Things are different now," she said, laying her hand over his. "We'll be touring arenas, mostly. I'll probably never see the inside of a monster's lair or set foot in the Heartwyld."

Her father shook his head, unconvinced. "There's a Horde north of Cragmoor, the remnants of those who survived Castia. Rose'll want her crack at it, sure as hell is cold. Ain't nobody loves glory like that girl. Except maybe her father. Gods, that guy was a piece of work."

"Rose wants nothing to do with it."

That caught him by surprise. "Really?"

Tam shrugged. "Fable's going to finish the last leg of their tour. They've got fights in every town between here and Highpool, and a contract in Diremarch after that."

"Diremarch? What's the contract?"

"I don't know. But whatever it is, I'll be a thousand miles away from the Brumal Horde." She had no idea whether that was true or not. She wasn't even sure where Diremarch was. Her father seemed halfway convinced, however, so she didn't bother mentioning Rose's warning: that whatever they were going up against might be just as dangerous as the Horde itself.

For a while her father's gaze remained fixed on the floor, roving the scatter of clay shards as though trying to decide whether or not he could piece them together again. As the silence stretched, Tam dared to hope she'd found the chink in the impenetrable armour of Tuck Hashford's embittered cynicism.

"No," he said finally. "You're not going."

"But—"

"I don't care," he said leadenly. "Whatever you're going to say, whatever reasons you think will justify leaving . . . None of them matter. Not to me. You don't get a say in this, Tam. I'm sorry."

I should have listened to Bran, she thought. *I should have left without saying good-bye.* The fire inside her was waning, and Tam feared it would go out forever if she didn't act now.

She stood and set out for the door. Chips of clay crunched beneath her boots.

"Tam . . ."

"I'll stay at the Cornerstone tonight." She pulled her cloak off its peg.

"Tam, *sit down*."

"We're heading for the arena first thing in the morning," she said, doing her best to keep the tremor from her voice, "and we start east the morning after. I doubt I'll see you before then, so I guess this is . . ." She turned, and froze.

Her father was standing, staring down at the object in his hands: the lute she'd left behind on the table. It looked small, so impossibly fragile, as though her dream of joining a band and following in her mother's footsteps—of escaping this city, this house, this prison of sorrow and its grief-stricken jailor—were but a toy in the grasp of a malevolent child.

"Dad . . ."

He looked up. Their eyes met. In hers, a plea. In his, a black rage rising. Something—another apology, perhaps—died on his lips, and then her father took her lute by its neck and smashed her dream to splinters.

Chapter Four

The Wyld Heart

Tam had a vague recollection of falling to her knees amidst the wreckage of her lute. Her father stood over her, his shadow thrown by lamplight in every direction. He was speaking, but she couldn't make out the words over the shrill roar in her ears. She was hoisted to her feet and dragged down the hall to her room, where she collapsed on the bed like a prisoner granted rest between sessions of torture. She glared at his silhouette framed in the hallway's dim light, and whispered (because she, too, was capable of monstrous cruelty), "I wish you had died instead of her."

His shadow slumped. "So do I," he said, and shut the door between them.

She cried for a while, great racking sobs that soaked her pillow, and once she screamed at the top of her lungs. Somewhere beyond her window a lonely trash imp echoed her cry.

Shortly after, Tam could have sworn she heard the muffled sound of her father's voice from his room on the other side of her wall. At times, when he was wildly drunk, he would rant at length, cursing himself and everyone he'd ever known. This was different. It sounded as though he was pleading with someone, arguing a lost cause against an intractable judge, and then he, too, fell to weeping, which wasn't uncommon at all.

Eventually, she slept.

When Tam awoke, the door was ajar. Threnody was nestled in the crook of her chin; the cat's tail tickled her nose, and when Tam dared to move the little jerk swatted her cheek. Dawn light filtered through the frosted pane of her window, painting the opposite wall in whorls of light and dark.

Tam lay there for a time, wondering if she would ever escape this place. It wouldn't be today. Her lute was destroyed, and she wasn't about to ask Edwick if he happened to have another she could borrow. She couldn't go to Fable empty-handed, and it wouldn't matter anyway, since Tam doubted even Bloody Rose could (or would) stand in Tuck's way when he came to take her back.

Instead, she would work at the Cornerstone or at the mill with her father—it didn't matter. She would squirrel away every coin she could spare until she had enough to get herself as far from Ardburg as possible.

She could hear Tuck bustling around the house: chopping in the kitchen, scraping something raw on the washboard, sweeping splinters and shards off the kitchen floor. Soon she smelled bacon frying and gods-be-damned if her stomach didn't demand she get up and eat. She clambered out of bed, got dressed, and padded out into the kitchen with the cat at her heels.

She spent a confused moment taking in the scene: laundry—*her* laundry—hissing itself dry on the flat top of the woodstove, a rucksack half-packed by the door, her father kneeling before the hearth doing his best to manage two pans at once. He glanced over his shoulder when Threnody announced their arrival with a tentative meow.

"Morning."

"What is this?" she asked.

"This," said Tuck, "is breakfast." He set a slab of toasted bread on a plate and heaped it with twists of almost-burnt bacon. He topped that with diced tomato and altogether too many brown onions, then set it on the table. "Sit. Eat. Please," he added, when she remained exactly where she was.

She sat. She ate. *Snakes on Fire* had been her mother's specialty, though she'd made it with considerably more finesse than this. Was it supposed to be a peace offering? *Sorry I dashed your hopes and ruined your whole life, dear. Here's the bottom half of a bacon sandwich . . .*

Her father vanished before she could ask him about it, or about the rucksack, or why he'd decided to wash her socks at the crack of dawn. Threnody nosed the door and whined until Tam let her out. When she turned back her father was standing across the table with a sealskin lute case in his hands.

"Is that . . ."

"*Hiraeth*. It belonged to your mother."

She knew that. Of course she knew that. Her mother once claimed that *Hiraeth* was her third favourite thing in the world, after Tam and Tuck. *What about uncle Bran?* she remembered asking, which had earned one of her mother's musical laughs.

I love Hiraeth *more. But don't tell him, okay?*

Her father laid the case on the table, unfastened its ivory toggles, and drew it open to reveal the weathered whitewood face of the instrument inside. *Hiraeth* was a thing of beauty. She was a hand longer than most other lutes, with polished bone tuning pegs and a shallow, heart-shaped bowl.

Tuck cleared his throat. "I want you to have it. To take it with you. She would want that, I think."

And then everything fell into place. The breakfast, her laundry, the pack waiting by the door.

She was leaving. He was letting her go.

Tam practically flew across the kitchen. She slammed into

her father and flung her arms around him. It was like hugging a great big oak, and when his arms encircled her she squeezed her eyes shut and loosed a breath she'd been holding for what felt like years. "Thank you," she murmured. "Thank you. I'll come visit whenever I can."

"No you won't."

"I will. As soon as we finish this contract in Diremarch, I'll ask—"

"No," he said. "Tam, you must never come back."

She backed off, bewildered. "What? What does that mean?"

"It means I never want to see you again."

The words hit her like a smack. "Do you hate me so much?" she asked coldly.

"Gods, no! Tam, I love you. I love you more than my life. But when your mother died...It hurt so bad it nearly killed me. It would have, if not for you." He reached out and took her face in his hands. "When you smile, I can see her. When you laugh, I swear to the Summer Lord I can hear her, still. As long as you're alive, Tam, then so is she. Can you understand that? I don't want you to go, but I can't keep you here. I know that now."

She took one of his big, scarred hands in hers. "Then why?" she asked. "Why can't I come back?"

"Because what if you don't? What if you never do? If you leave, and...and you die, I...I couldn't forgive myself. If never seeing you again means believing that you're alive, that you're out there somewhere, happy and free...then I can live with that. I'll have to. But I can't wait here wondering whether or not you'll return, worrying if you're gone too long that you're...I can't—" He stopped abruptly, choking on a sob. "Please, Tam. Don't make me live like that. It has to be this way."

"So I just...go?" she asked. She wasn't crying—not really—but she could feel tears spilling hot down her cheeks.

"Go," he said quietly. "Wherever your Wyld Heart leads you, go."

She ate the rest of her breakfast while Tuck folded her laundry and finished packing her bag. They talked all the while, but afterward she couldn't remember a thing they'd said to one another. Eventually they ran out of words, and before Tam knew it she was standing with her pack over one shoulder and *Hiraeth* on the other.

Threnody was outside when she opened the door. Tam scooped her up and buried her face in the cat's soft fur. "You take good care of Dad," she whispered. "Don't fight with the other cats, and watch out for trash imps." When her father wasn't looking, Tam snatched the piece of ribbon he'd been toying with the night before and tied a pretty little bow around Thren's neck.

She'd have tarried longer, soaking up a few more precious moments with her father, but Rose had said they were heading out first thing in the morning and Tam feared she might already be too late.

They embraced one last time. Tam clung to her father as if an abyss had opened up beneath her feet. It took all the courage she had to let go.

She was ten feet from the door when Tuck abandoned his sentimental stoicism and began dispensing fatherly advice. "Stay dry," he called to her. "And warm. And don't start smoking, or scratching, or drinking."

"Dad!"

"Okay, but don't drink too much. And don't sleep with anyone in the band!"

That turned her around. "You're joking, right?"

He shrugged, and then tried on a smile that didn't quite fit. "I'll always love you, Tam."

"I know," she said. Then she turned and ran without looking back.

The *Rebel's Redoubt* was still parked outside the Cornerstone when Tam arrived, short of breath, her shoulders chafed raw by leather straps. She doubled over, hands on her knees, and pressed a fist to her gut where a nasty cramp was settling in and hanging up art. She nearly yelped (okay, she *did* yelp) when the door to the argosy banged open.

A man dressed in a pale pink blouse and voluminous yellow trousers stomped down the rear steps. He wore a silk scarf—the same garish yellow as his trousers—tied beneath his pointed beard, and a farcically large hat that looked to Tam like a tree stump stuffed with white fox-tails.

He leaned against the wagon and watched her gasp for a while. He was holding a steaming teacup in one hand and a long-stemmed pipe in the other. After a few languid puffs he tipped the hat from his eyes and peered at her. "You must be the new bard. Tom, was it?"

"Do I look like a Tom?"

His eyes narrowed as he sucked the stem of his pipe again. "You people all look the same to me."

"What people?"

"Bards," he clarified. "Every one of you reeks of false confidence, blind optimism, and"—he sniffed the air—"is that bacon? Did you bring bacon with you? Because if that's the case then you and I have started off on the wrong hoof entirely."

"I—"

"Foot," he said. "I meant foot."

Rose came strolling out of the Cornerstone with Freecloud behind her. She wore a plain white tunic tucked into a pair of black leather trousers so tight Tam nearly bit her tongue off to keep it from lolling out of her mouth. The merc tossed a stunted halfpipe between her lips and slapped around for a light until Freecloud struck a match and lit it for her. "Morning, Roderick. I see you've met the new bard."

"What happened to the old bard?"

"Dead," said Rose.

"*What*?" Tam and Roderick voiced their surprise as one.

"She's kidding," the druin assured them. "Kamaris took umbrage with our decision not to rush off and fight the Brumal Horde. He's found a new band now. And we have Tam."

"Roderick's our booker," Rose explained to Tam. "Handler of contracts, wrangler of wranglers, arranger of lodgings, and lord of the Outlaw Nation."

"Also he bails us out of jail," said Freecloud.

Tam looked dubiously at Fable's booker. "What's the Outlaw Nation?"

"You'll meet them tomorrow," Roderick said, and then hollered, "Brune! Cura! The wheels are a-rollin'! Get your asses out here!"

Within moments Fable's final two members emerged from the inn. Brune was sporting a black eye and a broad smile. "Morning, Tam. Rod, what's brewing today?"

The booker helped himself to a noisy sip from the teacup in his hand. "A bracing green leaf from Lindmoor. It'll help with the hangover, but not the eye. Dare I ask how the other guy looks?"

The shaman dipped his head toward Cura. "She looks fine to me," he said, and hauled himself up the argosy steps.

The Inkwitch, meanwhile, was engaged in a protracted good-bye kiss with a man wearing a flail on his hip and a dead fox draped across his shoulders. She tore her mouth free like a jackal lifting its gory maw from a fresh kill. When the man leaned in, Cura slapped him, kissed him again, then pushed him off and strode away without looking back. The man—a merc, Tam supposed—stood dazed. He touched two fingers to his lower lip and frowned when they came away bloody.

Cura graced Tam with a wink as she passed, then plucked the teacup out of Roderick's hands and climbed aboard.

Rose took a final drag of her smoke before handing it off to Freecloud. "How long have we got to sleep?" she asked Roderick.

"The Ravine's an hour west of here. Call it two, accounting for traffic."

Freecloud sucked the dregs from Rose's halfpipe before flinging it into the snow. "That'll have to do, I suppose."

"Sleep?" Tam looked between the three of them, incredulous. "Didn't you all just wake up?"

Rose started up the argosy's steps. "Wake up?" she called over her shoulder. "We never went to bed."

Chapter Five

Necessary Vices

Tam had been to the Ravine once before, about a year ago. She'd been seeing an older girl named Roxa, who swung an axe for a band called Skybreaker, and had tagged along (without Tuck's knowledge, of course) when they auditioned for a big-time booker in search of new talent. A few hundred bystanders had been in attendance as Roxa and her bandmates dispatched a sleuth of underfed bugbears, but the booker had left unimpressed. So, too, had Tam. She'd heard tales of the great stadiums down south, like the Giant's Cradle, the Blood Maze of Ut, and the recently constructed Megathon, which was said to hover on tidal engines above the city of Fivecourt. By comparison, the Ravine was little more than a glorified canyon.

Her opinion changed the moment she stepped out of the argosy. Uncle Bran had told her once that the arena could hold up to fifty thousand souls, and she guessed it was over capacity today. Tam had never seen so many people in one place. The noise rolled and crashed between the steep canyon walls, which were riddled with cave mouths crowded with spectators. Higher up, daring Kaskar masons had hewn wide balconies of stone and timber that clung like fungal shelves to the sheer cliffs. Spanning the sky above those was a haphazard web of rope bridges and viewing platforms teeming with people pressed shoulder to shoulder and shouting at the tops of their lungs.

The mob surrounding the war wagon had been driven to frenzy by Fable's arrival. Everywhere Tam looked were ecstatic faces and waving arms.

"Stay with me, Tam." Brune laid a hand on her shoulder as they stepped into the throng.

"Is it always like this?" she yelled over the din.

"Pretty much." The shaman swiped his soiled hair aside and favoured her with his gap-toothed grin. "Welcome to the jungle."

The fights were already under way. Tam could hear the clang of metal on metal and see the occasional flash of spell-craft light the canyon walls. They skirted the sheer face of the northern bluff, escorted by two dozen men bearing cudgels and round wooden shields. Roderick was out front in that silly hat of his, strutting like a noble's pet peacock. The booker led them into a tunnel that climbed and curved until it opened into an expansive (and expensively furnished) armoury with a commanding view of the Ravine.

The place was bustling with bands, bookers, and bards. There was a bar near the entrance, and several games of cards or dice in session. Tam had expected to see mercenaries preparing for battle with focused calm, sharpening swords and polishing armour. Instead, she found a scene not unlike the Cornerstone commons on any given night. Fighters awaiting their turn in the arena were steeling their nerves with liquor, while those who'd fought already were celebrating in kind.

There was a broad window overlooking the Ravine, beside which a ramp descended to the canyon floor. The band that had just finished fighting was slogging wearily up it. Their leader wore a red cape and a comically large tricorne hat. He was limping on a bloodied leg, but smiling and waving enthusiastically at the crowd. The moment he entered the armoury, however, he wheeled on the man behind him.

"What the fuck was that? I told you to put those lizards to sleep!"

"I *tried*!" said a harried-looking man in mud-drenched robes. He was holding a broken stick that might once have been a wand. "It's the crowd, Daryn. They're too loud!"

"Too loud? It's a *spell*, you halfwit, not a fucking *lullaby*! And you call yourself a wizard? You couldn't turn ice into water on a hot day!" He stooped to examine a pair of ghastly puncture wounds on his leg. "Does anyone know if slirks are poisonous?"

"Only to assholes," said a woman stringing her bow nearby. "I'd start beggin' the Maiden's Mercy if I were you, Daryn."

The wizard chuckled at that, drawing a scowl from his injured frontman.

The woman slipped her bow over one shoulder and pulled on a pair of mismatched silk gloves. The fingers of each were cut off at the knuckle. She wore a luxurious, ermine-trimmed cloak over a rich-looking cotton tabard, a polished steel breastplate over a padded leather cuirass, and a blue silk surcoat under all of that, which seemed to Tam like too many things to be wearing at once.

When she caught sight of Fable she grinned toothily. "Well, bugger me with a manticore's tail, if it ain't little Rosie!"

Rose dragged a hand through her cropped red hair. "You *do* know I kill most people who call me that."

"Ah, but I ain't most people!" The woman, whose bow-legged saunter and backwater drawl were almost comically Cartean, slung an arm around Rose's neck. "Why, you and I are practically sisters, 'cept your daddy's a good deal prettier than mine. Freezing hell, girl, I crossed half the world to rescue you and this handsome devil from the Heartwyld Horde!" She beamed up at the druin. "Hiya, Cloud."

"Hi, Jain."

"All you did was step through a portal," Rose said dryly. "Like every other merc in Grandual."

"Fair point. But I did help ol' Gabe on his quest to reach you."

"My father said you robbed him. Twice."

Jain shrugged. "Builds character, getting robbed. Heck, if I hadn't—"

"Boss," said a woman nearby, who was also wearing armour on top of armour, and two helmets at once. "We're up next."

"Are we?" Jain spun on her heel. "Then let's show these northern louts how we do things down south, shall we?" She stomped toward the ramp, forcing Daryn to limp hastily out of her way. A dozen similarly overclothed women funnelled out after her.

Tam shot Cura a questioning look. "Jain?"

The Inkwitch scowled. "What about her?"

"As in *Lady* Jain? Leader of the Silk Arrows? First through the Threshold at Kaladar?"

Cura barked a bitter laugh. "Girl, there ain't a merc in Grandual doesn't claim they were the first to follow Golden Gabe through that portal. But yeah, that was Lady Jain." She narrowed her eyes and bit her bottom lip. "She's on the list, for sure."

"What list?"

The summoner arched a bone-pierced brow. "The list of people I'd like to fu—"

"Tam!" Uncle Bran nearly bowled her over with a slap on the back. His leathers were caked in mud, and there was an open gash below his left eye, so she guessed he and Iron-clad (or rather, the ragtag miscreants who called themselves Ironclad these days) had performed already. "I can't believe it! What are you doing here? I mean, I know what you're doing here, but how did you convince Tuck to let you go?"

She glanced over at Cura, hesitant to mention how much yelling, crying, and, eventually, hugging, had been involved. "Long story," she said.

"Right. Well, you're here now, so it's..." He trailed off when he saw the sealskin lute case on Tam's back. "Is that your mother's lute? I figured Tuck burned the thing!"

"I guess not," Tam said.

Her uncle took a step back, and a wistful look stole over his face. "Gods, you're the spitting image of Lily at your age. Except you've got your dad's height, obviously. And that go-fuck-yourself jaw of his. And his dirt-brown hair. Heck, I suppose you've got a fair bit of both of 'em in you."

Cura snorted. "That's the general idea."

Bran scratched the grey stubble on his jowls as he examined the ink on the summoner's arms. "I suppose it is. Say, is Roderick around?"

"Try the bar," Cura suggested.

"I always do. I'll see you later."

Bran staggered away, and Cura broke off to speak with a man in spiked armour who'd painted his face like a cat's, so Tam was left on her own. She wandered toward the window up front. She had it all to herself, since most folks in the armoury were too busy plying themselves with liquor to take note of what was happening down in the arena.

She watched Jain and the Silk Arrows swarm a bandersnatch, which looked like a huge fluffy dog with bone-white fur and bloodred eyes. Its tongue lolled between fangs as long as Tam's arm, and whatever it touched sizzled as though the creature's saliva was highly corrosive. The beast's stubby, spiked tail wagged excitedly whenever it was about to attack, which made the bandersnatch a fairly predictable adversary.

A few of Jain's girls baited it with spears, while the rest put a whole forest's worth of arrows into its hide. By the time they were finished the thing looked like a spinster's pincushion. The Silk Arrows trotted back up the ramp to thunderous applause.

Up next were the Dustgalls, who made short work of a minotaur who tripped while charging them and broke its neck in the fall. The beast twitched and howled until one of the mercs put it out of its misery, then a pair of wranglers came and dragged it off by the ankles.

Giantsbane, who Tam had seen arrive alongside Fable the day before, had a bit of sport before their match. The arena gate opened and the so-called cockatrice Tam had seen in the Monster Market came squawking out. The mercenaries, whose pockets were no doubt stuffed with seed, pretended to run in fear while the chicken flapped in hot pursuit. Laughter cascaded down the canyon walls, though it ended abruptly when Alkain Tor dared to pick the bird up and got pecked in the eye. The Giantsbane frontman hurled the chicken down and stomped it to death while the crowd cried foul.

Afterward, they faced off against a quartet of scrawny trolls. Branigan had told her once that trolls, which could regenerate lost limbs, were prized among arena wranglers, but Giantsbane dismantled them so thoroughly that Tam suspected the poor bastards might not remember what parts went where when it came time to grow them back.

While the Renegades took on something that looked like a giant, pissed-off cactus, Fable began preparing for the main event. *Preparing*, of course, being a relatively loose term in this case. Brune paced in circles, slugging a bottle of Aldean rum and whispering what sounded like self-assurances under his breath. Cura disappeared into an alcove with one of Jain's girls and returned a few minutes later with a pipe in her teeth and a languid smile on her lips.

Freecloud came to stand beside Tam at the window. He produced the moonstone coin he'd been toying with in the Cornerstone the previous night and thumbed it idly as he watched the current battle unfold on the arena floor.

Glancing past the druin's shoulder, Tam saw Rose sitting by herself on a low sofa. She was wearing her scuffed black armour, and her scimitars, *Thistle* and *Thorn*, were in scabbards on either hip. There was an open satchel on the mercenary's lap, and for long seconds she stared down at it, flexing her fingers like a thief about to test a lock. Eventually, she withdrew a glossy black leaf and, with the grim resolve of someone determined to swallow poison, placed it on her tongue.

Tam was about to ask Freecloud what Rose was doing, but the druin spoke up before she could.

"We all have our rituals," he said, without taking his eyes off the action below. "Necessary vices that enable us to conquer our fear. Or, if not conquer it, then to at least pile furniture against the door while we duck out the back. It's not enough to survive what we do, Tam. We must also *endure* it."

"What's the difference?" she asked.

"One concerns the body, the other the mind. Every battle has a cost," he said quietly. "Even the ones we win."

Tam didn't fully understand what he meant, but decided to pretend she did, and nodded sagely. "So what's your vice?" she wondered.

"Love," said Freecloud, flashing his jaguar smile. "And I suspect one day it will kill me."

The sun was sinking in the west as Rose led Fable into the Ravine. Freecloud was a few steps behind her, and Brune jogged after them both. The shaman was shirtless despite the cold, waving his arms and goading the crowd into a frenzy. His weapon, a double-bladed twinglaive he called *Ktulu*, was leashed by a leather thong to his broad back. Tam had examined the polearm earlier: The two halves of the weapon were attached in the middle by a metal screw, which allowed the shaman to wield each separately if he wanted to.

Cura brought up the rear at a walk. She wore a heavy black shawl and was unarmed but for a trio of sheathed knives she claimed were merely part of her outfit. The Inkwitch didn't seem to care that fifty thousand people were watching her every move.

"Thrill 'em and kill 'em!" Roderick shouted after his charges, then bullied his way to join Tam at the window. The ledge was getting crowded now that Fable was taking the floor.

"Is it true you don't know what they're fighting?" she asked the booker.

Roderick was half a foot shorter than Tam, and was forced to nudge his hat from his eyes so that he could peer up at her. "I don't, no," he admitted. "And I don't like it, either. My contact here said he had something special in mind. 'Rose is gonna love it,' he said, and of course she went ahead and agreed to it!" He pulled a long-stemmed pipe from the sash at his waist and began stuffing its bowl. "Sometimes I think that woman wants to die young," he muttered, and then fixed Tam with a sidelong glare. "Don't tell her I said so."

Her uncle Bran sidled up on her left with two tankards of beer.

"Thanks," she said, wresting one from his grip.

"What? Oh, yeah, sure," he grumbled.

Somewhere, a bell was tolling. Tam saw the portcullis in the opposite wall begin to grind open. As it did, those watching from window, bridge, and balcony went as quiet as so many people possibly could. Whatever emerged from that gate would be the best Ardburg's huntsmen could manage, a monster they hoped was capable of challenging one of Grandual's greatest mercenary bands.

Except it wasn't a monster at all. It was a man, one of the wranglers Tam had seen earlier, but now he was screaming and flailing the stump of what had until recently been his right arm. He stumbled and fell, splashing helplessly in a pool of his own blood.

Within seconds the window was packed with mercs desperate to get a view of the arena floor. Roderick's hands froze in the act of striking a match. The flame sputtered out; his pipe fell clattering to the ledge before him.

Something enormous ducked under the black iron portcullis. Its flesh was the sickly blue of mouldy bread. Its gangly limbs were corded with muscle, marred by welts and festering sores. It scooped up the thrashing groom and lobbed him against the wall. His body burst like a rotten orange, showering the balcony below with gore.

The creature straightened, but its shoulders remained hunched, as though it had lived for years in cramped captivity. In darkness, too, Tam concluded, since a swollen black pupil filled the entirety of its single vast eye.

"Fuck me with a Phantran's salty dick," muttered Roderick. "It's a cyclops."

Chapter Six

Wood and String

It was said that Bloody Rose had killed a cyclops when she was just seventeen years old. She hadn't been a mercenary at the time, just a scrappy young girl eager to escape the long reach of her father's shadow. There'd been no band to back her up, no bard to watch what transpired and record it in song. But grand deeds have a way of getting around, and so the daughter of Golden Gabe became a celebrity overnight, having earned the name by which she'd be known forever after.

Bloody Rose.

There were some who didn't believe it. They figured she'd found it dead, or used her daddy's gold and hired mercs to slay the beast on her behalf. But Tam had never once doubted the story was true.

She did now. The cylops was enormous—the size of a lord's keep, at least. How could a seventeen-year-old girl—how could *anyone*, for that matter—overcome something so monstrous as *this*? How did you even begin?

By running straight at it, evidently.

Rose took off at a sprint, charging unflinchingly into the creature's colossal shadow. She gripped the pommels at her waist, tore the blades from their scabbards, and hurled them into the empty sky. Before Tam could ask Bran or Roderick why, runes on Rose's gauntlets blazed to life—one blue, the other green. Matching glyphs flared along the edges of her scimitars as they came spinning back to her open hands.

"That's . . . incredible," Tam breathed. She glanced over at Roderick, who'd recovered his pipe and spared her a confident wink.

"Very," the booker agreed.

Freecloud was racing after Rose. He clenched *Madrigal*'s narrow scabbard in one hand and leaned as though he were running into a gale.

Cura tore her shawl from her shoulders, tossed it away, and shouted, *"AGANI!"* Tam marvelled that she could hear the summoner's cry over the noise bouncing off the canyon walls. The Inkwitch fell to her knees, face to the ground, hands raking furrows in the earth before her. Her back bent like a crone's, and *something* began climbing out of her.

What the . . . ? Tam set her mug on the window ledge, since her hand was shaking, sloshing beer over her white-knuckled fingers.

Segmented legs clawed the ground as a charred-black tree hauled itself from the summoner's flesh. In seconds it was the size of a bull, then a Brumal mammoth, until finally it towered over Cura, half the height of the cyclops itself.

Brune hadn't yet moved. His head was lowered, and it looked as though the shaman was speaking to himself, shifting his weight from foot to foot. He pulled the twinglaive off his back and planted one end in the ground. At last he set off after Freecloud and Rose. He tipped forward—not falling, but running on all fours like a beast.

"C'mon . . ." pleaded Roderick around the stem of his pipe.

The shaman was *changing*. His thighs tore through his trousers. The hair on his arms thickened into a shaggy brown coat that swept over his shoulders and across his back. His nose broadened into a wide black snout. His hands and feet sprouted curling yellow claws.

Tam was suddenly on the tips of her toes. "He's a *bear*!" she cried.

Brune roared, an earsplitting snarl that began like thunder booming through a mountain pass, but then dwindled to something like a newborn hatchling pleading to be fed. All at once his entire body shrank to the size of a dog.

A very small dog.

An overfed cat, even.

Tam frowned, perplexed. "He's a bear . . . *cub*?"

Dismay and laughter rippled up the canyon walls. Brune halted, obviously mortified, and buried his face behind tiny paws. A few mercs behind Tam were chuckling among themselves. Even Branigan snorted bubbles into his beer.

Roderick cursed under his breath as he hurriedly struck a match. "He gets anxious, sometimes," the booker explained, waving a hand to clear the smoke he exhaled. "The bigger the crowd, the smaller the bear."

"Here we go," said Tam's uncle, drawing her attention back to the arena floor.

The cyclops aimed a clumsy kick at Rose as she approached. She danced around it, sprang into the air, and stabbed one of her curved swords into the monster's calf. She used the weapon's leverage to haul herself up before planting her other blade an arm's length higher. Tam supposed that years of harsh captivity had inured the cyclops to pain, or else the monster was simply impervious to it, since it pivoted on its other foot, befuddled by Rose's disappearance, while she gouged her way up the back of its leg.

Cura remained prone as the creature she'd summoned stretched its skeletal boughs toward the sky. A face emerged from the mottled folds of its trunk and began shrieking—in anger or in agony, it was impossible to tell. There was a sucking *whoosh*—the gasp of fifty thousand stolen breaths—and its leafy crown bloomed into a storm of cerulean flame. It moved away from Cura, scuttling on roots that reminded Tam of a beetle's legs. Every plodding step shivered loose a hundred blazing leaves.

Tam turned to Roderick. "What is that thing?"

The booker puffed his pipe and regarded her frankly. "What are you, blind? It's a tree with its head on fire."

As Rose climbed the cyclops's leg, Freecloud positioned himself directly in front of it—an obvious target. The creature tried stomping him flat, but Freecloud—who still hadn't drawn his weapon—stepped clear with the unhurried ease of a pilgrim conceding the road to a farmer's cart. When the beast tried again with the other foot, Freecloud ducked casually aside.

At last, he drew *Madrigal* from its scabbard. The slender blade sang in the druin's hands, slashing across three of the monster's toes and severing them completely.

Tam leaned into her uncle, shouting to be heard above the baying crowd. "He's so fast!"

Bran was clapping, and paused to whistle between his fingers. Then he tapped the side of his head. "That's the prescience for you."

"The prescience?"

"Rabbits can see the future," he said, using a slang term for druin she doubted Freecloud would approve of. "They know what'll happen—or what will very probably happen—right before it does."

Since Branigan was obviously drunk and not making sense, she turned to Roderick instead. "Is that true?"

The booker shrugged. "More or less."

Freecloud was making a slow circle around his opponent. *Madrigal* hovered above his head, poised to strike. The cyclops tracked him warily. Strands of gore drooled from its jaw, slopping over the swell of its belly and into the matted loincloth below.

Rose must have hit a nerve in its buttocks, because the

thing yelped and slapped her with a meaty hand. She weathered the blow, gripping her hilts like a climber dangling above a yawning abyss. She was twenty feet from the ground now; a fall wouldn't kill her, but it would leave her dazed and in danger of being stomped to death in the meantime.

Determined to recover the beast's attention, Freecloud levelled another chop at its ankle. The cut was shallow, glancing off bone. It turned ponderously as the druin darted between its legs.

When Rose reached the monster's waist she let *Thistle* and *Thorn* tumble to the ground. Using its loincloth for purchase, she clambered onto the creature's back as it stooped to swipe at Freecloud. There was a ridge of coarse blue fur running the length of its spine, which Rose climbed hand over hand with alarming dexterity.

Below her, Freecloud was forced to retreat as the cyclops lunged at him with both hands. Fast as the druin was—and no matter how much warning the prescience gave him—the cyclops was simply too big to evade for long. Freecloud ducked a blow so narrowly his ears got clipped, and when the next attack followed Tam could have sworn he stepped *into* its path instead of out.

She gasped as Freecloud tumbled violently across the arena. Where he stopped he lay, unmoving.

The whole of the Ravine seemed to hold its breath. The cyclops loosed a chortling roar and advanced on the crumpled druin.

Roderick reached up and withdrew his pipe from his mouth. "This is bad," said the booker, with the bleak resignation of a man watching the neighbour's dog squat in his yard.

Tam turned on her uncle. "It can't kill him, right? They won't let it."

Branigan shook his head. "Who's *they*?"

She looked to either end of the canyon, where a cordon of spearmen stood guard in case the monsters made a break for it. None of them were eager to rescue Freecloud. In fact, she doubted they would challenge the beast even if it came right at them.

By now Cura's burning tree creature was bearing down on the cyclops. One of its boughs flung a clump of burning leaves at its enemy, but they bounced from its tortured hide like sparks glancing off iron plate.

Cura rose unsteadily, her face pale, her sweat-soaked hair plastered across her brow. Tam saw the woman's chest swell as she drew a breath...

When she released it, a gale ripped through the boughs of her summoned atrocity. It tore loose every leaf and sent them swarming around the cyclops's head, a cloud of fiery wasps that scorched its waxy flesh but skittered harmlessly off the leathery lid that closed over its bulbous eye.

The cyclops put off killing Freecloud long enough to deal with this latest irritation. The two monsters grappled briefly, but the cyclops was much larger and undoubtedly stronger. It hoisted the bare-branched horror overhead and smashed it against the ground like a club. Cura's creature splintered apart and dissolved into wisps of inky black smoke.

The Inkwitch slumped to the ground as the cyclops resumed its advance on the unconscious druin.

Rose was still lost to sight on the monster's back. But even if she'd guessed from the crowd's reaction that Cura's creature was dead and Freecloud was in mortal danger, what could she do?

No more than I, thought Tam miserably. She nearly jumped out of her skin when her uncle's hand settled on her shoulder.

"You might want to look away, Tam. This won't be pretty."

Look away...

She did. She looked away, and found her gaze drawn to something across the room.

A length of wood, a bit of string—an instrument begging to be picked up and played. Tam heard it whisper her name in a voice she could barely remember, and suddenly her fingers itched to hold it. Her heart ached to hear it sing.

She bolted from the window, pushing through the gaggle of mercs behind her. Branigan no doubt assumed she'd gone to retch, or to spare herself the sight of Freecloud being stomped to mush. In truth, Tam had no idea *what* she was doing, but she'd decided that she had to do *something*, even if it amounted to nothing.

She would apologize later to whoever it was that had left their bow unattended.

Tam shrugged her mother's lute from her shoulder and replaced it with a near-empty quiver. Then she was gone, past the guards at the armoury gate and sprinting down the ramp as fast as her legs would carry her.

The sound of the crowd hit her like a physical force, a percussive roar louder than anything she'd ever heard. The quiver bounced painfully against her side, so she chose an arrow at random and tossed the rest, running across the arena floor as if the Heathen's hounds were snapping at her heels.

She was already short of breath. Her heart was labouring. Her vision swam. She glimpsed her surroundings in scattered fragments: Cura on her knees, eyes widening as Tam hurtled past her; Freecloud stirring groggily as a bear cub nipped at his ear...

And then her gaze went up, and up, and Tam found herself looking into the baleful black eye of the cyclops.

She felt her knees threaten to buckle. Every instinct screamed at her to turn and run away. The monster was bleating at her—the hair-raising mewl of some demented sheep—but Tam could barely hear it over the noise sheeting down the canyon walls and the rasp of her own ragged breath.

Having concluded (and rightly so) that the bard with the bow presented no threat whatsoever, the cyclops took a final step toward the druin. One more, and Freecloud was dead.

Now, said the voice in Tam's head.

She skidded to a halt, put her arrow to string. On her first attempt to draw the bow she barely bent it at all, since it was much longer than the one she'd used to practice with Tera. She tried again, gritting her teeth as she pulled the fletching to the edge of her jaw.

The sun was in her eyes, so Tam had to squint to see clearly. She aimed the point of her arrow at the only target she could think of, because when you fought something with one big eye in the middle of its head, choosing something to shoot at was sort of a no-brainer.

Beyond her centre of focus she saw Rose gain the giant's shoulder. The mercenary reached out—the runes on her gauntlet burning blue—and a scimitar sprang to her waiting hand.

Tam took a breath, trying in vain to keep her hands from trembling. The muscles in her arms were on fire. She could feel the arrow straining against her grip, a trained falcon awaiting the command to kill.

She let it fly.

Chapter Seven

View from a Hill

Tam awoke with the roar of the arena echoing in her ears. Her head was throbbing, and her jaw ached as though she'd taken a punch. Memories began to surface in her mind, ghastly images, like cold corpses floating below the glassy face of a lake. She saw the cyclops toppling, its head cracking like a gourd as it hit the ground. There'd been blood—so much blood—and Tam had fainted dead in front of fifty thousand people.

So where am I now? she wondered.

For a moment Tam feared she'd been dreaming—that everything from the cyclops to her father's farewell had been nothing more than a cruel delusion. She dreaded to hear her father's voice beyond her door or feel Threnody's fluffy tail tickle her nose.

But no, she wasn't home. She was lying on a stiff cot in the dark. Distant music and fitful orange light filtered through a slatted window above her. She was aboard the argosy, then. The *Rebel's Redoubt*. And outside was . . .

Fighter's Camp.

Tam had heard stories of Fighter's Camp during her stint at the Cornerstone. It was an overnight celebration held whenever there were fights at the Ravine, attended by hundreds of

mercenaries, nobles, wealthy merchants, and just about anyone clever enough to slip past the loose cordon of parked argosies and careless sentries. Bran and Tiamax had sometimes,
after several drinks and a great deal of pestering, regaled her
with tales of dancing, drinking, and the sort of wild debauch-
ery usually reserved for the top floor of a Whitecrest brothel.

It was, simply put, the biggest party in Ardburg.

And she was missing it.

Tam sat up, groaning at the ache in her skull and waiting for her eyes to make sense of the gloom. Fable's fortress
on wheels was as impressive inside as out. There was a full
kitchen at the rear, and a lounge furnished with a well-
stocked bar, comfy sofas, and an honest-to-Glif fireplace with
a stone chimney and everything.

Farther along were the bunks belonging to Brune, Cura,
Roderick, and—as of this morning—Tam herself. The shaman's rumpled bed was piled with furs, while the Inkwitch
slept on black satin sheets and a plethora of luxurious pillows.
The booker's bunk, which was opposite Tam's, was a mess of
soiled straw, mismatched socks, and empty bottles.

Well, *mostly* empty bottles. Tam had spotted one beside
it earlier that contained a cloudy amber liquid she'd hoped to
hell was whiskey.

Rose and Freecloud shared a large bedroom at the front of
the argosy. The door was ajar, and Tam could see a glimmer
of light within. She thought about sneaking over and peeking
inside but decided to mind her own business and go join the
festivities instead.

She stood, wincing as a board creaked underfoot, then
started for the door. Her next step knocked over the half-
empty bottle beside Roderick's bed. The glass rolled noisily
down the corridor ahead of her, its contents sloshing onto the
floor as it did.

"Tam?" Rose called out behind her. "Come here. Let me
see you."

The bard turned, approached the door, and pushed it gently aside.

Freecloud was laying on a wide bed within. A sheet was drawn to his waist, and Tam stifled a gasp when she saw the bruises darkening the pale gold of his skin. His right shoulder was skinned raw, and a series of small cuts marred one half of his face. The druin's chest rose and fell with the slow cadence of deep slumber.

Rose, who was seated on a chair next to the bed, smiled weakly at Tam as she entered. "How you feeling?"

"Fine, thanks." She nodded toward the bed. "Is he . . . Will he be okay?"

"He will, yes. No thanks to me." She used a damp cloth to dab sweat from the druin's forehead. "Listen, Tam . . . What you did today was—"

"Stupid, I know."

"Very stupid, yes," said Rose.

"It was reckless," Tam added.

"Absolutely," Rose agreed.

"I'm a fool."

A smile split the mercenary's face. "Then you'll fit right in." She raised a hand before Tam could heap any more abuse on herself. "But seriously, what you did today was incredibly brave. Thank you."

Tam's face boiled like a kettle at the compliment. She swallowed to keep the steam from spewing out her ears. "My father'll kill me if finds out."

"Oh, he'll find out," Rose assured her. "I'd bet all of Ardburg is talking about the bard with the bow tonight."

Tam spent a moment gazing sightlessly at the candle on the dresser next to the door. Finally, she asked, "Did I really kill it?"

Rose dipped her cloth in a bowl of water at her feet. "The cyclops? No, you didn't. I cut its throat."

Tam didn't know whether to be disappointed or relieved. "I missed, then?"

"That depends what you were aiming for," Rose said. She motioned to a strip of cloth binding her right thigh.

It was a moment before Tam understood. "No..."

"Yep."

"I shot you?"

"You shot me," Rose confirmed. "Did a piss-poor job of it, though. I've had slivers that bled more when I pulled them out."

"I shot you," Tam repeated dumbly. The pain in her head was receding, crowded out by utter disbelief.

Rose wrung out her cloth. "Yeah, well, good luck convincing anyone of that. According to fifty thousand witnesses you killed a cyclops with a single arrow."

A silence fell between them. A pair of drunks were singing as they passed below the window to Rose's room. One of them stopped to relieve himself against the *Rebel's Redoubt* before hurrying to catch up with his friend. Tam was about to leave as well when the mercenary spoke again.

"I almost killed him today," she said, pressing the cloth to Freecloud's face. "I was sloppy. Irresponsible. We could have fought that thing together, but I tried to do it all by myself. I put my bandmates in danger, and I damn near killed my bard." She chuckled darkly. "Wouldn't Dad be proud."

"You were fearless," Tam said.

"Fearless?" Rose's voice was suddenly dagger-sharp. She glanced over, eyes lost to the shadow of her furrowed brow. "No, Tam. I was afraid."

Freecloud stirred on the bed. He murmured a string of sibilant words in a language Tam took for druic.

Rose stroked the soft fur of his ear with a callused finger. "You should go," she said, not unkindly. "Find Brune and Cura—they'll look after you. It'd be a shame to miss your first Fighter's Camp."

Tam nodded and turned to leave.

"They've named you, by the way."

She paused, tucking her hair behind her ear as she looked over her shoulder. Rose's back was to her, and Tam was struck by how small she seemed just now—this legend, the woman the world called Bloody Rose.

"Named me what?" Tam asked.

"Oh, I expect you'll find out soon enough."

"Well if it isn't the Bard herself!"

Winded from her walk uphill, Tam handed Bran the tin mug of coffee she'd brought him and cupped her own with both hands. "Mercy," she huffed. "Not you, too. What are you doing up here, anyway? I was looking all over camp for you."

"Stretching my legs," said her uncle. "Clearing my mind. Saying good-bye."

"To what? The city?" Ardburg was a hedge of grey stone to the east, crouched beneath a cloud of rising smoke.

"That too," he said.

The wind was brisk this high up, and Tam was grateful she'd woke up wrapped in someone's cloak—and a fine one, too, with a leather hem and silver scrollwork around the collar. She pulled it closed as she gazed over the sprawl of Fighter's Camp. Tam couldn't remember most of what transpired the night before (which was probably for the best), and the things she *could* recall (like pouring half a bottle of Agrian moonshine into the gory eye socket of Alkain Tor) seemed wildly far-fetched. The only thing Tam knew for certain was that she'd broken just about every rule her father had, and probably a few he hadn't dreamed up yet.

"What's wrong with 'the Bard'?" Bran chuckled. "It's a great name. You don't like it?"

"I don't deserve it," she grumbled.

"Don't deserve it? Tam, you killed a cyclops with a *single arrow*! Do you know how many arrows it took me to kill a cyclops?"

"How many?"

"None! I've never fought a fucking cyclops, are you kidding me? If I saw one in the Wyld I'd run so fast I'd leave my boots behind! Also, I can't shoot for shit."

"Yeah, well, neither can I, apparently."

Her uncle eyed her suspiciously. "How do you figure?"

"Because I missed! I missed the giant monster standing right in front of me, and I—" She paused to make sure they were alone on the hilltop. They were, but she lowered her voice anyway. "*I shot Rose.*"

Bran sputtered hot coffee down the front of his leathers. "You what?"

"I fucking shot Bloody Rose!" she hissed.

He stared at her a moment. "Is she dead?"

"No, she's not—" Tam scoffed, exasperated. "The arrow only grazed her. Anyway, it was Rose who killed the cyclops, not me."

"How?"

Tam used a finger to mime slitting her throat. "She cut an artery in its neck, but when it fell . . ."

"I remember." Bran grimaced. "Splat."

"Splat," she echoed. "And now everyone assumes I'm some kind of . . . Well, I don't know what they think I am, but I had three bookers try to recruit me last night. One of them promised he could have me skirmishing for the Stormcrows in Fivecourt next month! I'm just a bard!" she protested. "Hell, I'm barely even that!"

"You're *the* Bard," Bran corrected her. He snuck another sip of coffee and pondered the wall of whitecapped mountains to the north. "We don't get to choose what people think of us, Tam. You're a legend now, girl, and legends are like rolling stones: Once they get going, it's best to stay out of their way."

"Did you just make that up?" Tam asked.

Her uncle grinned impishly. "Of course not. I stole it from your mom."

Tam laughed, and then spent a long moment studying her uncle's face: his crooked nose, his grey-shot beard, the wrinkles crowding the corner of his eyes.

When did he get so old? she wondered.

"What?" Bran asked, when he caught her staring.

"Nothing," she said. "Thank you."

"For what?"

"For this," she said, gesturing down at Fighter's Camp. "For everything. After Mom died, Dad just sort of . . . gave up, you know?"

Her uncle scratched a scar under his jaw. "I know."

"I think he resented me," Tam said, "because I reminded him of her. It must have been hard on him. On you, too. But you were always there for me."

Branigan's grin returned. "That's because you worked at the bar," he said, and they both laughed.

The camp was bustling with activity. Tents were collapsing, teamsters shouting at one another as argosies began rolling onto the muddy road.

"But seriously," Bran said, "do me a favour, will you? Be careful. A bard's duty is to watch, not to fight. Never to fight," he repeated, a sadness creeping into his voice. "Which reminds me." He set his mug on the ground and reached beneath the back of his cloak, withdrawing a metal vial about as long as Tam's hand from top to bottom.

She frowned at it. "Where were you keeping that?"

"Not important," Bran said. "Listen: Just because Fable isn't going to fight the Brumal Horde doesn't mean you won't be in danger. How much do you know about Rose's past?"

"Pretty much everything," Tam replied.

"Everything that's in the songs, you mean. You know about the cyclops—everyone does—and you've heard about her duel with the centaur prince. You know she burnt the pirate fleet at Freeport and led the survivors of Castia in battle against Lastleaf and the Heartwyld Horde. But did you know that Fable isn't her first band? Well, it's not the band it used to be, anyway."

"Meaning..." Tam prompted.

"*Meaning* she killed them."

Tam blinked. "I'm sorry?"

"Well, she didn't *kill* them," he clarified. "But they died because she convinced them to fight at Castia."

"Bloody gods, Bran, that's not the same thing at all!"

"I know. I'm sorry. But my point is this: Rose is a fine leader and a brilliant fighter—one of the best I've seen, no doubt. But there's a chip on her shoulder. She's got something to prove—whether it's to herself, or her father, or the world in general, I don't know. It can't have been easy growing up the daughter of Golden Gabe. The man's got boots even a giant could wriggle its toes in, but that doesn't stop Rose from trying to fill them. *That's* why she takes on contracts that others won't touch. *That's* why she'll tour the Heartwyld when no one else will. It's why most bands settle for fighting wrangler trash while Fable risks their lives every time they step onto the arena floor."

Tam swallowed a mouthful of swiftly cooling coffee. "You mentioned a point?"

"So now a Horde is threatening Kaskar—and maybe Agria, too—and Rose is *running* from it? It doesn't make any sense."

"Fable has a contract in Diremarch, remember?"

"Exactly. And according to Freecloud it's something just as dangerous. Which is why I'm giving you this." He twisted the metal vial at both ends. It came apart to reveal a thin golden spine with a needle-sharp tip. "Do you know what this is?" She shook her head no. "It's the quill of a will'o'wisp. We call it 'The Bard's Last Refrain.' If things ever look dire...if Rose and the others get themselves into trouble they can't get out of ... I want you to take this quill and prick yourself with it. Hard."

"And then what?" asked Tam.

"You'll die. Or at least you'll *seem* to have died. The effect lasts for a day or two, and with any luck whatever killed your crew will be long gone. Unless it was cannibals, in which case those bastards'll clean you to the bone. Here." He screwed the two halves of the cylinder back together and offered it to Tam. "I pray you'll never need to use it."

Tam wasn't the praying sort, but she certainly hoped she'd never have to rely on playing dead to save her life. "Thanks," she said, palming the vial.

By now the track below was clogged with wagons and warriors trickling west beneath the dull iron sky. Considering how drunk most of them had been just a few hours earlier, Tam was surprised most of them could keep down breakfast, never mind hike uphill in armour. The argosies were headed back to the city, since their bulk would be a hindrance in the terrain between here and Cragmoor.

"I'd better go kick the boys awake," Bran said eventually. He and Ironclad were heading west along with everyone else. Her uncle wasn't overly keen on the idea (he'd been among those who'd liberated Castia, and the memory of Lastleaf's Horde still gave him nightmares), but his bandmates—the ones he'd hired to stand in when the old band broke up— were determined to go. They'd missed out on the greatest battle in living memory and were eager to earn some songs of their own.

"I should go, too," said Tam. And then, because she couldn't bear the thought of losing two people she loved in as many days, she said, "I'll see you again, right?"

He smiled. "Of course you will."

Uncle Bran had never been a very good liar (which was probably what made him such a shit gambler), but she appreciated the effort nonetheless.

*   *   *

Tam was halfway through the camp when she saw Lady Jain bearing down on her. The mercenary smiled and waved as she approached, so Tam responded in kind.

The thing about waving, though, is that it leaves you woefully unprepared to block a punch.

Tam doubled over Jain's clenched fist. Her breath puffed into the chill winter air and then fled as though it feared a beating itself.

Jain gave the bard a consoling pat on the head, stooping so that she and Tam were face-to-face. "You had that coming, girl. Care to guess why?"

"Wuhhh," Tam managed.

"Wrong," Jain said. "It ain't 'cause ya stole my bow yesterday. I've got more bows than problems, and I ain't short o' problems."

You bloody idiot, Tam berated herself. *Jain's bow!? You stole Lady Jain's bow?*

"No," the mercenary was saying, "the reason I suckered you is because *I'm* the best archer in Grandual. 'The greatest shot in all five courts,' they call me. It took me years to earn that title, but I *did* earn it: in the forests of Agria, on the battlefield at Castia, and every day the sweet Summer Lord has granted me since. But it was worth it, see? Because whenever some li'l girl picks up a bow and plays hero, guess who she's pretendin' to be?"

Tam's voice emerged as a shrill wheeze.

"Exactly." Jain planted a thumb on her chest. "Me. But then you went and dropped a fuckin' cyclops with one arrow! One of *my* arrows, no less! Which means that one day soon some snot-nosed brat'll pick up a bow and call herself *the Bard*, and before long these kids'll be copping your name from Saltbottom schoolyards to the Cartean steppe. So, no," she grated, "I didn't punch you for stealin' my bow. I punched you for stealin' my *whole goddamned identity*!"

Tam could finally breathe, albeit painfully. She blinked to keep her tears at bay. "I'm just . . . a bard," she rasped.

Jain leaned in close, looking skeptical. The woman's breath smelled like pipe smoke and southern oranges. "Just a bard, eh? Well I sure as heck hope so, Tam Hashford."

"Your bow's in the argosy," Tam squeaked. "I can—"

"Keep it," Jain said, waving dismissively. "Bard or not, if you're keeping company with Rose yer gonna need it. Her name's *Duchess*, by the way. She was my first bow, a gift from m'daddy, and besides these gorgeous brown eyes o' mine it was just about the only thing he ever gave me. Now *Duchess* is a lady, mind you, so you'd best treat her like one. Keep her warm, keep her dry, and don't string her up unless you mean to use her." This last remark was punctuated by a lewd smirk. "Got it?"

"Got it," said Tam. "Thanks."

"You're most welcome, Tam." Jain drew a knife from a sheath on her leg and held it a hair's breadth from the bard's nose. "Now, gimme that cloak."

Tam was shaking by the time she returned to the argosy, and not just because she was freezing. She'd heard men and women gossiping as she navigated the frenzied camp. Tidings had come from the city shortly after dawn, when a breathless rider on a frothing horse galloped into camp and informed anyone who'd listen that Cragmoor, the fortress whose ice-sheathed walls had repelled the horrors of the Wastes for hundreds of years, had fallen.

Brontide and the Brumal Horde were coming south.

The news—as she and Bran had witnessed from their hilltop vantage—had riled the camp like a boot to a beehive, and now mercenaries were moving west in a swarm. The plan, as Tam heard it from a man doling cold corn soup from a cast-iron cauldron, was to rally at Coldfire Pass. "We'll put a stop to 'em there," said the potbellied cook, as though he planned on leading the defense himself and smiting the giant with his wooden spoon. "Saga once held that pass for three days against a thousand walking dead!"

The *Rebel's Redoubt* hunkered like a rock amidst the camp's chaotic swirl, and Tam saw several mercenaries cast accusing glares at Fable's argosy, as if the band's refusal to fight the Horde was an outright betrayal of humankind.

Maybe they're right, Tam thought. After all, wasn't "fighting monsters" the whole point of being a merc? And now the monsters had been kind enough to gather in one place (having apparently forgotten the drubbing they took at Castia), except Rose was more concerned with finishing their tour and fulfilling a contract than confronting what might be the greatest threat to Grandual since the Reclamation Wars.

Forget it, she told herself as she climbed the steps at the rear of the argosy. *You're a bard now. You're here to play the lute—not to ask questions, or to lecture Bloody Rose on what it means to be a mercenary. So keep your mouth shut unless she asks you to sing.*

Tam had just shut the door behind her when she heard a strangled cry and saw, with eyes still adjusting to the wagon's shadowed interior, a monster lurching toward her.

Chapter Eight

The Villain of a Thousand Songs

Tam barely had time to register a pair of curling horns, the clomp of hooves, and the reek of stale wine before the monster shouted, "Move!" and barrelled past her. It crashed through the door, bowled down the steps, and landed on all fours in the mud below, where it promptly began vomiting.

A low chuckle drew Tam's attention. Brune was standing at the *Redoubt*'s kitchen counter, pouring hot water from a char-black kettle into a bowl of cut oats. "Welcome back," he said. "Jain was looking for you."

"She found me," Tam told him, then pointed to the thing throwing up outside. "What is that?"

"That's a very hungover satyr," said Cura, who was stretched out on a sofa near the crackling fireplace. She wore a short black shift that left her legs bare, offering Tam a further glimpse of the artwork inked on her skin. It was hard to tell in the dim light, but every piece looked as horrific as the thing she'd summoned off her back in the arena yesterday.

"A satyr? What's it doing here?"

Brune ambled up next to her, blew on a spoonful of steaming oatmeal, and shovelled it into his mouth. "Puking," he said, unhelpfully, and then called out to the creature below. "I told you not to eat that belt, Rod. Or at least to take the buckle off first."

Rod?

Tam looked from the shaman to the satyr, who she hadn't recognized without his ridiculous hat and outrageous clothing. Its legs were covered in coarse brown fur, its knees kinked backward like those of a deer. It had cloven hooves in place of feet, and a pair of horns curling from a wild mane of straw-coloured hair.

"Wait, Roderick's a—"

"Friend," said Freecloud, suddenly appearing at the bard's other shoulder. His bruises were concealed by a belted blue dressing robe, but the cuts on his face were already healed and fading fast. He flashed her a tight smile, and Tam recalled Bran telling her that druins could see a few seconds into the future. Which meant he would know the word she'd been about to use. "*What* Roderick is isn't important," Freecloud went on. "Not to us. It's *who* he is that matters. And despite his numerous shortcomings, he is honest, and loyal, and brave."

Tam frowned down at the satyr. "Brave?"

"In his way," said the druin. "Would you live among monsters with nothing but a pair of boots and a silly hat to disguise yourself?"

She sure as hell wouldn't, but since Freecloud knew that already, Tam didn't bother saying so.

"If you think *he* looks funny naked," Brune mumbled around a mouthful of porridge, "wait till you see Cura."

"Fuck yourself," said the summoner.

"*Way more hair,*" Brune whispered.

"That's rich," Cura drawled, "coming from a guy who spends his nights as a bear."

Freecloud laid a hand on Tam's shoulder. His long ears canted forward in what she took for concern. "You're shivering."

Tam realized her teeth had been chattering and clamped them shut. "Jain took my cloak."

The druin laughed quietly at that, as if robbing people at knifepoint was somehow an endearing quality. He studied Tam a moment longer, sizing her up. "Excuse me a moment," he said, and started toward the front of the argosy.

The privy door banged open as he was going by. A woman who most definitely wasn't Rose emerged wearing only bed-sheets, and barely even those. She was pale and freckled, with a curve to her hips that Tam might have appreciated more had the woman not let the sheet across her chest slip when she caught sight of the druin.

"Morning, Cloud."

"Morning, Penny." Freecloud skirted past her without a second glance.

The girl—Penny—shook her head, red curls bobbing, and cinched up her sheet. "Bear, was that you thumping the door just now?"

Brune spooned up the last of his oatmeal. "Roderick," he said.

"Oh." Penny's sour expression made it evident what she thought of the satyr. "Well, you can tell him I'm finished."

"Too late," said Cura, licking the tip of one finger and using it to turn a page of her book.

Penny crossed into the kitchen and threw her arms around Brune, then kissed him as though she were a dog and his face was an untended birthday cake. Tam shuddered and looked away. When it was over, Penny insisted on giving Tam a hug and a somewhat less vigorous kiss.

"You must be the new bard," she said cheerily. "I'm Penny, by the way. I'm an Outlaw."

"An outlaw? Really?"

Penny snickered, and Brune gave the girl a reproving look.

"There's some folks who follow us on tour," he explained. "They call themselves the Outlaw Nation, and they sort of . . ."

look after us, you know? They drink with us, cook meals from time to time, repair our weapons and whatnot."

Cura looked up from her book. "Penny here can't cook for shit, but she takes *very* good care of Brune's weapon. In fact, she polished it just last night."

Before Brune could muster a reply, Freecloud returned with Rose in tow. Fable's leader spared Penny a wan smile before addressing her shaman. "You know the rules, Brune. No guests in the morning."

"Mine left at the crack of dawn!" chirped Cura. "Like a good girl."

Penny looked expectantly at Brune, as if imploring him to speak up on her behalf. The poor man glanced to Rose (leaning casually against the wall) and back before offering Penny a cringing shrug.

"Rules are rules," he mumbled.

Penny huffed imperiously and whirled toward the door. Brune called after her. "Penny, your clothes!"

"I'll get them tonight," she said, hiking her stolen bedsheets to her knees as she stepped around the retching satyr.

Freecloud approached Tam bearing a leather longcoat the colour of a late autumn leaf. "Try this on," he said.

She took it from him. The leather was rough and worn, marred by scuffs and slashes. Parts of it looked charred by flame or ravaged by something corrosive. It smelled like a forest on fire, and Tam had the sudden sense of having taken something that didn't belong to her.

"Go ahead," the druin urged.

The others were watching closely. Brune's expression verged on disbelief, while Cura wore a lopsided grin Tam couldn't even begin to interpret. Rose was half-smiling as well; the window on the opposite wall threw bands of light across her face, but left her eyes in shadow.

Tam slipped the coat on. It was a little broad at the shoulders, a bit long at the sleeves, and the bottom nearly skimmed the floor as she turned from side to side, but it fit. It fit *pretty damn good*, actually, and she found herself wishing that Bran, or Willow, or Tiamax (really *anyone* who'd known her for longer than two whole days) could see her now, dressed like some warrior-poet in a druin's war-torn longcoat.

"That belonged to the Duke of Endland," said Freecloud.

Tam regarded him with a look of blank stupefaction she usually reserved for Cornerstone guests who ordered drinks in a foreign language. "You're not serious," she said. "*Are* you serious?"

The druin's long ears bobbed in affirmation. "I am," he said. "Rose and I found it on the battlefield at Castia, along with my sword, *Madrigal*."

The Duke of Endland was the villain of a thousand songs. His real name was Lastleaf, but no two bards could agree on his true identity. Some claimed he was the son of Vespian, who had ruled the Old Dominion before it fell. Others called him Heathen, and asserted that the druin warlord had in fact been one of Grandual's gods—none other than the Autumn Son himself. The only unassailable truth was that six years ago he'd led a host of a monsters out of the Heartwyld Forest and had very nearly wiped the Republic of Castia off the map.

"Why don't you wear it?" Tam asked.

"Because my ears invite condemnation enough," said Freecloud. "Between Lastleaf's rebellion and the fact that my kind once kept yours as slaves, people tend to treat us with a certain ... hostility."

"They're dicks," Rose translated.

"Nevertheless," said Freecloud, "dressing up as the Duke would be in poor taste, I think. Besides, you saved my life, Tam. Perhaps this coat will save yours one day. The leather is thick, reinforced at the breast and the back. It will soften most blows, and bear the brunt of all but the deepest cuts."

"It won't stop an arrow," said Cura matter-of-factly.

"You're scaring the girl," Brune grumbled.

Cura's grin was predatory. "I like scaring girls."

Rose pushed herself off the wall. "We should go," she said. "We're due in Woodford two days from now, and we'll be fighting traffic every mile east. Where's our driver?"

The sound of stamping hooves drew their attention. Roderick was swaying in the doorway, smacking his lips and scratching his furry arse. "Let's get this show on the road," he slurred.

Freecloud's ears dipped in concern. "You good to drive, old boy?"

"Of course! I just need..." He stumbled into the kitchen and began opening cupboards. "A spoon of honey, a mug of orange juice, and a bottle of white wine, preferably Agrian. Wait, is it morning still? Better make it rum."

Tam cleared her throat, pointedly *not* looking below the satyr's waist. "Aren't you forgetting something?" she asked.

Roderick, who'd been bending over the icebox, turned bleary, bloodshot eyes upon her. "What? Oh, right. Has anyone seen my hat?"

By afternoon they were on the road east of Ardburg. The *Rebel's Redoubt* was trailed by the self-proclaimed Outlaw Nation: a small army of followers on foot and horseback, as well as a convoy of smaller wagons bearing everything from casks of ale and crates of food, to cast-iron ovens and a portable forge, in case Fable needed a loaf of bread or some dents hammered out of their armour.

Tam went up to the roof, pulled an oiled tarp off a sofa there, and played a few songs on her mother's heart-shaped lute. The sun came out, and she shrugged off the Heathen's longcoat when she started to sweat. Brune joined her a while later. He scared a crow out of the upper hearth, got a fire going, and brewed a pot of tea for the others, who arrived one by one and amused themselves in various ways.

Rose and Freecloud huddled with their heads together, occasionally laughing and often kissing. Roderick swayed on the baseboard up front, smoking and swigging rum, munching contentedly on what Tam suspected was a leather glove. The satyr sang along as she played, replacing song lyrics with his own bawdy rhymes (except for *Kait and the Cockatrice*, which he sang *almost* word for word).

Cura sat alone with a book in her lap. Tam couldn't help but steal a glance at its title.

"*Pixies in Peril*? What's it about?"

"Pixies."

"Just pixies?"

"Also peril," said the Inkwitch dryly.

Tam tucked a strand of stray hair behind her ear. "Sounds cool."

Brune chortled, sipping his tea. "Does it, though?"

The day wore on. The blue sky faded to pink as the sun set behind them, and Tam looked over her shoulder to catch one final glimpse of home.

Except, of course, it wasn't home. Not anymore.

Chapter Nine

Woodford

Tam awoke the next day with yet another vicious hangover, since someone, at some point the night before, had opened a bottle of wine, and then a cask of rum, and then a keg of stout Kaskar beer, after which she vaguely remembered playing cards with Freecloud and losing a great deal of money she hadn't had in the first place.

Roderick's haystack was vacant, and sure enough she felt the rumble of the *Redoubt*'s wheels grinding below her. Brune's bed was empty as well, and the door to Rose's room was shut. Cura was still in her bunk, sitting with her back to the window, her nose buried in the final pages of *Pixies in Peril*.

"Morning," Tam ventured.

"Is it?" The Inkwitch didn't bother looking up from her book.

Good talk, Tam chided herself. *You're fitting right in.* She slipped out of her bunk, rummaged through her pack for a pair of fresh wool socks, and pulled them halfway to her knees before padding down the hall toward the galley.

Brune was crouched by the fireplace, waiting patiently for the kettle to boil. He glanced over as Tam crashed onto one of the sofas. "Tea?" he asked.

"Please," she groaned.

The shaman chuckled. "Feeling rough?"

"Aren't you?"

Brune shook his head, his expression veiled by his long hair. Something about him reminded Tam of the older mercs who practically lived at the Cornerstone. He had an easy smile, and moved with slow purpose, even when the kettle started howling like a wolf on fire. "I took it easy last night," he told her.

"Easy?" She sat up, wedging a cushion in the crook of her arm. "You and Roderick had a wine drinking contest, remember? You drank five bottles all by yourself."

He flashed her that gap-toothed grin of his. "Yeah, well, a bet's a bet. And it was his wine, anyway." Brune retrieved a set of four clay mugs from the cupboard, then swiped a glass jar off the counter and wrenched loose the lid. His tongue wedged between his teeth as he used two big fingers to pinch a ration of tea leaves into each cup. "Besides, I'm not allowed to get *really* drunk. Boss's orders."

"You mean Rose? Why not?"

The shaman went stiff as he poured hot water into one of the mugs, and Tam immediately regretted having pried.

"There was... an incident," Brune said. "Earlier in the tour. I got very drunk, and very angry, and..." He trailed off as he refilled the remaining mugs, and then set the kettle on a slate board. "Anyway, it won't happen again, so long as I drink responsibly from here on out."

Only a mercenary would call guzzling five bottles of wine drinking responsibly, she thought bemusedly. *Dad was right: These people are insane.*

Aware that she'd made the shaman uncomfortable, Tam decided to change the subject. "Those are beautiful," she said, nodding toward the cups, which were made of glazed white ceramic decorated with painted blue animals: long-necked, long-legged beasts with the barrel chests of horses.

"Aren't they?" Brune picked one up; the teacup almost

disappeared in his huge hand. "I bought them at the Winter Souk. Cost me a whole gig's pay almost, but it was worth it. They take their tea very seriously in Narmeer." He closed his eyes and inhaled a noseful of fragrant steam. "Every court's got their darling drink, come to think of it. The Agrians like their simple summer beer, the Kaskars their whiskey. The Phantrans have their coffee, and their rice wine, and their rum. Boy, do they love their rum. And the Carteans, well, have you ever tasted *sagrut*?"

"*Sagrut*?"

"Vile stuff," Brune declared. "Tastes like sour milk and horse blood."

Tam wrinkled her nose. "What's in it?"

"Sour milk and horse blood."

"Oh."

"Here." Brune came and handed her two cups. "Take one of these up to Rod, will you? I'll bring the other to Cura."

"What about Rose and Freecloud?" Tam asked.

"Don't expect we'll see much of them today," said the shaman with an exaggerated wink.

"Okay."

"If you know what I mean," he added, winking again.

"I do," Tam assured him.

"Because they're having—"

"Bye," she said.

"—sex," Brune finished, but she was already headed for the stairs.

"What's with the hat?" Tam asked Roderick as they sipped their tea and watched the wintry forest roll by on either side of the road.

The satyr, who'd produced a flask from somewhere and was adding a nip of some amber liquid to his cup, glanced over. "Fancy, right?"

The bard admired the bushel of stiff white fox-tails. "That's one word for it, sure."

The booker's eyes narrowed. "You think it's dumb."

"So dumb," Tam admitted. "It's maybe the dumbest hat I've ever seen."

Roderick snorted, and offered her the flask despite her remark. "Brandy?"

"No, thanks. I'm already hungover—"

"Best thing for it," he insisted, pouring her some anyway. He stowed the flask and sipped from his cup, sighing contentedly afterward.

Tam's tea was almost finished, so her next mouthful was mostly booze. It wasn't near as bad as she'd expected, however. The taste of plum lingered in her mouth and a pleasant warmth went coursing through her. Her gaze wandered north, where the Rimeshields marched across the horizon beneath snowy cloaks. The air was crisp, and the late-morning sunlight sparked off the barding of the horses hauling the argosy.

Roderick was right, she thought. *My head feels better already.*

"This hat," Rod said, reclaiming the reins from between his knees, "keeps me safe, as sure as any helmet. This shirt, these pants"—he indicated his offensively pink blouse and baggy white trousers—"protect me like armour. The boots, too." He stomped on the baseboard with his hard leather soles.

She inspected the hat again, trying to discern if there was a skullcap hidden beneath it. There might have been iron rods inside the tails to keep them erect. "How so?" she asked.

"By hiding what I really am. My horns, my hooves. All of this, really." He waved his cup over his legs. "If people found out what I was, they'd despise me."

A peal of laughter sounded some distance behind them. Tam turned to look at the train of carts and wagons snaking along the brown strip of road. "Do the Outlaws know?" she asked.

"Some of them. Penny does, obviously. Most of them have

toured with us for years—they're practically family. But if a wrangler caught me with my pants down?" He drank again and licked his lips. "I'd end up in a cage, or worse: fighting for my life in some backwater arena."

"Rose wouldn't let that happen," Tam said. *A silly thing to say*, she told herself, *seeing as you've known her for two whole days*.

The satyr eyed her sidelong, probably thinking the same. "You're right, she wouldn't. But it could cause the band a lot of trouble. They might have to find another booker, and I ... I don't know what I'd do, to be perfectly honest. Fable's all I've got. Well." He grinned at her. "That, and this fancy hat."

When they arrived in Woodford there wasn't much of a crowd to greet them. The townsfolk had no doubt assumed that Fable would forsake their tour and head west along with everyone else, so when the Outlaw Nation rolled into town they were met by a few dozen wary onlookers, including one very shocked young woman whose hair was hacked short and dyed hucknell-bean red. She took one look at Rose and screamed until her lungs gave out, then hit the ground like a sack of yams.

Word of their arrival swept through town like a spring flood, and before long Woodford's thoroughfare teemed with folk eager for a look at Bloody Rose and her bandmates.

Roderick came strutting down the *Redoubt*'s steps wearing flared gold trousers and a green silk shirt buttoned low enough to show off the satyr's unruly chest hair.

The booker, accompanied by a few burly Outlaws, barged his way toward Rose and Freecloud, who were being accosted by a cluster of innkeepers, tavern owners, and the hopeful proprietor of a local brothel called the Mindflayer's Mistress, all of whom were vying to provide lodging for the band.

Wherever Fable stayed, Cura explained to Tam as the

negotiations went on, they stayed for free. Not only would the lucky establishment reap a fortune selling food and booze to Fable and their entourage, but the notoriety of having hosted Bloody Rose would drum up business for years to come.

"They'll never wash the sheets she sleeps on," Cura said, and then smiled wickedly. "But they'd better burn mine."

The "lucky" establishment turned out to be an inn called the Crowded House, which certainly lived up to its name once Fable and their ilk moved in. The place was long and narrow, its walls hung with clouded glass mirrors that made it seem even busier than it was. There wasn't a proper stage, but a bard was crammed on a corner stool doing his damndest to contend with the noise.

Roderick left to meet the local wrangler. Freecloud managed to con a few of the inn's regulars into a one-sided game of Shields and Steels before he and Rose retreated to their room. Rose, Tam noticed, was clutching a glassy black orb to her chest as she and Freecloud climbed the stairs.

Cura was accosted by a full-lipped woman who declared herself the Inkwitch's biggest fan and was eager to prove it. The two of them disappeared, which left Tam and Brune to hold the fort on Fable's behalf.

Thankfully, the shaman was happy to keep her company. He polished off four tankards to every one of Tam's, and occasionally passed her a pipe of something that left her lungs burning and her body tingling. He drew the line at scratch, however. When a sallow-faced man offered Tam a knife coated with dazeworm venom, the shaman growled so deep and low she feared he might become a bear right then and there. The dealer skulked off, and Brune laid a hand on her shoulder.

"Promise me you'll never do that shit," he said.

She rolled her eyes. "You sound like my dad."

Brune laughed, but his grip on her shoulder tightened. "I'll take that as a compliment, then, 'cause your dad's a fucking legend. But seriously, promise me."

A legend? Tuck Hashford? Tam had to crane her neck to meet the shaman's eyes. "I promise."

"Good." He beamed down at her. "Let's get some grub."

They found a booth and shared a bowl of spiced potatoes. Penny passed out on the seat beside Brune, and Roderick slunk in next to Tam a short while later. The booker was lamenting the "slim pickings" he'd been offered by the local wrangler when a harried-looking woman approached the table.

"Excuse me . . ." she interrupted.

"You're excused," said Roderick. "Now fuck off."

"Rod." Brune's voice was a chiding rumble.

"Apologies, love," the booker muttered. He slapped on a feeble smile. "What is it you want? An autograph? Did you bring a quill? Parchment? If it's a tumble you're after, I'm afraid you're too skinny for Brune's tastes, and far too meek for mine. Though perhaps Tam here would fancy—"

The woman untied a leather purse from her waist and dropped it on the table with a very heavy *clink.*

Roderick's ears perked up at the sound. "Your room or mine?" he asked.

The woman ignored him, her eyes fixed on Fable's shaman. "Please, we need your help. My village is just south of here. We're under attack!"

Brune swiped hair from his eyes. "Under attack? By who?"

"Our dog! He's gone mad!"

The shaman eyed her skeptically. "You want us to kill your dog?"

"He's already dead!" she cried. "A pack of grill got him two days ago, stripped the poor bugger to the bone! We buried him in the yard, said our prayers to the Summer Lord, and stood vigil all night by his grave—"

"You stood vigil for a dog?" Roderick blurted.

"But he *came back*," the woman screeched. "Broke out of his coffin and dug free of his grave!"

"A coffin? Like a *dog* coffin?" The booker looked around, grinning. "Is this a joke? Did Cura put you up to this?"

"He killed our horses, then our pigs, then he went after our neighbour, Mary."

"Did he . . . kill her?" Brune seemed genuinely concerned.

"Poor Mary managed to escape," she said, "but in the dark she stumbled into the open grave and broke her neck."

A snort escaped Roderick before he slapped a hand over his mouth. "I'm sorry," he said, when Brune and the woman both glared at him. "Go on," he urged, "please. You said your dog—"

"Phoenix."

The satyr stifled a chuckle, smothered a giggle, then abruptly left the table. Tam could hear him cackling madly somewhere behind her.

"And now Mary's come back as well," said the woman, "only she's some sort of devil! My husband hit her with the shovel, knocked most of her jaw clean off, and she just kept after him. We've got her locked up now, and all she does is stare at us with those white-fire eyes. We don't—"

"Hold on?" The shaman forestalled her with a raised hand. "Did you say there was *white fire* in her eyes? The dog's, too?" The woman nodded, frantic, and Brune pushed the purse of coins back toward her. "Take your money," he said. "You don't need mercs, just a few strong men. Tell them to search the houses in your village. Keep an eye out for chalk drawings, candles, scrawny old men in black robes—things like that."

The woman sniffed. "What? Why?"

"Because Mary's not your problem, lady. Phoenix ain't either. You've got a necro in the neighbourhood."

"A what?"

"A necromancer," Brune said, but was met with a blank stare. "A sorcerer who uses dark magic," he clarified, prompting the woman to trace the Summer Lord's circle over her heart. "You could chop Mary's head off, or burn her. Same goes for the dog. But you're better off going after the one responsible for bringing them back. Find them, kill them, problem solved."

The woman retrieved her coin purse and clutched it tight. "So if we kill this nekkermancer—"

"Necromancer."

"—then Mary and Phoenix will be at peace? For good?"

The shaman nodded. "That's right. A puppet can't dance without someone pulling the strings."

She thanked him and hurried off.

Roderick returned a few minutes later and passed out cups of something he called "Corn and Oil." It was dark as coffee, but thick as syrup, and smelled cloyingly sweet.

"What's in this?" Tam asked, peering into the black mirror of her mug.

"Phantran rum, raw sugar . . . They drink the stuff like water back east." The satyr nudged his hat from his eyes. "You've never had one? My mother practically raised me on the stuff."

"What was your mother like?" Tam ventured.

Roderick stroked his pointed beard. "Like me, I guess, but with bigger horns, hairier legs, and a fouler mouth. Ah, and she could sing like a siren in heat."

"Mine too," Tam said. And then, because she was more than a little drunk—and because Rod had said *could* instead of *can*—she asked, "How did yours die?"

"Monsters killed her."

The bard blinked. "Monsters?" She'd assumed satyrs were monsters until yesterday, and wondered what exactly qualified as one to Roderick.

"Ever seen a raga?" he asked.

She had, back in Ardburg's Monster Market. "They're like great big cat-people, right?"

"Close enough. Well, a few of them killed my parents

when they refused to pledge allegience to the Heartwyld Horde."

Tam thought of the raga she'd seen in the market. He'd been imprisoned, but had smiled toothily at her through the bars of his cage. *Hey, kid!* she remembered him saying. *How many kobolds does it take to saddle a horse?* She'd ignored him, hastening on, and never did hear the end of that joke.

"Are all ragas monsters, then?"

Roderick didn't seem willing to meet her gaze, and instead took a long sip of his drink. "Only if they choose to be," he said.

Chapter Ten

The Spectacle of Suffering

Woodford's arena was called the Hysterium. It wasn't nearly the size of the Ravine, but it was shaped like a bowl and made entirely of metal, so in Tam's fragile state it sounded just as loud. Every stamp and scream from beyond the armoury split her skull like an axe through kindling. Her guts were a roiling cesspool of ale, wine, whiskey, and too many cups of Roderick's "Corn and Oil"—each of them vying to be the first one out.

Brune arrived late. There were dark circles beneath his eyes and a crimson smear across his lips that Tam hoped was cosmetic paint. He wore a loose leather cuirass over soiled, shredded clothes, and was using his twinglaive as a crutch as he hobbled into the armoury.

Cura raised a bone-pierced eyebrow. "Rough night, Brune?"

"Brutal," he growled.

"Are those even your clothes?"

"They are now."

"Where's your other boot?" Tam asked.

Brune resisted the urge to look down, but she saw him wriggle the toes on his bare left foot. "Right where I left it," he said defensively. "Say, does anyone have—"

"Here." Rodrick passed him a wineskin. The shaman

guzzled it empty, wiped his mouth with the back of one hand, and looked somewhat refreshed afterward.

Rose sighed. "What happened, Brune?"

The shaman rubbed at his face. Something haunted flashed in his eyes, brief as a wisp of cloud skimming past the moon. "I don't remember."

"Was anyone hurt?" asked Freecloud. The druin was studying his moonstone coin and didn't bother looking up.

"I . . . don't remember," the vargyr repeated. He seemed on the verge of tears. "I don't think so."

Rose chewed her lip, a gambler deciding whether outrage or empathy was her best bet. "Take it easy out there today," she told him. "I'm sure the rest of us can pick up the slack. Cloud? Cura?"

"Of course," said Freecloud.

Cura gently nudged the shaman's ribs. "Same as always, then?"

Brune dredged up a sheepish smile. "Thanks," he said, and then muttered, "Sorry," to no one in particular.

"Don't worry about it," Rose said. "Now let's kill 'em, thrill 'em, and get the fuck out of here."

"You only just arrived," said a woman descending the armoury steps, "and already you're plotting your escape!"

The newcomer was the Hysterium's wrangler, a severe-looking woman bundled in expensive furs. Her hair was bound in a thick braid down the length of her back. She wore a short sword in a jewelled scabbard on her hip, and the polished steel torcs she wore on each arm were a symbol of pride and wealth among the Kaskar elite.

Rose's smile didn't quite reach her eyes. "Hello, Jeka."

"Bloody Rose!" The two women clasped wrists. "I'm relieved you came. I was worried you'd renege on our contract and run off Horde-hunting along with every other merc in the north."

"Seen one Horde, you've seen 'em all," quipped Rose. "And Fable never breaks a contract."

Jeka dipped her head. "I'm grateful to hear it."

Freecloud was peering through the gate that opened onto the arena floor. "Who's out there now?"

"Men without helmets," said the wrangler.

Cura laughed. "We can see that much. He means what band is it?"

"Men Without Helmets," Jeka repeated. "It's an orc-shit name, I'll grant you that, but that's what they call themselves."

Tam took a step closer to the arena gate. Beyond, she saw three mercenaries doing battle with a pair of sinu—lithe, fox-like creatures armed with wooden clubs. A fourth merc was down and bleeding, having suffered a painfully ironic head injury. As Tam watched, one of the sinu deflected an attacker's sword and sunk its jaws into the man's wrist.

"They'll be Men Without Hands if they're not careful," mused Freecloud, and Cura snickered appreciatively.

Jeka swaggered over to peer through the gate as well. "Bloody amateurs," she swore. Tam assumed she was referring to the mercenaries, since their adversaries were driving them back against the far wall. "Thank the Holy Tetrea I thought to drug those foxes, or I'd have a fucking wipe on my hands."

Tam glanced over at the wrangler. "You drugged them?"

"Of course," she admitted, with no shame whatsoever. "These brats-without-helmets are barely mercs at all. They're too green for a real fight, or they'd be headed west along with everyone else."

"Not everyone," Cura muttered.

"So I mixed a little something into their morning eggs," said Jeka, "but it looks like I should have doubled the dose. Ah, there we go."

One of the sinu stumbled, clutching its head with a padded paw. The nearest mercenary seized his manufactured good fortune and drove the point of his sword into the creature's gut. It fell with a whimper, which spurred its partner to attack more furiously despite the poison coursing through its veins.

The crowd hadn't seemed to notice the sinu's sudden lethargy. *They've come to see bands triumph and monsters get killed*, Tam reasoned. *They wanted blood, and now they've got it.*

"Do you do this often?" she asked. "Drug the monsters?"

The wrangler shrugged. "With the new blood, yes. Although sedatives aren't always the best option. I might break a kobold's arm, or dump a bucket of sand down a slag drake's throat. With some of them—the smarter ones—you can pretty much call the shots if you've got their offspring on hand. They'll do just about anything to save them, even if it means throwing themselves on a sword-point. It's dreadfully convenient."

It's dreadfully something, Tam thought, disgusted.

Jeka went on. "Some bands—Fable, for instance—won't allow it. They think it's cheating. I think it's good for business."

As if to accentuate her point, the crowd began celebrating a heroic victory beyond the gate. The bloody corpses of the sinu were dragged away, while the mercs still standing basked in the adulation like beggars tossed a handful of courtmark coins. They didn't seem overly concerned that two of their fellows were down and bleeding.

"Give us a moment to clean up the mess," said Jeka. At a gesture from the wrangler, the gate clacked slowly open.

In the meantime, Rose had drifted to one corner of the armoury and was holding a satchel Tam recognized from the Ravine. She plucked a brittle black leaf from inside it, then stole a furtive glance at Freecloud—as if the druin might disprove of what she was doing—before pressing the leaf to her tongue and letting it dissolve.

Uncle Bran had once suggested that Tam's father try using Lion's Leaf to bolster his courage. This was shortly after Lily's death, when her uncle still nursed the hope that Ironclad would go on as they always had. As if they possibly could. There were side effects (addiction not least among them), but Bran had been certain that, with proper medication, Tuck could return to fighting form once again.

Assuming she'd identified the black leaves correctly, Tam couldn't imagine what use someone like Rose could have for Lion's Leaf. Here was a woman who'd faced down the Heart-wyld Horde, whose exploits were praised by every bard in Grandual. Even her refusal to face the Brumal Horde seemed courageous to Tam. Rose had chosen to honour her contracts instead of running off to gorge herself on the soon-to-be carcass of Brontide's army.

Jeka strode back into the armoury. "You're on," she yelled, pitching her voice to be heard above the arena crowd, who were chanting Fable's name. The sound of stomping feet echoed from the circling tiers, a hammering heartbeat of leather and steel. Dust shook loose from the armoury roof, glinting like sparks in the slanting light.

Rose, her gaze wiped of everything but constrained fury, stepped into the circle of her bandmates. "Death or glory," she said.

"*Death or glory*," they echoed.

"But preferably glory," said Freecloud.

Rose nodded, and led them out.

"Is that...?" Tam trailed off as she studied the creature against which Fable was pitted.

"A raga," said Roderick. "And yes," he added, before the bard could think to ask, "I chose it because I fucking hate ragas, and I'm really looking forward to watching this one die."

"It's not just any raga," Jeka was pleased to point out. "Temoi here was a pride lord. The Scourge of Heatherfell. He led a war party against North Court last summer. His warriors were slaughtered, but Temoi was taken prisoner, destined to die in one arena or another. I paid a small fortune to make sure it was mine."

The raga was enormous, heavily muscled, armoured in

scraps of sun-bleached bone. His head was framed by a mane of coarse black fur, and there was a festering scar bisecting his broad, leonine snout. Claws that could have crushed Tam to pulp gripped a pair of flat-topped iron swords as long as the bard was tall.

All this she discerned while the beast was charging Rose. His huge swords came slashing before him, and Tam briefly imagined watching her idol's torso go jetting skyward on a surge of blood. But Rose was already down, tumbling between his legs, deft despite her half-plate armour.

Freecloud flowed into the space behind Temoi's swords. *Madrigal* came singing from its scabbard, carving up through the raga's chest. Temoi's bone armour shattered like dishware. His flesh curled away from the blade's edge to reveal the blood-slick grin of ribs beneath.

That blow should have killed him, Tam knew—and so did the bowl of spectators, since they groaned in dismay. The people of Woodford had been anticipating this fight for months, after all. They wanted Fable to win, but they wanted a good story as well—something they could use to impress their grandchildren someday without having to embellish *too* much.

Fortunately for them, Temoi wasn't so easily killed. The pride lord remained on his feet, fangs bared, arms flexing as his swords came scissoring back at Freecloud.

The druin stepped clear of the blades, then danced back as the raga slashed again. Tam marvelled at Freecloud's casual grace. Every move he made seemed part of some indiscernible stratagem, the way a Tetrea master reacted with cold calculation to an opponent's clumsy advance.

Brune, bless his heart, made an effort to join the fight. He staggered forward on one bare foot, but then stopped suddenly and clamped a hand over his mouth to avoid spilling his guts on the arena floor. A pair of Cura's knives blurred past him. One clanged harmlessly off the raga's bone plate, but the other buried itself between two of Temoi's exposed ribs. The beast howled in anguish, and might have rushed the Inkwitch had Rose's swords not come bursting through his chest.

The raga slumped to his knees, still clutching his heavy iron swords. He bared his teeth again, but if he'd meant to roar defiance he failed miserably, since only a wheezing rattle escaped.

Rose left *Thistle* and *Thorn* buried in the monster's back. She turned away from his corpse, arms outstretched, face raised to the sky like a prisoner released to a rainstorm. Freecloud sheathed his keening sword and started back toward the armoury gate. He passed Cura on the way as she stepped forward to retrieve her knives. Brune slumped visibly, gripping *Ktulu* with both hands and doing his best to appear as if he might not topple at any moment.

"Such a pity." Jeka's disappointment was readily apparent. "Fable usually puts on a better show."

Roderick said nothing, only eyed the dead raga with grim satisfaction.

What would she have them do? Tam wondered. *Torture the thing? Make a spectacle of its suffering?* Mercenaries killed monsters because monsters killed people, not so that wranglers could recoup the money they'd spent taking them captive. At least that's what Tam had believed until today.

She watched Cura spend a moment appraising the raga's ruined chest, then plant one foot on Temoi's thigh and grip her knife's pommel with both hands.

And besides, Tam thought, *fighting isn't a game, and killing monsters—whether you do so in a cave or on an arena floor—isn't something to be taken lightly.* The bard knew this better than most; she'd lost her mother to a monster, after all. *A moment is all it takes. A heartbeat, and the world as you know it—*

She saw the raga raise its head, saw the white fires burning where its eyes should have been.

"Cura!" Tam screamed through the gate.

The Inkwitch spared a glance behind her, then dropped

like a stone as one of Temoi's grey swords swooped over-head. The raga's swing arced in a circle, and Rose turned just in time to raise an arm before the blade struck. Sparks flared as the cold iron edge met Rose's raised gauntlet, driving her arm against her breastplate. There was a dry snap as the bone broke, a wet pop as her arm wrenched loose from its socket, and a gasp of horror from the Hysterium crowd as Fable's frontwoman went skidding backward, slamming hard against the opposite gate.

Tam rushed to a rack on the armoury wall and lifted a broadsword clear, immediately wishing she'd chosen some-thing practical—something she could swing more than once before her strength gave out—but there was no time to be picky. "Open the gate," she said to Jeka.

"What?" The wrangler scoffed. "Are you mad?"

"I said *open the goddamn gate*."

Jeka laid a hand on the jewelled pommel of her own weapon. "Try me, *girl*. I was a merc for seven years before I built this place. You ever hear of Rockjaw the goblin king?"

"I . . . uh . . . no?"

"That's because I split that prick's head open when he was still just a prince. Now drop that sword or I'll show you how I did it."

"Hey." Roderick took Tam by the arm. "You're the *bard*, remember? You can't just jump in and fight whenever you feel like it."

"But—"

"They can handle it, kid." The satyr sounded more sure than he looked. "Trust me."

Tam shrugged out of his grip. She discarded the sword and closed her fingers around the iron bars, wishing she hadn't left her bow on the *Rebel's Redoubt*. "I thought that thing was dead," she grated.

Beside her, the wrangler was trying—and failing—to hide her growing smile. "I think it still is," she said.

Chapter Eleven

The Greater of Two Evils

Cura said something to Freecloud that Tam couldn't make out above the anxious babble sloshing around the arena bowl. The druin nodded and began skirting the wall slowly, so as not to draw Temoi's attention.

Assuming, of course, that the creature squaring off against Brune and Cura was still Temoi.

Tam had her doubts. She recalled what Brune had said last night about white-fire eyes. Had a sorcerer brought the raga back from the dead? Could it have been Jeka? No, Tam decided. Despite the wrangler's smug glee at the prospect of getting more than she bargained for, the woman was very obviously as suprised as anyone that the pride lord was back on his feet.

Was the person responsible hidden among the arena spectators, then? And what, if anything, did this have to do with the woman who'd come begging for Fable's aid last night? *You've got a necro in the neighbourhood*, Brune had told her.

Whoever this necromancer is, Tam thought, *they just knocked on the wrong fucking door.*

Brune, who sobered considerably in a matter of instants, hefted *Ktulu* and threw a searching glance at Cura. The Ink-witch gestured encouragingly toward the hulking raga, as if to say, *Be my guest*. The absurdity of their exchange drew a bout of nervous laughter from the tiers above.

The shaman spat a mouthful of phlegm onto the arena floor, rolled his neck from side to side, and charged. The thing that had been Temoi thrust one of its swords directly at him, and though the tip was blunted, Tam had no doubt the pride lord's strength could punch it right through Brune and out the other side.

The shaman, however, had something less suicidal in mind. He used one of *Ktulu*'s long blades to knock the raga's weapon aside and lunged after it, so that Temoi's other sword chopped down behind him. This left the shaman in the enviable position of being inside his enemy's reach with a razor-sharp twinglaive in hand, so he did what anyone (provided they were skilled enough to wield a twinglaive without gutting themselves) would do in that case.

He cut the bastard in half.

Or he tried to, anyway. The raga turned just as Brune attacked, so the bulk of his arm bore the brunt of the blade's edge. Temoi's severed limb, and the sword it held, dropped like a dead branch at his feet.

But *Ktulu* didn't stop there. It was halfway through the pride lord's torso before it got snagged on something— probably his spine. The shaman tried to tug his weapon free, but abandoned it as the raga, undeterred by the fact that Brune had chopped him mostly in half, raised his other sword.

"*KURAGEN!*" Cura's voice cut through the arena's clamour like the scrape of a sword drawn in a chapel hall.

A creature surged off her thigh, tendrils of ink coalescing into something twice the size of the undead raga. Its torso was distinctly feminine beneath a sculpted chiton breastplate, and she (assuming *Kuragen* was a *she*) clasped a two-pronged spear in one webbed hand. Her head was encased by a pearlescent white helm that concealed the upper half of her face. It reminded Tam of the seashells her mother had brought back from a tour of the Silk Coast. Hair like tangled weeds emerged from beneath *Kuragen*'s helm, and gills ribbed her long neck, gasping clouds into the cold air. Instead of legs, she possessed a dozen writhing tentacles, each as thick around as Tam herself. Two of them lashed out to coil around the raga's raised arm.

Next to Tam, Roderick withdrew a silver flask from inside his pants. He took a swig and closed his eyes as a shudder ran through him. "I hate this one," he muttered. "She gives me the creeps."

For a moment the two monsters—Jeka's unholy abomination and Cura's undersea horror—strained against one another, until the thing the Inkwitch had summoned snapped another of its coiling limbs around the raga's arm and hauled him off balance. Brune barely managed to tear his weapon free before the raga went down.

Tam felt the gate bars quiver in her hands as Temoi hit the arena floor. He dropped his remaining sword and scrabbled for purchase as *Kuragen* began dragging him across the ground. A fourth tentacle snagged the raga's leg, hastening his doom. Cura was kneeling now, breathing in gasps and trembling visibly with the effort of sustaining her inked monstrosity.

Freecloud had reached Rose's side. She roused at his touch, thrashing madly, but he pinned her down until she went still beneath him. Brune drifted toward the couple, weapon ready, in case Temoi managed to get free and go after them.

Which didn't look likely, since Cura's conjured horror lashed two more tentacle limbs around the raga's waist, hoisting him roughly into the air. Tam forced herself to watch despite the urge to turn away.

There was a sodden tearing sound as Temoi's remaining arm was ripped from his shoulder. The raga landed on his knees in a pool of blood, and the Hysterium spectators bellowed appreciatively.

Cura staggered to her feet, swaying like a tower rocked at its foundation. Tam could hear her speaking, but couldn't make out the words. Damp rot and the sharp tang of salt tickled her nose.

The raga roared up at *Kuragen*, who rammed her spear into his mouth and out the back of his head. The ghostfires guttered like windblown candles in his eyes.

"Incredible," Jeka whispered. "I've seen summoners fight before, but..."

"But?" Tam asked.

"Not like this," said the wrangler. "Never like this."

By now *Kuragen* had coiled half her tentacles around the armless raga. His legs kicked desperately, but he was helpless in the horror's grip. The Inkwitch extended a trembling arm as she surveyed the sea of howling faces around them. Cries of "*Kill it!*" and "*Finish him!*" were lobbed like stones from the circling heights, and at last the noise resolved into a single word, chanted over and again by the Hysterium crowd.

Death. Death. Death.

Cura bowed her head, an acknowledgment, and curled her open hand into a fist.

Kuragen squeezed. The muscles in her constricting limbs bulged beneath water-slick scales. Temoi gurgled around the spear in his throat, and then crumpled on himself like a suit of cheap tin armour. Bones snapped, blood slopped from the bursting seams in his flesh, and the fires in his eyes went out.

The raga was dead. Again.

Kuragen vanished in a swirl of blue-black mist, leaving Temoi's corpse to collapse in a broken heap as the sound in the arena reached a fever pitch.

"See?" Roderick stole another sip from his flask. The satyr was doing a piss-poor job of hiding the fact that his hands were shaking. "Business as usual."

They left the arena by way of a nondescript door normally reserved for Jeka's kitchen staff, a few of whom were seated on crates outside, sharing a pipe of something stronger than tobacco and trying to outdo one another with escalating inter-pretations of Fable's performance. Tam caught one of them leering at Rose as she went by, but the man found something exceptionally interesting about his crusty leather boots when Freecloud glanced his way.

Cura—weary, but flush with the thrill of victory—shared a lingering stare with a butcher in a bloodstained apron who'd been preening himself in the reflective surface of a knife. She met his devouring gaze with one of her own.

"You wanna go for a ride?" she asked, and the butcher, for all his affected cool, leapt to his feet like a dog who'd been promised a walk.

Freecloud turned on her. "Seriously?"

"What? Oh, I'm sorry, did *you* just use a sea goddess to kill a giant zombie-lion or was that me? I've earned this, Cloud. Besides, I'm sure he can find his way home when I'm finished with him."

The druin looked to Rose. Fable's leader had stripped the armour off her ruined right arm, which vaguely resem-bled a sausage savaged by quarrelling dogs. "Fine," Rose said through gritted teeth. "If he wants to come, he can come."

Cura crooked a finger and the butcher scurried over, trailed by a chorus of hoots and catcalls from Jeka's staff. He set his knife on a crate and began untying his bloody apron, but the summoner shook her head. "Leave it on," she told him. "And bring the knife."

Fable and the Outlaw Nation struck east for Rowan's Creek. Rose was consigned to the nursing wain and placed under the care of Fable's medic, a Cartean witch doctor named Dannon. Doctor Dan (as the Outlaws called him) purveyed a variety of ointments, unguents, and dubious concoctions that could cure almost anything, from blindness, to petrification, to early onset lycanthropy. According to Dan, even a missing limb could be regenerated with the right ingredients, though to Tam that sounded a little far-fetched. Freecloud took Rose's absence as an opportunity to gamble his way through Fable's legion of followers. Despite the druin's reputation for winning every game he played, there was no shortage of challengers willing to try their luck. And it wasn't as if the druin *stole* their money. When the tour passed through Bryton, a village famous for its sprawling orchards, he bought each and every Outlaw an apple pie and a jug of sweet cider.

Tam and Brune were left to entertain themselves while doing their best to ignore the groans, grunts, and occasional squeal from the direction of Cura's bunk. They tried playing Shields and Steels, only to find that every shield but one was missing. The remaining piece had a satyr-shaped bite taken out of it, and Roderick grudgingly admitted to having eaten the others.

"I get hungry!" he said defensively.

They settled for a game of Contha's Keep, the aim of which was to remove wooden blocks from the midst of a precariously stacked tower and place them on top without collapsing the entire structure—a task made even more difficult when the occasional bump in the road jolted the *Redoubt*'s kitchen table.

"Do you know who Contha was?" Brune asked as Tam was nudging a block free.

"You're trying to distract me."

"Is it working?"

The tower didn't so much as wobble as she set her piece on top. "Obviously not," she said. "So, who was Contha?"

The shaman chuckled, and began using the tip of one huge finger to push a block out through the centre. He was surprisingly dextrous for someone with hands the size of frying pans. "He was a druin. An Exarch, actually."

"An Exarch?"

"They were like governors of the Old Dominion," said

Brune. "An Exarch ruled over each city-state on behalf of the Archon, who was basically like the king." His block tumbled clear. He placed it on top and grinned triumphantly, then scooped up the bottle of rice wine near his elbow and drank directly from the neck.

Tam examined the tower. It was getting sparse near the bottom; she would have to choose her next block carefully.

"Contha was the Exarch of a place called Lamneth," Brune went on, determined to draw Tam's mind from the task at hand. "He was something of a recluse, apparently, but a brilliant engineer. When the civil war broke out, and the Exarchs began hurling hosts of wild monsters at one another, Contha fielded an army of golems instead."

The brick Tam had selected popped free. She put it on top and sighed in relief when the tower stopped swaying.

She'd seen the remains of a golem once, when she and her mother had gone exploring the forests around Ardburg. The massive construct had been blanketed by moss. The druic runes that once served it as eyes were dormant, and some animal had made a nest of its mouth. "Have you ever fought one?" she asked as Brune contemplated his next move.

The shaman shook his head. "We came across a live one, once. Runebroken. Running rampant and killing whatever it could find. Freecloud managed to get it under control. He carved a few symbols into a stone medallion, then used his sword to cut the same runes in the golem. Next thing you know, it's doing whatever he tells it to."

"How does Freecloud know so much about golems?" Tam asked.

Brune tried claiming a brick near the bottom, but the structure swayed dangerously, so he went after another instead. "Uh...I'm not—"

"Contha's his dad," came Roderick's muffled voice. The booker was laid out on a sofa behind them with his hooves crossed and his hat perched over his face.

"I thought you were driving!" said Brune, obviously startled. "This thing practically drives itself," Roderick assured him.

Tam was pretty certain that wasn't true, but her curiosity outweighed her concern. "Contha is Freecloud's *father*? Is he still alive?"

The satyr lifted his hat. A cloud of fragrant smoke came billowing out, and Tam was startled to see that Rod had been smoking a pipe underneath it. "So far as we know, yes. He and Freecloud aren't especially close. Most druins don't think too fondly of anyone who isn't a druin. They liked us all better as slaves. So if Cloud's old man found out he was shacking up with a human, or—God's forbid—that he and Rose—"

They heard a sharp yelp down the hallway. Seconds later, Cura's pet butcher appeared, naked but for a spiked leash trailing from his neck.

"That doesn't go there, you crazy bitch!" He froze at the sight of Roderick, who was waving his hat to clear the smoke around his horns. Revulsion made an ugly mask of the butcher's otherwise pretty face. "What the fuck are you supposed to be?"

The satyr spoke around the pipe stem in his teeth. "I'll be the guy with his hoof up your ass if you don't apologize to the nice lady."

The butcher scoffed. "Lady? That painted freak almost killed me! She's damaged goods, man. Bent as a grass sword! And you..." His lip curled in disgust. "You're a fucking *monster*. Go back to the Heartwyld where you belong. Or better yet, go rot in a wrangler's cell and wait for some merc to come along and srrkk—"

The man was dragged violently around by Cura, who'd given the leash on his neck a hard yank. She was holding the butcher's blade, and now pressed it against the prickling skin of his throat.

"You forgot your toy, *dog*," she told him. "Run and get it." The knife went *thunk* into the cupboard beside the door.

The butcher stumbled after it, aided by a kick in the ass from Cura, who was wearing only the bloodied white apron she'd stripped from her suitor—a look Tam found strangely appealing.

The man fled without retrieving his knife. He had a fuzzy, flat little bum that made the bard wonder (not for the first time) why the heck you'd want to see a man naked, much less allow one to crawl on top of you.

The door slammed shut, and the tower she and Brune were building clattered across the table.

The shaman glared accusingly at Cura as she padded over and claimed his bottle of rice wine. She gulped it empty, then set it down amidst the ruins of Contha's Keep.

"I'm playing the winner," she said.

Chapter Twelve

The Rock and the Road

Branigan had told Tam once that every town, village, and hamlet along the ingeniously named East Road was famous for something. Two days later the tour rolled into Rowan's Creek, a town known for its gargantuan lumber mill, which loomed like a lord's keep over the houses clustered around it. The arena here was a box of stepped benches called the Logger's Lair.

A band of adolescent boys named Five Rotten Apples skirmished for Fable against a quartet of dead gnolls. According to the Lair's wrangler, the hyena-headed zombies had been killed in battle three days before, but had risen from the dead with white fires burning in their eyes. Rumours floating through the Outlaw Nation suggested that Kaskar's necromancer-at-large had been performing this trick all over the north. Ancestors screeched from the prison of their tombs, while graveyards belched up the dead in droves. Country-wide exhumations were under way; columns of black smoke buttressed the sky above every town.

On Rose's orders, Roderick sent word east that Fable would fight only *living* monsters for the remainder of the tour.

While they watched the Five Rotten Apples dispatch the gnolls, Tam asked the booker why bands weren't hiring themselves out to the towns and villages in need of aid.

Rod pulled off his hat and scratched around the base of one curling horn. "Because villagers can't pay what a wrangler can," he told her. "There's more gold to be gained fighting in the arenas, and more glory in facing the Horde than hunting down some demented dark wizard."

"Well, what about us?" Tam wondered. "Fable, I mean. Is our contract in Diremarch more important than helping people here?"

The satyr replaced his hat. "Why don't you ask Rose yourself?" he said. "I'd suggest packing your stuff first, though, just in case."

Tam decided to keep her misgivings to herself for the time being.

When the undead gnolls were dealt with, Bloody Rose and her band made a show out of overcoming their own foe: a massive red toad with four eyes, stubby wings, and a tongue that turned to flame the moment it left the monster's mouth. Brune and Cura kept it flanked while Rose systematically destroyed all four of its eyes. Freecloud cut its flaming tongue in half before stepping in to put the poor creature out of its misery.

The crowd loved it, but Tam found the whole thing a bit contrived. She began to question every song she'd ever heard about heroic mercenaries and vile monsters doing battle on the arena floor. If those so-called battles were anything like the one-sided slaughter she watched from the comfort of the Lair's armoury, then the work of a bard was even more difficult than she'd been led to believe.

Something her father had said the night she joined the band resurfaced in her mind. *Mercenaries aren't heroes*, he'd warned her. *They're killers*.

She was beginning to understand what he'd meant by that, and to see the mercenaries she'd once considered heroes in a new and garish light.

They spent the night in Rowan's Creek. Fable secured

rooms at an inn called the Troubled Troubadour and threw a party that featured no less than four fights, three fires, and, implausibly, a birth. The child—a girl with natural red curls—was named Rose, prompting Tam to wonder how many baby Roses had been left in Fable's wake throughout their touring years.

The party was in full swing when Tam retired, so she barricaded the door with everything but the bed and a white bearskin rug. Despite her fortifications, Brune clambered noisily through her ground-floor window shortly before dawn. The shaman's clothes were shredded, his hands sticky with blood. He reeked of booze, and begged the bard not to tell the others.

Tam wondered if this had something to do with the "incident" he'd mentioned a few days ago. "Whose blood is that?" she asked warily.

"Not a who," Brune said, curling up on the bearskin rug. "A what."

"What, then?"

It seemed an effort for the shaman to open his bloodshot eyes. "You ever seen a beaver?" She shook her head no. "Lucky..." he murmured, closing his eyes and drifting off. "Vicious little bastards." His next breath was a ripping snore, so Tam let it lie and pulled a pillow over her head.

The tour rolled on.

In Barton, a village proudly claiming to have the "Tallest Watchtower in the North," Fable butchered a mob of malnourished goblins before a crowd of well-fed northerners. Afterward, they paid a visit to Barton's celebrated watchtower. They spent a few minutes catching their breath at the top, gazing out over the snowcapped forest around them, before Cura gave voice to what each of them was thinking.

"What a waste of fucking time."

The tour rolled on.

In Bell Mill (which boasted neither a bell nor a mill) the

band faced off against a giant spider by the name of Bigger Ted. "This here's the offspring of Big Ted," his wrangler explained to Tam while Fable hacked it apart, "who was the offspring of Ted, who was the offspring of Little Ted, who was hardly bigger than a housecat."

Bell Mill, it turned out, was famous for its spider hatchery, which everyone but Cura refused to visit. And since Cura saw rules as things *begging* to be broken, she stole one of the spiders—a fuzzy orange one about the size of her fist—which Tam watched Roderick eat later that night.

The satyr had been disappointed afterward. "That didn't taste like orange at all," he complained.

The tour rolled on.

Salt Creek touted itself as the birthplace of a legendary heroine named Wyld Willa. Everything—from the village cobbler (Willa's Wandering Feet) to the local pub (Willa's Wet Whistle)—was named in her honour, as were the villagers themselves, nearly all of whom were named either Willa or William.

Salt Creek's wrangler ("Call me Will!" he told them) offered up a trio of grizzled grey-bearded ogres. Rose killed one, Freecloud another. Brune and Cura played a hasty game of Rock-Paper-Scimitar over the last, which the shaman won. He managed to pull off the transformation into a huge brown bear, and made quick work of the band's final foe.

There followed another wild night, another weary morning, and the tour rolled on.

The weather took a turn for the worse. The clouds dumped snowflakes the size of saucers, and the entire train was stranded for almost a week in a town called Piper, whose illustrious "Golden Road" (which Freecloud claimed was actually limestone cobbles slathered with yellow paint) lay buried under several feet of snow. Fable was forced to share Piper's only inn with a dozen or so other bands intent on facing the Horde at Coldfire Pass. They were one and all keen to see a mercenary of Rose's calibre among them, but once word got around that Fable was running off east, she might have been a rotter for the scornful glares thrown her way whenever anyone was damned sure she wasn't looking.

Tam did a stint onstage one night, playing through her repertoire of Fable-inspired songs. When her audience learned she was the daughter of Lily Hashford, they insisted she play *Together* and proceeded to sing along when she did.

Piper's arena, called the Golden Gallery, was built like a theatre: The combatants fought on a stage fenced by barbed netting, while the spectators watched from a semicircle of tiered stone benches. The wrangler here either hadn't received Roderick's notice or had decided to ignore it, since his entire stable comprised of previously slain monsters.

Small wonder no one cares there's a necromancer on the loose, Tam pondered. *Killing him would be bad for business!*

Rose was livid, but instead of calling off the fight she chose a pair of wargs—great black wolves as tall at the shoulder as Brune—and set her summoner loose. While her bandmates passed around a bottle of Gonhollow whiskey, Cura took centre stage and called forth a monster of her own.

"YOMINA!"

Her scream split the air like a thunderclap. Ink curled off her arm and resolved into a figure hunched beneath the bowl of a broad straw hat. Cords of limp white hair fell past its shoulders, too thin to obscure the creature's vulture neck and black-toothed grin. It wore a blood-soaked robe that clung to its bony frame, and was impaled by no fewer than seven swords.

As the white-eyed wargs circled it, *Yomina* closed long-nailed fingers around two jutting hilts. Tam winced at the grating of metal on bone as it pulled the blades from its chest.

Despite its decrepit bearing, Cura's inkling (as she referred to the menagerie of horrors tattooed on her skin) was alarmingly fast. The wargs' jaws snapped shut on scraps of black cloth as *Yomina* dodged with such uncanny speed that Tam thought she'd blinked and missed it moving from one place to the next.

It buried a sword to the hilt in either warg, but still they attacked. One by one the inkling tore blades from its body and drove them into its snarling assailants. At last, as the pair lay crippled, the fire in their eyes fading like stars at dawn, *Yomina* withdrew the seventh sword from the centre of its chest and cut the heads off them both.

The inkling vanished, and Rose bent to help the summoner find her feet. She cupped Cura's face in both hands and said something meant for her alone. The Inkwitch nodded, then chuckled weakly at whatever Rose said next. The two of them embraced as the crowd dispersed into the chilly twilight.

Fable decamped to the inn to wait out the blizzard. When it finally passed, the tour rolled on.

Once, while Tam was fishing with her uncle Bran, they had come across a black bear wading through rapids thick with leaping salmon. The fish were headed upstream, drawn by instinct toward the spawning grounds of their youth. Tam was reminded of that now as the *Rebel's Redoubt* plodded sluggishly against the flood of westward traffic. The foul weather had frozen the road for days, but now it teemed with men and women bound for Coldfire Pass.

The sun peeked occasionally through the roof of clouds, so Tam and the others spent the day on the argosy's roof. The bard sat between crenellations, plucking idle music from *Hiraeth's* heart-shaped bowl and surveying the throng below for mercs she might recognize—either by sight or by reputation alone.

The Duran twins—big, brutish Agrians clad head to toe in spiked iron plate—were trailed by an escort of rough-looking goons they employed in place of a proper band. She saw the White Snakes as well, and Layla Sweetpenny, and Warfire, who coated their weapons in pitch and set them on fire before every battle. Tam wondered if it was by design or coincidence that all five of them were beardless and bald.

She whooped as the Sisters in Steel rode by on armoured white stallions, and waved at Courtney and the Sparks as the gang of chain-skirted spear-wielding women trotted by. Courtney blew her a kiss, and she wondered if the renowned warrior recognized Tam as the girl who'd served her wine at the Cornerstone when they came to Ardburg last summer.

Probably not, she decided.

Rick the Lion was given a wide berth as he navigated a cumbersome-looking war chariot through the crowd. An argosy bearing the name *Wyld Child* rolled past on iron-shod wheels, but the band to whom it belonged remained cloistered inside.

"Tam, look up." Brune drew her attention to a skyship sailing overhead. Its sails crackled with captured electricity, and its tidal engines rained streamers of fine mist that she could feel on her outstretched fingers.

Skyships were exceedingly rare, since the secret of their manufacture had been lost when the Dominion fell. Tam certainly had no idea how they worked, though she'd seen one up close a few times. Vanguard—the band Tiamax and Edwick had both been a part of—had discovered one intact in the Heartwyld years ago. They'd called it *Old Glory*, and when they retired after the battle at Castia, the skyship was sold for a pittance to Rose's father, Golden Gabe himself.

By now the road was so congested that Roderick was forced to halt the argosy as the river of westbound warriors flowed around them. As she watched them go by, dashing and dazzling in the bright panoply of war, something like shame stirred in Tam's gut. All these men and women were racing to save the world, to stand for all of Grandual against Brontide and his ravaging Horde...

And here we are, she thought dejectedly, *a great big rock in a river of heroes.*

"Hey, Rose!" someone called from below. "You're heading in the wrong direction!"

Rose came to stand beside Tam, who identified the speaker as Sam "the Slayer" Roth. On his back was the great-sword *Fang*. His embossed plate armour was strapped so tight over his bulky frame that he looked like a Narmeeri pineapple splitting at the seams. His horse, Tam noted, appeared to be struggling under its rider's considerable weight.

Roth was pointing west. "The Horde is *that* way."

"So I keep hearing," Rose drawled, "but I'm afraid we've got prior commitments. Besides, who's gonna keep the courts safe while all you selfless heroes run off to save us from the Horde? There's a necromancer on the loose, or haven't you heard?"

The Slayer tugged at the collar of his breastplate, clearly uncomfortable in the afternoon heat. "Aye, I did hear that. I also heard you've got a gig in Diremarch."

Mercenaries were an avaricious bunch, Tam knew. If there was a juicy contract up for grabs, Sam Roth would doubtless wonder why he hadn't got wind of it.

"That's true," Rose said.

"So what's more important than a giant with a host of monsters at his back? Don't tell me you'd rather earn a few lousy courtmarks than do battle with the Brumal Horde! Where's the glory in that?"

"This isn't about money, Sam."

"Ha! I knew it! So what's the gig? It must be something big. Something bloody vicious, right?"

"You wouldn't believe me if I told you," said Rose.

Roth's eyes narrowed. "Gods of Grandual," he breathed, "it's a dragon."

Rose said nothing, but her smile deepened just a little.

"It is, isn't it? You've got a fucking dragon on the hook!"

The man actually sounded jealous—as if doing battle with a winged, fire-breathing lizard the size of a house was in any way enviable.

Please let it not be a dragon, Tam thought. She'd wanted adventure, sure, but adventures tended to end rather abruptly when a dragon got involved.

"Which one is it?" Roth asked. "Konsear? Akatung? Wait, didn't your father kill Akatung?"

"It's the Simurg."

The Slayer's face dropped. "Say what?"

"The Simurg," Rose repeated. "The Dragoneater."

Was it Tam's imagination, or had the others—Freecloud, Cura, Brune, even Roderick on his driver's bench—gone very quiet all of a sudden? A coincidence, she decided, since the satyr began whistling to himself, and Cura flipped another page of her book. Even so, a chill went down Tam's spine, despite her thick leather longcoat.

Rose is kidding, Tam told herself. *Of course she's kidding.*

Sam Roth laughed for a good long while. When he'd finished he pulled off a mailed glove and wiped at his eye. "Fine," he said. "Don't tell me. Winds of bloody winter, Rose, you had me going for a second there."

"Something funny?" asked a woman who reined her charger in beside Roth's beleaguered mount. She was pretty, Tam thought. Her skin was deep brown, her hair dyed the colour of untarnished silver. There was a spear on her back, and a shield bearing a silver star on a black field was strapped to her left arm.

The Slayer was having trouble wedging his mail glove back onto his pudgy hand. "Rose here was just telling me why Fable is bound for Diremarch instead of Coldfire Pass. They're off to fight the Dragoneater!"

The woman didn't even blink at the name. The Dragon-eater was a made-up monster, and it was clear Rose had no intention of telling Roth (or anyone, for that matter) what awaited them in Diremarch. "It's true, then?" The newcomer raised her shield to cut the glare as she looked up. "Bloody Rose is running from a fight? Never thought I'd see the day."

Rose put on a frosty smile. "I'm not running from anything, Star. I've already fought one Horde, remember?" She glanced over briefly as Freecloud moved to stand at her shoulder. "This isn't our fight."

"Not your fight?" The woman—who Tam now knew was Lucky Star—sneered up at them. "I don't recall Castia being *my* fight, but that didn't stop me from coming to save your ass, did it?"

Rose's smile was melting like an ice chip in a clenched fist.

"But what if the Horde breaks through Coldfire Pass?" Star pressed. "What if it threatens Coverdale? Will it be your fight then, I wonder?"

All trace of mirth fled Rose's face. She glowered like a gargoyle with an incontinent pigeon perched on its head. "Good to see you, Slayer," she said, then stepped away from the battlement and called out to Roderick. "Get us moving," she ordered. "Run them down if you need to, I don't care."

"Runnin' 'em down!" Roderick cracked the reins, and the *Redoubt* lurched into motion.

"What's in Coverdale?" Tam asked Freecloud.

"Our daughter," he replied.

Chapter Thirteen

Highpool

After one final stop in a village bearing the unfortunate (and unfortunately accurate) name of Boring, Fable's tour rolled to its conclusion in Highpool, which rivalled the capital of Ardburg for size and dwarfed it for splendour. Constructed almost entirely of brilliant white limestone, it perched like an ivory crown at the top of a broad hummock.

The city was surrounded by the southernmost peaks of the Rimeshield Mountains, and rearing above it was a colossal figure carved into the sheer cliffs to the north. One of its hands clasped the hilt of a granite sword, while the other was extended over the city below. Channels carved into the rock allowed a steady stream of meltwater to pool in the palm of its hand before spilling between its fingers into a reservoir several hundred feet below.

The residents of Highpool called it the Defender, but as they approached the city, Freecloud apprised Tam of its true identity.

"The Tyrant?" She squinted up at the statue's face. It was worn almost featureless by centuries of harsh weather, but the long ears sweeping back from its head marked it as druin.

"His name was Gowikan," said the druin. "He was an Exarch who tasked his slaves—hundreds of men, women, and monsters—with rendering his likeness into the mountainside. They toiled for a dozen years and managed only so much as that hand, so he put thousands more to work. A decade later they'd chiselled out his chest, an arm, his head—all you can see now. But they never finished."

Freecloud was toying with that strange moonstone coin as he spoke. Tam wondered if the thing was some sort of lucky charm.

"By then the Dominion had begun to collapse. Civil war erupted, and the Exarchs turned on one another. Gowikan's army was untrained, ill fed, exhausted from years of gruelling labour. They were overrun, and the Exarch was killed." The druin's ears shivered when he sighed. "It makes me wonder, sometimes, if what we're doing really matters. The fighting, the killing, the *glory* we're all so desperate to claim. None of us decide how we are remembered," he said, and Tam recalled her uncle voicing a similar sentiment on the hill above Fighter's Camp.

"Gowikan was cruel," Freecloud continued. "And vain. He was a petty despot whose quest for immortality doomed both him and his people. And yet here he stands, long after his enemies are gone, revered by those he'd have treated as slaves. Immortal, after all."

Tam pulled a strand of windblown hair from her eyes. "Aren't all druins immortal?" Tam asked.

"Essentially, yes," said Freecloud. The coin in his hand vanished with a flick of his wrist. "It's too bad so many of us are pricks."

The road into the city ran a full circuit of the hill upon which it was built, and was flanked on the left by an earthen bulwark packed with exultant crowds. They cheered wildly as the Outlaw Nation wound its way toward the gate, and Fable's welcome inside the city was even more grand. People lined the streets as the *Rebel's Redoubt* ambled by, and Tam, who tried counting the number of women sporting the same bloodred hair as Rose, gave up after the first hundred. She doubted there was a single hucknell bean left in the whole damn city.

I should bring some with me wherever we go, she thought. *I could sell them and make a fortune...*

One woman (who ran beside the argosy for several blocks) begged the honour of having Brune's babies, while another, brandishing a wailing infant dressed in a makeshift bunny costume, claimed to have given birth to Freecloud's already.

"Should I be worried?" Rose asked the druin.

Freecloud favoured the woman with a wave and a wary smile. "I certainly am."

The balconies and rooftops were teeming as well. Dyed cloth streamers rained down from above, along with clumps of birdseed, and rose petals so frozen they fell like hailstones.

Tam leaned over the driver's bench. "What's with the birdseed?" she asked Roderick.

"No idea." The satyr scooped some up and tossed it into his mouth. When he saw her horrified expression he held out his hand. "I'm sorry, did you want some?"

She waved him off. "I'm fine, thanks."

"Suit yourself." Rod siphoned the seed in his hand, examining its contents. "Hey, I think there's corn in here!"

At last they halted before a three-storey inn called the Gnarled Staff, whose proprietor, a retired wizard named Elfmin, welcomed Fable in the yard outside and presented each of them with a bright red scarf.

"It's...warm," Tam remarked as the old man draped one across her shoulders. The thick wool actually radiated a mild heat as she drew it around her neck.

"It's enchanted!" said Elfmin. He adjusted the pair of gold-tinted spectacles he wore on the bridge of his nose. "A minor cantrip, but they'll serve you well in Diremarch, believe me!"

It took all afternoon for the Outlaw Nation to take up

residence in the Gnarled Staff. Once they had, everyone—
Tam included—spent the early hours of the evening fast
asleep since, as Rose bluntly put it, "We sure as hell won't be
sleeping tonight."

Since the Gnarled Staff would host the final party of Fable's
tour after the following day's fight, the band spent their pen-
ultimate night in Highpool exploring the city's seedier estab-
lishments. An entourage of Outlaws tagged along, but pretty
much anyone with the mental and moral fortitude to keep up
was welcome aboard.

Their first stop was the Basilisk, a brothel furnished with
statues of men and women in various states of fornication.
After that was the Gorgon's Den, which had a similar theme
but considerably more snakes lying about.

Next up was Mackie's, followed by the Bald Bard, and
then another brothel called the Longest Sword in Town,
where Freecloud, after a great deal of heckling and altogether too much wine, was persuaded to dance in a cage while
Tam played a sultry rendition of *Magic Boy*, a song usually
reserved for children's birthday parties.

The walls of the Shattered Shield were decorated with
broken swords and cloven shields. The place was full of grizzled warriors who told meandering stories of days and nights
spent touring the Heartwyld. All of them, it turned out, had
lost bandmates to the rot, the disease that had once preyed
indiscriminately upon those who entered the poisoned forest.
One old man brandished a hand he claimed had been infected,
before Arcandius Moog (a bandmate of Rose's father) began
producing his miracle cure.

Before moving on, Tam asked the room of weary vets
what song they'd most like to hear, and was touched when
they unanimously agreed on Lily Hashford's most famous
ballad—which suited Tam just fine. Not only did it remind

Tam of her mother, but it had earned her a place in Fable. If she'd played any other song but *Together* during her audition, she might still be back in Ardburg right now.

By the time she reached the song's final verse the old mercs were singing along with her. When she finished, there wasn't a dry eye in the place.

Their last stop was a tavern called the Monster Market. The staff were scantily dressed as various fey creatures, and instead of wax candles or oil lamps, there were *actual* pixies imprisoned in coloured glass jars suspended from the rafters. Following Rose's example, each of her bandmates and every Outlaw stole one on their way out the door. In the street outside they tore off the lids and set their captives free, laughing in wonder as the sky filled with the buzz of bright wings.

It was almost dawn by the time they started back toward the Gnarled Staff. Somewhere along the way Penny lobbed a snowball at Brune, who lobbed one back. He missed, but hit Rose instead. The street-wide snowball fight that followed raged until a platoon of white-cloaked watchmen arrived to break it up.

They arrested Brune, who couldn't hope to outrun them with Penny straddling his shoulders. Rose and Freecloud were discovered together in a snowbank and charged with lewdness, public nudity, and possession of an unsheathed sword.

Cura took Tam by the hand when the bard almost slipped on a patch of ice. The two of them fled together, ducking through alleys and skirting the edge of snowy squares. They managed to shake their pursuers, but Cura didn't let go of her hand. They were almost to the inn when the Inkwitch squeezed Tam's fingers and pointed skyward. "Look."

The moon's glow bathed the falls above Highpool in silver light, transforming the tumbling water into strands of whispering silk. Between each were swatches of starry sky that glimmered like a lake in the moment before it turned to ice.

"Beautiful," Tam said, but by then she'd turned away

from the spectacle of falling water and was looking at Cura instead.

The summoner glanced over, a sly smile spreading across her face. "Hey, you know what we should do?"

"It needs to be wet first," said Cura.

"Will it hurt?" Tam asked.

"It'll tingle a bit, but no—it shouldn't hurt. Not if we're doing it right."

"Have you done this before?"

"Of course," Cura said. "But usually just by myself."

"What if I don't like it?"

"You'll love it. I'm actually shocked you haven't done it before—a girl your age? Now close your eyes and hold still."

The summoner emptied a pitcher of water over Tam's head.

When her hair was thoroughly soaked, Cura disappeared from her periphery. Tam gazed up at the shadowed beams of the Staff's kitchen, the back of her neck resting on the edge of a ceramic basin. She heard the grind of a mortar and pestle, a quiet dribble of liquid, and then more grinding.

"All set," Cura said. She returned to Tam's side and began massaging the mixture into the bard's scalp. It started to tingle almost instantly.

Since this would likely take a while, Tam decided to press the Inkwitch for answers to the questions she'd been holding in like a breath since their encounter with Sam Roth the day before. "So Rose has a daughter?"

Cura's fingers froze momentarily before resuming their work. "She does, yes. Her name's Wren."

"Is she a druin?"

"She's a sylf. She doesn't have bunny ears, if that's what you're wondering."

"A sylf?"

"Sylfs are what happen when a druin male and a human female conceive a child. Druin women—lucky for them—can only get pregnant once, and only with another druin."

Tam hadn't known that. "Then how do they survive?" she asked. "If every woman only has one child they would die out eventually, right?"

Cura snorted. "They would, yes. They have, in case you hadn't noticed. But they're immortal, don't forget. Or near enough. Freecloud says they *can* die of old age, whatever that means to a rabbit. They're not from here, you know."

Tam *did* know that. According to her mother, the druins had come to Grandual from another realm—a doomed realm—using the sword called *Vellichor* to cut through the fabric of dimensions. Once here, they had quickly set about subjugating the natives—men and monsters too primitive to contend with the invaders' sorcery and superior technology. Their leader, Vespian, forged an empire that became known as the Dominion and ruled as Archon for a thousand years.

Tam supposed that an adult hearing that story for the first time might assume it was nothing more than a fable—a fairy tale pieced together from half-truths and superstition. But since her mother had been the one to tell her, Tam had believed it without question. Both Edwick and Tiamax had seen *Vellichor* firsthand, and both swore that you could see an alien world in the surface of its blade. The Archon, before he died, had gifted it to Rose's father, who owned it still.

"How old is Wren?" Tam asked.

"Four," said Cura. "Maybe five. She lives with her grandfather down in Coverdale. We stop in every few months for a visit."

Her grandfather? "You mean Golden Gabe? Why is she with him and not Rose?"

Cura raked her fingers through Tam's hair. The gentle tugging might have felt nice—*more* than nice, even—if it weren't for the tingling sensation, which was stronger now than it had been before. "Because," said Cura finally, "the road is no place for a child."

Then why are Rose and Freecloud on the road? Tam wanted to ask, but figured it was best to leave the subject alone for the time being. Instead, she asked something else she'd been wondering for a while. "Back in Woodford, Jeka said she'd never seen a summoner like you. What did she mean by that?"

"Have you *seen* me?" Cura's tone was thick with feigned arrogance. "I'm hot as red iron."

A smell like burnt vanilla tickled Tam's nose. "But that's not what Jeka meant. She said you fight differently than other summoners."

"That's because summoners don't usually fight," Cura told her. "They're entertainers, mostly. They carve things out of wood, or etch them into little glass bells, and then burn them, or break them, to bring them to life."

"Okay, so if a summoner carves a bird out of wood—"

"Then they get a wooden bird. And if they etch one into glass—"

"It's made of glass," Tam finished.

"Exactly." Cura left her side, and Tam heard her using the pitcher to scoop water from a barrel in the corner. "The things I summon are different. They're carved into my flesh, inked into my blood. So when I call on them"—cold water splashed over Tam's head—"they're made of flesh and blood. They're real. Or something close to real. It's hard to explain," she said, returning to the barrel and refilling the pitcher.

"But what are they?" Tam asked, as another jug of water went over her head. The vanilla smell was beginning to fade, which she took for a promising sign. "That burning treant, the sea monster, that . . . other . . . thing with the swords stuck through it. Why do you have such—"

"We're all done here," said Cura. There was a curt finality in her tone, an edge that threatened to cut if Tam dared to press any further. "Sit up and take a look."

The bard eased her neck off the basin behind her. Cura was holding up a hand mirror so that Tam could see her reflection gazing back at her.

Her face was unchanged. Her eyes were the same. Her hair, however, was no longer the plain, dull brown she'd inherited from her father.

It was platinum blonde.

Tam watched a smile like sunshine spear across her reflection's lips. "Oh my fucking gods, I *love* it."

Chapter Fourteen

The Big Deal

When Kaskar's old king died a few years back, his son and successor undertook several ambitious construction projects—one in each of the north's great cities—to help ingratiate himself to the people he now ruled. Grimtide got a grand new lighthouse, North Court a racetrack. East Bellows became home to the court's largest library, while West Bellows boasted its most comprehensive museum. Ardburg was granted a state-of-the-art bathhouse, complete with heated pools, steaming saunas, and a wrestling gym that, according to Tam's uncle, saw more sex than a brothel on two-for-one night.

In Highpool, King Maladan Pike ordered the restoration of the old arena, which had fallen into such disrepair that bands and bookers sometimes avoided the city altogether. Maladan's Stone Garden, as it came to be called, was a six-tiered cylinder dug into the bedrock of the hill itself. The top-most seating ring—the only one visible above ground—was given over to expensively furnished private boxes from which the city's well-to-do could watch the carnage below in lavish comfort. Conversely, the bottom tier was affectionately referred to as "the Pit," and it was not uncommon for those who dared its depths to emerge with injuries as grievous as those they'd come to watch fight.

The Garden's armoury was more extravagant than any Tam had seen thus far. There was a buffet fit for a king's banquet, and a bar stocked with every liquor imaginable. The tiled stone floor was thick with patterned carpets, the sofas piled with so many pillows she was forced to stack some on a nearby chair to make room for sitting. Tapestries depicting great battles of the arena's past were draped between lamplit dressing mirrors.

In one such mirror Tam found the reflection of a mercenary whose fame rivalled that of Bloody Rose herself. When Brune collapsed onto the sofa beside her, scattering pillows in every direction, Tam leaned over and whispered, "Is that the Prince of Ut?"

"The Prince of where?" asked Brune, too loudly.

The man in the mirror, his face obscured by a veiled purple cowl held in place by a golden circlet, glanced in their direction. His kohl-rimmed eyes were barely visible, and when they bored into Tam she did her best to disappear into what cushions remained to her.

The shaman scratched the back of his neck. "Did you do something with your hair?"

"Nope."

"Cool." Brune craned his neck to look past her shoulder. "Yeah, that's the Prince, all right. He doesn't have a band, you know. He takes on monsters all by himself—which is crazy if you ask me. Everyone, no matter how good they are, needs someone at their back once in a while. Even Rose—" He broke off, nudging her. "Oh, watch this."

The Prince of Ut's booker, a heavyset Narmeeri whose spotted fur cloak was cinched tight beneath several chins, called out to one of the Garden's stewards as she passed by.

"Excuse me? Hi, hello, yes." The man spoke with the shrill arrogance of a castrated king. One of his ring-choked fingers stroked the soft fur at his collar, while the other motioned to the spread of food laid out nearby. "There seems to have been a mix-up with the grapes."

The steward's expression told Tam she'd rather be anywhere but here at this moment. "The grapes?"

"Yes, indeed. The grapes."

She pointed. "You mean those grapes?"

"Yes—and no. You see, I specifically requested that the grapes be *purple*, and these, as you can no doubt ascertain despite your apparent simple-mindedness, are green."

If the steward cared that she'd been insulted, she didn't let it show. "So?"

"So..." cooed the booker, glancing pointedly toward his master. "His grace does not eat *green* grapes. He only eats *purple* grapes."

The woman blinked. She looked at the table and back again. "Those grapes are green," she said.

"Yes, I can see that. *Those* grapes are green. Which is why—"

A roar shook the Stone Garden, so loud the lamps overhead swayed on their silver chains. The steward made use of the distraction to slip out unnoticed. A moment later Cura descended the armoury stairs. "The Wererats are victorious," she announced.

"Victorious over what?" asked Freecloud.

"Wererats," she said, perusing the buffet table before selecting a peach and biting into it. "Crazy, right?"

Roderick came clopping down after her. "We're up next!" he announced.

"What are we up against?" Rose asked. She'd ingested her customary dose of Lion's Leaf a few moments earlier, which dulled her voice and robbed the light from her eyes.

The booker rubbed his hands together. "Orcs!"

"How many?"

"They've got a whole warband in the cells by the look of

it—I told them to choose the twelve biggest, meanest, green-
est bastards they could find. That's three for each of you, provided Tam doesn't run in and shoot them all first." He winked
at the bard. "Nice hair, by the way."

She beamed. "Thanks."

"I knew it!" said Brune, stroking his beard as he admired
her new look.

Rose looked into one of the dressing mirrors, locked in a
staring match with the void-black gaze of her own reflection.
"We'll fight all of them," she said.

The satyr's eyebrows nearly knocked the hat off his head.
"Say what now?"

"All of them. The whole warband."

Silence engulfed the armoury.

Rose's double looked out from the confines of the lamplit
mirror, searching out the eyes of her bandmates, one by one.
Brune took a breath that made a barrel of his chest before
nodding his assent. Cura smirked and sunk her teeth into her
peach. "I like those odds," she said.

"I don't," murmured Freecloud. "But I do like the stakes.
Death or glory, right?"

Rose's reflection grinned. "Death or glory."

The whole warband turns out to be seventy-seven orcs strong,
and though Tam never feels the need to embellish that number, many others do. It will be said, or sung, or slurred by
bards and boasting drunks in days to come that Fable took
down a hundred, a hundred fifty, no—*two hundred* orcs that
afternoon.

The truth, as far as Tam is concerned, is incredible enough.
One moment she is watching a wave of green, growling, iron-
edged madness rushing toward Bloody Rose and her bandmates, and the next...

...a brown-furred bear roars loud enough to rattle hearts.

His hooked claws reduce metal to scrap and slash open bodies as if they were skins bursting with brackish wine . . .

. . . a summoner braces herself as an inked stallion kicks free of her flexing arm. Metallic wings unfurl like sails behind its straining neck. Its hooves hum with lightning, drum like thunder, pound like rain as it plunges into the fray . . .

. . . a druin's sword sings like a struck bell as it cleaves the air. He moves with a predator's purpose: every step a calculation, every strike a certainty. His heart is a spinning coin with his lover's face on one side, his daughter's on the other, and whichever way it lands, he loses . . .

. . . a woman cuts, hacks, slashes, and strikes—a whirling storm of fire and steel. Born in shadow, her destiny eclipsed by the brightest of stars. What else can she be but a comet, burning bright enough to draw every eye as she streaks toward some unfathomable fate?

When the bits and pieces of seventy-seven dead orcs are carried, raked, and scraped from the blood-soaked stone of the arena floor, it is announced that the Prince of Ut, unwilling to be overshadowed by Fable's extraordinary feat, has withdrawn from the title match.

The crowd boos their dismay, until Rose re-emerges, alone, from the armoury gate. She will fight in his stead, she declares. Eager to please the baying crowd, the wranglers set loose a marilith: a snake-tailed woman with six sword-bearing arms that looks, Tam thinks, like she belongs among the abominations inked on Cura's flesh.

Rose destroys it, but she does so with dramatic flair, as if the arena is a stage and every witness a bard who, when they leave this place, will sing her praises to any who'll listen. When she finally permits the marilith to die—hewing its head off with both swords—she drops her blades and stands with arms outstretched as the crowd clamours like supplicants before their god.

A rain of purple petals flutter down from the sky, spiralling

through slanting tiers of sun and shadow. Tam plucks one from
her hair and cannot help but smile.

Roses. Of course.

There was a party at the Gnarled Staff afterward. The Outlaw
Nation would disperse in the morning—some of them heading
home, while others would find another band to attach themselves to while Fable set out alone to fulfill their contract in
Diremarch. One by one the Outlaws paid a visit to the long
trestle table at which Rose and her companions sat, and said
their good-byes. Penny was particularly upset that Brune was
going north without her. She clung to the shaman's arm like a
shipreck survivor to the last spar of her shattered craft.

Plenty of mercs showed up as well. The Wererats, who'd
skirmished for Fable in the Garden earlier today, were around
somewhere, as were Youth Gone Wyld, who were actually four
men in their late fifties whose idea of "touring" had regressed
to attending parties they weren't invited to.

Korey Kain, who was the archer of a band called Shark's
Breakfast, stopped by to say hello, and to show off the swell
of her baby bump. "Her daddy's gone off to put a boot up
the Horde's ass," she declared proudly. "I'd be there too if my
armour still fit!"

Tam was wedged on a bench between Cura and Brune.
Rose and Freecloud were seated opposite, while Rod's chair
capped the end. Their table was crowded with brimming tankards, empty bottles, and plates littered with the scraps of
an epic meal. The shaman and summoner were arguing over
which of Grandual's courts was best to retire in if the Diremarch contract proved as lucrative as they hoped it would.
Roderick was eating something that crunched like a mouthful of chicken bones and was probably a mouthful of chicken
bones.

Tam, meanwhile, was doing her best not to make it obvious she was listening in on Rose and Freecloud's conversation.

"...needless danger," the druin was saying. "We'd done our part. There was no reason to fight the marilith."

"No reason?" Rose took a drag on her halfpipe and sneered through the smoke. "Did you see that crowd? Did you hear them chanting my name? Do you think Golden Gabe ever killed a marilith by himself?"

The druin's ears were rigid with anger. He opened his mouth to retort, but then clamped it shut, as if the prescience had warned him that whatever he was about to say would earn more ire than it was worth. "The tour's finished," he said with forced composure. "Remember, you promised—"

"No more Lion's Leaf." Rose traced the sign of the Summer Lord over her heart. "I promise."

"It made you careless."

"It made me entertaining," she replied, exhaling another stream of smoke into the air above her head. Her expression grew serious. "And I needed it, Cloud. You know that."

The druin put a hand on hers. "Listen, you've got nothing to—"

"Bloody Rose!" The voice—gruff and gravelly—belonged to Linden Gale, who swung an axe for the Wererats. He was a hulk of a man, and his broad face had the look of leather chewed to scrap by a starving dog. "Settle a bet for me, will ya? Rumour has it you're headed to Diremarch. They say you've got a contract with the Widow of Ruangoth."

Rose didn't bother turning to face him. "We do."

They had an audience, Tam noticed. Conversations nearby lapsed into silence. Drinks paused on the way to lips. Pipes were forgotten, their smoke languid in the loaded air.

"What's in Diremarch?" Linden asked.

"Snow," said Cura.

"Rocks," said Brune.

"Your whore mother," said Roderick.

There was a collective gasp from the tables around them.

"What?" The booker raised his hands, pleading innocence. "His mother's literally a whore! Linden, back me up here!"

The big mercenary gave a grudging nod. "That's right."

"See? I told you. She works at that hole-in-the-wall brothel up in Fetterkarn, right? What's that place called again?"

Gale looked mildly embarrassed. "The Hole in the Wall."

"Lovely establishment," said Roderick. "And their goat's head soup is"—he kissed his fingers—"to die for."

"I've heard another rumour, too." The Wererats' axeman seemed eager to steer the subject away from his mother. "I've heard you're going after the Simurg."

"That's right," Rose answered.

By now most of the room was listening in, which meant that most of the room laughed when she said so—even the Outlaws. Everyone except Fable themselves, in fact.

Linden laughed hardest of all. "I can't believe it!" he cried, once he'd regained his breath. "I mean, I'd heard you were craven. Every merc in Grandual knows that Bloody Rose couldn't start a fistfight with a trash imp without a mouthful of Lion's Leaf."

Freecloud shifted, preparing to rise, but Rose clamped his hand to the table.

Linden scoffed, and Tam could smell the liquor on his breath even from so far away. "The *Simurg*, though? You can't be serious. The least you could do is come up with something reasonable. Hells, they say the Winter Queen is back from the dead—why don't you go hunting her instead?"

"Show me the contract," said Rose. "I'll bring you her head."

Another uneasy smatter of laughter came and went.

"You were in Ardburg when the Horde hit Cragmoor." Gale's voice was angry, accusing. "You should be at Coldfire right now, along with every other merc who could make it in

time, ready to give that whoreson Brontide a taste of mercenary might."

"Whoreson?" Freecloud's good cheer hadn't quite vanished yet. "Really, Linden? That seems a poor choice of word,
considering."

"Fuck yourself, rabbit." Gale spat on the floor, and then
stooped to leer in Rose's face. "But here you are in Highpool,
making a big fucking deal of yourself. Well, you ain't that big
o' deal, Rose. You're a coward who'd rather get paid instead of
admitting there ain't enough Lion's Leaf in the world for you
to face another Horde. Not after what happened at Castia."

A wiser man might have said his piece and walked away.
But Linden Gale, as it happened, was not a wise man.

"Your father would be ashamed," he added. "Golden Gabe
would never run from a Horde. He crossed the Heartwyld to
save you from the last one, and he'd be at Coldfire now if he
wasn't babysitting your half-breed bastar—"

He shut up then, because Rose's fist was halfway down
his throat.

Chapter Fifteen

The Bard and the Beast

Gale swallowed the rest of his sentence, along with most of his teeth. He staggered back, lashing out with a meaty fist, and caught Rose's jaw with the heel of his palm. She might have fallen had Freecloud not been there to prop her up.

Cura was on her feet, then the table, then airborne. She landed on Gale's back and started boxing his ears. Roderick, doing his best impersonation of a body suddenly deprived of its skeleton, went slithering beneath the table.

Linden's bandmates leapt to his aid. Two of them jumped Brune as he stood, dragging the shaman to the floor and raining down blows as Penny screamed obscenities. Another one hoisted a chair above his head and looked for the weakest target he could find.

Me, Tam realized, too late.

Freecloud vaulted the table, putting himself in the chair's path. As it broke across his shoulders, the druin, impossibly fast, caught a splintered leg before it spun away. He whirled and smote Tam's assailant across the temple, dropping him.

"Thanks," she said.

"You're welcome. Have I mentioned I love your hair?"

"You haven't, no."

"I do," said Freecloud. "It suits you."

By now he was surrounded. The druin spent a moment assessing his aggressors: three men and one very muscular woman. For a heartbeat the five of them—the gang and the ganged upon—seemed rooted to the spot, but then Freecloud, with the feral glee of a fox in a chicken coop, exploded into motion.

Rose, on the other hand, didn't bother waiting to be preyed upon. She socked the closest merc to her (who, to be fair, had been wearing an especially threatening scowl) and threw herself low at another man rushing at her with a bottle in hand.

Cura had given up punching and opted to choke Linden Gale to the ground. It worked like a charm; the big man sagged to his knees, swatting futilely at the summoner's ink-sleeved arm, before pitching face-first onto the tavern floor. The Ink-witch had barely gained her feet when Gale's girlfriend jumped her from behind. The two of them went tumbling out of sight, but Tam could hear them screeching like a pair of cats behind a fishmonger's stall.

Pockets of fighting had erupted all over the Gnarled Staff, as mercenaries, Highpoolers, Outlaws, and those too drunk to remember which of those factions they belonged to picked sides in the melee. The serving staff crouched behind the bar like soldiers on the ramparts of a city under siege. There'd been a trio of musicians onstage when the brawl started, and instead of fleeing for cover they played determinedly on. To their credit, they even upped the tempo to better suit the chaos of the common room.

Motion in her periphery drew Tam's eye: Roderick reached up from beneath the table, fumbling from one item to the next until he found the arm of his tankard, then pulled it to safety below.

Brune was down, rolling among tipped-over chairs and discarded bottles as he tangled with half a dozen assailants. Penny leapt to his defense, seizing a woman by the hair and dragging her from the pile. The two of them grappled for a moment before Penny threw a haymaker that sent the woman crashing into the bar.

Brune had just gained his knees when Gord Lark, the Wererats' scrawny frontman, smacked him across the face with the flat of his shield. The shaman's head snapped back, and Lark flipped his shield sideways, angling it for a chop at Brune's exposed throat.

Tam reached Lark in time to wrench the shield from the man's bony grip, though she found herself at a loss as to what to do next.

Lark offered one alternative. "Gimme that back!"

"Come and take it," she snarled.

Come and take it? Tam's inner voice harangued her. *Why the hell did you say that? What if he comes? What if he takes it?*

She cringed behind the stolen shield as Lark lashed out, and was gratified to hear his knuckles crack against the iron-studded oak. While the merc bemoaned his busted fingers, the bard hefted the shield and brought it down hard on his head.

"Fuurgk," he remarked, then his eyes rolled back and he collapsed in a heap.

Edwick had told her once that Slowhand, Golden Gabe's lesser-known sidekick, used a shield called *Blackheart* in battle rather than an actual weapon. Though not completely sold on the notion, Tam had to admit that a heavy slab of wood certainly had its uses.

Brune was back on his feet. He sidestepped the rush of a wailing attacker and used the man's momentum to heave him headlong over a nearby table, then raised an arm to deflect a ceramic plate. The woman who'd tossed it lobbed two more, but went scampering off once she ran out of dishware. When one of the men he'd downed earlier climbed groggily to his knees, the shaman grasped his neck in one huge hand and hoisted him, legs thrashing, off the ground.

The man gurgled a plea for mercy, but Brune's reply was a growl so deep it set Tam's hair on end. Terror fluttered like a bird against her ribs. She looked from the Wererat's rapidly purpling face to Brune's. Fear and ferocity warred across the shaman's features. His eyes seized Tam's, wild with desperation.

"*No*," Brune grated behind a cage of clenched teeth.

The Wererat fumbled for the knife strapped to his chest.

"*I can't...*"

A slash drew blood from the shaman's arm.

"*Can't...Tam...run—*" Brune managed, before the cage of clenched teeth sprang open, and the beast within came raging out.

The shaman's face transformed in an instant, broadening beneath swatches of coarse brown fur. His arms bulged, the muscles rippling like snakes in a sack. The hand around the Wererat's throat doubled in size. Claws like black knives punched from shaggy, padded paws. Brune's tunic shredded as his body underwent a catastrophic change. What began as a snarl of defiance became an earsplitting roar that hushed the entire room at once.

For the space of a breath, anyway.

Then the screaming began.

The place dissolved into pandemonium. Doors and windows became clogged for the press of bodies eager to escape the room. Even the musicians forsook their song and fled the stage. Weapons were drawn, steel blooded by guttering lamplight.

Tam felt something jar her arm and looked down to find a serrated steak knife quivering in her shield. She wrenched it loose, briefly considered using it to defend herself, but decided that stabbing someone in a bar fight wasn't something she'd feel good about tomorrow morning, so she tossed the knife to the floor.

Brune roared again, a sound like plate armour tearing along a rusted seam. His hands spasmed open, and the man dangling in the shaman's grasp pulled free and tried to scurry away. The beast knocked him to the ground, speared his calf with its claws, and pinned him there as it mauled him with its jaws.

Glancing over her shoulder, Tam saw Freecloud helping

Cura to her feet. The summoner's lip was split, and she was cradling her head as though stunned. Rose was scrambling against a mob of fleeing patrons. The frontwoman was shouting, but her voice was drowned out by the noise all around them: shrieks and stamping feet, the thunderous tread of paws pounding across wooden floorboards...

Tam wheeled to find Brune charging directly at her. The shaman's massive head was levelled like a battering ram. She barely had time to lift her shield before the impact sent her soaring. Her ankles caught on a bench seat, her back slammed hard on a tabletop. Her momentum kept her rolling—a lucky thing, since she flipped over the opposite side as the beast crashed through the table, cracking it in half, hurling cups and cutlery skyward.

She kept moving, rolling out from beneath a wooden bench an instant before it was smashed to splinters. She scrambled to her feet, took two sprinting steps to the next table over, and slid on her hip across it, which must've looked pretty fucking cool until she slipped, flailing, off the other side. The beast followed, crushing chairs to kindling, ploughing through cedar planks like they were palm fronds.

Tam, from her knees, saw a black iron boot stamp the table in front of her, then Rose was vaulting overhead, a moon-bright scimitar in either hand. She slapped the flat of one sword against the beast's head, dazing him, then smacked it hard with the other. Its eyes lolled. Blood spilled in strands from its frothing jaws, but the stupor was momentary.

It swiped at her with one huge paw. Rose turned her blade so its edge scored the pad on his palm. It tried to bite her, but she danced wide, and brought the rune-traced flat of both swords hammering against its skull.

Rose had expected to knock it out, Tam guessed, since she was woefully unprepared when he attacked instead. The warrior clattered to the floor with four fresh gouges in her black iron breastplate. The beast that wasn't Brune pounced before she could recover, but Tam hurled herself into its path, crouched behind her stolen shield. The snout bashed into it and drove her sliding backward across the floor, kicking wildly to keep her legs away from those awful jaws. She hit something—Rose—and the two of them snowballed ahead of the raging goliath, crashing together into the stone base of a buttressing pillar.

Rose swore and swung above Tam's head, opening a gash in the beast's snout. It reared onto its haunches, bellowing in fury.

Tam's eyes caught the glint of metal near the monster's feet. A pellet of some sort, or . . .

A vial.

It was the one Branigan had given her on the morning after Fighter's Camp. "The Bard's Last Refrain," he'd called it. Tam had put it in the pocket of her new coat shortly afterward and hadn't thought of it since.

I could use it on Brune, she thought. *If I can get to it, that is . . .*

She would need a distraction. Something to draw the beast's attention long enough for her to recover the quill inside. Maybe Rose could—

"Brune, stop!"

The beast whirled and lashed out at the woman who'd dared to lay a hand on its ragged flank.

Tam froze in a crouch, staring in mute horror as ribbons of red bloomed across Penny's chest. The girl's blouse was in shreds, her eyes wiped of everything save the shock of pain and betrayal.

Move, Tam told herself, *now!*

She dropped the shield and dived forward, skidding between the bear's hind legs. She plucked up the vial and yanked its halves apart. The quill slipped out, bouncing once on its end before Tam swiped it from the air and plunged it as hard as she could into the beast's flank.

It staggered, turning ponderously to regard her with beady black eyes. It attempted a roar that emerged as a yawn instead, then collapsed on top of her.

Chapter Sixteen

Some Wild Thing

They'd entered Highpool like heroes returning from conquered lands, but left it like thieves desperate to escape the gallows. Rose and Freecloud purchased a pair of spare horses from Elfmin, who bore them no ill will despite the havoc they'd caused. Rod disappeared for a while and arrived outside the inn driving a cart drawn by two sturdy Kaskar ponies.

Good idea, Tam thought, since Brune was a burden and neither she nor Cura were in any shape to ride a horse in the dark.

"Please tell me you didn't steal this." Freecloud's face was wary in the torchlight.

"Of course I didn't steal it!" The satyr rounded the wagon, inspecting the bed. He was chewing lazily on what looked like a sequined slipper. "I bought it. And cheap, too."

Rose looked suspicious as well. "From who?"

Rod plucked a severed hand from inside and tossed it casually over one shoulder. "Corpse collector."

"Are you serious?" Cura was nursing a bloody lip and a swollen left eye. She'd come out worse than any of them—except for Brune, obviously, who'd returned to human form bearing a serious goose egg, a vicious slice across the bridge of his nose, and bruises colouring most of his face.

Don't forget Penny, Tam's mind chimed in. The girl would live, apparently, but she would bear the scars of Brune's attack for the rest of her life, inside and out. Tam's injuries were much less severe. Her ribs ached, and her head felt like some spiteful gambler was rattling dice against the inside of her skull. Still, she'd got off easy considering a monstrous bear had landed on her not half an hour ago.

"You couldn't find anything nicer?" Cura asked.

Roderick spit out a silver button. "Whaddaya want, a gilded carriage? We're trying to be inconspicuous here."

"It's fine," said Rose. "Cloud, help me get Brune on board. Rod, take the *Redoubt* north. We'll meet you in Coltsbridge. Tell the Widow's man we had something to take care of first."

"Who's the Widow?" Tam asked. "And where are we going?"

"The Widow is our contact in Diremarch," Rose said, then made a gesture that encompassed the unconscious shaman, Cura's battered face, the smashed windows of the inn behind them, and the fact that they were skulking in disgrace from a city that had welcomed them with open arms just two days ago. "We're going to make sure this never happens again," she said.

"We should teach you to fight," Freecloud said to Tam over breakfast the following morning. The two of them were seated by a dwindling fire, eating quail-egg hash out of wooden bowls and sharing a clay pitcher of Bryton's apple cider back and forth. Rose and Cura, whose monthly cycles had synced after so long together, had gone searching for a creek in which to rinse. They'd found one nearby, Tam guessed, since she could hear their voices whenever the wind picked up. Brune was still out cold in the bed of the corpse cart. According to what Bran had told her, it might be several hours yet before the quill's effects wore off.

"Why?" Tam asked. "I'm just a bard."

"You're *the* Bard," Freecloud reminded her. A wry smile snagged his lips as he speared a wedge of potato with the tip of his knife. "Besides, bards hide under tables. They climb trees, or cower in bushes, or run for the hills at the first sign of trouble. They don't take on professional mercenaries with nothing but a shield. They don't bring down bears. Or a cyclops, for that matter."

"I didn't—"

"I know," he cut her off. "But still."

Tam gazed down at her bowl. Once, a few years ago, she'd dared to drag her father's sword out from under his bed. She'd spent the afternoon practicing with it, swinging the heavy blade until her arms ached, and when Tuck had come home she'd been standing in the kitchen, brandishing it overhead like some triumphant hero.

He'd been upset, to say the least. He'd wrested the sword from her hands and hacked one of the chairs (the one Bran used to sit in) to pieces. Though perhaps not a master class in sensible parenting, the lesson had been an effective one. Tam had been afraid to pick up a sword ever since.

"Okay," she said eventually. "Sure."

The druin's eyes—usually a deep, emerald green—went the colour of a sunlit leaf. "Excellent." He reached for the cider and took a long swig, baring his teeth at the tartness. "This doesn't mean you're off the hook when it comes to being our bard. If I so much as step on a lizard you'd better tell the world I kicked a dragon to death. Sound good?"

She nodded. "Sounds good."

"Rose can teach you the sword," he said. "I'll show you how to hold that bow of yours properly."

"I—"

"No you don't," he cut her off again. Damn, but the pre-science could be annoying sometimes. "Anyhow," the druin went on, "it's best you learn to protect yourself. We're not on tour anymore. If something happens, we won't have Doctor Dan to patch us up. Things could get dangerous from here on out."

Tam stood, swiped the crumbs from her lap, and went to retrieve her bow. "Let's get started, then," she said.

They travelled east, winding through wooded foothills along a track Tam suspected had been made by goatherds. Rose and Freecloud led the way on horseback, while Tam and Cura took turns driving the corpse cart. Brune remained unconcious in the wagon's bed, rendered death-like by the effect of the will'o'wisp's quill.

They avoided towns, in part because Rose feared the mercs they'd tousled with back in Highpool might come seeking retribution, but mostly because she was sick and tired of explaining to every person who asked that no, they weren't heading west, and yes, she was well aware there was a Horde invading Grandual.

Instead, as the sun set and violet clouds piled over the star-spangled wash of deepening blue, they found a remote steading and paid the farmer handsomely for use of his barn.

Tam was leading one of the ponies into a stall when Freecloud took the reins from her hand. "I'll finish this," he told her. "Rose needs you outside."

"For what?"

The druin's ears bobbed in imitation of waggling eyebrows. "Go see."

Rose was waiting in the yard with her swords drawn. She passed *Thistle*, which was the smaller of the two, to Tam and then backed off a step. "Hit me," she said.

But Tam was too busy marvelling at the weapon in her hand. *I'm holding Bloody Rose's sword*, the girl in her fairly shrieked. It felt lighter than it should have, and up close she could see the flowing druic script etched along the blade's cutting edge. The scimitar's hilt was slightly curved as well, bound in black leather worn raw by Rose's grip.

"Where did you find these?" she asked breathlessly.

"Conthas. I stole them from my stepfather on my way to Castia."

Tam blinked. "You have a stepfather?"

"Had. He fell out of a skyship."

"Oh. I'm sorry . . ."

Rose's armour clanked when she shrugged. "He was an asshole," she said. "Now, hit me."

Tam raised her sword. "Hit you where?"

A low chuckle. "Wherever you can."

"What if I hurt you?" Tam asked, genuinely concerned.

"You won't."

"I might get lucky."

"You won't," Rose repeated.

Tam lunged, angling a backhanded chop at Rose's left arm, and found her hand suddenly empty. *Thistle* arced through the sky and landed in the snow several yards away.

"What was your first mistake?" Rose demanded to know.

"I, uh, dropped my sword?"

"That was your last mistake. Your first was telling me where you would strike."

Tam shook her hand, trying to rid the tingling numbness from her fingers. "But I—"

"You did," Rose said. "With your eyes. With your body. Hell, you may as well have sent me a letter. *Dear Rose, I'll be attacking from the left shortly. Please knock the sword out my stupid hand. Yours truly, Tam.*"

Tam might have laughed were she not so thoroughly embarrassed. "All right, so I'm terrible at fighting," she muttered. "I bet you're terrible at playing the lute."

The gauntlet on Rose's left hand flared green. *Thistle* flew into her hand and she returned it to Tam with a grin. "Try again."

And so Tam tried again. And again. And again. After each failed attack (one of which left the bard sprawled on the ground with a mouthful of snow), Rose helpfully pointed out where she'd gone wrong.

Whack. "You're too slow."

Thump. "You're off balance."

Crack. "You're holding that sword backward."

Freecloud and Cura emerged from the barn and shared a wineskin between them while Tam's humilation continued. To make matters worse, the farmer's daughter trotted across the yard and stood watching as well. The girl, who looked to be about Tam's age, was dragging a huge iron broadsword sheathed in rust. After a dozen more disastrous defeats, Rose declared the training session at an end.

"You did well," she said. "Better than I expected."

She must not have expected much, Tam grumbled to herself. She scanned the slush at her feet for any trace of her dignity, but it was nowhere in sight.

"Bloody Rose!" called the farmer's daughter. She had the lilting accent of folk from Bellows, east beyond the Silverwood. "Will you spar with me some? Just until dark?"

To Tam's surprise, Rose obliged. "Pay close attention," she told the bard. "This girl might teach you a thing or two."

The farmer's daughter was good. Or at least she *looked* good to Tam. She was certainly fast, and obviously strong, considering the size of that bastard sword she was using. After going several rounds with Rose, the muscles in her arms stood out like stone carvings on a temple wall. She was graceful, too. Rose even went so far as to praise her footwork, despite pointing out that she angled her left foot before every thrust.

When the girl paused to catch her breath and twist her long hair into a knot, Tam found herself studying her sleek neck and smallish ears, the tips of which had gone red for the chill in the air.

The girl caught Tam staring. "I like your hair," she said.

Tam offered a tight smile in reply, since her voice was off gallivanting with her dignity and nowhere to be found.

When night fell in earnest, the girl—sweat-slicked, her breath gusting in rapid bursts—shook hands with Rose, shot Tam a grin, and jogged off home.

"Use dirt," said Rose, as she and Tam headed toward the barn.

"Sorry?"

"Tonight, at her window. A stone might break the glass— or, worse, wake up Dad. If there's no glass, make sure she knows you're there before climbing in, or she might take your head off with that pig-sticker of hers."

"What are you talking about?" Tam asked, feeling heat flood her cheeks. "Why would I throw dirt at her window?"

"Because," Rose said, wearing a smile Tam couldn't quite interpret, "that girl might teach you a thing or two."

Tam went for a walk after dark. She headed toward the treeline first, despite Rose pointing out that the farmhouse was in the opposite direction. Cura offered her a curious, two-finger salute as she left the barn, which the bard realized afterward had been either a lewd gesture or a helpul pointer.

She wandered in the forest for a bit, and nearly screamed in fright when a dark shape settled on a bough overhead. *It's only an owl*, she realized. The bird's round face swivelled to watch her, its eyes glinting green in the shadows.

Tam stumbled upon a trapper's lean-to shelter, barely discernible for the tangled thatch disguising it. Fearing it might be home to some wild animal, she hurried back toward the barren field. Her route, fortuitously, took her near to the farmhouse, where she couldn't help but notice a lantern glowing on the sill of an open window.

She almost yelped when someone took hold of her arm.

"Sorry," the girl whispered, sliding her hand into Tam's

own. Her grip was strong, and her skin was ice cold, as though she'd been waiting outside for a while. "It's dark," she whispered, pulling Tam toward the treeline. "Wouldn't want you to trip and break your neck."

The moon had disappeared behind a cloud, so Tam could see nothing at all once they entered the forest. Her guide, at least, knew where she was going, and before long they came to the trapper's shelter Tam had fled from earlier. The girl knelt by the entrance, unfastening the toggles before slipping inside.

Tam stood for a moment outside the mound, listening to the crack and crackle of the winter forest and waiting for her nerves to settle. She hadn't been intimate with many people—mostly because trying to pursue romance under her father's regime was like trying to throw a party in prison. There'd been Saryn—her first—and then Roxa, who Tam suspected had been more interested in boys than girls, but had made an exception because Tam's father was a famous mercenary. Occasionally she'd fooled around with the daughter of a cook in the Cornerstone kitchens, but she could never for the life of her remember the girl's name.

Something her uncle once told her sprang to mind. *Boys are like raccoons,* he'd said. *They're pesky, and not to be trusted around food. Also, they're more afraid of you than you are of them.*

When Tam had told him she fancied girls, Bran had offered a revised theory almost immediately. *Girls are like coyotes. They run in packs, they make noise when you're trying to sleep, and if one comes near you it's best to scare them off with fire.*

"What are you waiting for?" The girl's voice was muffled by the skins stretched over the hut's wooden frame.

Tam banished Bran and his rubbish advice from her mind, then ducked through the flap. It was dark inside and smelled like pine needles. Something grazed her cheek, and then there were fingers in her hair, a mouth on her lips, wet and warm.

The girl's tongue slipped through her teeth, probing, and Tam felt a tingling in her belly as it grazed her own. A callused hand slipped between her legs and her thoughts blew away in an instant.

Tam returned the favour, was rewarded with a throaty gasp, and soon after that the girl's body spasmed as if a lightning bolt had struck her bathwater. Panting, the girl pulled her tunic off, and Tam, perhaps a touch overeager, writhed from her coat like a snake desperate to molt a season early. She finally got it off, along with her tunic. She'd expected to freeze, but she burned instead.

They spent something like an hour within the humid confines of the shelter. By the time they emerged and walked hand in hand to the edge of the wood, Tam had, in fact, learned a thing or two.

The girl kissed her once more before sprinting toward the house. Tam took her time rejoining the others, in part because her legs were quivering so badly she could barely walk, but also because it gave her time to turn the last hour over in her mind, as though examining a bauble from some foreign land, or a pure white shell plucked from the grey-stone strand of her days.

She was almost to the barn when Brune awoke, screaming like a man gone mad.

Chapter Seventeen

The Bringol's Bridge

The farmer arrived just after dawn with a basket of eggs, a wheel of soft cheese, and a ration of fragrant, freshly ground coffee beans. "All the way from Bastien," he announced proudly. "I brought the harvest in a week early thanks to this stuff."

Freecloud thanked the man and set about making breakfast, while Rose smoked a pipe and watched the water boil. Cura teased Tam about her encounter with the farmer's daughter ("Did you hold hands?" "Are you two getting married now?"), while Brune sulked alone in one of the empty stalls. The shaman's hair obscured his face, but his bowed neck and slumped shoulders made his shame evident. He sniffed now and again, wiping his nose with the back of one huge hand.

When breakfast was ready, Rose brought him a bowl of scrambled eggs and a tumbler of strong black coffee. Tam had expected Fable's frontwoman to berate him for what had happened back in Highpool, but instead she laid a hand on the shaman's ruddy cheek and used her thumb to swipe a falling tear. They spoke at length; Brune's voice an anxious grumble, Rose's the soft murmur of a groom trying to soothe a skittish horse.

"What?" the shaman blurted suddenly. "Are you serious? What about the contract?"

"The contract can wait," Rose assured him. "But if the

Widow is telling the truth, and we're to stand any chance of surviving what's to come, we need you to figure this out."

Brune's heavy brow knitted. He fixed Rose with as serious a look as Tam had ever seen him wear. "Thank you," he said.

"Of course." Rose put the steaming mug in his hand. "Now go thank Tam for saving your life. I was this close"— she held two fingers an inch apart—"to killing you the other night."

Around noon that day they spotted a hamlet nestled between two hills. Rose called a halt and sent Brune into town on an errand. Shortly after he left, one of Rose's saddlebags began yelling at her.

She rushed to her mare's side, rummaged through her satchel, and withdrew the small glass orb Tam had seen her holding back in Woodford.

It had been dark and dormant before, but now it contained the face of a man whose lean, angular features were framed by a tumble of blond hair gone grey at the temples. He was wearing an impish smile, and although she'd never met him before, Tam knew Golden Gabe the moment she saw him.

"Rosie! Hi! It's me, Dad."

Rose held the orb at arm's length, as if expecting it to crack open and hatch a hell-spawned demon. "Dad, you know I can see you, right? You don't need to tell me it's you. And you don't need to shout, either. I can hear you just fine."

"Where are you?" Gabe shouted. "Are you safe? Did you hear about the Horde?"

"We've been through this, Dad. I'm *not* going to fight the Horde. I promise."

Her father looked relieved. "Good," he said. "But . . ."

"But . . . ?" urged Freecloud, his ears stiffening.

"It broke through Coldfire Pass. I don't know how," he said, before either Rose or Freecloud could ask. "It's possible not enough mercs made it in time. The winter's been especially harsh, and roads through the mountains... Well, the snow slows our people down, but not the Horde, apparently. Not with a giant to clear a path."

Tam briefly imagined Brontide kicking through mountainous drifts like a toddler after the season's first snowfall.

"So what now?" Rose asked. "Which way are they headed?"

Gabe was shaking his head. "No one knows. They might—"

"*Mommy?*"

Rose flinched. She glanced at Freecloud, who came to stand next to her. Where before she had held the orb at arm's length, Rose now cradled it like a bird she'd found fallen from a nest.

"Mommy, are you there?"

Another face loomed in the glass, too close. Tam saw a green eye blinking, then a mouthful of teeth, then nothing as a palm smothered the image within.

"Here," came Gabriel's voice, muffled. "Hold it like this."

The scene in the orb jostled a while longer, but then a little girl's face looked out. She was fine-featured, with her father's narrow nose and sun-struck emerald eyes. Her hair was long and fine, a colour between silver and green. The sylf's smile, however, was all Rose. "Hi, Mommy! Where are you?"

"Hi, Wren. Daddy and I are way up north, in Kaskar. Where are you?"

"I'm right here!" the girl squealed, once again pressing her face to the glass. "Can't you see me?"

"We can see you," said Freecloud, leaning in beside Rose. "You look beautiful, honey."

An impish giggle. "Grandpa says I'm the prettiest girl inside of the Harpwild."

"Prettiest girl *this side* of the *Heartwyld*, love," Gabe corrected. "And what did we say about calling me Grandpa?"

"You said not to because it makes you seem, um, old."

"Exactly."

"But you *are* old!"

They heard Gabriel scoff. "Go talk to your mother!"

"We're visiting Aunt Ginny and Uncle Clay," Wren announced. "They have all the horses here! Your horse, and Daddy's horse, and Grandpa's horse. And Tally took me for a ride, um, yesterday." The sylf held up three fingers. "She's fourteen already!"

"I see Grandpa's been teaching you to count." Freecloud laughed.

"I could teach her swordplay instead," Gabe mused from beyond the sphere's vision. "Though she's not quite strong enough to lift *Vellichor* yet."

Vellichor! Tam got chills just hearing that name. *The Archon's fabled weapon! The sword he'd used to cut through—*

Cura nudged her in the ribs. "Let's take a walk," she said. "Give these two some privacy, huh?"

Despite wanting to stay and sate her curiosity about Rose and Freecloud's relationship with their daughter, Tam grudgingly followed.

Up ahead was a shallow stream spanned by an ancient stone bridge. Instead of crossing it, Cura picked her way down the steep bank. Tam followed, slipped, and went tumbling through snowy brush toward a hard landing on the ice below. The summoner skidded down to her, laughing, and nearly slipped herself when her boots hit the glazed surface of the stream. Tam caught her before she fell, and the two of them stood clasping one another until they were sure of their balance.

In the shadows beneath the stone arch they found the frozen corpse of a bringol, which Cura explained was a kind of troll. He was enormous—or would've been, were he not hunched against the stonework with his legs splayed and his chin on his chest. His copper-brown scales were sheathed in ice. Rime sprouted from the deep shelf of his brow, and an icicle as long as Freecloud's sword clung to the tip of his nose.

There were a few skeletons trapped in the ice around him: a pair of cows, dozens of birds, and an assortment of small animals. In the bringol's lap was a calcified copper bell cut with crescent-moon-shaped holes.

"See this?" Cura picked it up, being careful to keep it very still as she did so. "When a bringol rings its bell, whatever hears it is dazed by the sound and drawn to its source. We're lucky this one's dead." She reached inside and wrenched the clapper loose, then tossed both it and the now-harmless bell to the ground.

They poked around for a bit. Cura found some chests buried in the snow, while Tam studied a series of crude drawings the monster had scratched on the underside of the bridge, many of which depicted the bringol mating with what she assumed were cows.

"Who exactly is the Widow of Ruangoth?" Tam asked eventually. She'd heard the name from Linden Gale back in Highpool, then again in the barn this morning. "I mean, besides being the one holding our contract up north."

Cura closed the lid on a trunk of mouldy clothes. "I don't know much about her either. She was married to the Marchlord— his second wife, apparently—and when he died she got it all: his castle, his money, his land. Lucky girl, if you ask me."

The bard managed a weak smile. "I guess."

"You guess? She got a castle, Tam. A *castle*. I'd say that's worth losing a husband, wouldn't you?"

Tam was gazing sightlessly at the broken bell. The deep-buried memory of her father's racking sobs echoed in her mind. "No," she said.

For a few seconds Cura's voice was nothing but a droning hum, like the sound of someone speaking through a closed door.

"...called in every debt in the March," she was saying as Tam snapped out of reverie, "which drove the farmers farther south. A year later she lost half her sworn shields to an avalanche in the Brumal Wastes. The rest of them deserted her shortly after. Since then, no one has seen her."

The bard turned and started back toward the bringol's corpse. "How did she get in touch with Fable?"

"She's got a man. The Warden. He's the one who offered Rod the contract."

"What *is* the contract?" The bringol's toenails were the size of dinner plates, yellowed and chipped beneath a layer of frost. Tam stepped onto one, arms outstretched, and tried to keep her balance. "What are we going there for? Rose lied to Sam Roth, and again to Linden Gale. Every time someone asks about the contract she tells them we're going after the Dragoneater."

Cura chuckled. "Yeah."

"So what is it, really? Why doesn't Rose want anyone to know the truth?" Tam's boot slipped off the toenail. She turned to face the Inkwitch and tried again with the other foot. "I bet the Widow killed her husband," she declared, angling her arms to steady herself. "I bet she married him just to steal his wealth. But now he's back from the dead or something, and she's hired Fable to put him down. Am I right? I'm right, aren't I?"

The summoner wore a strange grin. Granted, *all* of Cura's grins were strange, but this one looked almost pitying. As the child of a dead parent, Tam knew a pitying smile when she saw one.

"She wasn't lying, Tam. The Dragoneater *is* the contract. We're going to kill the Simurg."

Tam lost her footing again, and her temper, too. "It's because I'm new, right?" she asked. "Or is it because I'm just the bard? Is that why you won't tell me? I think I deserve—"

"We're going after the Simurg," Cura repeated, dead serious this time. A cold wind swept under the bridge, ruffling the black feathers at the collar of her cloak.

"The Simurg's not real," Tam said. The gust had blown her anger out, and she struggled to rekindle it.

The Inkwitch shrugged. "The Warden says it is. He says the Widow knows where it makes its lair. Beyond the Rimeshields, in the Brumal Wastes."

"That's..." *Impossible*, she'd have said, if she could find the breath to do so. *Ridiculous* would've worked as well. *Outrageous, preposterous*—any of these fit just fine.

Unless it's really true, Tam thought. *Unless the Simurg is more than just a fairy tale.* In which case Rose's intent to go after it was all of those words, along with one more: *suicidal.*

What was it Rod had said back in Woodford? That he sometimes thought Rose might *want* to die young? If so, she was certainly taking the necessary steps to make sure that happened.

A growl startled her, followed by a ripping snort. Tam yelped, spinning, and saw the bringol shift where it sat. She half-expected to see its eyes spring open, white fires flaring in empty sockets, except...

It's not dead, she realized. *It's asleep.*

A metallic hiss announced that the Inkwitch had drawn a knife. *"Tam,"* Cura whispered. *"Stay. Very. Still."*

The beast mumbled something, though the only word she caught was "kitty," and then scratched the pale-gold scales of its belly. Its hand fumbled absently for the bell in its lap, but the bell wasn't there—it was lying in the snow, too far away for either Tam or Cura to reach quickly. When the bringol's hand swatted empty air, it frowned, grumbled again, and began to stir awake.

Tam motioned frantically for Cura to give her something—anything—to replace the missing bell. The summoner cast around desperately, then put her knife between her teeth and picked up a cow's skull. She threw it to Tam, who turned and set it gently between the monster's legs.

The bringol's hand fumbled over it. Its fingers—each as thick around as Tam's wrist—searched out the skull's hollow eyes, which it must have mistook for the moons cut into its copper bell, since the creature grunted contentedly and settled back to sleep.

The bard allowed herself a relieved sigh, and was about to

remark on how near they'd come to disaster, when the monster loosed a loud snore and the icicle on its nose broke loose.

Never in her admittedly short life had Tam moved so fast. Her hands darted out, fingers clamping around the cold shaft before it struck the ground between the bringol's legs. The icicle was massive, and the muscles in her arms, weary from drawing *Duchess*'s string these past few days, were already trembling with the effort of holding it.

Slowly, she backed away from the slumbering monster, gently easing the icicle into the crook of her arm. She glanced at Cura, who jerked her head back the way they'd come, and the two of them crept stealthily out from under the bridge. Tam set the icicle down, and then, after admiring the melted grooves her grip had left behind, scrambled after Cura up the snowy bank.

Rose and Freecloud were right where they'd left them. The scrying orb was dormant in Rose's hands, and the mood between the two of them was strained. The druin said something Tam couldn't make out and put a hand on Rose's shoulder, but she slunk from his touch and stuffed the orb roughly into her saddlebag.

The shaman returned a few minutes later, plodding across a fallow field with a bulging sack over one shoulder. "Every apple in town," he announced, dropping the sack into the wagon and climbing in after it. "Half are brown, most are soft, but they'll do the trick, I think."

Tam climbed onto the driver's bench. "What are they for?"

"A bribe," said Rose, putting heels to the horse beneath her. "Let's move."

Chapter Eighteen

A Home Beyond the Heartwyld

Shortly before dark they turned onto a rutted logging trail that led into the westernmost reaches of the Silverwood. Before the trees swallowed the sky behind them, Tam cast a lingering look over her shoulder. In the distance, the half-hewn statue of the Exarch Gowikan loomed stark against the setting sun, a shadow framed by the red-gold fury of the fading day. From so far away, the Tyrant's outstretched arm could be mistaken for a gesture of benevolence, a sheltering hand hovering over those scratching out lives in the city below.

Funny, Tam thought, how different a thing could seem at a distance—how beautiful, despite the ugly truth. Was it worth it, she wondered, to look closer? To examine something, or someone, if doing so risked changing your perception of them forever after?

She was young enough to think the answer was yes, but too young to know if she was right.

Tam spent the next two evenings sparring with Rose. The result of each session was distressingly similar to the first, but she *did* manage to fumble her sword onto Rose's foot on the second night.

"I meant to do that," she insisted.

"Sure you did," Rose drawled, helping Tam to her feet. She summoned *Thistle* to hand and gave it back to the bard. "Again."

Not content with merely witnessing Tam's degradation, Brune and Cura decided to contribute as well.

The Inkwitch taught her how to hide a knife, hold a knife, and use a knife to stab, slice, or slash one's enemies. Fortunately, she and Tam used sticks to approximate the knives in question. *Un*fortunately, Cura insisted on using a knife to whittle those sticks into dagger-sharp points.

When Tam pointed out they'd might as well use real blades after all, Cura laughed harshly and told her, "Grow a pair."

"A pair of what?" Tam asked. "Ow! Frigid fucking hells, you didn't tell me we were starting!"

Brune, meanwhile, showed her how to fight like a true vargyr, using trips, takedowns, and grapples to pummel an enemy into submission. Tam proved surprisingly adept at this, since she was fast for her height, strong for her size, and not at all afraid of fighting dirty.

"Very good," said Brune after a bout one afternoon. He touched a finger to the ear Tam had been boxing moments earlier and seemed surprised it didn't come away bloody. "You've got a knack for this. Now remember, a boot to the balls won't work on a basilisk, but it's your bread and butter in a tavern brawl."

Tam continued to practice with her bow as well. She carried *Duchess* as she walked, keeping pace with the corpse cart and taking aim at targets as her bandmates called them out.

"That slanting oak," said Freecloud on their second morning in the forest.

Her shaft skimmed the bark and bounced away.

"That ugly knot that looks like Brune," Cura pointed out.

"Hey!" Brune shouted, taking offense, but then he saw

the knot and nodded appreciatively. "Never mind. That's me, all right."

Tam's arrow struck it dead-on.

"Ouch," said the shaman.

Freecloud beamed. "Well done, Tam." He yanked the shaft free as they passed and inspected the tip before returning it to her.

"That rabbit." Rose gestured to the animal bounding through the brush ahead of them.

Tam skewered it a heartbeat later. The round of applause she earned from her bandmates didn't quite eclipse how awful she felt for having killed something so fuzzy and adorable. Not until lunchtime, anyway.

Shortly after dusk they arrived at what appeared to be an old mill: a large, thatch-roofed warehouse attached to an open-air sawing station. There were logs stacked to either side of the track, and a pile of felled trees waiting to be chopped. The bard could see no evidence the mill was currently occupied, and no light at all was visible through the shed's open windows.

Freecloud slipped from his saddle. "I'll look after the horses," he said quietly.

Rose dismounted as well. She looked around warily, one hand hovering over *Thorn*'s pommel. "Don't tie them too close," she warned. "He doesn't like horses, remember."

"I think the feeling is mutual," said Brune, as Rose's mare gave an anxious snort. The animal calmed a bit when the shaman placed a soothing hand on her neck.

Tam wondered who it was that lived here, in an abandoned mill at the edge of the Silverwood. She'd been about to ask when Rose hissed at Freecloud, who'd struck a match and was using it to light his halfpipe.

"No fires," she said.

The druin winced, waving at the smoke and stamping out his pipe. "Shit, sorry. I forgot—"

"Who is that!?" said a voice from inside the building.

It was deep and sonorous, like someone shouting down the length of a hollow trunk. "I smell smoke, and horses, and the stink of a wet animal!"

Brune sniffed at an armpit. "That might be me."

"Timber, it's Rose!" The mercenary dared a few steps toward the darkened mill. "The band and I are just passing through. Thought we'd spend the night, if you've got room for us."

"Who is *us*?" the voice demanded. "You haven't got that bloody satyr along, do you?"

"Roderick's not here, no."

"Good! That ogre's ass ate my favourite tapestry the last time you were here. And most of my apples, too."

"Speaking of which..." Rose beckoned to Brune, who reached into the cart and passed her the sack of apples he'd purchased earlier that morning. "I have a present for you."

A silence, while the wind conferred with the rustling leaves.

"Is it apples?" The voice sounded hopeful.

"*Hundreds* of them," said Rose. She plucked one from the sack and sent it rolling underhand toward the building.

One of the doors cracked slowly open. A face appeared: rough bark features scrunched beneath mossy brows, and a stumped nose poking out above a beard of bone-white lichen. The thing stooped; an arm reached out and closed curling twig-like fingers around the apple at its feet.

Maiden's Mercy, Tam thought, suddenly breathless. *Timber is a tree.*

While waiting for her nerves to settle, she volunteered to help Freecloud tie up the animals. The druin could see in the dark, but Tam was essentially blind, so instead she petted the horses while Freecloud unhitched the ponies that pulled the wagon.

"What are we doing with the cart?" she asked.

"We can leave it here. This road is seldom used."

"What about the loggers?"

"There are no loggers," said Freecloud, leading the first horse away. "Timber operates the mill himself. Highpool sends a convoy each month to collect the wood."

"You mean he cuts down trees?"

"Yes."

"And then stacks them in piles?"

"Evidently." The druin guided her hand to a bridle and then returned to unhitch the second pony.

"But isn't that . . . uh . . . murder? I mean, he's a—"

"Treant," the druin finished for her. "Not a tree. They look similar, in the way you and I look similar, even though we are not. Trees and treants are very different."

"How so?"

"Well, treants have eyes."

"Okay."

"And mouths. They can speak—do you know many trees that can speak?"

"No, but—"

"They have hands, and feet, and names . . ."

"I get it."

"They sleep, eat—"

"What do they eat?" Tam asked, genuinely curious, but also wanting Freecloud to stop listing things.

"Anything, really. Berries, nuts. Squirrels dumb enough to wander into their mouth. Timber loves apples, obviously." He finished securing the mounts and returned to her side. "Anyway, don't call him a tree."

"I won't," she promised.

Freecloud spoke quietly as they started toward the mill. "When humans ran this place they clashed with the treants who'd settled here. They attacked them unwittingly because they mistook them for trees. Now Timber selects the trees himself. He trades the lumber to Highpool and spares them risking men by sending them into the forest."

"Is the Silverwood that dangerous?" Tam asked, suddenly conscious of the sounds around them: creaking, cracking, snapping, shuffling, and, distantly, the shriek of something dying in the dark.

Freecloud took her arm. "We should get inside."

Timber, whose body was made of highly flammable things like wood and leaves, had a perfectly reasonable aversion to open flame, so the band was permitted only a single enclosed lantern by which to see inside the treant's home. The mill warehouse reminded Tam of Ardburg's public museum. The rafters were hung with tapestries, some of which—namely those depicting scenes from the Reclamation Wars—were so threadbare that a strong gust of wind might reduce them to dust. Others portrayed more recent events, such as Saga's epic arena battle against the chimera.

Now that she'd been on tour, however, and had seen first-hand the sorry scraps that passed for "epic" these days, Tam wondered if even that infamous battle, which had culminated with the destruction of two skyships, countless fishing boats, and the Maxithon itself, had not been hopelessly embellished.

There probably wasn't even a chimera, mused the cynic inside her. *Just an overfed goat, an underfed lion, and whatever sickly lizard the wrangler passed off as a dragon.*

Mounted on the wall were a collection of battered, leaf-shaped shields bearing emblems the bard didn't recognize. A pair of dummies dressed in archaic-looking armour stood vigil by the door. Their helms, she noted, bore chain-link sleeves to accommodate a druin's distinctly long ears. Rounding out the furnishings were several cluttered bookshelves and dense carpets that may once have been fine but were now tracked in sawdust and scuffed raw by Timber's heavy tread.

Lacking a fire over which to cook, the band shared a meal of cold cucumber soup and yam mash spiced with cinnamon. Timber served cool beer in ornate wooden mugs: a deep red lambic that tasted like sour cherries and horse blanket in the best way possible.

Their host's eyes—knotted orbs that glistened wetly in the lamplight—examined the mercenaries as they ate. They lingered for a while on Tam, and then settled on Rose. Timber cleared his throat before speaking, a sound like a damp board cracking in half. "I'll confess, I'm surprised you're not headed west to fight that Horde."

"I'm surprised you didn't head west to join it," said Rose. "You're getting old, Timber. This could be your last chance to get blood on your branches."

The treant chuckled, causing one of the few leaves still clinging to his gnarled boughs to shake loose and fall into his lap. "They're plenty soaked already. Have I told you I used to run with Blackheart back in the day?"

"Several times," said Freecloud.

"He was a vicious bastard," Timber told him anyway. "Though I guess with a name like Blackheart you aren't likely to grow up charitable. He bullied half the Shaded Mire into invading Agria. We sacked a dozen towns and twice as many villages. Spirits, we were already plotting to march on Five-court once we'd torn down every brick in Brycliffe. Alas, we got no farther than Hollow Hill . . ."

"I've heard the tale," Rose grated. "Too many times. My father wouldn't shut up about it. Did you know Saga couldn't keep a bard alive for the life of them? I used to think my dad let them die just so he could tell the stories himself."

"Saga . . ." There was reverence in the treant's rumbling voice. "They held us off for three days, you know. *Three days!* There were only five of the bastards, and a whole forest of us. Blackheart was furious, and your father certainly did his part. He felled dozens of us, and gave me this to remember him by." Timber patted a malformed stump on the side of his head. "But it wasn't him that hewed old Blackheart down. 'Twas that evil bastard, Slowhand."

Tam sipped at her beer. "You mean Clay Cooper?"

"Aye. He chopped Blackheart to bits and turned him into a shield! And thus our ill-fated invasion came to an end." The treant took a draught of his own beer from a wide wooden bowl. "Most of the lads returned to the Mire, but a few of us decided to settle here in Grandual. But you are right," he said to Rose. "I *am* old. Too old to run off and join some fool giant's Horde. Most of the young trunks went, mind you, and the rest followed when the birds brought news of Cragmoor. A gang of 'em came around here a while back. I guess they figured it would help the cause to have an old-timer along. They were *insistent* I join them. Rather too insistent, in fact."

Brune was pouring himself a second mug. "Oh yeah? How did that work out for them?"

"Not well," replied Timber. The bag of apples was by his side. He reached to claim one and popped it into his mouth. Tam heard a hollow clunk as it landed somewhere inside him. "You passed them on the way in."

Tam recalled the piles of neatly stacked logs flanking the road outside. "You...killed them?"

Timber thumped the carpet beside him with a barrel-sized fist. "I did! And didn't so much as snap a twig in doing so! It hardly matters, though. They'd have died out west anyway, along with the rest of those leafless twits. Firewood now or kindling later—dead is dead."

"You think the Horde will fail?" asked Cura. "They've won two battles already. They're probably marching into Agria by now."

"Then they'll *die* in Agria," bellowed the treant. "The same as we did. They had their chance at Castia, and they blew it. If Lastleaf had brought down the Republic...Well, he'd have taken all of Endland by now. My kind"—he made a grumbling sound that Tam recognized as a belch, and the scent of apple wafted into the air—"*monsters*, as you call us, would finally have a place to call our own. A home *beyond* the Heartwyld. I might have made the journey west myself, were that the case. Put down roots at last, and welcomed winter into my soul."

Rose was staring into her lap. Her hands were clasped, the muscles in her jaw working as she ground her teeth. She'd rushed to Castia's defense six years ago, had been trapped in the city for months as Lastleaf's army gorged themselves on the dead outside the walls.

At least that was the story as Tam had heard it. But stories, she'd come to learn, were different depending on who did the telling. Lastleaf's name was infamous throughout the five courts. He was a vengeful warlord—the Villain of a Thousand Songs. But to the denizens of the Heartwyld, or the so-called *monsters* of Grandual, who couldn't feel safe in their homes for fear of mercenaries kicking down their door, he'd been a saviour.

You didn't get to be the villain of one story, she supposed, unless you were the hero of another.

"Although I doubt Lastleaf would have stopped there," ventured Freecloud. He was toying with that coin of his again, thumbing the profile etched onto one side. "I knew him, remember. He was charismatic, ambitious, cunning, and clever. But he'd suffered too much indignity, endured too many concessions to his pride. He was angry and spiteful, driven mad by hatred." Freecloud's ears drooped as he spoke. His eyes went the colour of summer plums in the wavering light. "Lastleaf despised humans—as many of my kind do—and would have led his Horde into Grandual eventually."

Tam shifted uncomfortably. Her coat—the Heathen's coat—weighed on her like it was made of lead instead of leather. Her whole body tingled, and she suddenly felt as if the spectre of Lastleaf himself sat in her place, looking out from behind her eyes.

Chapter Nineteen

Prints of the Past

Tam slept poorly that night, for several reasons. Timber's snoring rivalled Brune's for sheer volume and sounded like two porcupines fighting to the death inside a hollow log. Once, after a fit of harsh coughing, the bard heard what she assumed was a bat come flapping from the treant's mouth. It winged among the rafters for a bit before escaping through a window.

She lay awake for a long while after that, clutching her blanket as she grappled with what Cura had told her under the bringol's bridge—that Rose hadn't been lying when she'd told Sam Roth they were going after the Simurg.

A part of her *still* didn't believe it. The Simurg wasn't a typical monster. It didn't steal children or terrorize villages. No one claimed to have seen it skulking in the woods at night, or to have glimpsed it soaring over the mountains on a clear day. There were no songs about it. None that Tam knew of, anyway.

But there were stories. Children's tales, mostly, spawned from half-remembered myths of a time even before the Dominion, when the Heartwyld was called by another name, and Grandual was but a small part of a greater realm.

When she was very young, Tam's mother used to regale her with tales of knights who rode into battle on the backs of dragons, except the dragons in these stories weren't evil, or greedy; they didn't reduce whole towns to cinders like the asshole dragons of this age. They were wise, kind, and colour- ful, and at the conclusion of each story the knight and her dragon would fly off together into the sunset.

When she was older, Tam heard new endings to the old tales. Darker endings, in which the knights were vanquished and their dragons devoured by an implacable foe who laid waste to their cities and buried them beneath an ocean of ice.

The stories weren't particularly frightening—they were fairy tales, after all. The priesthood of the Winter Queen claimed the Goddess herself was the one responsible for the Brumal Wastes, and Tam had heard numerous wizards assert (usually while drunk) that the endless expanse of snow and ice was the result of a weather spell gone terribly wrong.

"One minute you're conjuring clouds," she'd heard one sorcerer say, "and the next: *Whoosh!* You've ended civilization as you know it!"

And in the unlikely event the stories were true? How many centuries had passed since then? If the Simurg ever had been real, then surely it was long dead now. As dead as the knights and the dragons Tam dreamed of when she finally fell asleep.

She awoke sometime later convinced she could hear the horses screaming, until she remembered they were tied far down the road and realized it was just the wind howling through gaps in the warehouse walls. The treant's home grew colder as the night stretched on, and the bard was grateful when Cura, tossing restlessly on her own bedroll, pressed her back against Tam's.

The summoner's warmth was a welcome comfort.

Her nearness, even more so.

Tam woke up freezing. The warehouse doors were wide open, and although the day had dawned bright, the air was icicle-crisp. She dragged her blanket with her as she rose, and Cura, who was huddled next to her, mumbled disapprovingly.

Everyone else was gone, and so Tam, wearing her blanket like a cloak, shuffled around the treant's home, inspecting in daylight what she'd only glimpsed in the dark the night before. She scanned the spines on Timber's bookshelf: *The Company of Kings*, *The End of Empire*, *Fables of the Greensea*. She picked up a volume entitled *Birch Without Bark* and flipped through it, but there were no words—only page after page of trees whose bark was either peeling or stripped away entirely.

On another shelf was a toy golem, a miniature replica of the runebound constructs Freecloud's father had employed during the Dominion's civil war. The figurine was cloaked in dust, and when she tried blowing it off the thing clattered to pieces.

Tam tried in vain to reassemble it, but settled instead for hiding the scattered limbs behind a musty old book. Afterward she abandoned the blanket, slipped into her leather longcoat, and ventured outside.

There was blood on the road, splashes of vivid red across stark winter white. To the west, Rose and Freecloud were standing near to where Tam and the druin had tied up the mounts the night before. The corpse cart had been overturned, two of its wheels smashed beyond repair. One of the ponies lay dead nearby.

Down the road to the east, Brune was kneeling beside the carcass of the other. The animal's corpse had been savaged. Its ribs were cracked apart, and its entrails strewn across the track like decorations at a zombie's birthday party. Something—Tam had no idea what—had dragged it a long way from where they'd left it.

The shaman stood, clawing a knot from his tangled hair. He glanced up and grimaced as Tam approached. "Guess we're walking from here on out," he said.

Tam went to inspect the dead pony and instantly regretted it. She looked into the forest instead, and saw crows—dozens of them—loitering on the bare branches. They shuffled and cawed and flapped their wings, eager as beggars at a bakery door.

Cura joined them a short while later. She examined the pony's corpse, more intrigued than revolted as she surveyed the carnage. "What could have done this?" she asked. "Not wolves."

"Not wolves," Brune agreed. "Look." He pointed to a trail of deep prints in the muddy road that Tam hadn't even noticed until now. They were huge, spaced so far apart Tam would be hard-pressed to imagine an animal big enough to have made them.

Cura stooped beside one. "An ogre, maybe? A monster of some kind, for sure."

The shaman shook his head. "An ogre wouldn't have left a such a mess. And they don't eat raw meat. It makes them sick, the same as us. They'd have taken the horses and butchered them properly, not slaughtered them. A bear did this," he said eventually. "A big one."

Cura hid a yawn behind the back of her hand. "Bears aren't monsters. No matter how big."

The shaman sighed and started back toward the mill. "This one is."

They bid farewell to Timber. The old treant waved distractedly with one branching arm while the other sprinkled raw salt over the bloody slabs he'd cut from Fable's dead mounts. In return for the horsemeat, the treant had traded them a large canvas tent and furs—cloaks, shawls, hats, and mitts—to keep them warm on their journey north.

Freecloud's grey was gutted as well, but Rose's mare had snapped her leash and escaped into the forest. She returned a short while later, and was unfairly rewarded by being relegated to the role of pack mule. She bore most of the band's gear, as well as *Hiraeth* in its sealskin case.

Tam carried *Duchess* strung and hung over one shoulder, and a full quiver on her hip. She'd donned a scratchy wool sweater beneath the rugged red longcoat, and a pair of boiled leather boots lined with fur and laced to her knees.

Rose had added a layer beneath her armour, and fastened a hooded crimson cloak to her battered pauldrons. Cura was wearing something between a robe and a shawl that was part fur, part feathers, and, as usual, all black. Brune bundled himself in furs, while Freecloud wore nothing but his gold-green scale and sky-blue cowl.

Everyone but Cura wore the enchanted warming scarf Elfmin had gifted them outside the Gnarled Staff. When Tam asked the Inkwitch why she refused to do so, Cura eyed the bard's bright red scarf as though it were a snake coiled around her neck. "Not my colour," she said.

They left the track behind, following trails marked only by hooves and padded paws. Brune led the way. He used to live in this wood, Tam gleaned, but if he relished the thought of a happy homecoming he was doing a damn fine job of hiding it. The sight of those horses had rattled him. Every snapping twig drew his attention, every scuttling creature compelled his hand toward the twinglaive on his back.

From time to time Brune would stop and listen to some snatch of birdsong, or trace his fingers over scratch marks in the face of a tree, or kneel in the snow and make ridiculous chittering noises at a chipmunk hiding in the underbrush.

"What the fuck are you doing?" asked Cura.

"I'm asking him something," Brune whispered.

The summoner laughed. "Are you serious? You can't talk to animals!"

"Shut up, witch, or you'll scare him. Hey!" he called after the scampering critter. "Hey, wait! Get back here, you cheeky little shit!" Cursing, the shaman stood and dusted snow off his knees. "I can so talk to animals," he said defensively. "They just don't always listen." He tramped off angrily, calling over his shoulder as he went. "Dogs hate you, by the way."

The summoner scoffed, but her grin dropped away as she started after him. "Wait, that's not true, is it? Brune? Hey, are you serious?"

As Tam made to follow, a clod of falling snow caught her eye. She glanced up to see an owl perched on a branch above. It was round-faced, its eyes a vibrant green in the forest gloom. There was something odd about its feathers—they had the dull gleam of tarnished coins, and curled at the tips like metal shavings.

They must be frozen, she reasoned.

The owl tracked her as she moved past it, its head swivelling until it faced backward.

Owls do that, Tam told herself, ignoring the prickling chill crawling up her spine. *That's a thing that owls do. Isn't it?*

She heard a whirring hum, the flap of wings, and when she glanced back over her shoulder, the bird was nowhere to be seen.

"You used to live here?" Tam asked the shaman as they walked.

"I did," said Brune. "There's a settlement up ahead."

"Do you have family there?"

A brusque nod. "My dad."

"Is he like you? A vargyr, I mean."

"He is. A bear. Those were his footprints we saw this morning."

"Your *dad* killed our horses?" Tam asked. "Does Rose know?"

"She does, yeah."

Tam tried to push a branch from her path and was rewarded with a stinging slap that left a bit of twig in her mouth. "Why did he do it?" she asked, once she'd spit it out.

"Because he knows I'm here. He can smell me, probably, or else one of the others told him. The horses were a warning. A message, actually."

"What's the message?"

Brune chuckled, rubbing at his bearded chin. *"Hi, son. Welcome home. Now get the fuck out of my forest.* Or something to that effect."

"You two don't get along, I take it?"

"We used to. We were close, once, back when I was just a boy. He and I used to range all over the forest. He taught me to hunt, and to fish, and to sham. Sometimes—"

"Wait," Tam cut him short. "Is that where *shaman* comes from? As in you *sham* into animals?"

"Obviously. What the hell did you think it meant?"

"I don't—I mean, I've never..." She gave up trying to explain herself. "Forget it. So what happened, then? With your dad?"

Brune's sigh wreathed his head in white cloud. "The Silverwood vargyr are led by the Clawmaster, who is typically the strongest warrior of the tribe. When I was a kid, that was a man named Berik. He was wise, and kind, and had been Clawmaster for more than twenty years, until one day my father challenged him, killed him, and assumed leadership of the tribe."

"Wow," Tam said.

"Wow is right. I couldn't believe it: My old man was the king! And being the stupid little runt that I was, I was actually *proud* of him. I didn't care that he'd killed a better man than he would ever be, or that he challenged anyone he thought might threaten his reign. He and I never went hunting after that. Or fishing. For a while he lost interest in me completely. I begged him to help me find my *fain,* but—"

"*Fain?*"

"It means..." Brune frowned, swiping hair from his eyes.

"There's no other word for it, really. Soul mirror? Eh, that sounds stupid, doesn't it?"

"Pretty stupid, yeah," Tam agreed.

They came upon the ruins of what looked like an ancient dwelling: a crumbled shelf of flat stones beneath a torn turf roof. Nearby, a tree was marked with the same four slashes Tam had seen elsewhere on trunks and boulders. She'd thought nothing of them earlier—they were in a forest, after all—but now she could guess who'd made those gouges, and could interpret their meaning.

Get the fuck out of my forest . . .

"Hold up," yelled Cura behind them. "I need to pee."

"Same," said Freecloud. "I'll go up," he said, since the trail they'd been following skirted the waist of a wooded hill.

"Such a gentleman," said Cura, already threading her way down the slope to their right.

Rose looped her horse's line around a branch before sparking a halfpipe and going to explore the ruins of the old home.

Brune pulled the stopper from his waterskin and drank deep. "Anyway, the *fain* is our true nature. It allows us to transform into whatever animal we identify with the most. My father wouldn't teach me to find mine, and when I sought help from the others, he accused me of plotting to overthrow him. He couldn't challenge me directly—I had no power to speak of, and it would have made him appear weak—so he exiled me instead, and promised to kill me if I ever returned."

"What?" Tam was aghast. "So why are we here?"

"Because I have no idea what I'm doing," said Brune. He took another pull from his skin and then offered it to Tam. "I never found my *fain*, or learned how to sham properly. I fled the forest and went east till I hit ocean. One night I drank myself blind before the owner of the tavern found out I had no money. Hell, I didn't even know what money *was*. Some goons of his started doing a number on me, and . . . out came the bear. I was so drunk I don't even remember it, but some lowlife booker saw it happen, and the next thing I know I'm fighting monsters in a Freeport pit. Brune the Beast, they called me."

Tam drank from the skin and discovered Brune had topped it up with the treant's sweet red beer. She stole a second mouthful before handing it back. "And that's where you met Rose."

The shaman nodded. There were half a hundred songs about the Battle of Freeport, and every one of them ended the same way: with Rose and her brand-new band burning the pirate fleet to ashes.

"I need my father to show me what I'm doing wrong," Brune said, watching as Freecloud made a cautious descent from the escarpment above. "Assuming the Widow's contract is for real... Assuming the Simurg exists and we somehow manage to find it, I can't afford—" He paused to sniff their air, and was about to say something further when the sudden boom of Cura's voice rattled the forest and shook the snow from the trees.

"KURAGEN!"

Chapter Twenty

Strange Animals

They found Cura kneeling by an icy stream at the base of the hill. *Kuragen* loomed over the summoner, salt water sluicing from her scalloped helm. Two of her tentacle limbs held thrashing prisoners—a pair of oversized badgers—and her spear was levelled at a snarling white lynx the size of a small horse.

There were half a dozen animals surrounding Cura's inkling. Vargyr, Tam guessed, judging by their size. The beasts scattered as Rose led a charge down the snowy bank—all but a giant skunk, who bared its fangs and leapt at Brune. The shaman levelled his glaive, but one of Rose's scimitars—*Thistle*, blurring green—brought it down with a yelp.

The lynx bounded away from *Kuragen*'s spear. When it reached the opposite bank it turned and settled into a crouch.

"Wait!" Brune laid a hand on Rose's shoulder before she could hurl *Thorn* as well. She glanced up at him, eyes wild, her face as white as the ice skirting the stream's edge.

She's terrified, Tam realized, scarcely believing her eyes. *How long has it been since she's fought stone cold sober, without the false courage of Lion's Leaf coursing through her veins?*

And yet, fearing for Cura's safety, Rose had rushed in without hesitation. Only now, as she lowered her arm, did

Tam see the warrior's hands trembling, or notice the sheen of cold sweat that plastered her hair to her face.

By the time the bard's eyes snapped back to the lynx, it was gone. In its place was a woman. She was powerfully built and utterly naked. Her pale skin was laced with scars and daubed with paint markings intended to resemble those of her *fain*.

Assuming I'm using that word correctly, Tam thought.

"Brune, son of Fenra!" the woman yelled. "I am Sorcha. I speak for Shadrach, who is Clawmaster of this Wood."

"So, speak," Brune said impatiently.

The woman's eyes flickered to Cura's inkling, betraying the barest hint of . . . fear? Uncertainty? Morbid curiosity? It was hard to tell from so far away, but Tam guessed it was probably all three.

"You were exiled. Ordered never to return. You have returned."

"Your people have a startling grasp of the obvious," said Freecloud.

"For this transgression. You are summoned. To the Faingrove." The lynx-woman had a curious way of speaking, as if barking orders to someone who could comprehend only a few words at a time.

Rose slammed *Thorn* back into its scabbard. Her other hand gripped the collar of her armour as if it were constricting around her throat. "The Faingrove?" she asked her shaman. "What is it?"

Brune's expression hovered somewhere between devastation and determination. "It's an arena."

"Not alone," said Rose, for the seventh time.

"Yes, alone," Brune insisted for the eighth.

"This isn't a negotiation," she told him. "I'm not asking."

"It's not my rule! Our laws forbid—"

The white lynx turned to yowl at them, which Tam

assumed was Sorcha's way of telling her charges to shut the fuck up. The bard might have thanked her for it were she not afraid that doing so would earn her a reprimand as well.

A whine to her right drew Tam's attention. The skunk Rose had wounded earlier limped alongside them, the only one of their escort (aside from Sorcha) who was not embodying their *fain*. She was a middle-aged woman, scrawny, with twin streaks of grey in her ratty black hair. Her breasts swayed beneath stooped shoulders as she hobbled, a bloodied hand clutching the wound on her leg. She was barefoot in the snow, but that seemed the least of her concerns.

When she caught Tam staring, the woman spat at her feet. *"Fabhik du ik arhsen klak."*

"What did she say?" the bard asked.

"She likes your coat," Brune translated, obviously lying.

When they reached the vargyr settlement the shaman staggered to a halt. Brune's village was populated by trees taller than any Tam had ever seen. Even this late into winter they retained a full complement of scarlet leaves. Even so, a few shafts of falling snow pierced the canopy here and there. Between the paths were great mounds of green and brown peat, fronted by walls of flat stones like the ruin they'd seen in the forest this afternoon. Before each arched doorway was a carved wooden totem depicting the *fain* of its inhabitant.

More than half of the homes were destroyed, their roofs caved in, their stones scattered or blackened by fire. The totems in front of these dwellings were wrecked as well, burnt or smashed into pieces.

"What the hell happened here?" Brune asked. Since Sorcha didn't seem the talkative sort, he directed his question toward the skunk-woman. She answered with a sneer, but when the shaman took a threatening step toward her she found her voice awful quick.

"Your father. His enemies. All of them, broken. Broken in Faingrove."

Tam's flesh crawled as the skunk-woman spoke. Her voice was a shrill and grating whimper that sounded barely human. As they proceeded along the winding trail between shattered homes, the bard quickened her pace until she was shoulder to shoulder with Fable's shaman.

"Is she . . . um . . . normal?" Tam asked him. "I mean, normal for a vargyr?"

Brune shook his shaggy head. "No. None of this is normal. I don't understand what's happened here."

They were forced to step around the charred remains of a spider totem, and Tam took a moment to thank the Holy Tetrea that Brune's "spirit-mirror" wasn't some sort of hideous insect.

"Vargyr use their *fains* to hunt, or to defend themselves. These people"—he gestured toward the twin badgers who'd attacked Cura at the stream, now snarling and nipping at one another's flanks—"they should be *people*. If they stay shammed for too long . . . Well, they'll end up like her."

The skunk-woman was crouched on all fours, sniffing around the base of a shrub.

Brune stopped before one of the crumbled mounds. Its stones were worn smooth and cloaked in green lichen. The totem before it was missing most of its head. The lower half was gouged by four deep claw marks, but it was still possible to discern the likeness of the animal it was meant to signify.

"A wolf?" Rose was squinting to see in the growing dusk.

"My mother lived here," Brune said. "She left when I was very young."

"Where did she go?" Tam asked.

The shaman reached to run fingers over the totem's disfigured face. "She wasn't from here. She and her pack were wanderers. Wyld Hearts, we call them."

Tam's breath caught. She could almost hear her mother's voice whisper in the evening breeze blowing through the leaves overhead.

"She stuck around long enough to see me whelped, but after that..." Brune sighed, and seemed somehow diminished for it. "Not everyone loves their children, I guess."

Tam's heart ached to imagine a child growing up believing such a thing. Even when she and her father were at odds—when something one of them said wounded the other deeper than intended—she had always known that he loved her.

Freecloud shifted uncomfortably, his ears drooping like flowers dead of thirst. It occurred to Tam that he and Rose had left their own daughter behind.

Another of Sorcha's barks got them moving again. Tam could see a vast cavern up ahead, its walls and ceilings thick with foliage.

The Faingrove, she assumed.

More and more vargyr joined their procession. Most of them loped or scuttled on paws and claws and hooves, but a few of them remained human, or something close. Tam spotted a man with a ridge of grease-spiked hair who cackled like a hyena as he clambered over the peat mound beside them. Another woman walked on her knuckles and beat her chest when Cura dared to meet her gaze.

Brune's expression was bleak. "How could my father allow this to happen?"

"Animals tend to favour instinct over intellect," Freecloud pointed out. "It makes them prone to subservience."

"What do you mean?" Rose asked.

"The longer they remain in this form, the more susceptible they become to the commands of someone stronger than them," Freecloud suggested. "You can tame most dogs in a matter of hours, but it can take months to break a human's will. Or so I've heard," he added, when Rose eyed him askew. "I've never trained a human, just so we're all clear on that."

"So what are we doing here?" said Cura. "We came so that Brune's dad could set him straight, didn't we? So the old bear could teach him how to find his..."

"*Fain*," Tam provided.

"Whatever. But now Brune's dad wants to kill him. Coming here was pointless—so why not leave? Fight our way out of here?" She nodded at the skunk-woman, who was stumbling along with her eyes closed, no longer bothering to clutch the wound that would almost certainly kill her. "I doubt these runts could stop us."

"Except it's almost dark," said Freecloud. "We'll be blind, and lost. They won't."

Rose looked up at her shaman. "It's your call," she told him. "You don't have to go through with this if you don't want to. But if you're staying, then so are we."

Brune peered into the Faingrove ahead. A damp heat radiated from inside, but there were no fires burning that Tam could see. "I'm staying," he said eventually. "I've been running from this place long enough, I think. It's time to settle this."

"Then let's settle it," Rose said. She didn't bother asking whether or not the others agreed. She didn't need to. Freecloud offered Brune a reassuring nod. Cura was scowling into the dark as if her own demons were waiting inside. If the Clawmaster intended to challenge his son, he would have to go through Fable first.

Sorcha relinquished her *fain* and fixed Brune with a sneer. "No fangs inside," she said, indicating the twinglaive strapped to his back. "No outsiders, either."

"Try and stop us," said Rose, already pulling off her gauntlets.

The vargyr bared her teeth. "You think I can't?"

"I know you can't."

The two women glared at one another until the shaman cleared his throat. "Maybe you could wait outside..." he began feebly.

"Like hell we could." Rose wheeled on Brune. "Now would you please tell this *kitten* to get out of my fucking face before I drag her back to that stream and drown her in it?"

Sorcha growled. Her hands flexed into claws, but before she could embrace her *fain* a deep voice boomed from inside the cavern.

"LET THEM IN."

The vargyr around them cowered. Their ears flattened, and those with tails tucked them between their legs.

Cura sniffed. "Let me guess: the great and powerful Shadrach?"

Brune, who'd gone rigid, only nodded.

"Fine," Sorcha conceded. "But no fangs. No shells."

"No fangs, huh?" Freecloud sounded amused. He laid *Madrigal*'s scabbard on a stone shelf and began unlacing his armour.

Cura relinquished no fewer than six knives, and Brune gave up his twinglaive. Tam leaned *Duchess* against the rock wall and unbuckled her quiver.

It took Rose several minutes to peel off every piece of warped black metal she'd strapped to herself. When she finished, Sorcha examined the pile of discarded gear.

"Clawmaster demands tribute," she sneered.

Rose looked dubious. "Fine," she said. "It's mostly junk anyway. He can have anything except my—"

"These." Sorcha picked up the rune-etched gauntlets.

"Of course," Rose said curtly, but Tam saw the barest hint of a smile curl her lips.

The lynx-woman sniffed the gauntlets before passing them off to a weaselly-looking man whose *fain*, Tam guessed, was probably a weasel.

"You really don't need to come in," Brune told his bandmates. "A challenge is sacred to the vargyr. It can't be avoided, and it can't be interfered with. Shadrach and I will fight one-on-one. I'll kill him, or he'll kill me, but you can't help me in there." He looked pointedly at Rose. "None of you can."

"It doesn't matter," she told him. "You're not going through this alone, Brune. That's not how a band works. Where you go, we go."

Sorcha gestured at Rose's wool longshirt. "No shells," she repeated, as if speaking to a child. "Only skin."

Rose frowned. "Only skin?

"You want us naked?" Freecloud asked.

The lynx-woman nodded. "Naked. Yes."

Rose gave Brune on a friendly clap on the shoulder. "Good luck in there," she said. "We'll be here if you need us."

They stripped.

It was awkward.

Tam (immensely grateful for the heat rolling out of the Faingrove) did her damndest to look the others directly in the eye, and they attempted to do the same. Nevertheless, she couldn't help but gawk at the scars lacing Rose's lean frame, the bizarre horrors inked over Cura's pale skin, and the tattoo of a butterfly axe on Brune's lower back.

"A girl made me do it," explained the shaman, when he caught Tam looking.

Of all of them, only Freecloud's body was left unblemished by the band's misadventures. The druin healed quickly, Tam knew, but also she'd never seen him take a blow unless he deliberately put himself in harm's way, as he had back in the Ravine, and again during the brawl in Highpool.

A group of vargyr gathered around Brune, each bearing a wooden bowl of coloured liquid that began to radiate as dusk gave way to night.

"It's made of bloomshrooms," said the shaman, as an old woman with milk-white eyes slathered the glowing paste over his arms, chest, and legs. "We can't enter until we're done up in likeness of our *fain*. Hence the claws." He raised his hand to show off the red stripes on the back of his hand. She painted his face as well, sketching fangs around his mouth and a long white snout between his eyes.

He didn't particularly *look* like a bear, but Tam decided

it wasn't worth pointing out that a blind woman had done a lousy job of getting his *fain* right.

At Sorcha's orders, the bowl-bearing vargyr surrounded the rest of the band as well.

Freecloud arched a brow. "They're painting us, too?"

"Painting us like what?" Tam asked.

Brune shrugged. "I guess we'll see," he said.

Chapter Twenty-one

The Clawmaster's Cave

They walked five abreast into the waiting dark. Brune's mountainous frame was marked by white whorls and the plume of a tail up his broad back. Rose bore the jagged red stripes of a Rushfire tigress, while Cura sported violet feathers and a raven's wings in blazing blue across her bare shoulders.

Tam was a raccoon, or something like one. Her legs were striped green and gold, with cuffs at her wrists, and a bandit's mask around her eyes.

Freecloud's nose was a red slash between fans of vibrant blue. The same colours were applied to both his groin and rear (which the druin found hilarious), while his chest was splashed a lustrous white.

"What are you supposed to be?" Tam had asked him outside.

"A mandrill, I think."

"Is it a monster?"

"It's like a monkey," he explained. "A very angry, very dangerous monkey."

There were no fires in the Faingrove. The only light came from its inhabitants (painted in semblance of their respective *fains*) and from a collection of glowing skeletons bound by gut string and arrayed throughout the cavern. Each set of bones belonged to an animal much bigger than it ought to have been.

Tam recognized at least three bears, a snake, a wolf, a southern ape, and several large cats.

Shadrach's trophies, she presumed. *How many challengers, willing or otherwise, have stood in this place and wondered if they'd soon be nothing more than a despot's decoration?*

It was sweltering inside. Brune had explained that the Faingrove was home to a hot spring, and Tam could feel steam curling around her as they moved deeper in. They were told to stand near one of the lower pools, while Brune proceeded alone to the open space in the centre of the grotto.

Mighty Shadrach, Clawmaster of the Silverwood vargyr, reclined on a throne made of glow-in-the-dark bones. The skulls of conquered enemies gleamed like morbid lamps across the back, and the wings of some vanquished avian adversary reared against the darkness above him.

Brune's father was painted almost entirely red, so it was impossible to mistake how enormous he was. There were slashes of white on his forearms and calves—each of which were as thick around as Tam at the waist—and a mane of gold across the breadth of his shoulders.

Sorcha knelt at his feet. She had given him Rose's gauntlets, but the Clawmaster seemed to think they were nothing more than trinkets, since he cast them aside as he stood to greet his son.

"You should not have returned." Shadrach's voice came from all directions at once. It enclosed them like the heat of the hot springs, oppressive and smothering.

"You should not be Clawmaster," Brune shouted back. His words incited a discordant choir of yelps, snarls, growls, and barks. There were more than a hundred vargyr present, by Tam's estimation. They were all in human form, but their *fains* had long since come to dictate their nature.

"I have earned my rank by sacred rite!" boomed Shadrach. He swept his bulky arms to indicate the hanging skeletons. "Behold, my unworthy challengers."

"Your victims, you mean. You are mad, Father. There's nothing sacred about what you've done here." Brune called out to those gathered along the shelves and ledges of the cavern. "Look at what you've become! Listen to yourselves, grunting and shambling like beasts. We used to sing in this place. Do you remember? We used to dance, and feast, and celebrate our second natures. And now?" He turned ponderously. "It's nothing but a killing ground. A wicked shrine to a god you didn't ask for, and you sure as hell don't deserve."

"*Be silent!*" Shadrach shouted down the slope before him. "I will not tolerate these slurs from an outcast!"

"*You* made me an outcast, Father. *You* turned me away. Your own son!"

"*My* son?" The Clawmaster sounded incredulous. "No. You were never mine. Not truly. And the day I realized that is the day I cast you out."

Brune staggered beneath the hammerblow of his father's words. "Not yours? You would disown me now?"

"I've seen your *fain*, boy. I saw it then, and I see it now, plain as fresh tracks. You bring your filthy pack to this place and claim to be *my* son?"

"I *am* your son!" The shaman was livid.

"Come, then!" his father goaded. "Show me!"

Brune was already running, roaring at the top of his lungs.

Shadrach bellowed, triumphant, and charged to meet him.

He'd wanted this, Tam knew. He'd kindled Brune's anger, adding fuel until it burned white-hot. Rage was something the Clawmaster could predict—something he could channel, and therefore control.

The whorls on Brune's back began to swell as the shaman's body grew. His limbs bulged, fur bristled through the paint on his arms, splashed in the same glaring colours.

The Clawmaster burst his seams the way a firebomb

exploded from a clay pot, doubling in size, tripling, towering over Brune as he stampeded down the ramp.

Fury cracked between them like a peal of thunder, a sound so deeply primal Tam nearly pissed the pants she wasn't wearing. Yet she couldn't look away: not as the two bears crashed into one another with the force of rockslides tumbling down opposite slopes.

Their impact shook the cavern, drawing cries of savage glee from its occupants. The two monsters grappled, huge on their hind legs, straining against one another as their claws raked and their jaws snapped, and then Shadrach had Brune by the scruff and threw him to the ground.

Fable's shaman halved in size as he landed. He'd barely righted himself before the bloodred bear was on him, scoring his flanks with talons like scimitar blades. Brune made a weak lunge for his father's throat, but Shadrach skewed away. His teeth clamped onto Brune's shoulder and the Clawmaster twisted, hurling his son halfway across the arena floor.

Brune hit the ground hard, tumbling over stone and scree, and then vanished.

"What?" Tam heard herself cry.

"He's in the water," Cura muttered.

Fable's shaman had rolled into one of the cavern's pools. Tam could see ripples of white phosphorescence as the shaman's paint bled away. He emerged as a man, coughing and gasping, near invisible now that his colouring was gone. He hauled himself onto the stone and lay there panting.

The Clawmaster's exultant roar became a husky laugh as he relinquished his animal form. "You're more fool than I thought, boy. Are you really that naive? Or are you so eager to usurp me that you would deny your true nature?"

Though his words were barbed, Shadrach's manner of speaking was elegant in contrast to his fellow vargyr. Tam recalled what Freecloud had said about animals being easy to manipulate, and wondered if the druin's supposition was true. Did the Clawmaster demand that his subjects spend more time as beasts than they did as men and women? Was he deliberately dulling their minds to make them more pliant to his commands?

To do so would be evil, of course. Unforgivably cruel. But Brune's father, from what little Tam knew of him, seemed like exactly the sort of asshole to try it.

"You want to know what you really are?" the Clawmaster asked his son. "You're not mine," he snarled. "You're hers."

He pointed to one of the skeletons suspended from the cavern roof. It looked to Tam like a dog, except it was longer, leaner, with a narrow snout and sharper canines...

"Oh, Brune, no," she heard Rose whisper. "Don't look up. Please, don't look up."

But Brune did, and after a stunned silence he murmured hoarsely, "Is that...?"

"She came back for you," the Clawmaster said. His tone was lighter now, almost conversational. As though he wasn't eviscerating his son with words. "This was three, maybe four years ago. She was furious when I told her I'd cast you out. She was always big on loyalty, your mother. The 'pack' meant everything to her. It was why she left you and me in the first place," he said. "To be with her *real* family."

Brune was on his knees in a puddle of oily light. "You..."

"She called me a tyrant," Shadrach said, chuckling darkly. "And a few nastier things, besides. She dared to challenge my right to lead." He craned his huge neck. "You see how well that worked out for her."

His grandstanding earned an ovation of yips and growls, but it was Brune who growled loudest. Tam could barely make him out against the steam rising from the paint-lit pool behind him, but she could see his shoulders quaking, his hands trembling as they curled into claws. A sound escaped him that was part moan, part anguished wail.

Tam felt the hairs on her neck rise.

The light from the pool disappeared, lost behind the shadow of something suddenly huge, and Brune's wail of sorrow became a blood-chilling *howl*. It echoed back and forth across the Faingrove, bouncing from water and stone until the mournful cry of a hundred wolves surrounded them.

"Now you see," his father said. "This is what you really are. I should have—"

Brune barrelled into him, a snarling void amidst the riot of garish colours. The Clawmaster sailed backward, crashing through the skeleton of a boar whose glowing gold tusks were as long as Tam's bow. Shadrach rose in a rage, shamming in an instant into the great red beast he'd been before. When the wolf lunged next, he was ready.

At least he'd thought he was ready.

Shadrach's claws swiped at nothing. His teeth snapped shut on empty air. Brune juked, diving low, snagging the Clawmaster's heel in his jaws and dragging at it. Tam heard the tear of sinew, the grisly pop of sheared tendons, and the bear roared in agony.

"Get ready," said Rose.

Tam stiffened. *Ready for what?*

Shadrach collapsed onto all fours, twisted, lashed out with an arm the size of a tree trunk—which might have levelled Brune were he not airborne, springing with a speed and grace he had never possessed as a bear. Fable's shaman landed directly on top of his enemy. His fangs found purchase in the muscle around Shadrach's throat, and he leapt again, flinging himself over his father's head, writhing in the air so that he landed on all fours.

The Clawmaster couldn't manage to right himself. Brune had him by the collar and was wrenching him from side to side, dragging him to the ground whenever Shadrach made to rise. His father tried clawing at him, but the wolf was too fast, ducking away before the bear's talons could reach him.

Shadrach roared again, a shuddering cry that—from anyone else—might have implied that surrender was imminent. Except the vargyr lord was too prideful for that, too insufferably arrogant. And he'd been *grooming* his adherents for exactly this moment.

Shamming, the Clawmaster slipped from Brune's jaws. He scrambled away, clutching his throat.

"*Now,*" Rose hissed.

"Kill him!" bawled Shadrach. "Kill the traitor! Do it now! Your master commands you!"

And then, chaos.

Chapter Twenty-two

Shadow of the Wolf

Sorcha leapt and was a lynx before she landed, powering down the ramp and lunging at the black shadow that was Brune. Several others joined her—dropping from bluffs or splashing across pools to heed the Clawmaster's call—but not all of them.

Not yet, anyway.

"ABRAXAS!" Cura called forth the inking she'd summoned in Highpool: a metalwork stallion that kicked free of her arm. The jointed struts of its wings snapped open, crackling with violet light as it rushed to intercept Brune's assailants.

Freecloud sprinted toward the scattered bones of the boar, while Rose turned and—

"Sorry," she said, then shoved Tam hard with both hands.

The bard plunged into the pool behind her, and because she'd been in the midst of asking, "Sorry for what?" she gulped down a mouthful of hot water. She heard muffled screaming, saw clouds of green and gold swirl above her—and then Rose was dragging her from the pool, squeezing her to force the water from her lungs.

For an absurd moment, all Tam could think about was the

fact that she was wet and Rose was warm and neither of them were wearing anything but paint.

Well, Rose is wearing paint, she thought. *I'm just naked.*

"Why?" she spluttered.

"Because I need you invisible," Rose told her. "Or near enough."

"I don't understand."

"My gauntlets. I need you to get over there and grab them for me." Rose pointed at the Clawmaster's throne. She was trembling, Tam noticed, her whole body begging for a dose of Lion's Leaf.

A scrawny, redheaded woman was creeping toward them. When Tam caught her eye, the girl bared her teeth and shammed into a mangy-looking fox.

"Go," Rose ordered. She pushed Tam away and turned to face the vargyr. As she did, Freecloud returned bearing a glowing gold tusk in either hand. He heaved one at Rose as the fox pounced. She caught it two-handed and clubbed the beast from the air.

Tam took off running. Tiers of stone climbed like colossal steps on her right, and she stayed near the wall to avoid the battle raging in the middle of the cavern.

Cura's static stallion was circling the grotto floor, discouraging those who hadn't yet joined the fray from doing so. It trampled, kicked, and thrashed wildly, skewering foes with the spikes cresting its head.

It was hard to see how Fable's shaman was faring. He was swarmed by lesser beasts: a wolverine, a weasel, and Sorcha, whose spotted claws moved so fast they blurred. Two more cats—an orange cougar and a sleek purple panther—were bounding toward them. Brune was bigger—much bigger—than any of them, and fuelled by manic rage, but his enemies were ferocious. The wolverine and the weasel were clinging to his hide, spitting and clawing, while the lynx attacked him head-on. Tam saw the shadow of Brune's head swoop beneath

Sorcha's swiping paws, snag her belly, and rip it open. Offal splattered the stone floor beneath her, but Sorcha fought on, heedless of how grievous her injury was.

Tam, now just a slender shadow in a cave full of colour, ran as fast as she could, staying well clear of Brune's vicious struggle and keeping an eye out for Cura's stallion. She skirted the edge of another hot spring and pulled herself onto the lowest shelf ringing the cavern floor.

Someone—a vargyr—dropped down in front of her. Tam registered a pair of bright green stripes, but it was the *smell* that told her who it was. The skunk-woman didn't notice her until the two of them collided. She squealed in surprise, and Tam saw black-and-white-fur sprout from the woman's face.

How do you stop someone from shamming? she wondered. She tried a straight jab to the throat first, and was delighted when it did the trick. The vargyr gurgled something before toppling off the ledge and into a pool below. Tam hurried on.

Rose and Freecloud were back to back, wielding the boar's tusks like dull swords to bludgeon whoever came close. They'd barely bought themselves a reprieve when the twin badgers sprang at them. Rose went down beneath one, but managed to lodge her bone in the crook of its jaw. The other attacked the druin, attempting to butt him with its head and knock him prone. Freecloud evaded it, but his concern for Rose kept him from pressing the advantage.

Something gold-bellied and white-faced went soaring past Tam and hit the rock wall on her right. Brune had flung the weasel away, and now it crouched, dazed, on the path before her. Tam brained him with a heel to the head and ran on.

She sought frantically for Shadrach, and found him below, lying on his side with both hands pressed to his ravaged neck.

Is he dying? she wondered, and was so preoccupied by the Clawmaster that she almost ran headlong into a wall of bristling, bright pink spikes. Instead, she skidded onto her bare ass, wincing as the skin was scraped raw.

What the fuck is this? The hedge of spines advanced on her, and it took the bard a moment to realize what she was facing. *A bloody porcupine!* Tam scrambled to her feet and tried edging around it, but the foul thing chittered at her and swung its rump like a spiked flail.

"Fuck," she swore, frustrated. When one of the pink quills stuck into her arm, she swore again—in pain, this time.

The thing was backing her up, costing her precious seconds. The drop on her left was too far to fall safely, and the shelf on her right too high to reach. She could jump, but the nearest pool was full of flailing skunk, and there was a weasel stirring groggily on the path behind her.

A tingling sensation warned her that Cura's inkling was coming before it arrived. Shadrach dived from its path as it stampeded past. Tam thought about calling for help, but *Abraxas* was already rearing. Its wings fanned open—filaments of electricity arcing between the barbed metal struts—and then swept forward, pinching like the legs of a spider into electrifying spears. They impaled the porcupine, wreathed it in a net of blue-white energy, and hoisted it skyward.

Tam bolted underneath it. She didn't look to see what became of the creature, but she could smell it frying from the inside out, and heard shooting quills clatter against the stone all around her.

Glancing left, she saw the wolverine's body flopping in the air, trapped between Brune's shadow-jaws. The lynx was still after him, but Fable's shaman was dancing in circles, and Sorcha's wound was tiring her quickly.

Freecloud had dispatched one of the badger brothers—its body was floating in the pool behind him—and as she watched, he brought his tusk down across the back of the one attacking Rose.

Tam leapt from her precipice onto the ramp. She pounded up it, bare soles slapping on the damp stone. She found Rose's gauntlets on the ground near Shadrach's throne. Scooping them up, she turned, and—

A huge hand seized her throat. The bard felt her stomach drop; she kicked frantically as her feet left the ground.

No air.

Shadrach's face loomed before her: red skin, black beard, the same gap-toothed grin as his son, except malicious. Hateful. Merciless.

No. Air.

Shouldn't he be saying something? Making a threat? Telling her how weak she was? How pitiful? Where was the fun in just wringing someone's neck!?

No.

Should she kick him in the groin? That always worked in stories.

Air.

She heard one of the gauntlets clang on the stone below her. Her grip on the other was loosening, so she slid it on. Couldn't lose both. Rose would kill her.

Like Shadrach was killing her.

Something hit her palm, and Tam's fingers closed instinctively around it. It was metallic. Cold. Like catching a fish you couldn't see with your bare hand. Her vision was dimming, but she lifted her hand to see. The runes on the gauntlet were glowing green.

And so was the sword in her hand.

She wondered briefly whether she or Shadrach was more surprised to see it there, before she drove it, with every ounce of her strength, into the wound on his neck.

It didn't kill him (because *every ounce of strength* didn't count for much when you were a skinny seventeen-year-old girl) but it obviously hurt, since the Clawmaster wailed and let her go. Tam landed in a crouch, snatched up the other gauntlet, and ran like the fucking wind down the ramp.

One of the huge cats—the cougar—looked her way. Light glazed its eyes as it tracked her in the dark. It prepared to lunge at her, but Cura's inkling barrelled into it, trampling the beast beneath thunderstruck hooves.

"Tam!" Rose was running at her. "Behind you!"

She didn't look. Didn't need to look. She could hear the heavy thud of Shadrach's feet as he closed on her.

She was running too fast to pull *Thistle*'s gauntlet off, so she lobbed *Thorn*'s at Rose and then prayed to the Summer Lord's flea-ridden beard that Shadrach slipped, or tripped, or decided to pick on someone his own size.

Rose caught it—of course she caught it—and slammed it on. *Thorn* answered her call, shining blue as it streaked like an arrow to her open hand.

"Down!" she screamed.

Tam dove, rolling over grit and stone as Rose hurled the scimitar sidearm. The bard watched, breathless, as it whipped overhead, spinning like the moon struck loose from the sky. It went clean through the Clawmaster's side. He stumbled, balancing on one leg to keep from slewing sideways, and Rose threw herself shoulder-first into his knee.

It snapped, and Shadrach barely started screaming before his face hit the ground with a sickening crunch.

Her mother's voice notwithstanding, Tam had never heard a sweeter sound in all the days of her life.

Brune's father remained where he was, motionless. Nearby, Cura's inkling fizzled and disappeared. The summoner was leaning heavily on Freecloud, who had gone to watch over her.

Rose offered Tam a hand up. "Nice throw," she said.

"You too," Tam replied.

The fight was over. Or ending, in any case. There were still many dozens of vargyr watching from the outskirts of the cavern, but if they hadn't attacked at the Clawmaster's command she doubted they would do so now.

Shadrach had controlled them through fear, and although

fear bred subservience, it did not beget loyalty. Tam wondered who it was that told her that. Her father, probably. It was too wise to have come from her uncle Bran.

The panther was dead. The wolverine was lying in halves. One of the badgers was whimpering piteously, soon to expire. Sorcha, somehow, was still on her feet, but giving up ground, hissing defiantly as the wolf advanced on her. At last she relinquished her *fain* and fell to her knees, baring her throat in a gesture of submission.

A groan from Shadrach drew Brune's attention. He stalked over, lips peeled back from sabre-length fangs. His growl shredded the air, and Tam was nearly overcome by the urge to run.

Except she could see Brune's eyes in the ruddy red aura emanating from Shadrach's paint. There was pain there, and grief, and so much anger. But no *rage*. No mindless fury. They weren't the eyes of a beast, she thought—only a heartbroken son on the cusp of killing his father.

Freecloud lowered the tusk in his hand. "Brune," he said softly. "Come back to us."

The shaman's head swivelled toward the druin. The two of them regarded one another for a long moment before the wolf conceded, and Brune's shadow shrank into that of a man. He dragged blood-matted hair from his eyes as he gazed down at Shadrach.

The Clawmaster's face was a ruin. Several of his front teeth were missing, and his nose was crushed to pulp. Both the wound in his shoulder and the tear in his side were bleeding freely. He would die before long, Tam guessed, if Brune didn't kill him first.

"End it," he grated. "Take . . . my place."

"You think I want this?" Brune shook his head. "I don't. I'm not like you. I know that now."

Shadrach sneered. He tried to speak, but his words dissolved into a fit of coughing. When it subsided, his features slackened. The black clouds in his eyes blew away like smoke, and one of his hands scrabbled weakly toward Brune's bare foot. "Son," he gurgled.

"I'm not your son." The shaman's voice was cool, emotionless, but for the barest sliver of pride. He looked up at the bones of his mother, hanging in the dark like a distant constellation. "I'm hers."

They found a pool unsullied by dead badger or bloody skunk and rinsed themselves clean. Brune, who the surviving vargyr insisted on naming Clawmaster despite his protestations, ordered the bones decorating the Faingrove taken down and buried.

Outside, they dressed unhurriedly, reclaiming their armour, their weapons, their musical instruments, and their poor frightened horse, who had shit a small mountain in their absence.

Tam was considering Sorcha: the way she'd been cringing when they'd left her, and how the other vargyr—the ones who'd stood by while Shadrach and his lieutenants were slaughtered—had begun slinking down from the circling heights as the band filtered out of the cavern. What crimes, the bard wondered, had the white lynx perpetrated in the Clawmaster's name? With her master dead, would she still have a place among her people?

Tam's answer came by way of a tormented yowl that cut off abruptly and was followed by the wet slop of tearing flesh.

The band, Brune especially, was keen to put the village behind them, but since they were thoroughly exhausted and it was after dark, Rose deemed it best to spend the night. They each laid claim to the home of one of Shadrach's minions, and though Tam hadn't taken notice of what likeness was carved on the totem out front of hers, she knew as soon as she bedded down that it had belonged to the skunk. The place was warm, at least, so she did her best to ignore the smell and went to sleep.

They set out the next morning, striking north and west by paths they'd have never found if not for Brune, who grew less and less sullen as the days passed. At night he would sham into a wolf and pad off into the forest alone. They heard him howl sometimes, though not at the moon.

Come dawn there would always be something—a hare, a grouse, or a gasping trout—lying by the embers of the evening fire.

"Careful," Cura warned the shaman as they broke their fast on quail eggs over hot porridge one morning. "I may start to like you if this keeps up."

The next day they were roused by the summoner's terrified scream as she awoke to the skewed jaw and glassy eyes of a deer's head lying on the pallet next to her.

"Better?" Brune asked, wearing his old smile again.

"Fuck yourself," said Cura, and thus was order restored.

That afternoon, as they ascended the forested foothills that would soon give rise to the Rimeshield Mountains, Tam sidled up beside the shaman.

"Brune?"

"Mmm?"

"Do you think . . ." She trailed off, tried again. "Would it be okay if I wrote a song about you? About what happened with your father?"

Brune chewed it over a moment. "Of course," he said eventually. "That's what you're here for, right?" And then, after a while, he asked, "What will you call it?"

"I don't know." She hadn't given it any thought as of yet. "*The Howling of the Sky*?"

A wince. "Nope."

"*Brune and the Big Red Bear*?"

"Ha. Terrible."

She deliberated a moment. "How about *Shadow of the Wolf*."

The shaman smiled. "That'll do," he said.

Chapter Twenty-three

Hawkshaw

Coltsbridge calling itself a city made as much sense as Tam branding herself a swordmaster, but it did so anyway.

Nestled in the boreal bosom of the Silverwood's westernmost reaches, the self-proclaimed metropolis was almost buried by snow. It was surrounded by a stone wall so shoddily put together that the local children climbed it for fun, using its uneven stones as dreadfully convenient handholds. Aside from the graveyard (which boasted a bigger wall than the city and was patrolled by guards charged with keeping the dead inside), the city's most remarkable feature was the armoured war wagon parked in front of the inn.

Rose tried the *Redoubt*'s door and found it locked, so she rapped it with her gauntlet. When no answer came, she did so again, harder, and shouted, "Open up!"

"Piss off!" came a familiar voice from inside. "I swear by the Frost Mother's frozen tits, I've told every one of you furboot bumpkins a dozen times: The band ain't here!"

"Yes they are!" Rose yelled.

"No they fuckin' aren't!"

Cura shouldered past Tam and approached the argosy. "Rod, if you don't open this door in the next ten seconds I'll summon *Kuragen* and put a tentacle so far up your ass it'll knock the teeth outta your mouth." The Inkwitch waited, hands on hips, and actually counted under her breath. She was up to eight when the door banged open and Roderick, wearing nothing but his fox-tail hat and an improvised bed-sheet skirt, came clomping down the steps.

"Yer back!" The booker, obviously drunk, reeked like a rotter's chamber pot. "Yer a day late," he slurred. "The Wid-ow's warning . . . er, her Warden, that is. The windows War-den warned me—wait, gimme a sec." The satyr rubbed a hand over his face, apparently trying to blink himself sober, and then tried again. "The Widow's warblen—*warblen*? Gods, that's not even a word . . ."

"The Widow's Warden?" Freecloud provided. "What about him?"

Roderick fixed his bleary eyes on the druin. "He's pissed as Glif, is what! He says time is of the effense." He hiccupped. "Essence."

When Rose took a step toward the door, the booker threw an arm across her path. "One moment, please. I have guests. Ladies!" he hollered into the wagon's dark interior. "My mom's home! Party's over! Collect your stuff and get the fuck out!"

Before long, three scantily clad women came stumbling from inside. The last kissed Roderick on the mouth before scampering away. Rose started forward again, and again Rod raised a hand to forestall her. Two more women sauntered down the steps, then another, and then four more in various states of undress.

"Is that everyone?" Rose asked.

"Just about." Roderick grinned sheepishly as another five girls trundled out, their clothes and hair in disarray.

The booker snatched a cream-coloured smock from one of them. "That's mine, dear."

"This is actually pretty impressive," said Cura.

Freecloud pinned his pipe between his teeth. "I'm not even mad."

At last the booker sketched an elaborate bow, gesturing expansively toward the stairs behind him. "Welcome home," he said.

The Widow's Warden had taken a room at the local inn called Tiffany's. The place was surprisingly busy, probably because it was the only spot around to enjoy food, drink, and song—although the song in question was being sung by a drunk who'd forgotten he was holding an instrument at all. He bellowed lyrics about unrequited love while big fat ogre tears streaked his rosy cheeks. Tam wondered if the woman who'd broken his heart was within earshot.

For her sake, I sure as hell hope not.

They found the Warden standing before a pingball table. The slab of slanted wood was topped by a small maze built around clusters of coloured glass jars, each one filled with varying amounts of water. The Warden's hands—clothed in black leather gloves that left the tips of his fingers bare—operated two brass paddles he used to send a marble pinging through the maze, eliciting a chorus of scintillating notes that were all but drowned out by the wailing bard.

"Hold up," Rod said to Rose. "He hates to be interrupted."

When the marble finally evaded his paddles and clattered into a locked slot by his waist, the Warden gazed sullenly at the table for a long time before Roderick mustered the nerve to speak up.

"Excuse me, Warden? May I introduce Bloody Rose, Freecloud, Cura, and Brune—better known as Fable: the Greatest Band in Grandual. Fable, this is Hawkshaw, the Warden of Diremarch and Tiffany's reigning pingball champion."

Hawkshaw turned without a word and moved to sit at a round table in the corner behind him.

"Have fun," said Roderick, as the band moved to claim seats at the table. "I'll be at the bar."

The Warden wore a black leather snowmask, the kind worn by Kaskar huntsmen to protect their skin from the biting cold. It concealed most of his face, leaving only his left eye, his wide mouth, and the iron-shot whiskers on his chin visible. His head was covered in a rusted chain-link hood.

"You're late." His voice was raspy, his tone more statement than accusation.

"We had something that needed taken care of," said Rose.

"And is it? Taken care of?"

"Yes."

A nod. "We'll leave tonight, then. My lady—"

"Tomorrow," Rose cut him short. "We're hungry, and thirsty, and tired. It's not as if the Dragoneater's going anywhere, right? It's been waiting a few thousand years for us to come and kill it," she said wryly, "another night hardly matters. I assume the Widow hasn't offered the contract to any other bands?"

"Not since you accepted her invitation," said Hawkshaw. "But there were others. Before. My lady's first choice rejected her offer. Her second choice accepted."

Freecloud's ears perked up. "Who accepted?"

The Warden turned his head fractionally. "The Raincrows attempted to kill the Simurg last year."

"Attempted?" Brune sounded as shocked as Tam felt. "And what, they failed?"

Hawkshaw's silence was answer enough.

Tam was grateful for the tavern's gloom, since it helped to hide the pang of grief on her face. *The Raincrows...dead*. She'd met them on several occasions in the Cornerstone. Their axeman, Farager, used to spike drinks with a potion that could turn a mercenary's gruff voice into a piercing mouse squeak and then pick a fight with them. He had an odd sense of humour, did Farager.

The Raincrows were a great band, sure, but had they been skilled enough to take on the Simurg?

You were fools, Tam cursed them. *And so are we.*

"Who was her first choice?" Rose demanded. "Who refused her offer?"

"Excuse me." Freecloud flagged down a barmaid. "We'll need a round here, please."

Hawkshaw's half-gaze swallowed the lamplight like the depths of a well. "Your father," he said.

The druin stole a glance at Rose's face and flinched at what he saw there. "Better make it two."

The *Redoubt* was too cumbersome to follow where Fable was headed, so everyone but Rose (whose mare had survived the Silverwood) and Roderick (who despised horses just a little less than they despised him) was furnished with a brand-new mount, courtesy of Hawkshaw's generous purse.

Brune chose a sturdy, barrel-bellied garron that seemed amenable to having a mountain-sized man straddle its back. Cura, unsurprisingly, chose a sleek black filly with a temperament to match the summoner's own. Freecloud—who had a type, apparently—chose another pale grey.

Tam had never been a strong rider, so she selected a docile brown gelding the trader tried to talk her out of.

"This is a child's horse!" he claimed, intent on selling her a larger, more expensive animal.

"Perfect," Tam said. "Sold."

"Don't bother naming him," said Cura as Tam climbed into the saddle. "You won't know each other long enough to get attached."

Tam nodded, waited until the Inkwitch was out of earshot, then scratched the gelding behind one ear. "Don't listen to her, Parsley. We'll be friends forever."

Hawkshaw rode a roan stallion he called Bedlam, whose white coat was speckled red down its legs and across its muzzle, so it looked as if the beast had stomped through

a bloodbath and stopped for a drink. The Warden wore a
soiled straw cape over black leather armour strapped tight
to his lean frame, and carried a scabbardless bone longsword
on one hip. His snowmask seemed a permanent fixture,
and Tam wondered if the man was hiding a disfigurement
other than his missing eye. Considering the constant glower
employed by the eye he *did* possess, she figured it was best
not to ask.

They started north at a trot, while Roderick, carrying his
boots in the crook of one arm, clopped alongside them. The
satyr claimed to have no trouble keeping up, but whenever
Hawkshaw called a halt (which was rarely) he collapsed in a
heap and gasped like a beached fish.

"You could try not smoking while you run," Tam suggested when they made camp that evening in the husk of a
burnt-out farmstead.

The booker, busy dislodging a stone from one of his
hooves, didn't bother looking up. "And you could try keeping
your mouth shut unless you've got something useful to say."

The following day they turned east, skirting the forest's
edge and climbing the evergreen flanks of the Rimeshield
Mountains. The land here was riddled with steep ravines and
sheer bluffs. The trees were dark, dense, and tall. There were
no birds that Tam could see, save the occasional crow.

That night they stayed in the shell of an empty keep.
Brune offered to go hunting, but Freecloud insisted he and
Tam would do it, so the bard could practice with her bow.

"Two for the pot," she announced, returning to camp
with a pair of white rabbits in hand.

Hawkshaw said hardly a word to any of them. He tied
Bedlam apart from the other horses ("He's a biter," the Warden explained) and sat removed from the rest of the band,
hunched like a crone beneath his black straw cape. When
Roderick offered him a smoke, he refused. When Cura passed
him a wineskin, he waved it off.

"You want soup?" asked Brune. The shaman had some-how managed to turn two scrawny rabbits, four frozen car-rots, a stalk of brown celery, and a handful of salt into a shockingly delicious meal.

"No," said the Warden.

Cura, who'd had nothing to do with preparing dinner, decided to take his refusal personally. "What's the matter with you? I'm all for a little brooding—believe me, I do it bet-ter than most—but there's brooding, and then there's being a total sack of dicks."

The masked man said nothing in response.

"You're being a sack of dicks," Cura said, in case her implication wasn't obvious.

Hawkshaw regarded her coolly.

After supper, Rose pulled *Thistle* from its scabbard and passed it to Tam. "Follow me," she said.

"What? We're training at night?"

"You think monsters only attack in broad daylight?" she asked, sounding amused.

"I—" The bard clamped her mouth shut, followed Rose out beyond the keep's ruined walls, and proceeded to get her ass kicked in the cold for the next hour.

Hawkshaw was in the saddle by the time Tam awoke. The band ate a hurried breakfast of stale scones and cold tea before getting under way. They climbed higher into the range of foothills bordering the northern edge of the Silverwood. The trees thinned, and the ground beneath Parsley's hooves became less earth and more stone. Fearing game would soon become scarce, Freecloud took Tam ranging again while the others led their horses at a walk.

There was a double-decked crossbow atop the Warden's packs, and a quiver of bolts fletched with white feathers on the hip opposite his sword, but Hawkshaw never offered to hunt. The Widow's man reminded Tam of an old dog out for a walk: He didn't bother to stop or sniff at every stump and bush, just padded determinedly toward home so he could collapse on a rug and rest his weary bones.

"Crossbows aren't a hunter's weapon, anyway," Freecloud told her, leaving Tam's imagination to reach its own ominous conclusion as to what the druin meant by that.

"I love this," remarked Brune at some point in the afternoon. He was smiling contentedly, swaying on the back of his stocky garron. "This feels good, doesn't it? To be off the tour, away from the stink and the noise, riding under an open sky."

Even Rose, who'd grown increasingly solemn the farther north they went, smiled at that.

"It used to be like this all the time," the shaman said to Tam. "The old bands had it best if you ask me. No arenas, if you can imagine that. No schedule to keep, or seedy wranglers. No bloodthirsty crowd howling for blood . . . Just an honest-to-goodness *adventure*, with a big bad beast waiting at the end."

"The Dragoneater," Tam murmured.

"Yes!" Brune slapped his knee, startling his horse. "The bloody *Dragoneater*! Who in the world can say they've gone head-to-head with the Simurg and lived to tell the tale?"

"Not the Raincrows," said Cura.

Some people knew how to kill a conversation. Cura, on the other hand, could make it wish it had never been born.

They took shelter that night in an abandoned village. There were four buildings more or less intact, and the party split themselves among them. Hawkshaw claimed a round guard tower on the outskirts of town, while Rose and Freecloud drove a fur-covered lizard the size of a dog out of an old forge and settled down there.

Brune and Roderick (dubbed "the snorers" and sentenced to endure one another's company) took up residence in what had formerly served as the local tavern. The satyr unearthed a crate of cheap white wine, which tasted to Tam like the worst possible combination of sugar and water. Roderick declared it "perfectly chilled!" and by morning he and Brune had polished off all six bottles.

Tam and Cura were relegated to a small home at the edge of an iced-over pond. It was close quarters, but after they dug the snow and bramble from the hearth and got a fire going, it was pretty damned cozy. The dwelling must once have belonged to an herbalist, Tam reasoned, since the shelves were stocked with jars of basil, buckthorn, and catmint, while the skeletal remains of various flowers hung like thieves from the rafters overhead.

Since they'd left the Silverwood, the bard had begun composing (in her head, at least) a song about Brune's trial in the Faingrove. She picked out the opening chords on *Hiraeth*'s strings and sung the first verse. Cura, her nose buried in the memoir of a goblin torturer entitled *Grime and Punishment*, seemed not to mind.

"Not bad," said the Inkwitch, once Tam had played it through a few times. "You could try singing a bit lower, maybe? It might sound more ominous, less frivolous, if that's what you're going for." She shrugged. "Up to you, though."

Tam grazed her fingers over the strings. "Show me," she said.

Cura closed her book. "Let's sing it together," she proposed. "Stay under me, okay?"

"Sorry?"

"Take the low notes, dummy."

Tam swallowed, blushing, and wondered why her heart had just skipped a beat. Two beats, actually. "Right. Okay. Yeah."

She repeated the intro twice before Cura picked up the words. Tam joined in tentatively, careful to keep her voice pitched lower than Cura's. The summoner wasn't a bad singer, actually. Her voice was untrained, raspy and raw, but now and again a note of airy sweetness slipped through like a cooling breeze.

At first the two of them stumbled along, but soon enough they were flying, soaring wing to wing and riding the music's current until, inevitably, they ran out of sky.

"That's all I've got so far," Tam said.

"It's good." Cura returned to reading her book by firelight. "For a song about Brune, I mean."

Tam considered it a compliment. She replaced her lute in its sealskin case and went to sleep.

Chapter Twenty-four

The Woes of Diremarch

It snowed the next morning, but thankfully not for long. They headed northwest now, making straight for Ruangoth. The mountains reared, monolithic, to either side, dotted here and there with hollow towers or sacked outposts. They were passing through the ruins of another village when Tam's curiosity finally got the better of her.

"What happened here?" she asked the Warden.

Hawkshaw didn't answer, though his flat gaze slid over the barren houses around them.

"Was there a war or something?"

"Not a war," said the Warden.

"What, then?" Brune asked, reining his garron in beside Parsley. "I've met a few Marchers in my day. They were proud, and tough as old leather. And Diremarch is said to be the hardest place in the north. I'd bet half the king's bodyguards are from around here."

Hawkshaw glanced over. "So?"

"So, what happened? Where is everyone? Marchers are supposed to guard the realm against the terrors of the Brumal Wastes, but it looks as if the Horde itself rolled through here."

"It did," said the Warden.

"How do you mean?" asked Rose, riding a few paces behind them.

Their escort cocked his head. "They mustered up north, beyond the mountains. But most of them weren't there to start with. They were down here." By *here*, Tam assumed he meant Grandual. "They fled north to escape the hunters, so they wouldn't end up as arena meat. Brontide offered them refuge, and promised them a shot to put right what went wrong at Castia. To die fighting, instead of just . . . dying."

It was as many words as she'd heard Hawkshaw say at once. Speaking out loud seemed to cause the Warden pain.

That, or he doesn't enjoy explaining the woes of his land to strangers.

"We always expected an attack would come from the Wastes." Sunlight sparked on his coif as the Warden shook his head. "We were facing the wrong direction."

These people, Tam thought, surveying the devastation around her, *should have been able to rely on mercenaries to defend them. Isn't that why we have bands in the first place? But Diremarch is remote, and bitterly cold. Why would anyone come so far north to rescue a few measly villages when they could entertain an arena crowd and then visit a tavern to drink and dice and whore until their stupid dicks fall off?*

Was *that* why Hawkshaw was so hostile? Did he resent Rose's notoriety, or hate that she and her ilk had been elsewhere while his country fell prey to the monsters mercs were supposed to fight? She was deciding how best to get answers to these questions when the Warden brought Bedlam up short and reached for his crossbow.

"What is it?" Rose squinted up the slope before them. Up ahead was a roadside chapel that looked relatively intact. Standing before it was a cluster of what Tam at first mistook for people.

Except they weren't people.

"Sinu," said Freecloud.

Hawkshaw slipped a bolt into the crossbow's upper slot, then another in the lower. "I'll deal with this," he growled, even as Rose cantered past him. Freecloud went after her, so Brune and Cura did the same. Tam, unwilling to be left behind with only Rod and Hawkshaw for company, nudged her own horse forward.

"Frozen fucking hell," she heard Hawkshaw mutter behind her.

All but two of the fox-like sinu retreated into the chapel as Fable approached, but the bard guessed there were around eight in total. Four of those who'd gone inside had been smaller—females or pups—and one of the two who remained was female as well. She was sleek and slight, white-furred, with untrusting green eyes. She wore a sword-belted tunic and a hooded wool cloak. Her companion was male, and much older, his colouring more grey than white. The fur around his neck was coarse and shaggy. He carried a short sword in one hand and a small buckler in the other.

He began speaking, but in a series of shrill yips and clipped syllables Tam couldn't understand. It sounded as though the creature were speaking a foreign language backward.

"They have nothing of value," Freecloud began translating, because *of course* he could understand the Sinu tongue. "They mean us no harm, and merely wish to shelter here overnight."

The pair of fox-creatures shared a glance, seemingly amazed the druin could comprehend them. The male said something more before lowering his sword.

Freecloud related his words. "They will happily go elsewhere if we'd like to stay here instead."

The entire band looked to Rose, who palmed the back of her neck and chewed her bottom lip. The sinu appeared harmless enough, sure—but if they'd encountered a party of helpless travellers instead of hardened mercenaries, would they still have been so gracious?

The female barked a series of guttural yaps.

"They were cast out of their clan for refusing to join Brontide's Horde," explained Freecloud. "They were once"—he struggled to translate the word—"more, but are now few. They clashed with four-arms recently—I'm guessing she means yethiks—and were attacked by a warg two days ago." He paused as the sinu vixen finished speaking. One of her hands withdrew a talisman from beneath her tunic.

Do the monsters have gods? The thought occurred to Tam out of nowhere.

Freecloud relayed the female's final words. "The warg killed three of their leash, but those who perished do not . . . uh, rest. She says the dead hunt them now."

Rose exhaled a frozen breath. "Ask her—"

Something whizzed past her, and a white-feather bolt sprouted from the vixen's throat. Blood spilled over her hand and the talisman clasped within it. The male barked something in anger, or grief, and rushed them.

Hawkshaw's crossbow shuddered as a second bolt streaked over the snow, burying itself in the sinu's shoulder and spinning him around. The Warden abandoned the bow and drew his bone sword as he strode forward.

"Warden!" snapped Rose.

The sinu recovered, snarled, and lunged.

"Hawkshaw, stop!"

The Warden caught the creature's blade with a gloved hand, yanking it off balance, and drove his sword up through the sinu's belly. The old fox whimpered, blood frothing over his mangy whiskers, and died as Hawkshaw dragged his weapon free. The Warden released his grip on the sinu's blade.

Before anyone in Fable could stop him, Hawkshaw stepped into the chapel's shadowed interior. A chorus of snarls and painful howls followed, and then a menacing silence. Tam couldn't have said which of the two was louder. Eventually he reappeared, his sword sheathed in gore. He was dragging a dead sinu behind him, and tossed it unceremoniously on top of the vixen's corpse.

"Bloody gods, man!" Rose was livid. "They were harmless!"

Hawkshaw was peering down at the gloved hand with which he'd caught the sinu's blade. The leather was shredded, but not deep enough to cut, obviously, since he wasn't bleeding everywhere. "They were monsters," he said finally. "Their presence here is strictly forbidden."

Freecloud's ears were stiff with supressed rage. "You could have asked them to leave. There was no need for violence."

"Says the merc who kills monsters for a living," said Hawkshaw gruffly. "What's the problem? Doesn't feel right without a crowd to cheer you on?" He plunged his sword into a snowbank, then knelt and wiped it clean on a sinu's cloak. "Or maybe you only kill when someone pays you? I'll toss you a few courtmarks if you help me clear the bodies out of here. We're spending the night."

The druin's fingers tightened on *Madrigal*'s hilt, and for a moment Tam feared he might draw it and cut the Warden into two equally dour halves, but at last he relaxed his grip.

Hawkshaw grunted and walked back into the chapel.

Rose was the first to dismount. She walked to where the sinu lay dead in the snow and examined the corpses. Her gaze lingered longest on the female with the iron bolt in her throat. When Hawkshaw emerged from inside—hauling two smaller bodies this time—she charged him, punched him left-handed, then pinned him against the stone wall. He struggled against her, but found a scimitar's edge tickling his throat.

"The next time I tell you to stop, you stop. Got it?"

The Warden bared his teeth. "You have no—"

"*Do your fucking ears work?*" Rose asked him. Her blade must have nicked him, because Hawkshaw jolted wildly and made a strangled sound.

"Yes," he growled.

"Do you understand what I said?"

"Yes."

"Good." Rose gave him a hard shove and backed off. "Because if you piss me off again—and I am *very* easy to piss off—I will kill you. For free. And I won't need a crowd to watch me do it."

That night Tam dreamt of being chased by a leash of wild sinu whose eyes burned with ghostly fire. When she awoke, gasping a lungful of frigid air, Freecloud was kneeling by her side. The druin laid a comforting hand on her shoulder.

Brune and Roderick were snoring—one slow and steady, the other sporadic and sputtering. Cura had her head buried under her saddlebags in an attempt to drown them out. Rose was asleep, but tossing fitfully. Hawkshaw was standing in the chapel door, his frame cast into shadow by the pale snow beyond. Since they didn't have the means to burn the sinu, the Warden had offered to keep watch in case they came back from the dead.

"You were dreaming?" asked Freecloud.

Tam nodded.

"Me too," he said.

The chapel's interior was lit by bands of bright moonlight streaming through high windows. Considering the state of every other structure in Diremarch, the hall was in surprisingly good condition. There were no pews here, like in the Summer Lord's shrine in Ardburg, though there was a bowl-shaped altar. Freecloud stood and went to stand before it, indicating with a tilt of his ears that Tam should join him.

"Something's rotten in Diremarch," he said, once they were side by side and as far away from the Warden as possible.

"Rotten how?" she asked. "I mean, besides the fact that everything's in ruins and everyone's dead."

The druin sniffed. "That's just it. Hawkshaw says monsters passed through here on their way north. He claims they attacked towns and drove the Marchers from their homes. But the monsters are gone. The Horde is on the other side of the country, so where are the people now? Why haven't they started rebuilding? Humans are nothing if not stubborn."

"I think you mean resilient," Tam said teasingly.

The druin shrugged. "Manticore, monticore."

"It's definitely *man*ticore."

"Agree to disagree?"

"Or we could just agree that it's manticore."

Freecloud's ears twitched dismissively. "I think there's more to what happened here than the Warden is letting on, and I fear it's got something to do with Brontide's Horde, and with Kaskar's undead dilemma." He glanced over his shoulder. "Are you pious, Tam?"

She almost laughed. Considering the behaviour she'd either excused or indulged in since joining Fable (vulgar language, excessive drinking, rampant drug use, and indiscriminate sex with total strangers—not to mention frequent acts of extreme and unwarranted violence), the druin had probably guessed her answer already.

Tam could remember praying as a child. She'd asked the Frost Mother (who southerners called the Winter Queen) for lots of snow to play in, and beseeched Vail, the Autumn Son, to make all the pumpkins as big as he possibly could. She'd attended festivals to Glif each spring and watched fireworks crackle in the sky above Ardburg, and hadn't missed one of the Summer Lord's parades in years.

Once, when she was much younger, she'd asked her father if the gods were real. *Real enough*, he'd answered.

Unsatisfied by his reply, she'd gone to Lily instead. Her mother had told her the same story the priests had, except she told it better, so that Tam nearly wept when the Frost Mother died giving birth to the Spring Maiden, and again when the Autumn Son, who was abhorred by his father, sacrificed himself so that his mother might be reborn.

And so, her mother concluded, *goes the cycle of seasons. And so it always will.*

Is that story really true? Tam had asked.

She could still remember the sorrow in her mother's smile. *I hope not*, she'd said.

Freecloud, Tam realized, was still waiting for an answer.

"No," she said. "I'm not very pious at all."

The druin put a hand on her shoulder. "Good. Because the gods are a lie."

Chapter Twenty-five

Something White

As Freecloud explained to Tam why the Holy Tetrea—who were worshipped in every court of Grandual—were false, she watched specks of slanting moonlight move across the altar before them, slow as stars wheeling in the night sky.

"So the druins are gods?" Tam asked, once he'd finished speaking.

"The gods are druins," he corrected. "It's not the same thing."

"But the Summer Lord is actually the Archon of the Old Dominion?"

"Vespian, yes."

"And the Winter Queen is really his wife..."

"Astra."

"Astra," Tam repeated. She saw the Warden's shadow stir in the doorway.

"The Archon's wife died giving birth to their daughter," Freecloud was saying, "and Vespian, driven mad by grief, instilled a sword he called *Tamarat* with the power to bring her back from the grave."

"Like necromancy?" Tam asked.

"The druins are immune to necromancy," he told her. "Whether it's because we're immortal, or not native to this world, I have no idea. And yet the Archon found a way. He was a powerful sorcerer, and many of the weapons he crafted were not merely weapons. They were *tools*, created to serve a specific purpose. *Vellichor* is one. *Tamarat*, another."

"*Tamarat*," breathed Tam. The bowl of stars whispered the name back to her. "It can bring people back from the dead?"

"Not people. Only Astra. But to do so, the sword requires an immortal's life in exchange."

Considering how precarious the druins' tenure in this realm was (since each female could give birth to but a single child), the Archon forging a sword that consumed his own kind seemed to Tam like kind of an asshole move. "So Vespian killed one of his people?"

"His daughter," whispered Freecloud. "He killed his daughter, Glif."

"What? Why?" Tam was horrified.

"I suspect he was trying to keep Astra's death—and her revival—a secret. Or else he was ashamed of what he'd made and hoped to conceal it. It's possible he *blamed* the child for Astra's death. But I think . . ." Freecloud paused, gazing down at the altar. "I think Vespian surrendered a piece of himself when he forged that sword. He'd been a hero, once." The druin sighed heavily. "But he did what he did, and so granted Astra a second life."

Tam, who considered herself something of an expert when it came to stories, had a strong suspicion this one didn't end with the words *happily ever after*.

"Suffice it to say, Astra was no longer the woman she'd been before. She was different, darker. She took her own life several times in the years that followed, and each time the Archon brought her back. But with every incarnation there was less of the woman she'd been and more of . . . something else. Eventually, she bore Vespian another child. I know," he said before Tam could interject. "It shouldn't have been possible. But nevertheless, Astra gave birth a second time. To a son."

Tam pulled her eyes from sweep of moonlight constellations. "Holy shit," she said, her voice amplified by the bowl in front of her. "It was *you*!"

She heard the druin draw a sharp breath and then stifle a laugh. "No," he said. "Nice try, though."

They both turned at the sound of a scuff by the door. The Warden's shadow remained where it had been throughout the night, but its shape had changed. His head was canted sideways, the rough planes of his mask cut in profile against the luminescence outside.

He was listening.

"Who was Astra's son?" Tam asked, a whisper.

The druin turned his back on the altar. "Ask me tomorrow."

Tam took a last look at the chapel as they rode north the next day. She wondered which of Grandual's misappropriated gods had been worshipped there, and why, assuming there were others who knew the Tetrea were false, belief in them persisted. Most people, she figured, sized up the truth when it came knocking, decided they didn't much like the look of it, and shut the door in its face. And who could blame them, really? Better to worship a fictional Summer Lord (who had a kick-ass beard and threw a damn fine parade every year) than his factual counterpart: a druin who'd killed his own daughter to resurrect his dead wife.

A bank of heavy grey clouds rolled in, and by midmorning it began snowing again. Tam was no farmer, but she'd have bet her lute the weather would get worse before it got better.

The bard waited patiently as Rosc and Freecloud rode knee-to-knee and conversed between themselves for the better part of the morning, but when Rose cantered up to speak with the Warden, Tam reined Parsley in beside the druin's grey.

"It's tomorrow," she reminded him. "Who was Astra's son?"

Freecloud grinned. He'd drawn his cowl up over his ears,

and without them to soften his appearance, he looked decidedly feral. His eyes—which changed to suit his mood, she'd noted—were a pale blue. "Lastleaf."

"I figured," she said.

"Because he's the only other druin you know?"

"Pretty much, yeah."

"Lastleaf—or Vail, as he was named at the time—was born sickly, and grew into a spiteful child. His father despised him, probably because the boy reminded Vespian of his awful sin. But Astra doted on him. To her, Lastleaf was a miracle. A balm to ease the pain of her broken heart. She never again tried to take her life, but even still . . . Her previous resurrections had taken their toll. She began dabbling in necromancy, and soon became obsessed. It's said she would kill servants who displeased her and then bring them back as loyal puppets. If necromancy is an art, which I'm not saying it is, then Astra was its greatest master."

The storm abated as the Warden led them into a broad defile. Steep cliffs climbed to either side, their upper reaches lost in a wintry haze. On the trail ahead, Brune and Cura were playing a game of Cyclops. The shaman clapped a hand over the left half of his face. "I spy, with my cyclops eye, something that is white."

"Snow," said the Inkwitch.

Brune withdrew his hand, blinking above his gap-toothed grin. "Lucky guess."

Freecloud peered up as he spoke. "Inevitably, the Exarchs discovered Vespian's secret, and when they did they rebelled, thus beginning the war that would seal their doom. The Dominion was broken, the capital besieged, and while Vespian rushed to defend Kaladar's walls, his slaves—humans and monsters both—revolted as well. They overwhelmed Astra, who was a formidable warrior in her own right, and killed her."

Parsley was starting to lag, so Tam gave her ribs a gentle nudge. "But Vespian brought her back, right?"

"He would have, yes. Except Lastleaf stole *Tamarat* and fled the city."

"What?" Tam's disbelief drew the word out slowly. "Why would he do that?"

"To spite his father. Or because he knew what his mother was. What she might become if Vespian managed to revive her."

It was Cura's turn to cover one eye. "I spy, with my cyclops eye, something that is . . . white."

"I just did white."

"So?"

"Snow," Brune tried.

"Guess again. Idiot."

"This snowflake?"

"Nope."

"That snowflake?"

"The Archon was furious," said Freecloud. "He abandoned Kaladar to its destruction, interred his wife's body until such time as he could reclaim *Tamarat*, and set out after his son. Lastleaf, meanwhile was hiding out in the Heartwyld. He spent centuries there, evading his father's agents, befriending its inhabitants, and laying the foundation for what would one day become the Heartwyld Horde. By the time Vespian caught up to him, Lastleaf had become too powerful. The Archon escaped, but was mortally wounded. Which was how Saga found him."

"And that's when he gave *Vellichor* to Rose's father?" Tam knew this part. *Everyone* knew this part. The dying Archon had offered up his weapon on one condition: that Gabriel use it to kill him before he succumbed to his wounds. She'd never wondered why until now.

"You said Vespian's weapons were tools. Does *Vellichor* do something?" she wondered. "I mean, besides, you know . . ."

"Carving doors between worlds?" The druin looked amused, but then scratched his chin as though pondering something. "Gabriel said once that if a druin is slain by *Vellichor*'s blade they will return to our own realm—or to a fragment of it, anyway—an everlasting memory of what we had, and lost."

"Do you believe that?" Tam asked.

His ears perked hopefully. "I'd like to."

"My teeth!" Brune shouted, still trying to pinpoint something white.

"No."

"Your teeth?"

"How the fuck could I *spy* my own teeth?" Cura snapped.

"Tam's hair!"

"Damnit."

"So what does any of this have to do with the Brumal Horde?" Tam asked. "Or with the dead rising all over Kaskar? I mean, if you're telling me the gods are a joke then you'd better damn well have a punch line."

The druin blinked. "Did you just come up with that?"

She hadn't. It had occurred to her last night as she was falling asleep. "Uh-huh."

Freecloud's expression was equal parts dubious and impressed. "When Saga fought against Lastleaf at Castia he was carrying three swords. One of them was *Scorn*, a rare gift from his father. Another was *Madrigal*, which he took from the Exarch of Askatar, and I took from him. The last was *Tamarat*. When it became clear to Lastleaf that his rebellion had failed, he took his own life."

Now *that* was news to Tam. According to every bard between Endland and the Great Green Deep, Rose's father had slain the self-styled Duke of Endland in single combat, with sixty thousand mercenaries there to witness it.

And how many people would swear they saw you kill a cyclops? Tam asked herself. "I still don't—"

"He used *Tamarat* to do it," said Freecloud.

It took the bard a moment to process the words, and another to respond with one of her own. "Oh."

Ahead of them, Brune slapped a hand over half his face. "I spy, with my cyclops eye..."

Freecloud's eyes had grown dark as they spoke; they were the leaden grey of stormclouds now. "I believe the Winter Queen has come back from the dead," he said, "and that *she*—not Brontide—is leading the Brumal Horde."

"...Ruangoth," Brune announced. His neck was craned, his uncovered eye fastened to the towering citadel rearing from the mists ahead of them. "I spy Ruangoth."

Chapter Twenty-six

Grudge

Because Grandual had once been plagued by roaming monsters, Tam had seen more keeps, castles, and fortresses on their journey than she could count, but every one of them paled in comparison to the stark majesty of Ruangoth.

It was imposing and alien, a soaring spire of what looked liked raw obsidian. Every fractured pane gleamed black, violet, green, or blue, reminiscent of the aurora that sometimes glowed on winter nights beyond the Rimeshield's frosted limits. The centre spire was surrounded by concentric battlements of descending height. The whole thing resembled a colossal flower, its towering style rising from a swell of black petals.

It was almost dusk by the time the band navigated the ring of fortifications and reached the courtyard at the spire's base. No groom dared the rising storm to assist them, so the band stabled their mounts themselves before following Hawkshaw across the yard and entering the castle through an unlocked servants' door.

They found themselves stamping snow from their boots in a kitchen dominated by a four-sided hearthstone column. Someone had stoked a fire inside it, but there were no staff present that Tam could see.

There was, however, a great big turtle coming at them with a cleaver in its hand.

Tam screamed, put an arrow to string with a speed borne of sheer terror, and shot it in the chest. The arrow cracked off its mottled plastron, pinged from a hanging pot, sparked off a stone column, and splintered on the ground between Roderick's legs.

"*Hold!*" Hawkshaw imposed himself between Tam and the turtle, whose reaction to being shot mirrored someone who'd accidentally spilled gravy on an already soiled sweater—it merely frowned down at the latest gouge in its shell. "This is Grudge," said the Warden. "He's the steward here."

Brune was laughing—either at Tam's reaction, or at Roderick, who'd crossed his knees and was covering his crotch with both hands.

Freecloud stepped forward to examine the creature, careful to stay beyond the reach of its cleaver. It was roughly the size of Brune, with bowed legs and stubby arms. Its head looked like a lump of stone at the end of a long, wrinkled neck, and behind its puckered beak Tam spotted one or two teeth, which suggested it may once have possessed an entire mouthful. Its nostrils were cavernous holes between huge, heavy-lidded eyes that blinked sluggishly as it beheld the newcomers.

"An aspian." Freecloud's voice was breathless with awe. "I'd thought there were none left in the world."

The aspian's head swivelled toward the druin. "Eh?" it said.

"I said I thought the Great Mother's hatchlings were—"

"I was chopping carrots," the turtle announced with an old man's croak.

The druin's ears wilted visibly. "I see . . ."

Hawkshaw scratched the iron-shot whiskers below his snowmask. "Grudge," he said, "show the lady's guests to their quarters. I've a report to make. And put that cleaver down before you slit your throat."

"I'm going to put them...in the soup."

Cura bristled. "Put who in the soup?"

"I think he means the carrots," Rose pointed out.

The Warden sighed impatiently. "GRUDGE!" he shouted into the turtle's ear (or at the side of its head, anyway, since it didn't have ears), "TAKE THEM TO THEIR ROOMS! Breakfast is a bell after dawn," he told the rest of them. "I'll come for you then." Hawkshaw turned and stalked off. His boots left shimmering puddles on the stone floor behind him.

The steward watched him leave, blinking several more times before remembering he'd been assigned a task. He set the cleaver down beside a pile of diced carrots and took up a brass lamp from the counter beside him. "This way," he said. The band started after as he turned, but then stopped as the turtle wheeled ponderously back toward them.

"Eh?" he asked.

No one moved. Grudge's rheumy eyes blinked once, twice, before finally he plodded off in the direction Hawkshaw had gone.

They followed the doddering steward through Ruangoth's expansive interior, though he moved so horrendously slow that they were forced to loiter in his wake. At every branching path Grudge would raise his lantern and peer down each shadowed avenue, before finally (and, it often seemed, arbitrarily) choosing one and dawdling onward.

The Widow's citadel was as majestic within as it was without. Though the lords of Diremarch had lived here for generations, they'd done little in the way of redecorating. The rooms were cavernous, the ceilings panelled with murals depicting ancient druins doing ancient druin things, which tended to involve drinking, fornicating, and holding random objects (scythes, sheaves of wheat, lightning bolts) above the hunched backs of prostrate slaves. The hallways were wide enough for the entire band to walk abreast, and Grudge led them up several broad (and excruciatingly long) stairways.

The entire place was eerily quiet. They'd been in transit for almost half an hour and Tam had yet to see any servants or soldiers. The sconces set along the walls were thick with dust; only the steward's swaying lamp kept the darkness at bay. Their footsteps echoed in the emptiness, scampering out ahead of them and creeping up behind.

Brune whistled, and the shadows whistled back at him. "I'd heard the Widow let things slide when the Marchlord died, but this"—he brushed his hair aside, gazing up into the gloom of an airy gallery—"seems like a waste of a perfectly good castle."

"Be careful we don't lose him," warned Rose, indicating the aspian with a nod. "We'll be lost in the dark otherwise."

"*Lose* him?" Roderick scoffed. "Lose *him*? Gods almighty, I've seen thieves drag themselves to the gallows faster than this one!"

"Eh?" Grudge stopped and turned, bathing them all in flickering lantern light.

"Heathen help us all," sighed the booker, doffing his hat and pushing his mop of greasy hair back between his horns.

"IS THERE A BATHROOM SOMEWHERE?" Cura yelled.

The aspian cocked his block-shaped head. "Eh?"

"A PRIVY?" she tried. "A LATRINE?"

"A SHITHOLE?" suggested Brune, which earned him an exasperated glare from Rose. "What? Some people call it that."

The old turtle nodded. "Just ... ahead," he promised.

Just ahead turned out to be a quarter of an hour later. The aspian lurched to a halt at an intersection, peering past his feeble light into the dim recess of each branching hall. He blinked slowly (he did everything slowly) and then mumbled, "Eh," more to himself than anyone else. "I seem ... to have taken ... a wrong turn."

The entire band groaned as one. The Inkwitch, standing

with her knees together, looked as if she were considering squatting to pee right then and there. Even Freecloud tugged an ear and sighed like a sulking child.

Eventually they became aware of a low, rattling wheeze. The aspian's wide mouth crinkled at the corners.

"A jest," he rasped, and went so far as to very ... slowly ... wink. "The hatchlings of Bentar ... are known for ... our quick wit."

Roderick muttered something under his breath. Tam caught the words *not* and *fucking* and *quick* and *anything*, so she had a fair idea as to what the satyr had said.

Grudge lifted his lantern to indicate the passage on their left. "This wing here ... is yours."

"What, the whole wing?" Rose asked.

The aspian bobbed his sagging neck. "Yes," he said. "Take whichever rooms ... you wish. I shall see you all ... at breakfast."

Having fulfilled his duty, he turned a tedious half circle and ambled off in the direction they'd come. Tam wondered briefly if aspians were as long-lived as their reptilian counterparts. She hoped so, or else they'd waste half their lives getting wherever it was they were going.

Cura, desperate to relieve herself, had already disappeared down the hallway. "See you at breakfast!" her voiced echoed back to them.

Their designated wing consisted of more than a dozen spacious rooms, including two dining halls, a kitchen, four bedchambers, a library, and three lavishly decorated areas that seemed suited for nothing more than sitting around on expensive, albeit dusty furniture. Several windows had blown open, allowing snowdrifts to pile in some rooms and cold drafts to haunt the halls like ghosts. Since Grudge appeared to be the castle's only servant, there were no fires lit, but plenty of things (stacked kindling, moth-eaten bedsheets, paintings of pastoral countrysides) on hand to burn. They found a stash of cold wine and hard cheese in the pantry, and since the quality of both were improved by neglect, it turned out to be, as Roderick put it, "Quite the lucky find!"

Rose and Freecloud took the largest bedroom, while the satyr ensconced himself in another, slamming his door while grumbling about the shameful lack of maids to seduce. Brune claimed a bed as well, and Tam assumed Cura would want the last, so she laid her bedroll out on the library floor.

She went to sit by the window, watching snowflakes swirl beyond the frosted pane. She drank some wine and chewed a strip of Brune's thrice-salted beef jerky, which made her wish her wine was plain old water instead.

She thought about Ardburg—farther away now than it had ever been—and had a sudden yearning to be back in her old bed, to hear her father's voice beyond the bedroom door as Threnody's tail tickled her face. She cried for a while, because she was young, and lonely, and terrified of the future.

After that she started browsing the shelves. She leafed through a book about the Fall of Kaladar, then found another speculating on the disappearance of the Exarch Contha following the destruction of his golem legions. She set it aside, thinking Freecloud might want to read it, and then replaced it, figuring he probably wouldn't.

Tam groaned at the weight of a volume entitled *The Hatchlings: A History*. Its brittle pages told the story of Bentar, the Great Mother of the aspians, whom Freecloud had mentioned in the kitchen earlier. The Great Mother had accompanied the druins (as a beast of burden, naturally) when they first came to Grandual—the only member of her species to survive the cataclysm. Bentar had given birth to seventy-seven hatchlings, and the book went on (in excruciating detail) to tell the life story of each. They were listed alphabetically, so Tam thumbed her way to the entry on Grudge.

Grudge, Hermonious, it read. *Born seventy-first of seventy-seven. Shell-brother to Shrack, Timanee. Perished (undocumented) during the Battle of Ter—*

A hiss drew Tam's attention to the shelf above her head. In the space from which she'd pulled the tome was a skeletal rat with white-fire eyes. She screamed (though she doubted anyone heard her) and swung the book, clipping the creature's skull and knocking it to the floor. She pounced, slamming the hatchlings' heavy history again and again onto the undead rodent. Once its bones were shattered and its eyes burnt out, she hit it six more times to make sure it was dead.

So that was it for sleeping alone in the library.

Chapter Twenty-seven

Monsters Under the Bed

Tam carried her bedroll into the hallway. Her eyes searched the darkness for demon-rats, but the only light she saw was a flame's red-orange glow flooding the hall up ahead. She walked toward it, and found herself in a lavishly furnished parlor where Cura was sitting cross-legged before a whispering hearth. The summoner was hunched over, little more than a shadow against the fire's light, so Tam couldn't tell what it was Cura was doing until she was just behind her.

The other woman glanced up briefly. "If you plan on using 'bad dreams' as an excuse to share my bed . . . Well, to be honest it's worked before—a few times, actually—but I'm busy right now."

She was wearing a black half-robe tied with a dark blue sash, and had shrugged one shoulder free. Tam did her best not to stare at *Agani*'s flaming crown arching across Cura's shoulders. A selection of knives and needles were laid out on a cloth beside her. An array of coloured ink vials was clustered just shy of one knee, a bottle of wine near the other.

She's carving a new tattoo, Tam realized, discerning lines of black ink on the inside of Cura's left forearm. The flesh around it was raw and red, so she couldn't quite make out what it was supposed to be. A woman, maybe? Or a twisting flame?

The summoner looked up again, her expression pained, and Tam was suddenly struck by the impression she'd intruded on something profoundly intimate.

"I'm sorry," she said. "I'll go."

"Stay. If you want to," Cura added, before returning her attention to the work in progress. "I heard you scream," she said eventually. "Roderick's not sleepwalking naked again, is he? He does that, sometimes, and I'm never sure he's actually asleep."

"There was a rat," Tam explained. "It was dead, but . . . not."

Cura set one needle down and selected another, smaller one. "Like a zombie rat?"

"Exactly like that."

"Did you kill it?"

She nodded. "With a book."

Cura's grin became a wince as her eyes strayed from her work. "You're a real hero, Tam. Now sit. Or sleep. Whatever you wanna do, do it quietly. I need to concentrate."

The bard sat down on the rug beside her. The fire's heat washed over her like bathwater, seeping through her skin and warming her bones. Tam hadn't realized she'd been cold until she wasn't anymore.

For a while she reclined on her elbows, listening to the fire's crackle and the *scratchscratchscratch* of the summoner's needle gouging the skin of her arm. Cura's eyes were narrowed as she worked, her teeth bared in a grimace. Now and then she would stop, gasping in quiet anguish. She discreetly brushed a tear from her cheek, and Tam pretended not to notice.

"My uncle Yomi was a summoner," Cura said eventually, drawing Tam's gaze from the fire. "He was a plainsman from out west. He and my father were both flagged to be Raven-guard, but my father—fool that he was—got caught stealing horses, and was sentenced to death."

Tam was shocked. "For stealing a horse?"

"The Carteans take their horses very seriously," she said. "If you kill a woman's husband you owe her ten sheep, or six goats, or two camels. If you kill her horse . . . Well, then you'd better kill her before she kills you."

"So your dad was executed?"

"No. He ran. And my uncle ran with him."

"To Phantra," Tam presumed.

Cura nodded, dipping a needle in crimson ink. "They met my mother in Aldea. She was a sailor. A smuggler. Fierce as a squall, and pretty as sunrise on the open sea—or so my uncle used to say. They were both in love with her, but since Yomi was kind and caring, and my father was a self-obsessed piece of shit, she chose him." A snort. "Obviously."

She wiped gore from her needlepoint on the rag beside her, dipped it, and continued her work. Tam had yet to get a good look at whatever it was she was drawing, and didn't try to.

"Remember when I told you about summoners? How they use wood, or glass, to give shape to their summons?" She didn't bother waiting for Tam to nod. "Well, my uncle did things differently. He would make these little figurines out of clay, and then glaze them in a kiln, like teacups. He painted every one with painstaking detail. Birds, snakes, dolphins . . ."

Tam was dying to know what a dolphin was, but she dared not interrupt—not when Cura's rambling monologue was answering every question she'd been dying to ask since they'd met.

Also, it was best not to piss the Inkwitch off when she had something sharp in her hands.

"We used to make them together," Cura went on. "His were brittle, beautiful, perfect. Mine were ugly, misshapen things." A throaty chuckle. "Monsters, really. I brought one or two of them to life—Yomi showed me how to smash them and summon them into being."

"Does it hurt?" Tam asked.

Cura paused, eyes roaming the blood-blurred lines on her arm. "Yes," she said finally. "But not in the way you think. It's exhausting, yeah, but it takes a mental toll as well. To bring something to life—whether it's made of stone, or glass, or whatever—you have to imagine it's real. You have to see it, and smell it, and feel it. And it requires... a spark, or something. I don't really know how to describe it. You need to give yourself over to it. The more you give, the more powerfully whatever you're trying to summon manifests. Does that make sense?"

"Sure," Tam said. "Sort of. Not really, no."

Cura snorted. "And that's why I don't bother explaining it," she said. "Anyhow, I couldn't bring myself to break all the monsters my uncle and I made, so I hid them in my room, under my bed." *Scratchscratchscratch.* "We got by for a time—my parents and Yomi and I, all living under the same roof—before things inevitably went to shit. My uncle picked a fight with one of the nastier dock gangs. They were trafficking boys along the Silk Coast, and Yomi set a whole shipload free and then burned their boat. He staggered in the door one day, still alive, but stuck through with so many swords it was a wonder he could even walk. And you know what my dad's last words to his dying brother were? He said, *You're too good, Yomi. You had this coming.*"

Cura wiped her needle down before using it to apply a colour close to gold. "My mother was away most of the time, smuggling swords across the Bay, and with Yomi gone my dad got worse and worse. He fought more, drank more, stole more, and started"—*scratch ... scratch*—"taking liberties, with me, that he wouldn't have dared with his brother around. Or Mom, for that matter."

She said nothing for a few moments. The fire muttered and Cura's needle turned her blood into ink.

"It didn't last long. I was never very good at playing the victim. One night I fought back, so *he* fought back. He might have killed me, except I grabbed all those monsters I'd hidden under my bed and I *smashed every one of them.*"

Tam shivered. Her skin prickled, and she tried not to envision Cura's father being torn apart by a child's disfigured nightmares. She failed, miserably.

"Funny thing is, my mom never did find out what a vile sack of shit she'd married. A pair of the Salt Queen's corvettes intercepted her run. They chased her out to sea and into a storm. Her ship was destroyed. Every woman but one was lost to the sea, and the girl who survived was stark raving mad. When I sought her out in the infirmary she told me Kuragen herself had killed my mother. Said the Goddess of the Great Green Deep rose up from below and broke the ship in two."

Cura straightened, examining her work. "I was twelve years old. I'd lost my uncle, murdered my father, and this salt-crazed bitch tells me a sea monster killed my mom?" The Inkwitch scoffed and shook her head. "I had nightmares for months."

Her needle nipped the gold ink again. *Scratchscratch-scratch.* "I went a bit mad myself, after that," she said. "I'd got a taste for summoning and wanted the whole feast, but I was on the street by then, with no clay to mould, and no kiln to fire it. But I *did* have knives, and needles, and a powerful urge to hurt myself." She set her tool aside and brushed ink-stained fingers over the tattoo on her thigh. "So I used my body. My own flesh and blood. Kuragen was first. My uncle Yomina was next."

Yomina? It was a moment before Tam recalled where she'd heard that name before. *The vulture-necked creature she summoned to fight the wargs back in Piper.*

"So that's what these are," Tam said. She reached out and grazed her fingers over the ink on Cura's calf: two women with scales for skin, linked together by heavy iron manacles. "Your fears . . ."

Cura put away her needles and returned the ink vials to

her pack. She began coiling a waxed bandage over her latest tattoo, regarding Tam with a bemused expression.

"What?"

Cura's eyes flickered to the bard's hand, which was still pressed against her bare leg.

"I'm sorry," Tam said, but before she could remove it, Cura clamped hold of her wrist.

"Are you?" She was on her knees, and used her leverage to pull the bard toward her. She placed Tam's hand where it had been before—on the portrait of two women coiled around, and bound to, one another—and then guided it up, around her knee, to the blues and golds and greens of *Kuragen*'s scales.

Tam could feel Cura's skin raise beneath her touch. The summoner's thighs were trembling, her nails digging in hard—drawing blood, maybe. Tam didn't care. Glancing up, she felt Cura's eyes hook her own and hold them captive as their fingers traced the swirl and scar of *Kuragen*'s snaking limbs.

By now Tam was unsure which of them was the guide and which the guided as they followed the trail of ink where it led, up and up, curling beneath the summoner's robe. Tam's heartbeat was as slow and measured as a thief's footsteps. Her breath dripped like honey from her lips. A brush of her fingertips drew a harsh gasp from the woman above her, and then Cura was opening like a flower to her touch.

A log in the fire snapped, throwing a handful of cinders onto the carpet beside them.

Cura hissed and put them out with her fist, then stood, swaying, as though in danger of losing her balance. She clutched her satchel of inks in one hand, and with the other pulled the sash from her robe, revealing a swathe of pale skin and the sickle curve of her breasts.

"Put the fire out," she said to Tam. "I'll go get the bed warm."

*   *   *

Never in the long, hot history of fires was one so thoroughly extinguished as the scatter of stamped-out ashes Tam left behind in that room.

She tried to blow it out at first, but soon realized she knew less about how fires worked than a girl her age ought to. The flames flared brighter, and Tam got a face full of ash for her trouble. Driven to resourcefulness, she used an iron poker to knock the logs to char, then stomped the coals to a fine dust. By the time she finished her pants were soot-blackened, her boots crusted with clinging ash that she tracked half-way across the carpet before stopping, sitting, and yanking them off.

Her hand struck something, knocking it over.

The wine bottle, she realized, snatching it up before it could empty itself onto the carpet. She set it down carefully, but then thought better of it and took a swig, then another, before eventually deciding to finish the bottle.

"I've been around these people too long," she muttered, getting to her feet.

Boots in hand, she padded down the cold, dark hall. As she passed the library, she spotted the moon-glazed bones of the rat she'd bludgeoned to death earlier that evening.

Wish me luck, pal.

She eased open the door to Cura's room. A candle's fitful light greeted her along with the summoner's familiar scent: a heady blend of lemon, liquorice, and sugarcane rum. Tam closed the door and shuffled slowly forward, hoping her eyes would adjust before she tripped over a stool or cracked her knee against the edge of the bed. She was about to say something, to offer an excuse for how long it'd taken her to put out a simple fire, when she heard the soft, unmistakable sound of Cura snoring.

Well, *damn.*

Tam considered waking her, but decided against it. Cura

would be exhausted, she knew—drained both physically and mentally by the act of engraving her latest tattoo. The bard set her boots on the floor, stripped off her sooty clothes, and lowered herself onto the bed as gently as she could. Her head had barely touched the pillow before Cura stirred restlessly, murmured something unintelligible, and threw a leg across Tam's waist, effectively pinning her.

It wasn't the welcome she'd been hoping for, but nor was it unpleasant. Tam lay awake for some time. Her thoughts were racing, her heart a quiet clamour in her breast. She'd been offered a rare glimpse of Cura's true self tonight, a peek behind the black silk curtain at the shattered mirror of her soul.

Are all of us broken? Tam wondered. *Each of us scarred in some way by our fathers, our mothers, our harsh and heartless pasts?*

After a while Tam could feel herself dozing, drifting toward sleep as she listened to the deepening rhythm of Cura's breathing, as slow and steady as waves crashing and crashing and crashing upon some faraway shore.

Chapter Twenty-eight

A Cold Breakfast

It turned out that Grudge was not just Ruangoth's only remaining servant, but its cook as well. Which meant that by the time the old turtle made breakfast for six and pushed it on a rattling cart from one side of the castle to the other, everything was cold. There were chilly eggs and lukewarm sausages, frigid porridge topped with dollops of crunchy brown sugar, and slabs of stale toast that were not much improved by spreading hard, saltless butter across them.

Cura, too, was acting cool. She'd been up and gone before Tam awoke this morning, and had responded to the bard's cheerful hello with a curt nod.

So that was shitty.

The others—Rose, especially—were too preoccupied to notice the tension between Tam and the summoner, although Brune gave them each a suspicious glare when he pretended a sausage was an erection sprouting from his forehead and neither of them laughed.

"What's the matter with you?" he asked Cura.

"Nothing."

"Nothing my ass. You love when I do the dickhead joke."

The Inkwitch shrugged and spooned cold eggs into her mouth. "It got old."

The shaman scoffed at that. "Dick jokes never get—"

He clammed up as the Widow of Ruangoth swept into the room. Their host wore a high-necked black gown beneath a shawl trimmed with glimmering green scrollwork, and a layered cravat of dark blue silk fastened beneath her chin by an emerald brooch. Her fingers were sheathed in sharp silver talons, and Tam made a mental note to find a set of those for herself if they survived long enough to see a city again.

The Widow's black hair was bound in a silver net studded with smaller versions of the emerald at her throat. Her face was masked by a mourning veil weighted with tiny silver bells.

Hawkshaw entered after her and took up position by the door. The Warden had shed his straw cape, but was wearing the same scuffed leathers as before. The snowmask remained in place, all but confirming Tam's suspicion that he was hiding some gruesome defect.

"Thank you for coming," said their host. The bells on her veil tinkled softly as she took her seat at the head of the table. Roderick, Brune, and Tam were seated on her left; Rose, Freecloud, and Cura on her right. Tam tried to catch Cura's eye, but the Inkwitch seemed to be pointedly avoiding her gaze.

Rose cleared her throat and pushed her plate away. "Yeah, well, a shot at the Dragoneater is a hard thing to pass up."

"Is it?" The Widow's voice was guileless. "I think many of your fellow mercenaries would balk at this contract. Despite their conceit, most of your kind are afraid to face a monster beyond the confines of an arena."

Tam expected Rose to bristle at the remark, but she only shrugged.

"You're right. But we aren't. The Raincrows weren't either, apparently."

"Would that they had been," said the Widow, inflectionless. "They might still be alive. I hope you prove more capable than they did."

She didn't sound like she *hoped* anything as far as Tam was concerned.

Rose's chair creaked as she leaned back and crossed her arms. "So what did the Simurg do to warrant this contract?"

"Warrant? The beast's very presence *warrants* its destruction. It is a monster in the truest sense. A threat to this world and everything in it."

Something mischievous tugged at the corner of Rose's mouth. "Philanthropy, then? How noble of you. Your late lord husband would be proud."

"My late lord husband was killed by the Simurg," said the Widow. "Compassion is no motive of mine, I assure you."

Roderick rapped the table. "Revenge it is, then."

"Revenge it is," she echoed, and something in her voice sent a chill up Tam's spine.

The silence stretched until Freecloud spoke up. "We're sorry for your loss. The Marchlord—"

"Was an intolerable dullard when he was sober," said the Widow, "and an insufferable boor when drunk. He was lonely, and bitter, and still very much in love with his previous wife. *Sara*." She spat the name like a fly from her mouth. "He never intended to marry again, but men like him are expected to pass their titles on through their children. And so he wed me, and assumed I would bear him sons to carry on his line. Alas, I would sooner swallow a blade than bring another child into this world."

"Here's to that." Rose drained her cup as though her cold tea was a shot of whiskey.

Freecloud shot her a withering glance before putting on a smile for their host. "You're a mother already, then?"

"I am," said the Widow without elaborating further.

The sound of slapping feet preceded Grudge into the dining hall. The ancient aspian began recovering plates, stacking them on the cart he'd used to bring them in. Tam ducked as the turtle's flabby arm reached over her shoulder. The steward smelled like radishes and rain-soaked leather.

Brune stole one last link of sausage before Grudge cleared them away. "If you disliked the Marchlord so much," he wondered out loud, "why marry him in the first place?"

Tam discerned the flash of teeth behind the Widow's veil. "Because he was rich. And had a very big castle. Also, in case you hadn't noticed, it's rather cold outside."

Across the table, Cura grinned. "I'd marry that smelly old turtle for a castle this big."

Grudge's head swung ponderously at that. He regarded her a long moment as his jaw hinged open like a drawbridge lowering in surrender. "Ha," he croaked, before resuming his task.

"The Dragoneater has been growing restless these past few years," said the Widow. "Likely because of that halfwit Brontide and his pitiful excuse for a Horde."

"That halfwit has won two battles already," Roderick pointed out. "And his pitiful excuse for a Horde gets less pitiful by the day. You're lucky Brontide didn't come through Diremarch on his way south."

The Widow clicked a silver claw against the lacquered tabletop. "Truly," she said dryly, "we count our blessings every day. Don't we, Hawkshaw?"

The Warden bowed his head. "As you say, my lady."

"I care nothing for the Horde," snapped the Widow. "It's the Simurg that concerns me. It has cost me a great deal already. If it decides to come south it will lay waste to all of Kaskar, at the very least. I, of course, will be held accountable, and Maladan Pike will appoint a new marchlord in my stead. Or worse: insist I wed myself to one of his brutish cousins."

Judging by the revulsion in her voice, their host would

rather drink an orc's bathwater than welcome another man into her bed.

Can't say I blame her, Tam thought ruefully.

The Widow laid a taloned hand on Freecloud's arm. "I don't suppose you'd like to be a lord?" she asked him. "I'm rich, you know. I have a very big castle, and I can be warm when I wish to be."

Freecloud calmly reclaimed his arm, but his ears may as well have been pinned to the roof. "I'll take my chances with the Simurg," he said.

"Speaking of gold," said Rose brusquely. "You promised us an awful lot of it."

Roderick, who'd bitten the corner off his cloth napkin, swallowed noisily. "Fifty thousand courtmarks, actually."

Fifty thousand courtmarks! Tam's mind struggled to comprehend such a fortune. A thousand gold coins could last you a lifetime, provided you didn't sprinkle gold dust on your food and buy every one of your friends a horse for their birthday. *Or maybe it could*, she amended, *if you threw in a nag here and there*. But fifty thousand? Fable could retire in luxury on that kind of money, provided they were still alive to spend it.

"And you shall have every coin," the Widow promised, "once the Simurg is dead." She spread her arms as she said this, and the bard noticed a web of crisscrossing scars on the inside of her forearms. Small cuts, razor-straight; she'd seen similar scars before.

She's a scratch addict, Tam concluded. *No wonder she's doing a shit job of looking after her march*.

Rose leaned over the table. "So where's it been hiding all these years?" she asked. "Callowmark? The Frostweald?"

"Mirrormere."

Rose blinked once. Then blinked again. Her lips quivered, torn between smiling and snarling. Tam knew almost nothing about Mirrormere, save that it was a perpetually frozen lake somewhere to the northwest. Somewhere *very far* to the northwest, judging by the look on Rose's face.

"Mirrormere is two hundred miles from here," said Rose. "Why have us trek all the way here just to send us west again?"

This is it, Tam thought. *This is where the trap gets sprung, where the veil is swept aside and we discover that the Widow of Ruangoth is in fact Rose's cunningly disguised arch-nemesis, or one of Freecloud's jilted lovers, or the Frost Mother herself, come to wreak vengeance upon the world.*

Her mind began racing: How could she arm herself? More importantly, how could she arm Rose? Grudge had left with the cutlery just a minute ago, but knowing how fast the aspian moved, he was probably still right outside the door. If she could reach him and reclaim their knives...

The Widow dispelled Tam's fears with an exasperated sigh. "How amusing," she cooed. "So eager, are you, to get from here to there? Even when *there* is the Dragoneater's lair?" She waved a hand airily. "You'll fly, of course."

Chapter Twenty-nine

The Spindrift

"Did anyone else see her arms?" Brune asked as Fable marched hastily toward their rooms. They were to leave for Mirrormere within the hour aboard the Widow's own skyship.

"She's a scratch addict," said Roderick. "Nasty habit."

"Not scratch," murmured Cura. "Suicide."

Rose glanced over. "You're sure?"

"I'm sure. Those scars..." She trailed off, and Tam saw the summoner clench and unclench her hands. "I'm sure," she repeated.

Brune scratched at the scruff on his chin. "Must be lonely up here in this drafty castle, with only Hawkshaw and the aspian for company."

"You feel sorry for her?" Rose asked.

"I do," Tam said, siding with the shaman. "I mean, yeah, she's awful. But no one's born bad, right? And we don't always get to choose who we become, if that makes any sense."

"It doesn't," Roderick assured her.

"It does," said Freecloud.

When they reached their wing, the bard tugged on Cura's sleeve to slow her. "What's up with you?" she asked, once the two of them were alone.

Cura shrugged. "Nothing. Why?"

"Well, I thought...I mean, last night—"

"What about last night?"

Tam snapped her jaw shut before it hit the floor. "We slept together," she said.

Cura's laugh cut like a knife. "We slept *beside* one another."

"But...naked," Tam said. Maiden's Mercy, this conversation was going downhill fast.

"Look, just forget about it, okay? What happened, happened. And what didn't happen...Well, it was probably for the best."

Tam was stunned. She felt as though she'd been punched in the gut, and it was all she could do not to curl up around the pain. "I thought we—"

"I'm sorry if my snoring kept you up," said Cura, breezing past her. "I'll see you on the ship."

Daon Doshi, captain of the skyship *Spindrift*, struck Tam as a man trying to be many things and failing at most of them. He had the tapering squint of a Phantran pirate, the braided moustache of a Kaskar thane, the bowlegged swagger of a Cartean horse lord, and was outfitted like an Agrian bandit who'd robbed a Narmeeri prince of his pyjamas. He wore a striped skullcap fixed with blue-glass goggles, a tattered yellow robe tied with a red sash, and a suit of shoddy ringmail draped over a padded patchwork gambeson.

Doshi greeted Fable one by one as they climbed on board, shaking hands and smiling like a brothel owner hosting a princeling's birthday party.

"And what have we here?" He met Tam with a rattling handshake, his dark eyes darting between *Hiraeth*'s sealskin case and *Duchess*, which she carried unstrung in her hands. "An archer? Or a warrior-poet?"

She smiled tightly in return, her stomach still clenched

from her encounter with Cura. "I'm just the bard," she told him.

Doshi sketched a deep bow as Freecloud arrived at the top of the gangplank. "*Itholusta soluthala!*" he said in what Tam assumed was druic.

"*Isuluthi tola,*" Freecloud replied.

"What did he say?" Tam asked the druin.

"He asked how much the toilet costs," said Freecloud, clearly amused.

Tam knew very little about ships, and even less about skyships, but she could tell at a glance that the *Spindrift* was a junkheap. Its hull, nestled in an iron cradle atop one of Ruangoth's black-shard towers, was about the size of a cutter. It was scuffed and splintered, patched in more places than a treasured old blanket. Its name was splashed in red across the side, and her sails—two larger and one smaller—were in obvious disrepair. Their metal ribbing was warped and rusted, the panels tattered and, in some places, ravaged by fire. Woodchips littered the deck, and though the bard couldn't fathom their purpose, the scent of cedar shavings was the *Spindrift's* most appealing feature thus far.

There was a tidal engine mounted on either side of the rear deck, which Cura pointed out was curious without explaining why. Tam headed over for a closer look.

"Duramantium," declared the captain, sauntering up behind her. Doshi's boots, she noticed, were soled with thick slabs of wood, though he was still several inches shorter than Tam. He placed a gloved hand on the hollow outer ring of one engine. "They don't make 'em like this anymore."

"Make what?" she asked. "Engines?"

"Anything!" Doshi stroked one of his moustaches. "Swords, armour, engines—the rabbits dug up every nugget of duramantium they could find and left none for the rest of us! And yet"—he took in the derelict cutter with an adoring gaze—"they sure left us some wonderful toys to play with."

Tam grazed her fingers against one of the duramantium rings. The metal was blue-black, grained with tiny flecks that sparkled like silver. She'd heard blacksmiths back in Ardburg reference the rare metal with an air of sorrow, the way old mercs grieved for comrades lost to battle, or bald men mourned their once-lustrous locks.

Hawkshaw stamped up the gangplank, having once again donned his black straw cape and scabbardless bone sword. A quiver of white-feathered bolts and his double-decked crossbow were slung from straps over either shoulder.

"You here to make sure the Widow's work gets done?" Rose asked.

"Indeed," he said, then stalked off toward the front of the ship. There was a figurehead mounted on the prow: a winged woman with a missing head. Tam suspected she and the Warden would get along just fine.

Doshi showed them below, which was reminiscent of the argosy's dim interior. The stairs descended into a long, low-ceilinged hallway with rooms on either side. There was a cluttered galley at the stern, and a locked door toward the bow, behind which were Daon Doshi's private quarters.

The bunks in each bedroom were so small that Rose and Freecloud were forced to sleep separately. Cura disappeared into one room and closed the door behind her. Brune, whose size made it difficult to manoeuvre in the ship's close confines, unpacked his belongings in a room opposite Tam's. After struggling for several minutes to find a place to store *Ktulu*, he eventually wrenched the twinglaive into halves and put them each beneath his cot.

Tam stowed her things, anxious to be back on deck before they set sail. She laid *Duchess* on the bed, and put *Hiraeth* under it. When she turned to leave she found Rose blocking her path, leaning not so casually against the doorframe.

"Did something happen last night I need to know about?" Tam hesitated. Sweat prickled across the small of her back, and she suddenly wondered if there was some unspoken rule among Fable's members that she wasn't aware of: *No fucking the bard*, for instance. Cura was already acting strange; the last thing she wanted was to get her in trouble with Rose.

"Nope," she answered. And then, in case that wasn't emphatic enough, she added, "No," and "Nothing," and "Definitely not"—which was, in hindsight, probably overkill.

Rose spent a long moment examining her fingernails—or her knuckles, maybe—while Tam began formulating a plan that involved squirming through the small circular window behind her.

"I heard you slept in Cura's room last night."

"She invited me," Tam blurted, tossing her moral integrity out the window instead.

Freecloud appeared beyond Rose's right shoulder. "She invited you?"

"Nothing happened," Tam insisted. "We only slept."

"Slept?" The druin looked skeptical. "Really?"

"It's true!" she told them. "We were in one of the other rooms, just talking, and then—well, I . . . and she . . ."

"She what?" Roderick poked his head around the edge of her door. "You know, for a bard you can't tell a story for shit."

Just then Brune emerged from his room. He saw his bandmates crowding Tam and grinned. "Did you ask her?" he said excitedly. "Did something happen?"

The satyr hushed him. "Quiet, fool! She's getting to the good part now."

Tam flapped her arms in annoyance. "There *is* no good part!" she cried. "I told you, we just—"

The world—*no, the ship*, Tam realized—listed violently. Roderick stumbled into Brune, who bumped into Rose and knocked her sideways into Freecloud. Tam seized the chance to make a break for it, bolting past them and hurrying up the stairs to the deck.

It was snowing fiercely now, and the wind threatened to

blow her off balance. Overhead, the skyship's sails fanned open like webbed fingers. Lightning leapt from spine to spine, rippling down the mast and spitting along the cutter's rail. A mild jolt of electricity surged through Tam's feet and up her spine.

So that, she realized, *is what the woodchips are for.*

The tidal engines whirled to life: one a blur of concentric rings, the other spinning so slowly she could see the hollow hoops turning laboriously inside one another. Daon Doshi stood at the helm near the rear of the ship. He was frantically palming a pair of spherical steering orbs, and when he caught sight of the bard he waved her over.

The stuttering engine was making an awful clatter, and whatever the captain shouted as Tam climbed the steps to the rear deck was lost between the racket and the buffeting wind.

"What?" she called back.

"*Hold on!*" Doshi screamed, as the *Spindrift* tipped free of its cradle.

With nothing but the steering console nearby, Tam grabbed hold of Doshi himself—and barely in time, since they'd begun a barrelling nosedive toward the canyon floor. Her longcoat thrashed behind her. Her scarf flailed madly. A flurry of woodchips blew past, swirling like cedar cinders into the sky behind them.

Doshi spat a mouthful of curling flakes and yelled over the wind's roar. "The water inside freezes!" His moustaches whipped across his cheeks as he glanced toward the faltering tidal engine. "It just needs to warm up a bit. Which it will," he promised, "any second now. Probably." He yanked a lever, cinching the sails, and their freefall gained momentum.

Squinting against the blowing snow, Tam saw Hawkshaw crouched at the stern. The Warden was gripping the rail with both hands as the gale tore at his straw cape.

Doshi was muttering something beside her; she heard him speak the Summer Lord's name.

"Are you praying?!"

"Of course I am!"

"For what?" Tam hollered, as the ground rushed up to meet them.

"For this to work!"

Doshi slammed the lever. The sails snapped open, crackling with power, and the bard's teeth clenched as the ship's unbridled current—stronger now that the woodchip carpet was gone—hummed through her bones.

The slow-spinning engine screamed like a boiling kettle, belching a cloud of white mist as it whirred into a silver blur. The captain's hands danced over the steering orbs, and the *Spindrift* veered away from the floor of snow and stone like a diving hawk deciding at the last second that it wasn't hungry after all.

Slowly, Tam pried her fingers from the captain's arm. She could have sworn she felt static snap between her teeth as she unclenched them. "That was..."

"Exhilarating," said Doshi, "I know. But if you think that was fun, just wait until we hit the Stormwall."

Chapter Thirty

The Rum-Go-Round

"There are three things," her uncle Bran told her once, "you never want to hear a woman say." Tam hadn't quite finished rolling her eyes before he raised a finger and told her the first: "*I'm pregnant*."

"That's ridiculous," Tam said. "What if you want a baby?"

"Then you need a better helmet, because your head is cracked. The world needs more humans like an orc needs a second asshole."

"Well, I doubt I need to worry about that one anyway."

Bran regarded her narrowly above his raised tankard. "I suppose not. Anyhow, the second is, *Did you remember?*"

"Did you remember what?"

"It doesn't matter what," Bran said. "To buy her a birthday present, to take out the trash, to pick up that thing from that place on your way home from the bar. Whatever it is, you *most certainly did not* remember. Your best bet at that point is to run and buy flowers. Or skip the flowers and buy a fast horse."

The final thing, in Bran's estimation, was the worst.

"*We need to talk*?" Tam frowned. "What's so bad about that?"

"It can mean only one of two things. Either you've fucked up big and are on the cold brink of hell itself, or . . ."

"Or what?" she asked impatiently, as he paused to sip his beer.

"Or you're about to get your heart broken."

"We need to talk," Cura said from the doorway.

Tam was sitting cross-legged on her bed with *Hiraeth* in her lap. She'd finished writing the words to Brune's song, and was trying to get down the music for the final verse. It required her to play the same tune over and over, experimenting with various notes, listening for branching paths and following them to see if they ended anywhere good. Often, they didn't, so she'd wander back to the beginning and start over.

"Sure," she said.

Cura glanced up and down the hall before stepping inside. She closed the door behind her and put her back against it. "What happened last night was a mistake."

"Nothing happened," Tam said, doing her best impression of casual indifference. "You fell asleep, remember?"

"I meant before that. In front of the fire . . ." She trailed off, and as the ensuing silence lengthened it was obvious to each of them what the other was thinking about. "I was in pain," she explained. "I was feeling vulnerable. And also a little bit drunk. I shouldn't have done what I did."

"I'm glad you did," Tam said, too quickly. "I—"

"Don't," Cura cut her off. "Just . . . don't." She left the door and came to sit on the edge of the bed. For a while she said nothing, only picked at the cloth strip binding her left arm. "I'm broken," she said finally. "There's something missing inside me. I don't know what used to be there. My mother. My uncle. A normal fucking childhood, maybe." A hollow laugh escaped her. "I don't know. But it's like a . . . a hole that I keep trying to fill. And yet no matter how many drinks, or drugs, or people I consume . . . it's still there. An empty space that nothing can fill and no one can fit."

"Maybe I fit."

"It doesn't—"

"Please," Tam said, wishing to hell that hadn't sounded so desperate. "Don't you want something real? Something that lasts longer than just one night? You say you've used people, but those people have used you, too. And you deserve better than that, Cura, whether you think so or not." The summoner remained silent, and so Tam went on. "Let me try, at least. And maybe let yourself *actually care* about someone instead of just giving yourself away to whoever—"

Cura drew her knife.

"Shit. I'm sorry. Please don't stab me."

"I'm not going to stab you, Tam." She unbuckled the blade's black leather sheath and slid the knife back into it. "This is *Kiss*," she said, offering it to the bard. "I didn't name it. It was a gift from my uncle Yomi. I want you to have it."

When Tam only glared at the knife, Cura set it down on the bed between them. After another uncomfortable silence she stood and went to the door.

"See you 'round, Tam," she said, and then left.

For several long minutes Tam stared at the weapon the summoner had left behind. Its blade was straight, its handle carved into the likeness of a raven. The lute in her lap lay silent. The song could wait; she didn't feel like making music just now.

I gave her my heart, Tam thought, miserably, *and she gave me a knife.*

The captain strolled into the galley that evening while the band was pitting itself against a half-cask of Tarindian rum. A search of the *Spindrift*'s cupboards had revealed a great deal of smashed glassware and one wooden cup, so they were sharing it around.

"Doshi?" asked Freecloud, glancing up from stuffing his pipe.

"Yessir?"

"Who's flying the ship?"

"No one," he answered. "No need to worry, however. I've checked our altitude, corrected our course, battened the hatches—"

"What hatches?" asked Cura. "Where are there hatches?"

"The point being," Doshi went on saying, "we are not going to crash. The Warden is up there, and Hawkshaw is nothing if not vigilant. If anything goes amiss I'm sure he'll let us know. We're clear of the mountains, not quite into the Brumal Wastes. The only thing we're likely to hit is a few clouds."

"How long will it take us to reach Mirrormere?" asked Rose.

"Two days, weather permitting," said Doshi. He claimed a seat at one end of the galley's trestle table, sidling up next to Cura, who in turn scooted closer to Tam, who tried to pretend she didn't notice the summoner's sudden proximity.

"Could we be attacked on the way?" asked Freecloud.

"We could," Doshi granted, "though it ain't likely. If it's ugly and it's got wings, it's probably out west with Brontide's Horde. Besides, the *Spindrift* may not be the fastest bird in the sky, but she's got a few tricks up her sleeve."

"Tricks?" Brune looked dubious. "Like what? Falling to pieces in a storm?"

"There's two dozen barrel bombs stowed in her belly," said Doshi breezily, as if he hadn't just admitted they were in a flying boat loaded with explosives. "And I keep a chest in my room stocked with enough alchemical grenades to set half the Heartwyld on fire. Also, I've got a few bolt-throwers stashed here and there."

"In the hatches, no doubt," said Cura.

Doshi favoured her with a shit-eating grin.

"Sounds like you're ready for trouble," said Roderick,

who was eating a handful of snow he'd scooped from the ice-box. "What are you? A pirate or something?"

Tam half-expected one of her bandmates to reprimand the satyr for being impolite, but they all looked pretty damn eager to hear the captain's answer.

"I was," he said, adjusting his goggles. "That's how I came to possess this fine vessel for the first time."

"The first time?" Brune passed Doshi the wooden cup. Since the shaman was sitting closest to the cask, he was in charge of refilling it each time someone finished it off.

"My crew and I found her beached on the Barbantine coast," said the captain. "We were plying the shallows, collecting the Salt Queen's toll from whoever crossed our path—"

"You were robbing them," Freecloud clarified.

"All tolls are robbery. Whether a king takes his share or a dashing young swab holds a blade to your throat, your purse is lighter all the same. But yes, we were robbing them. And one morning we spotted the *Spindrift* laid up on some rocks. Her hull was rotted through. Her sail was in shreds. At first, we mistook her for just another wreck—until we saw the rings."

"You mean the tidal engines?" Tam asked.

Doshi swallowed the last of his rum and returned the cup to Brune. "Right. The crew agreed to strip them and sell them off in Aldea. They're pure duramantium, remember. We'd have been rich as southern princes, every one of us. Could have done anything with that kind of money. Except the one thing I wanted to do."

Brune passed the cup off to Cura. "And what's that?"

"Fly," he said, looking through the cracked glass of a port-hole window. "There was a storm that night. I was on watch when a bolt struck the water near the wreck and set one of those engines whirling. Next thing I knew I'd stolen a dory and rowed to shore. I filled the other engine up with salt water and rigged the orbs so I could take her up. By morning

I'd fixed the steering, if you could call it that. I headed for Askatar, flying backward the whole time, and only able to turn right. I couldn't afford to repair her, and figured my old crew would come looking for us anyway, so I sold her off to some fat Narmeeri merchant for so much gold I had to buy three kolaks just to carry it all."

Tam raised a hand. "What are kolaks?"

"Like a scaly camel with no humps," said Cura, handing back the cup.

"What's a camel?" asked Tam.

"Like a furry kolak but with humps," Rose said, though she didn't take her eyes off Doshi. "So you took the money after all?"

The captain shook his head. "I meant to. I really did. Except I couldn't shake the feeling I'd given up more than I'd gained. I had more coins than a dragon could count, but..." His fingers toyed idly with the sash at his waist. "When you grow up as I did, without two coppers to rub together, being rich means being free. Free to go where you want, to eat what you want, to be whoever it is you'd like to be. But where I wanted to go, who I wanted to be"—he made an encompassing gesture—"is right here. I'd tasted *true freedom*, and I was hungry for more."

It was Tam's turn at the cup. Tarindian rum was a luxury she'd never experienced before this evening. She thought it would taste like the oversweet swill Roderick and Cura drank most of the time, but it didn't. The stuff was appallingly smooth, with notes of vanilla and honey, coupled with a subtle woodiness inherited from the inside of its cask.

Okay, she thought for the second time in as many days, *I've been hanging around mercenaries for too long.*

"The merchant fixed her up—or made her airworthy, anyway—and turned the *Spindrift* into a pleasure barge, his own flying harem. He called her something different, mind you—*The Gilded Palace*, or some rubbish name like that.

He filled it up with lots of booze, plenty of women, too few guards, and took to the skies."

Tam finished her cup—her fourth, in fact, or maybe her fifth?—and handed it back to Brune.

"Let me guess," said Freecloud amiably. "You stowed away?"

The captain stroked one of his moustaches. "Not quite. In fact, I bribed his guards, dressed up like a woman, and paraded aboard with the rest of his girls. Once we were airborne I staged a mutiny. We trussed him up and set him down in some bung-hole village downriver, then spent the next few months sailing all over Grandual. We split the merchant's fortune among us, and I dropped the girls off wherever their hearts desired."

Brune downed his measure of rum in a single gulp, then tapped the cask again and passed the cup to Rose. "Sounds lovely," said the shaman.

"It was." Doshi's smile turned wistful. "One of the girls and I fell in love. Anny, sweet Anny. I'd have jumped overboard if she asked me to. Well, probably. She had eyes like black pearls, hair like Satrian silk, and could cuss like a sailor with a stubbed toe. The third time I stole this ship was from her, but that's a tale for another sky."

Freecloud swirled the cup Brune gave him, gazing at it rather than drinking. "So you fly for the Widow now?"

"I fly for the Widow *for now*," the captain amended. "I've managed to piss off quite a few powerful people down south. The Widow pays well, asks no questions, and I ask none in return. It's a marriage of convenience—not that anyone with more wits than a lobotomized gremlin would marry that ice-hearted shrew."

Cura smirked. "Turned you down, did she?"

"Numerous times." Doshi wore a smirk of his own. "The woman's bloody rich, you know. Anyhow, it's lucky I ran into Hawkshaw when I did. He was in North Court at the time. I mistook him for a bounty hunter, because...Well, you've seen the fucker: grim as a grey sky, ain't he? Turns out he was down there to recruit a band for some super-secret gig."

"The Simurg," said Rose.

"The Raincrows," said Freecloud, finally downing his rum.

"Indeed and indeed!" Doshi pushed his goggles farther up and rubbed at the red mark they'd left on his forehead. "The Warden offered me work, and if you're looking to lie low you can't do much better than Diremarch these days. Also, the Widow has made me a very wealthy man. Once the Dragoneater is slain, I'm free to go where I please."

"And where will that be?" asked Roderick. Like Brune, he finished his allotment of rum all at once.

"I'm thinking Castia."

Freecloud's ears shot up. "You would risk flying over the Heartwyld?"

Doshi shrugged. "Why not? Oh, I hear the storms are the stuff of nightmares, and the sky above the forest is home to all kinds of fiends, but the Brumal Wastes ain't exactly smooth sailing either, and what's a journey without a little danger?"

"I'll drink to that," said Cura. It was Doshi's turn at the cup, but the Inkwitch stole it from under his nose. She and the captain shared a smile, and Tam felt a sensation she barely recognized—something very much like a raven-handled knife twisting in her guts.

Jealousy? The voice in her head *tsked* disapprovingly. *Maiden's Mercy, girl. Get a grip . . .*

"Besides," Doshi said, "I hear Castia's new emperor is some sort of paragon. The arena was torn down, slavery abolished. He's even granting citizenship to monsters so long as they promise to behave themselves."

"Dogs and cats living together!" Roderick threw up his hands. "What's the world coming to?"

The captain smiled, stood, and smoothed the wrinkles from the lap of his yellow robe. "Anyhow, should Castia fail to amuse . . . I suppose I'll just keep on sailing west."

"There's nothing west of Castia," Cura pointed out.

"There's something west of everywhere, my dear," Doshi countered.

Rose leaned over the table. "So you've seen the Dragoneater?" she asked. "You were there when the Raincrows took it on?"

The captain scraped his teeth over his bottom lip. "I was there, yes. I watched the Raincrows take their shot. The Simurg is not like other monsters—and I've seen plenty, believe me. This thing is . . ." He cringed at some horror only he could see. "Would you like to know how long the Raincrows lasted against the Dragoneater?"

The muscles in Rose's jaw flexed. "How long?"

"Seventeen seconds."

Chapter Thirty-one

The Final Verse

They sailed through the night. Tam went to sleep drunk and woke up hungover, grey light punching through the porthole window like a spear. The moment she opened her eyes she heard Daon Doshi's voice in her head.

Seventeen seconds.

She stayed in bed until her head ceased pounding, one hand on the raven knife she'd stowed beneath her pillow. Finally she roused herself, and when her feet hit the floorboards a mild current kicked up her legs.

Fuck this fucking shitbox skyship.

She lowered her feet again and waited until the tingling sensation went away, then got up and dressed.

Roderick was still asleep—Tam could hear the booker snoring through the walls. She found Brune and Cura in the kitchen sharing a cup of tea in the *Spindrift*'s single intact mug. The Inkwitch had started a new book—*A Ghoul on the Side*—and was still wearing a bandage over the tattoo she'd given herself two nights prior. She favoured Tam with a tight smile, but said nothing.

Topside, the air was brisk, but the skyship's high prow cut the worst of the wind. It was snowing, still; flakes whipped by, fleeting as half-remembered dreams, fizzling as they struck the sails above.

Rose and Freecloud sat amidst the scatter of Rose's red-and-black armour. The druin was speaking, gesturing grandly with his hands, while Rose examined the pieces of her armour one by one, knocking out dents with an iron mallet. She hadn't repaired it since she and the band had taken on the tribe of orcs back in Highpool, and Tam figured she'd be at it for hours. Every so often Rose would pick up a pauldron or a battered greave and yelp as it shocked her, then glare either at Doshi or the crackling sails above.

It was, remarkably, like any other morning she'd spent with Fable—except, of course, that they were thousands of feet in the air. You'd have never guessed they were a day away from a date with the Dragoneater.

Hawkshaw was sitting exactly where she'd seen him last, hunched in his black straw cape against the base of the headless woman.

Tam joined Doshi on the rear deck, and the captain commented on various landmarks as they passed overhead.

"See that glacier? The dragon Neulkolln is asleep inside— gods help the north if that thing ever melts. Look!" he said a short while later. "The Spires of Balmanak! They called it the Silver City. Every tower boasted windows of mirrored glass, and at sunrise the whole place would light up like it was made of crystal."

"Also it was built on a silver mine," said Freecloud, who'd left Rose alone to curse at her armour.

"What happened to it?" Tam asked. The so-called Spires of Balmanak were sheathed in ice, jutting like icicles from colossal white drifts.

Doshi grimaced. "The Simurg happened to it."

Eventually Brune and Roderick wandered up as well, and the four of them marvelled as they soared over the snow-capped tombstones of a giant graveyard. Doshi brought the *Spindrift* low, so they could read the weathered slabs as the skyship swooped between them.

"*Kathos Ironfoot,*" Brune recited. "*Never killed a merc that didn't need killing.*"

"*Here lies Bert,*" said Tam. "*We put him here because he died.*"

Freecloud grinned as he pointed out his favourite. "*I'd rather be dead than cold.*"

Roderick, clutching his hat against the grasping wind, rattled off another. "*One satchel of dried yeast. Two and half satchels of wholemeal flour. Two cups*—fuck me," he swore, "this is a recipe for walnut bread!"

Around noon Doshi's mood began to sour. Tam followed his gaze and saw dark clouds piled on the horizon. "The Stormwall," he announced, lowering his goggles and tightening the sash at his waist. "You'll want to get below. Things are about to get interesting."

Interesting, according to Daon Doshi, meant hailstones the size of kettles drumming against the *Spindrift*'s hull. It meant winds that screamed like a tone-deaf banshee while the ship rattled, rocked, and shuddered unnervingly. *Interesting* meant plummeting a thousand feet in a matter of seconds with the band nailed to the galley roof, screaming—or, in Roderick's case, laughing hysterically.

Once they'd broken through the storm, things grew calm again. One by one the band trickled topside and gathered at the rail. According to Doshi, the land over which they flew had once been an inland sea. There were ancient boats and the bones of leviathans locked in the ice, and the captain pointed out the frosted domes of Carthia. "Once a thriving island city-state," he remarked sadly. "All gone now. Nothing good lasts forever, they say."

"Nothing bad, either," said Freecloud, which drew a wry smile from Daon Doshi.

When the sun went down the band shared a quiet meal, during which Cura's foot brushed Tam's beneath the table.

The Inkwitch muttered, "Sorry."

Tam spared her a polite smile. "Don't worry about it."

Later, when Cura had trouble sawing the fat off a pork shank Brune had cooked up, Tam cleared her throat. "I've got a knife in my room if you need a sharper one."

"No, thank you," said Cura.

Their bandmates looked between them, bewildered.

Rose tried using the scrying orb to reach her father after dinner, but the sphere only crackled with static grey.

They retired to their rooms early. The cots were bolted to the floor, so Tam was relieved to find *Hiraeth* in sound condition underneath. She lit the shortest candle she could find and sat on her bed with the lute in her lap. The music to the final verse of Brune's song, which had proved elusive these past few days, tumbled suddenly into her head. She felt like an angler who'd come to the river's edge and found her quarry already flopping on the bank.

Tam played the song in its entirety for the first time. At the end, she let one note slide against another in a long, mournful howl, and imagined her mother might've liked to have heard it.

When the candle burned out she retuned *Hiraeth* to the sealskin case and stowed it away. She stood for a while, swaying with the ship and listening to the hull groan. Inexplicably, Tam found herself at the door to her cabin. Her heart was drumming in the dark. When she reached out to lift the latch, a spark licked her hand. She swore quietly (at the latch, and at herself) before going back to bed.

Tam dreamed she heard footsteps outside her door. She saw the glimmer of candlelight, the shadow of feet. But then the light went out, and the feet padded softly away on a floor that sang like a nightingale.

"Mirrormere!" Doshi announced, freighting the word with more menace than an iced-over lake probably deserved.

"It's huge," said Tam.

"It's the biggest freshwater lake in all of Grandual," the captain boasted.

"How interesting," said Cura, in a tone that implied she wasn't interested in the least.

The *Spindrift* hovered half a mile from the southernmost edge of the lake. Her sails were closed, the engines whirling slowly. As Fable prepared to confront the Dragoneater, Doshi toured the deck with a pair of tin buckets, filling them with snow and carrying them below.

"When the snow melts, I fill up the engines," he explained to Tam. "Water, as the Narmeeri are fond of saying, makes the world go round. Have you ever been to Satria?"

"I'd never even been out of Ardburg until recently," she confessed.

Doshi pushed his goggles up past his raised eyebrows. "Really? That's a shame. There's a whole wide world out there. It's messy, and ugly, and strange...But it's beautiful, too. Especially from the sky. Except Conthas," he added ruefully. "Conthas is a shithole no matter how you look at it."

Tam chuckled, for lack of any better response.

The captain regarded her a moment. "So this is your big adventure, hey? Touring with a band, flying in a skyship, slaying monsters and whatnot?"

"I guess it is," she said.

Doshi rubbed the red marks around his eyes. "Well, for what it's worth, I hope it doesn't end here."

The captain went on collecting snow, leaving Tam to wonder whether Doshi's words or the knifing cold was the reason she found herself shivering.

Her bandmates were pacing the deck, obviously anxious. Brune wore flimsy leather boots, loose wool trousers, and his warming scarf. Cura was dressed in ragged skirts, tearaway furs, and a pair of black leather moccasins tied at her ankles to keep the snow out. She'd finally consented to wearing her own red scarf, but had coiled it tightly around her left arm.

Tam decided to wear her scarf as well—out of solidarity, sure, but also because the wind coming off the lake was freezing. She headed downstairs, stepping carefully around the buckets of melting snow Doshi had left in the hall.

She was passing Rose's room when a hurried movement drew her eye. Glancing in, she saw Fable's frontwoman sitting on her bed. There was a familiar satchel on her lap, and a pair of glossy black leaves in her hand.

Tam stood rooted to the spot until Rose looked up, and even then she remained paralyzed, groping desperately for some excuse to leave, but finding none.

"This is the last of it," Rose said eventually. "I was saving it for today. Hiding it from Cloud, because I know he would disapprove."

"Why does he?" Tam asked.

Rose's pauldrons clanked when she shrugged. "He says it makes me reckless. I say it makes me brave. He thinks I don't need it . . . but I do." She pressed the leaves to her tongue, closing her eyes as they dissolved.

Tam considered leaving now, but didn't want Rose to think she'd gone to tell Freecloud her secret—not that she ever would. What Rose did was her own business, and if she thought she needed Lion's Leaf to take on the Dragoneater, then who was Tam to say otherwise?

"What does it do?" she asked.

"Focus," Rose said. Already Tam could hear the change in her voice—a sound like a song without melody. "After what happened at Castia I couldn't fight without worrying about the people around me. I was so afraid of losing them . . . I could hardly think." Rose's eyes, usually a shade of very dark brown, had gone the fathomless black of deep water. "Fable was a different band, once. Did you know that?"

Tam's nod drew the thinnest of smiles.

"Of course you did. There were five of us. Friends I'd made back in Fivecourt. Good friends. Good fighters, too, but...not great. When the Heartwyld Horde invaded Endland, I convinced them to go after it. We'd be heroes, I told them—except all I cared about was making a name for myself, being somebody other than Golden Gabe's daughter. But they believed in me. They followed me across the Heartwyld, to Castia. And they died."

Someone—Brune or Roderick—plodded heavily across the deck above them.

"After Wren was born, Freecloud and I started over. We got a new band going and began touring again, but things weren't the same. I was too cautious, afraid of doing anything that might put the others at risk. I started turning down gigs that sounded too dangerous, which would have doomed us to obscurity, and I could feel them getting restless, wanting more."

"Not Freecloud," Tam said. A guess.

"Not Freecloud," Rose admitted. "He's only here because I am. He'd rather be a father than a fighter." She stared absently at the empty satchel in her lap. "He deserves better than me. They all do."

The joints of her armour scraped as she stood.

"I won't be a slave to fear," Rose said. "I can't afford to be. Not today. Can you understand that?"

Can you keep it secret, she means.

"I can."

The effects of the drug turned Rose's smile into a snarl. "Good," she said, and left.

Tam lingered for a while afterward. Had it been mere months, she pondered, since she'd been a girl infatuated with Fable's frontwoman? With the whole band, really. She'd considered them heroes, the infallible gods of her own personal pantheon. While on tour, however, and during the hard, harrowing weeks since, she'd come to realize that those heroes were human after all—as fallible as anyone she'd ever met. More so, even.

Freecloud had been made a slave by his devotion to Rose, who in turn was enslaved by her single-minded pursuit of glory for glory's sake. Cura was marred in myriad ways by a horrific past she'd condemned herself to remembering every time she looked in the mirror. Brune had spent most of his life trying to be something he wasn't, and had risked his sanity to stake his place in the band.

And yet here they all were: at the cold edge of the world— each of them vying to be worthy of one another, to protect one another, to prove themselves a part of something to which they already, irrevocably belonged.

And me? Tam mused. *I'm just the idiot that followed them here.*

She moved on to her room, found her scarf on the floor near the foot of her bed, and hurried back toward the stairs.

As she stepped into the hall something creaked behind her. Turning, she saw that the captain's door, which Doshi locked fastidiously every time he left his room, was ajar. Though Tam could see nothing but darkness within, she'd have sworn there was someone watching her, and was mustering the courage to call out when the door closed.

It's the wind, she told herself. *The wind who opened it, the wind who closed it, and the wind who just locked it*, she thought, hearing the quiet click of a bolt sliding home. *Regardless, it's none of your business, Tam.*

By the time she returned to the deck, Fable was preparing to go overboard. Tam strung and shouldered her bow, then moved to peer over the rail. The slope was a good twenty feet below, and she guessed the snow here was fairly deep. A survivable jump, then, but she was nonetheless grateful when the captain tossed a rope ladder over the side.

Hawkshaw pointed at a cleft in the cliffside across the lake. "The Simurg makes its lair inside," he said to Rose. "It emerged from there the last time, as the Raincrows were rounding the lake."

And seventeen seconds later they were dead, Tam thought.

"How thick is that ice?" asked Freecloud.

"Very," Hawkshaw said. "Mirrormere is frozen year-round."

"Let's get moving," said Rose. Tam saw the druin's ears perk at the leaden growl Lion's Leaf had given her voice.

Brune went over first, throwing his twinglaive down before him. Cura was next, and then Freecloud. When Tam made to follow him over the rail, Rose pinned her with a glare.

"Where are you going?"

"Um . . . with you?"

Rose shook her head. "Not this time. You can see fine from here."

"But—"

"But what? You're the *bard*, remember. Or did you plan on killing the Dragoneater with a single arrow?"

"I just thought—"

"Listen." Rose moved close, near enough that Tam could smell the burnt-coffee tang of the Lion's Leaf on her breath. "I want to kill this thing and go home. I want it like I've never wanted anything in my life. But this might go bad." Her blunted gaze flitted toward the Simurg's lair. "It might go very bad. And if it does, I'll need you to write me a song."

Tam felt her heart clench like a fist. "A song?"

"Something that will make my daughter proud," Rose said.

The bard nodded, not trusting herself to speak.

Rose shared a hard grin with Roderick, a glance with Doshi, and a glower with Hawkshaw before throwing a leg over the rail.

"The song," Tam finally managed to say around the lump in her throat. "What should I call it?"

Rose paused. The wind whipped her hair like a blaze around the sharp edges of her face. "I've always thought *The Ballad of Bloody Rose* had a nice ring to it," she said, and was gone.

Chapter Thirty-two

Lurking Below

Tam stood at the rail of the *Spindrift* and watched the others make their way down the slope and onto the ice. Roderick came to stand beside her, bundled against the cold in a bulky fur cloak and his ridiculous fox-tail hat.

"Worried?" the booker asked.

"Of course I am."

"Well, don't be," Roderick told her. "I'm not a gambling man, but—"

"Just this morning you bet Freecloud you could fit inside the icebox," she pointed out.

"Okay, sure, but—"

"And yesterday you bet Cura you could spit from one side of the ship to the other."

"Impressive, right?"

"And last night you bet Brune you could eat a handful of glass . . ."

"Never bet against a satyr when food is on the line!"

"Glass isn't food!"

"All right, fine, I get it—I may have a *teensy* gambling problem. My point is this: I won every one of those wagers. And I'm telling you that Bloody Rose is a sure bet, every time."

"Even against the Simurg?"

"Against the whole damn world," he said. "Watch and see."

She hoped the booker was right. Out of the blue, Tam remembered the captain's creaking door, and the unseen presence she'd encountered below. She was about to tell Roderick when Doshi and Hawkshaw came to join them at the rail.

"Listen," said the captain, "if this goes sideways, I want you two downstairs on the double—and hang on to something. That thing let us go last time, but I can't imagine he'll take kindly to us dropping mercs on his doorstep a second time."

Roderick stroked his beard. "You think the Dragoneater's a *he*?"

The captain shrugged. "Probably?"

"I'll bet you ten courtmarks it's a she," said the satyr.

Tam slapped his arm. "Roderick!"

"What? Okay, yeah—I *for sure* have a gambling problem."

The four of them stood in silence for a while, alternatively watching the entrance to the monster's lair and the band of mercenaries making their way across the frozen lake, until finally Doshi grunted and began chewing a nail.

"What?" Tam asked.

"Hmm? Oh, it's nothing." Long moments passed. "It's just..."

"Seriously, what?"

"Well, I'd bet my sails the Simurg knows they're here by now." He scratched under one of his goggles. "So, where is he?"

"She," murmured Roderick into his scarf.

"Maybe it's not here?" Tam suggested. Part of her hoped it was true. A fairly large part, actually.

Doshi frowned. "I should think—"

"There." Hawkshaw's voice sawed through the captain's like a blade through bone. The Warden was pointing directly at the band. "It's there."

"Where?" Tam squinted into the blustering wind. Squalls whirled across Mirrormere's frozen expanse, leaving drifts wherever they blew apart. Where the ice was clear it gleamed like polished silver, though just now a cloud was obscuring the sun, its shadow passing swiftly overhead.

No. Tam's breath caught in her throat. *Not overhead.*

Under.

"It's under the ice."

Roderick glanced at her. "It's what now?"

"It's in the lake!" Tam shouted. "The Simurg is *underneath them*!"

"Oh dear," said Doshi. "This is bad."

"We've got to warn them!" Tam wheeled on the captain. "Now! Hurry!"

Doshi started toward the stern.

"No," growled Hawkshaw. "We go no closer than this."

"Why not?" Tam asked, but the Warden ignored her. "Captain, please," she said to Doshi. "This is your ship, right? *You* decide."

Doshi wilted under Hawkshaw's threatening glare. "Sorry, kid. I may be the captain, but I'm not the boss."

Roderick cupped his hands around his mouth. *"Hey! Rose!"* he shouted, but they were too far off to hear. The satyr began stomping in circles, rambling off a stream of expletives that would make a stone blush.

For a desperate moment, Tam considered hurling her bow overboard and jumping out after it, but then another idea (though not necessarily a *better* one) occurred to her. She took three measured steps backward before charging and shoving Hawkshaw as hard as she could.

The Warden went headlong over the rail.

He didn't make a noise as he fell, but Doshi cried out and rushed to Tam's side. They both looked overboard at Hawkshaw, who had landed upside down and was trying to wriggle free of the snow.

"He's going to kill you for that," the captain warned.

"I don't care," said Tam. "We're running out of time. I need you to—"

Doshi yelped as he went tumbling over the side. Roderick, who'd pushed him, pumped his fist and yelled, "Ha!" then looked to Tam. "Now what?"

Tam stared back, dumbfounded. "I was going to order Doshi to fly us down there!"

The booker scowled. "But I just pushed him overboard!"

"Why would you push the *pilot* overboard?"

"I thought we were pushing people overboard!" Roderick shouted defensively.

Tam pointed at the helm. "Get up there," she ordered, then pointed at the lake. "And get us down there."

The satyr opened his mouth to protest, but Tam bolted toward the stairs that led below. She took them at a flailing slide, bracing herself against the wall at the bottom and eye-balling the door at the far end of the hall. She'd heard it lock earlier, but if that door was anything like the rest of this boat it was very likely flimsy and probably half-broken already.

She ran as fast as she could down the hallway, lowering her shoulder and hurling herself at the door.

Which opened just before she hit it. Tam crashed into someone and drove them to the floor beneath her.

"Get off me!" said a woman's voice. Imperious, angry, oddly familiar.

"I—" Tam began forming an apology, but trailed off as her eyes relayed to her brain what it was she was looking at.

Pale skin, plum-dark eyes the shape of sickle moons, long ears sheathed in fine white fur . . .

A druin. Tam gaped in disbelief.

The bard sprang to her feet as if the woman beneath her was a bed of hot coals. "What are you doing here?" she asked the Widow of Ruangoth.

"I could wonder the same of you," said the druin. The

Widow. The *bloody druin Widow*. She rose and retreated to stand beside the larger of the room's two beds, arms folded, clutching her elbows. She was barefoot, Tam noticed, wearing nothing but a black silk shift that might as well have been painted on for how tightly it clung to her body. Her ears draped almost to her shoulder. "Well?" she prompted.

"Grenades," Tam managed, her mind still racing. "Alchemical grenades. The captain said he kept them down here."

"Why not come get them himself?" she asked.

"He's, uh, busy," Tam lied.

The druin eyed her skeptically, but then nodded at the rumpled cot behind the bard on which Doshi presumably slept. "Under there," she said.

Tam dragged a chest out from beneath the bed and threw open the lid. Inside, wrapped against breaking in sleeves of padded wool, were dozens of glazed earthenware spheres about the size of a large apple, each splashed with a painted red X. She quickly began loading the crook of one arm.

The skyship lurched; she heard Roderick whoop distantly as it did. *Good*, thought Tam, *he's figured out the controls*. Except then the ship pitched violently sideways and Tam nearly lost her balance. The Widow hissed like a snake yanked from its burrow.

"Who is flying the ship?" she asked.

Tam stood, careful to keep her feet apart. "Roderick."

"The monster?" There was venom in her voice, an ugliness that made the bard's skin crawl.

"The satyr," Tam said. *He's not a monster*, she considered adding, except she didn't have time to explain the difference. The Widow's prejudice was hardly an unusual sentiment— which was why Rod went to the trouble of disguising himself in public—it just struck Tam as odd coming from someone with pointed teeth, moon-shaped pupils, and bunny ears.

"Why do you need those?" asked the Widow as Tam kicked the chest closed and booted it back under the bed.

"I'm not sure yet," she answered—and truly, she had no idea how she planned on using the captain's stash of explosives, but she suspected they'd be a great deal more effective against the Simurg than her bow and arrows. With her arm full, she turned and fled the room.

Thanks to Roderick's haplessness at the helm, the hallway slanted abruptly as Tam ran down it. She almost fell into Rose's bedroom, but clutched frantically at the doorframe and managed to stay upright. As she vaulted up the stairs to the deck, another jolt sent her stumbling forward. One of the firebombs popped out of her arm and clacked onto the step below. Tam watched, winded, as it rolled and bounced, rolled and bounced, rolled and bounced down each and every step, until it landed (without exploding, thankfully) at the bottom and came to a stop against the Widow's bare foot.

The woman bent to picked it up, turning it over in her hands. Tam saw her lips part, her tongue flit like a serpent tasting the air for prey. A hungry gleam stole over her eyes, while the bard's gaze flickered to the hatching of pale scars on her wrists. She remembered Cura attributing those scars to suicide, and wondered if the Widow might not hurl the thing at her feet right now and let the ensuing blaze devour them both. Finally, and far too slowly for Tam's liking, she offered it up.

"I believe you dropped this," she said coolly.

"Thanks." Tam tucked it firmly back into the crook of her arm. She considered ordering the Widow to remain below, but since she was only a bard and the druin was mistress of her own castle and probably several hundred years her senior, Tam figured the woman would probably do whatever the hell she wanted anyway.

Up top, Roderick was braced at the helm. The satyr's hat had blown off; his mane of greasy hair whipped between his curling horns. He was grinning and pawing clumsily at the steering orbs like a teenage boy up a girl's tunic for the first time. The *Spindrift* weaved from side to side as it hurtled out over the ice, and Tam, now at the rail, searched the frozen face of the lake for sign of the Dragoneater.

She found it dead ahead, right beneath where the band was standing—a shadow that spread like spilled wine beneath Mirrormere's glassy sheen.

The Simurg, Tam knew, rising from the depths below.

"Roderick!" she shouted.

"On it!" the satyr hollered. He gripped two levers on the skyship's console and yanked them in opposite directions, at which point two things happened, both of them bad.

Chapter Thirty-three

Seventeen Seconds

First, the engines stopped whirling.

Then the sails snapped closed.

They dropped from the sky, and Tam nearly lost her footing as the hull hit the ice. She recalled Doshi bragging about the barrel bombs stowed down below and was momentarily grateful the ship hadn't yet disintegrated in a ball of fire. Her gratitude evaporated as the *Spindrift* tipped over, slewing sideways over the frozen lake. Tam clung desperately to the rail, saw her bandmates scatter from the skyship's path—Brune and Cura one way, Rose and Freecloud another, ducking as the cinched sails passed overhead.

The Widow, she saw, had wrapped both arms around one of the masts, while Roderick was hanging from the console like a climber from a cliff's edge.

Out of control, the *Spindrift* spun all the way around, so that Tam was looking over the bow when the sum of all her fears exploded from the ice.

Since Rose had first mentioned the Simurg by name, Tam had begun to seriously imagine what it might look like. She'd expected it to be big, but *big* didn't even begin to describe it.

Ragas were big. Ogres were big. The cyclops Rose had killed back in Ardburg was enormous, but beside the Simurg it would have looked like a child standing next to a warhorse. She had wondered what kind of monster could terrorize a city, or bring whole civilizations to ruin. Even dragons tended to avoid cities, since even bards with a bow got lucky from time to time.

But now—seeing it—she knew.

You didn't fight something this big. You didn't even *dream* about killing it. You packed your things, gathered your family, and hoped traffic wasn't too bad on the way out of town.

Tam had assumed that seeing the Dragoneater would leave her paralyzed by fear, incapable of doing anything but cowering in abject terror. But instead, she felt a kind of hopeless resignation, as though she were standing in the path of an avalanche, or adrift at sea as a tidal wave curled overhead. The danger it represented was so extreme, so *inescapably profound*, that her mind could scarcely comprehend it.

The *Spindrift* kept on spinning, so Tam was forced to twist around to keep the Dragoneater in sight. Its head was twice the size of Fable's argosy, with a broad white snout and deep-set yellow eyes that reminded Tam of the Palapti lions she'd seen at market from time to time. The lower half of its jaw was distinctively reptilian; a trio of spiny fringes—red, orange, and yellow—were layered to protect its gills. Behind its head was a flared mane of feathers, bright red fading to molten gold at the tips.

Its underbelly was armoured in pitted gold scales seamed with white down, while its feet were a hybrid of paw and claw, furnished with talons that could carve a house to kindling. Four white-feathered wings shivered open as the Simurg hauled itself from the water, each one vast enough to throw a whole village into shadow.

Rose and the others were scrambling for safety as the ice groaned under the monster's weight. The Simurg made a lunge for Brune, but the shaman, clenching the haft of his twinglaive between his teeth, embraced his *fain* with the effortless grace of a bird taking flight. His boots and wool trousers shredded as the white wolf leapt clear of the Simurg's shearing bite.

He still wore the scarf, though. And it *did* look adorable.

Before the creature could attack Brune again, Rose spun and hurled *Thorn* at the back of its head. The blade tore through one leathery fringe and the Dragoneater bellowed in pain.

Fairy tale or not, Tam thought, *it can be hurt*.

Now that it had fully emerged from the freezing water, Tam could see a tail, or something like one: a profusion of feathers the same sunset colour as those in its mane, as long again as the Simurg's entire body. It flexed its wings, showering the lake around it with shards of splintering ice, then turned its golden glare on Rose.

At which point, unable to help herself, Tam started counting to seventeen.

One . . .

Rose turned on a heel and began running *at* the Simurg, and the behemoth stalked to meet her. Its wings churned the air into snowstorms. Its talons raked gouges in the ice. The feathers behind its head fanned threateningly.

Freecloud started after Rose, no doubt cursing her (or rather, the drug that had stripped her of rational fear) under his breath. He clasped *Madrigal*'s scabbard in one hand, its hilt in the other. His sky-blue cloak snapped in the gale coming off the Simurg's wings.

"*KURAGEN!*" Cura went to one knee, black skirts parting, and the sea goddess burst from a cloud of ink. The horror was already in motion, afloat on a bed of tentacle limbs. One of her arms snapped out, and *Kuragen*'s broad-bladed spear traced a shining arc against the dull iron clouds.

Brune was doubling back. He'd planted *Ktulu* in the ice behind him and was racing on all fours toward the Dragoneater's flank.

...two...

The *Spindrift* turned another full circuit. Snow came sheeting over the rail beside Tam, and the folded sails hissed under the deluge. Roderick managed to get a hand on one of the steering orbs, and suddenly they were upright, still spinning, but heaving skyward. The satyr pushed the lever he'd pulled earlier and the sails stormed open. A booming thunderclap startled Tam, and one of the grenades couched in her arm jumped loose. Without thinking, she swatted it over the rail.

...three...

Kuragen's spear deflected harmlessly from the Simurg's white feathers, which were glazed in armouring ice. The sea goddess dove into the freezing water from which the Dragoneater had emerged, while Brune, racing on all fours, was forced to skirt the hole's splintered edge.

The Simurg, meanwhile, was bearing down on Rose, who summoned *Thorn* back to her open hand. She was about to launch it again when the monster opened its mouth and unleashed a torrent of white frost.

...four...

Tam squinted, disbelieving.

Rose was gone. Freecloud, too. Where they'd been just a second earlier was nothing but a strip of crystalline hoarfrost. The Dragoneater was already veering away, turning its attention toward the others.

...five...

Roderick regained control of the *Spindrift*. The skyship banked sharply, affording Tam an unobstructed view of the battle below. She scoured the scene for any sign of Rose and Freecloud.

They can't be dead already, she told herself. *Even the Raincrows lasted seventeen seconds.*

She was right. They weren't.

...six...

A glimpse of blue drew Tam's eye. In a snowdrift next to the frost-burned strip she saw Freecloud, who'd managed to tackle Rose before the Simurg's coldfire swept through. Even from so far away, the bard could tell they were shouting at one another.

...seven...

Kuragen came surging from the black waters of the lake, huge and horrific. As she did, the Simurg caught her with a swiping claw. The sea goddess slammed onto the ice, fracturing it, and before she could rise, the Simurg's head swooped down.

...eight...

Its jaws clamped down on *Kuragen*'s torso, pinning her arms, cracking her carapace armour. A scream like a squall echoed inside the mollusk helm, and the sea goddess's tentacle limbs reached frantically for the Dragoneater's throat, coiling, squeezing, strangling.

...nine...

But to no avail. The Simurg wrenched its head from side to side like a hound wresting a bone from its master's hand, and *Kuragen* went limp. Tam's eyes darted to Cura and found her facedown in the snow. Brune was lost to sight beneath the creature's tail-feathers, but beyond the monster she saw a lone figure step onto the ice.

Hawkshaw, she guessed, since she doubted Doshi was brave enough to come anywhere near the Simurg.

...ten...

The *Spindrift* was headed straight for the Dragoneater now. The creature tossed *Kuragen*'s body aside and fixed its molten regard on the approaching skyship.

Tam swallowed the dread that rose like bile from her gut and screamed over her shoulder at Roderick. "Up! Take us up!"

"Going up!" the satyr hollered.

And down they went.

"Bloody fuck—" Tam managed, as she half-stumbled, half-fell toward the front of the ship. She might have tumbled overboard had the headless figurehead not broken her fall. Half the arrows in her quiver slipped out and went spinning away. She wrapped both legs around the woman's waist and hoped to hell it proved sturdier than her neck. Before she could congratulate herself on not being dead or having dropped her armful of firebombs, she saw the Dragoneater's ruff rise again as it readied to pounce.

... *twelve* ...

Wait, had she missed eleven? She must have, though to be fair she'd been busy trying to stay alive.

Now they were going up. The *Spindrift* groaned. The tidal engines roared like a storm, streaming mist. Below the prow, Tam saw the Simurg's gold eyes leering hungrily at the ascending skyship. Before it could leap, the bard dumped her armload of alchemical grenades toward its open mouth.

... *thirteen* ...

They fell for what seemed like forever, but in fact it was only a second. Tam held her breath, still counting.

... *fourteen* ...

The Dragoneater turned its head at the last moment; the brittle clay firebombs shattered against the side of its face, scorching its snout with liquid fire. One of the bombs hit the creature's eye, detonating on impact.

The monster howled in agony.

Tam howled in triumph.

Roderick was cackling as well, looking backward as they climbed beyond the Simurg's reach, and so didn't see its wing come scything across to smash the *Spindrift*'s sails apart.

... *fifteen* ...

The skyship's masts came down, dragging a mess of mangled struts and shredded sailcloth that sparked with deadly currents. Tam looked for the Widow, but couldn't find her anywhere on deck. Roderick had abandoned the helm and was backed against the stern rail. The skyship was skewing sideways again, gaining speed as it plummeted toward the frozen face of Mirrormere.

...*sixteen*...

She would jump, Tam decided, right before they hit the ground. She swiped silver hair from her eyes and squinted into the flurry of blowing snow, trying to determine where that was likely to happen. Somewhere between the patch of freezing water and where Cura lay prone on the ice—which was better, she supposed, than landing on the water or the witch.

A glance told her that Rose—with Freecloud in tow—was rushing the Simurg again. Brune was halfway up its foreleg. He'd managed to get his teeth into something and was holding on for dear life.

And in case it wasn't clear to every one of them how totally and completely fucked they all were, several much smaller versions of the Simurg were emerging from the watery pit, directly in the skyship's path.

Roderick had been right, after all: The Dragoneater was a *she*.

And *she* was a mommy.

Seventeen, Tam counted, though she was pretty sure that second had come and gone. She launched herself from the skyship's prow as the ice rushed up to meet her, flying for one moment, falling the next.

Chapter Thirty-four

Soul on Fire

Tam landed on her shoulder in a heap of drifting snow that wasn't quite deep enough to pillow her fall, so it hurt like hell. She didn't hear anything (an arm, a leg, her bow) snap, so that was lucky. She gained her knees in time to watch the *Spindrift* come down and, in a stroke of good fortune that felt like finding a penny in the burnt-out husk of your home, it landed directly on top of one of the tiny Dragoneaters.

The hull crunched as it hit the ice. An instant later the front half of the ship (along with another young Simurg) was vaporized in a succession of *whump*ing blasts.

Poor Doshi, Tam thought, as the heat off the wreck seared her face. *There's no stealing your ship back from this . . .*

The Simurg—who'd lost an eye and two offspring in a matter of seconds—was shrieking in rage. She beat her wings and stamped the ice so violently that Tam feared it would crack and dump them all into Mirrormere's freezing waters.

Roderick poked his head from a nearby snowbank. "Have you seen my hat?" he asked, touching a hand self-consciously to a curling horn.

Shrugging *Duchess* off her shoulder, Tam pointed wordlessly at the creatures shaking water from their wings at the edge of the ice. Three of them had survived the skyship's crash. The raptors looked like smaller, snow-white versions of the Dragoneater, except without crests or feathered tails. The smallest was roughly the size of a horse, while the largest looked big enough to haul an argosy all by itself.

"Simurglings!" The booker's voice was shrill with disbelief. "Fuck me with the business end of a battle-axe, where did they come from?"

Simurglings? Tam was actually a little pissed she hadn't thought to call them that first.

She drew an arrow from the quiver on her hip and nocked it. When one of the creatures made a move toward Cura (now climbing groggily to her feet), she let it fly. The arrow pierced the muscle beneath the creature's wing, slowing it, and Tam ran to intercept.

Cura was standing by the time Tam slid to a stop beside her. The summoner's gaze, heavy with exhaustion, took in the trio of Simurglings, the wreckage of the *Spindrift*, and then the Dragoneater herself—vast as a mountain above them. She said nothing, but the thin line of her lips spoke volumes. She began pulling at the scarf binding her arm.

"Get behind me, Tam."

The bard reached for another arrow. "I think we should—"

"I said get behind me," Cura snarled, and Tam leapt to obey.

Two of the raptors came scampering toward them. The other went after Roderick, who jumped behind his snowdrift like it was a fortress wall. The young Dragoneaters moved with feline grace, prowling over the ice like feathered cats. Tam took aim at the nearest, but figured she'd best leave it to whatever Cura had planned. She switched focus to the one closing on Rod instead. She drew, fired, and swore beneath her breath as the shaft skipped off the ice between the creature's legs.

The echoing *shing* of *Madrigal* leaving its scabbard drew Tam's eye back to the Simurg. She couldn't find Rose or Freecloud at a glance, but Brune was in dire straits. The

Dragoneater had pulled him from its leg and had him in a tightening grip. The bard watched in horror as the monster plunged her fist—with Brune trapped inside it—into the lake. She imagined the shaman thrashing madly, desperate to wriggle free as cold water filled his lungs.

Her eyes snapped back to the Simurglings advancing on her and Cura. They seemed to be fighting over which of them got to take the first bite of bard. The smaller of the two nipped at the other, but was bullied aside as they drew near.

Cura was still furiously uncoiling the scarf, so Tam reached for another arrow. She'd nocked it, drawn it, and was exhaling to steady her trembling arm when the scarf finally came free. She watched, mesmerized, as it sailed skyward like a pennant torn from its pole, then stole a glance at Cura's latest tattoo.

And gaped. "Is that—"

"*BLOODY ROSE*!" Cura screamed. She stumbled into Tam as the thing carved into her arm stepped from a cloud of ink and fire.

It was discernibly female—rounded at the hip, broad across the shoulders—but decidedly inhuman. It didn't *look* like Rose, because Rose wasn't twelve feet tall and wreathed in flame, but it *felt* like her, exuding an air of boiling menace that left the bard gasping for breath.

The smaller of the two Simurglings drew up short, but the larger attacked, undeterred.

Bloody Rose leapt to meet it. Scalding swords bloomed in her hands. One smote the raptor across the face, battering its downy snout aside, while the other cleaved most of the way through its neck. The wound was cauterized instantly, but the Simurgling fell to the ice, skidding just short of Tam and Cura. It shuddered, squawked miserably, and died.

Cura's inkling turned on them. Snowflakes dissolved in the air around it. The ice beneath its feet was already softening to mush. There was, Tam could see, a figure *within* the fire, though she was little more than a silhouette behind the burning veil. The bard couldn't make out its face, but Tam was certain it had locked gazes with Cura.

The Inkwitch stood her ground. Her hands balled into fists at her side. Her eyes went wide and wild above flaring nostrils and gnashing teeth.

She's terrified, Tam thought. *She admires Rose. She must, or she wouldn't have followed her all the way here. But she fears her as well, and this*—the bard supressed a shiver—*is how Cura sees her.*

A soul on fire. A woman imprisoned by her nature, a danger to those nearest her...

Whatever silent struggle transpired between the summoner and the summoned was cut short as the smaller Simurgling pounced, driving *Bloody Rose* to the ice beneath it. The inkling twisted as it fell, catching the creature's lunging bite with one arm. The space between them was a flurry of scratching talons and flaming swords.

Cura slumped to the ground, shrugging Tam's hand away when she reached for her. "Go help Rod," she muttered.

Rod? Roderick! Fuck! Tam had forgotten all about him.

Whirling, she saw the booker was still alive, having adopted the surprisingly effective tactic of lying on his back and pinwheeling his feet in the air. The Simurgling managed to clamp down on one, only to find itself with an empty boot in its mouth and a cloven hoof in the face. It reared—

—and Tam's arrow punched through the soft scales on its belly. The Simurgling screeched and leapt away, shielding itself with a pair of wings as it used its teeth to pull the barb free. Roderick was up and running by the time it did.

Following the satyr's retreat, Tam found Hawkshaw closing in on her. The Warden hoisted his double-decked crossbow.

"Hey, I—"

Click.

Tam heard a whine in her ear as the bolt that should have killed her missed by mere inches. A gust of wind had saved her life, but there wasn't time now to thank it.

"Hawkshaw, listen—"

Click.

Tam juked right, and heard a second shaft buzz like a hornet past her nose.

The Warden tossed the spent crossbow away and drew his scabbardless bone sword without slowing.

Tam backed away, drawing Hawkshaw away from Cura—though she was fairly certain the Warden's ire didn't include the Inkwitch anyway. "Bloody gods, would you listen to me? I'm sorry! I didn't know the Widow was—"

Given the choice between finishing that sentence or evading the blade thrust at her head, Tam chose the latter. She leapt to one side and was turning to run when the Warden's sword slashed her shoulder. The blow drove her to her knees. She thought at first that her leather longcoat had borne the brunt of it, but a stripe of searing pain assured her that wasn't the case. A kick sent her sprawling facedown on the ice. Her bow clattered ahead of her, out of reach.

She rolled onto her back and found Hawkshaw looming. He reversed his grip on the rag-bound hilt of his sword and prepared to drive it through her.

Tam fumbled beneath her coat, found the raven-carved hilt she was looking for. She lashed out, hurling Cura's dagger at the Warden's face—which might have helped if she could throw worth a damn, but since she couldn't, the pommel glanced off his cheek and dropped at his feet.

That'll leave a bruise, remarked the cynic slouching in the corner of her mind.

Hawkshaw watched the knife fall, then grunted as a pair of flaming swords sprouted from his chest. He was lifted from the ground. The bone sword dropped from his twitching fingers. The fiery spectre of Bloody Rose pushed the Warden from her blades with a foot, and he hit the ground like a sack of meal, dead beneath his smouldering straw cape.

For a span of heartbeats Tam and the inkling stared at one another. This close, the bard could feel waves of heat rolling off the woman inside the fire, and...something else—a radiating aura that boiled with angst, and anger, and pride. Tam was overcome by the sense of being torn into halves. She felt *love*, and the need to *be* loved, warring inside her. The reconciliation of the two seemed an impossible thing, and yet if she could only grasp the one...

The apparition cocked her head, as though aware of how deeply she was being perceived. The shrouding fire burned from orange to blue. The ice beneath her puddled and sloughed. Tam knew she should get away, or at the very least *look* away, but the woman's presence compelled her to watch...

The flames vanished suddenly; the woman inside them dissolved into ash and was pulled into strands by the raking wind.

Tam sucked in a mouthful of cold air. She reclaimed her knife, then scrambled to where her bow lay. Suddenly, the ice beneath her lurched, and she was thrown to her backside.

Between the Simurglings and Hawkshaw trying to kill her, she'd been too preoccupied with her own survival to worry about the citadel-sized juggernaut they'd come here to kill.

But Rose hadn't. Nor had Freecloud.

From this side of the ice-water abyss, their fight against the Dragoneater looked absurd—like a pair of overly optimistic mice trying to bring down a lion. Tam could make out Rose, red-haired and black-armoured, striking at it from below. She was hurling her swords as fast as they returned to her hands, but it was hard to tell if her attacks were having any effect whatsoever.

Freecloud remained just inside the Dragoneater's reach, an

obvious target. *Madrigal*'s music bounced across the ice, the singsong warble of a bird drunk on brandy. The druin was using the prescience to anticipate the creature's attacks, running and leaping to avoid swiping claws, while occasionally finding time to retaliate.

A splashing figure drew Tam's eye: Brune, naked but for his drenched red scarf, was dragging himself from the lake. By the time she reached his side the shaman was sprawled on the ice, gasping for air and shivering like he'd seen his own spectre swimming in the depths below.

"Brune! Are you okay?"

"T-T-Tam? The f-f-fuck are you d-doing here?"

The bard opened her mouth to tell Brune that she'd spotted the Dragoneater lurking beneath the ice, then pushed Hawkshaw overboard, discovered the Widow hiding in Doshi's room, put the Simurg's eye out with a firebomb, crashed the ship, helped Cura fight off the Simurglings, and then watched the summoner's inkling (which was Rose, but not *really* Rose) kill Hawkshaw with a pair of flaming swords.

"T-Tam?" the shaman urged.

She blinked. "Sorry, what?"

"Where's C-Cura?"

"Here."

The Inkwitch shambled up beside them. Tam couldn't help but glance at the tattoo on Cura's arm and recall the fury of those flames against her skin. The ink was faded, indistinct, and would remain so for the next several hours. Though she'd never thought to ask, she suspected the Inkwitch couldn't summon the same inkling twice in one day.

"And R-Roderick?" Brune asked.

Roderick! Fuck! She'd forgotten him all over again. "He's..." Tam glanced around, and found the booker running flat out while the injured Simurgling limped after him. "There."

The shaman tried to rise. "I'll get him."

"Let me," said Cura, slipping her right arm free of her shawl.

Tam stepped ahead of them both. "I've got this," she said, and then barked, *"Rod!"*

The booker veered toward her. The Simurgling skidded behind him, wings flapping to keep it stable.

There were three arrows left in Tam's quiver. She chose one and drew, angling her shot to arc over the satyr's head. She took a deep breath, and her whole body flexed as she took aim.

Roderick was a flailing blur. The target, clear as crystal.

She released the breath and the arrow at once, and if the ice underfoot hadn't shuddered violently Tam was certain she would have hit the Simurgling.

But it *did* shudder violently, so she missed by a mile.

She pulled the second-to-last arrow from her quiver, swore when it snapped in her hand, and hastily threw it away.

Cura asked her something. Roderick was shouting words she couldn't hear. The Simurgling nipped at his heel, fouling his step, and the satyr went down.

Tam withdrew her last arrow. There wasn't time to draw the way Tera had taught her to draw or breathe the way Freecloud had told her to breathe.

She let the shaft loose the moment its fletching grazed her cheek. It whistled over Roderick's head and tore a gory hole through the creature's neck.

Which left only one Simurg to kill.

Chapter Thirty-five

The Damndest Thing

"What in the Frost Mother's frozen hell is Rose doing?" asked Roderick, squinting across the circle of shattered ice.

"Is she r-running?" Brune asked. He was still crouched, still naked, still shivering in the blowing snow. He'd be warmer as a wolf, Tam suspected, but unable to speak.

"Not running," said Cura. "Not Rose."

Roderick sniffed. "Really? Because I've done a lot of running today and that"—he pointed—"looks an awful lot like running to me."

The booker was right: Rose was running, weaponless, *away* from the monster, while Freecloud went on the attack. *Madrigal* was a sun-bright blur in his hands, humming as it hewed into the Simurg's foreleg.

Running or not, Tam marvelled that Rose was moving at all. Her own limbs were leaden with exhaustion, her every breath clipped by the cold. Rose was wearing plate armour, and had been dancing with the Dragoneater for several minutes now.

Brune looked up. His hair and beard were frozen stiff. Even his eyebrows were frosted with ice. "So what is it she's doing?"

"She's going to kill it," Cura said, "or die trying."

"Should we help?" Tam asked.

The Inkwitch shook her head. "I think it's too late for that."

They watch, helpless to intervene, as Rose runs flat out across the ice. She leaps a few smaller drifts, but a larger one looms ahead. The Simurg, its left eye a smoking ruin, must turn its head sideways to assess her flight. Then it points its muzzle at her, and Tam sees the red-gold feathers behind its head unfurl with the splendour of a courtesan's fan.

"It's going to—"

"We see," Cura says.

"But she—"

"We know."

She's going to die, Tam tells herself. *Unless . . . is she running for that snowbank? Can she make it in time?*

The Simurg spreads its wings, bracing itself. As Rose clambers desperately up the sloping face of the drift, it expels a stream of splashing frost so bright it hurts to look at.

"D-did she make it?" Brune asks. "D-did you see?"

"No." Cura's voice is hoarse.

"No *what*!?" squawks Roderick. "No, you didn't see? Or no she didn't—"

"There she is!" Tam shouts, pointing.

Rose is climbing back over the drift, which has been transformed by the Simurg's breath into a battlement adorned by spikes of crystallized ice. She stands there, red hair whipping in the frenzied wind, and screams. Not words. At least, no words Tam can make out.

The *Simurg*, however, understands just fine. It is wounded, badly. Its offspring are dead. It has wiped out cities, buried *civilizations* beneath centuries of ice—and this *woman*, this tiny, *insignificant* thing, has the gall to challenge it?

At least that's what Tam *assumes* it's thinking, because

when Rose skids down the icy drift and begins running toward it, the Simurg charges to meet her.

Freecloud makes no move to hinder it. Instead, he returns *Madrigal* to its scabbard and takes a knee. Whatever his part was in this, Tam suspects it is over.

Rose flings her arms out, beckoning *Thistle* and *Thorn* to her grasp—little good may they do her. The Simurg's hide is too thick. Its feathers, glazed in ice, are harder than scale.

The monster lunges, its head skewing sideways. As its jaw unhinges, Rose hurls one sword overhand, the other sidehand, directly into its mouth, and then slips—no, *drops*—onto her back, grinding along the ice as the Dragoneater's teeth snap shut above her.

"Oh," Brune says, very quietly.

Rose is on her feet again—Tam has no idea how—and running. The Simurg lifts its head, unleashes an ear-shattering screech that sounds at first like triumph, but becomes a strangled cry as Rose —gauntlets blazing—sprints beneath it, dragging her swords deeper into the creature's stomach with every step.

It swipes at her, but she throws herself between two of its talons and keeps on running. It lifts a rear claw to try again, but Freecloud is leaping to attack its other leg. *Madrigal* shears through bone and tendon. The Simurg screams, drags itself in a half circle, trailing blood and sweeping the lake with the bright feathers of its tail.

Rose slows, stops, turns. Freecloud hovers beside her, and Tam sees him say something she cannot hear.

The Simurg twitches violently, curling instinctively around some kernel of invisible anguish. It collapses, rises, fixes its lone eye upon Rose, who holds both hands before her like a supplicant begging favours of her god.

Except Rose needs nothing from the gods.

She only wants her swords back.

The runes on her wrists flare, and the scimitars to which

they are linked come spinning, slicing, and tearing through lung, through heart, through all the tender things in the behemoth's throat, and then burst in a shower of blood and bile from its gagging mouth. At last they arrive, slick with gore, in the hands of the woman the world calls Bloody Rose.

The Simurg is convulsing. Its wings shudder like sails in a storm. Its tail-feathers thrash, its talons rake trenches in the ice. It tries to roar, to shriek indignation at the woman who has severed the golden thread of its immortality, but can only heave more of its shredded innards onto the ice.

At last, the Dragoneater crashes to its side, spilling back into the freezing water from which it emerged. It claws feebly at the fractured ice before slipping and sinking into the cold depths of Mirrormere.

For a while no one speaks, and then Roderick chuckles. "Fuck me, would you look at that!"

The satyr's fox-tail hat, which he'd lost while piloting the *Spindrift*, comes tumbling across the ice and lodges in a snowdrift near his hoof. The booker scoops it up and sets it firmly on his head. "Well, if that isn't the damndest thing I've seen all day!"

Cura scoffs. "Seriously? *That* was the damndest thing you've seen all day?"

Roderick looks mildly affronted. Whatever reply he is about to offer, however, dies on his lips. "Actually, no," he says, pointing toward the flaming wreck of their skyship. "That is."

The Widow was alive, but on fire.

Stranger still, she seemed indifferent to the flames eating at her shift as the wind dragged it out behind her. She was barefoot, striding with slow purpose toward the open water.

Cura gawked. "Who the hell is *that*?"

"It's the Widow," Tam said. "She was hiding in Doshi's quarters."

Brune was shivering violently now. "Sh-she's a d-d—"

"Druin," Tam finished. "I noticed."

Roderick frowned over at the shaman. "Here, take this." He shrugged off his bulky fur cloak and offered it to Brune, who was busy glaring at the duplicate cloak the satyr had been wearing underneath it.

"Y-you've h-had t-two c-cloaks this whole t-time?"

Rod snorted. "Um, yeah. We're in the *Brumal Wastes.*"

Brune looked ready to throttle the booker, but the urge to survive compelled him to reach for the cloak instead.

"Guys," Cura demanded their attention, "look."

The Widow was standing over Hawkshaw. Strands of black hair obscured her face as she gazed down at his corpse, so it wasn't clear whether or not she grieved. She didn't seem the sort to mourn a servant's death, but she lingered long enough for the flames chewing her shift to go out.

"Get up, you miserable lout," she said.

Tam was about to point out that the Warden was quite obviously dead, but since Hawkshaw was in fact getting to his feet she decided that staring openmouthed was a better idea.

"Gremlins on a fucking stick!" Roderick turned on Cura. "I thought you killed him!"

The summoner scowled. "I *did* kill him."

"Well then how . . . ?" The booker gasped. "Wait, so she's a—"

"Necromancer," Brune finished. "She's a godsforsaken necromancer."

Hawkshaw fingered the wounds in his chest. His flat grey gaze fell on Tam first, then he looked across the water at the lake of blood vomited up by the Dragoneater.

Why is his eye the same? Tam wondered. Why wasn't it burning, like every other undead thing they'd encountered these past few months?

The Warden turned on the Widow. "The Simurg is dead?"

"It is," she replied.

"Then why am I still here? You said *no more*. You said that once the Dragoneater was killed I could be with Sara. You swore—"

"I lied," she said blithely, as though addressing a man who'd found celery in his egg salad sandwich instead of one whose soul she'd enslaved with foul magic. "Oh, don't pout, Hawkshaw. It makes you look so sinister, and we both know what a puppy dog you are." The druin grazed his leather-masked cheek with a pale hand. "I have need of you still. You're my *champion*. At least until I find a better one."

The Warden gave a grudging nod.

The Widow's fingers took rough hold of Hawkshaw's bristly chin. "And if you ever utter your first wife's name in my presence again I will bring her back from the grave so you can see what a beauty she's become. Do you understand me?"

Something—a lingering remnant of the Warden's free will, perhaps—glinted in his eye like a knife in the dark. "Yes, my queen."

"Good." She kissed the hard line of his lips. "You may be a slave, dear, but you are still my husband."

"Did she say *husband*?" Brune asked.

"Did he say *queen*?" Cura wondered.

"Queen?" Roderick said, loud enough to draw the Widow's attention. "Queen of *what*? And whose husband is he? Would someone please tell me what the frosty hell is going on here?"

"He's the Marchlord," said Tam, who'd put the pieces of the puzzle together and wished she could unsee what they revealed.

Brune frowned. "The one that died?"

"The one that died, yes."

Cura looked perplexed. "So then she's—"

"She's the Winter Queen."

Her bandmates looked at Tam as if she'd suggested they go skinny-dipping in the lake.

"At least I *think* she is," Tam explained hurriedly. Hawk-shaw was busy recovering his sword and crossbow, but the Widow was eyeing them with a sly smile on her lips. "Free-cloud told me the Winter Queen was really a druin. The Archon's wife. She ... uh, died." Tam opted to skip the part of the story where Vespian killed their infant daughter. "But the Archon used a sword called *Tamarat* to bring her back. Only she wasn't ..."

"Wasn't what?" pressed Cura.

"Sane," Tam whispered. "Anyway, she's been dead since the Dominion fell, but then Lastleaf used *Tamarat* to kill him-self at Castia, which means ..." She trailed off, since it was obvious from their expressions that the others understood where she was going with this.

"So you're saying this mousy little witch is really the Frost Mother?" Brune asked.

"I'm not particularly fond of that name," said the Widow, all but confirming Tam's outlandish conjecture. "It makes me feel so *old*."

"I don't believe it," said Cura.

The druin raised her chin, which lent her a chillingly imperious air. "Do you not?"

Her eyes gleamed cerulean. She whispered something undecipherable, and black smoke curled from between her lips. The corpse of the Simurgling Tam had killed with an arrow stirred to life. Its eyes burned away in wisps of white fire. Whatever subtle magic she'd used to lend Hawkshaw the semblance of life, this creature didn't seem to warrant it. It shambled to the woman's side and laid its head at her feet.

Mirth writhed like a maggot on the Widow's lips. "And now?" she asked.

Cura sneered, and Tam hoped to hell she wasn't about to say anything that might provoke the sorceress into killing them. "Now *what*? Do I think you're a goddess?" She feigned a laugh that was too harsh to be credible. "No, I don't. I think you're an orc-shit crazy bitch who spent too long alone in her castle with no one but a dead guy and an old turtle for company." She gestured at Hawkshaw. "I think you're so totally repulsive that your own husband would rather die than stay married to you." Cura glanced briefly at Brune. "I bet dogs hate you, too," she added.

Tam winced. *So much for pleasantries.*

The Widow's amusement vanished like a silver coin lost to deep water. "Perhaps this will convince you," she said, and started toward the circle of shattered ice.

What happened next was, without a doubt, the damndest thing Tam had seen all day.

Chapter Thirty-six

Lost and Found

The Widow spoke another string of sibilant words. Dark vapour streamed from her lips into the frigid air.

They waited. Moments passed. Cura had just opened her mouth to say something snide when a massive claw burst from the lake and grappled the cracked ice. The living corpse of the Simurg boiled up behind it, water sluicing from fur, feather, and scale. Flames like funeral pyres blazed in the cavernous sockets of its eyes. It reared above them, glacial and silent. The feathers on its crest had faded from the brilliant reds of sunrise to the bruised violet of dusk.

The sight of it drove the band to their knees. Cura swore. Brune muttered a prayer under his breath. "Gods fuck me," said Roderick, managing the impressive feat of swearing and praying at the same time.

Tam didn't say a thing. She couldn't. Her tongue felt like a stone in her throat, threatening to choke her. A faithless tear slipped from her eye and froze to crystal on her cheek.

The Widow gazed up at the Dragoneater, her hard features slack with rapture. She was wholly engrossed by her new pet, and it occurred to Tam that she should probably try to kill the woman here and now, except...

Except you spent your arrows. You have only a knife, and no chance at all of getting near her before Hawkshaw cuts you down or that Simurgling tears you limb from limb.

Judging by the grim set of their faces, her bandmates were coming to similar conclusions. Tam couldn't see Rose for the bulk of the Dragoneater, but she and Freecloud had been kneeling in exhaustion when the bard had seen them last. If the Widow decided to kill them now, there was little they could do to stop her.

Roderick steadied his hat and craned his neck to look up at the Simurg. "She duped us," he said despairingly. "The contract was never about *killing* the Dragoneater. It was about *controlling* it."

Before Tam could grasp the implications of why someone would want a world-wrecking monster at their beck and call, the Dragoneater lowered its head and buttressed it against the jagged edge of the ice.

The undead Simurgling scurried onto its mother's neck, and Hawkshaw climbed into the shelter of its feather crest before offering a hand to his mistress. The Widow's limp ears perked a little as she stepped onto the monster's back. She looked cautiously ecstatic, like a plainswoman at the prow of a seaborne vessel.

"Exquisite," she said breathlessly, then called down from her perch. "You will thank Rose for me, won't you? She really was the perfect woman for the job. So capable, so brave, so hopelessly insecure. I'd have preferred to lure her father here, but this"—the Widow bared her teeth and gestured to the empty landscape around them—"has a certain poetry to it. Gabriel's beloved daughter, so desperate to prove her worth, left to die in obscurity."

"Go fuck yourself," snapped Cura, which seemed to Tam like an ill-advised thing to say to someone who'd just made a pet of the world's most fearsome monster. The druin scowled down at them as though Cura and her bandmates were rot-ridden urchins begging alms on her doorstep.

"Why do you hate Gabriel so much?" Tam blurted, hoping to temper the Widow's wrath into something less likely to get them all killed.

"Because"—the druin's glare was cold enough to snuff a fire—"he killed my son."

The Simurg beat its wings, rising on a storm of sleet and swirling feathers that blew Roderick's hat from his head yet again. The monster climbed ponderously skyward, until it pierced the grey veil above the Brumal Wastes, and was gone.

"We're still alive," breathed Roderick.

"But now what?" asked Brune. He blinked around them, eyelashes heavy with frost.

Cura was still watching the sky, her expression bleak. At last she lowered her gaze: to the snow-clad mountains, and the barren tundra stretching away to the north. "Now we die."

Something was very wrong with Rose.

Tam and the others had skirted the rough circle of open water, wary of cracks that could—as Roderick discovered the hard way—split apart and leave one stranded on a slab of submerging ice. Fortunately, the satyr was an excellent jumper, and they'd been sure to give the water a wide berth afterward.

Rose was lying on her back with her head in Freecloud's lap. The druin's ears were slumped like a child sulking over a plate of steamed cabbage.

"Is she hurt?" Roderick asked. "What happened?"

But it was obvious the moment Tam laid eyes on Rose what was wrong. Her irises filled the whole of her eyes. Her lips and tongue were black—the latter so swollen it lodged like a lump of coal in her mouth—and dark blood trickled from her nostrils.

Tam's stomach turned. She could have stopped Rose from taking the Lion's Leaf earlier, or told Freecloud what she'd seen belowdecks. But she'd decided to trust that Rose knew what she was doing. She'd believed, like a fool, that Fable's leader placed more value on her life than on defeating the Simurg.

"She's going to die," said Freecloud.

"I'm fairly certain we're all going to die," Roderick was quick to point out.

The wind was getting stronger, the snow piling up around their ankles, and the sky to the east glowered like a priest when a harlot came to worship.

There's a storm coming, Tam surmised. *And when it gets here, we're done for.*

Brune dragged off the fur cloak the satyr had spared him earlier and placed it over Rose.

"You'll freeze," said Freecloud, but the shaman only shrugged.

Cura pulled the sable fur from her shoulders and draped it across Rose as well. Her teeth rattled as she flashed the druin an assuring grin.

Tam slipped out of her red leather longcoat before kneeling and laying it carefully over Rose.

"You needn't suffer because of her," said Freecloud. "She wouldn't want that." His voice wavered as he spoke, betraying a grief he was loath to reveal even to his closest comrades.

"But she's earned it," said Roderick. He removed his foxtail hat, then stooped and pulled it snugly over Rose's head.

They stood there shivering, grim as mourners at their own funeral. Tam was about to suggest they try carrying Rose into the shelter of the Simurg's lair when the yethiks attacked.

The monsters shambled through curtains of blowing snow. They were huge, shaggy brutes with four arms and faces that looked like boiled leather masks. Each was as big as Brune, except their leader, who was curiously smaller than the others, and currently howling something unintelligible as they approached.

Or not *quite* unintelligible, since it sounded a lot like . . .

"Wait!" Tam shouted, before Brune could sham or Cura summon one of her inked atrocities. "Listen!"

"Rooooose! Rooooose!"

Roderick poked his bare head out from behind the shaman. "Rose?" He looked to Freecloud. "Does Rose know any yethiks?"

"That's not a yethik," Tam said. She stepped out in front of the others and hoped she was right about that.

The figure that slowed to a halt in front of her was thickly bearded and draped in matted fur, but clearly human. His bottom two arms were merely stuffed sackcloth limbs linked by twine threads to the man's wrists. His face was burned a ruddy red by overexposure to the cold, and his mangy beard was thick with rime. Even still, Tam recognized the Raincrows' axeman almost immediately.

"Farager?"

The man scrutinized her through frosted lashes. "Tam? Tam bloody Hashford?"

"What are you doing here?" she asked, glancing warily at his apish companions. Unlike him, they were real live yethiks, with jutting brows, fanged underbites, and four arms apiece.

"We're here to kill you!" said Farager, but when Tam's hand strayed to her knife he dragged his stuffed arms skyward in a gesture of surrender. "Ha! I'm kidding, obviously. Gods, you should have seen your face!" He turned and signalled something to the yethiks behind him. They laughed uproariously and jostled one another with their copious elbows. "Actually, we saw you fighting the Dragoneater and figured you could use some help."

"You're too late," Cura told him. "It's already dead."

"We saw," said Farager.

"Well, not exactly dead," Brune grumbled.

"We saw that, too." The axeman squinted, surveying the swathe of gory red ice before looking skyward. "What the heck happened out here?"

"Rose is sick," Tam said impatiently. "Dying, maybe. Is there somewhere we can take her? Someplace warm?"

"There is," said Farager. He did something curious with his hands, bumping one into another before dragging it toward his chest. "Follow me."

The Yethiks lived in a warren of caves accessed via the cleft Hawkshaw had identified as the Simurg's lair. Tam's recollection of getting there was hazy. She remembered collapsing in the snow and then being loaded, along with Brune, Cura, and Rose, onto sleds pulled by Farager's yethik cohorts. She vaguely recalled Roderick complaining about *not* getting to ride on a sled until their rescuers relented and offered to tow the satyr as well.

The rest of the journey passed in a series of weary glimpses: a shadowed crevasse of sheer ice; snowflakes glittering against a narrow strip of sky; bones heaped in drifts against stone walls; bestial faces peering into hers; and finally, the warming kiss of a fire.

Its heat suffused her, enveloped her like a returning tide that carried her out to sea and dragged her down, and down, and down to sleep.

Tam woke to a gentle prodding on her back. The bard tried to turn over, but a pair of strong hands held her down. She realised she was shirtless, panicked, and wriggled violently in an attempt to seize the knife at her waist.

"Easy, Tam," said Freecloud from somewhere nearby. "She's only trying to help. You've been wounded. A sword cut, looks like."

A sword? Oh, yeah. Hawkshaw cut me. And kicked me. And tried to shoot me. Twice.

She felt something warm and tacky being spread over her shoulder blade. A salve, she guessed, wincing as her caretaker kneaded it gently into the wound. After that, a strip of something that crinkled like parchment was pressed onto her back. The salve doubled as an adhesive as it cooled, and the parchment hardened into a glaze over the gash.

When she was permitted, Tam rolled over and sat up. She found her thick wool tunic and pulled it gingerly over her head. The fire was reduced to a steeple of glowing logs, but the small cave in which she found herself was blessedly warm.

Cura was asleep on a fur mat beside her. Rose lay a short distance away. There was a clay bowl beside her head. Tam could see black slop glistening within, and more of it staining the stone beneath the bowl. The frontwoman's face was waxen in the dim light, slick with sweat. Her breath came in rapid bursts, and her fingers twitched around the hilt of imagined swords.

Freecloud was sitting by her side, toying with that moonstone coin of his. Tam wondered if the druin had slept at all since they'd been rescued.

Brune and Roderick were nowhere in sight.

Next to her was a yethik with pale brown fur spotted white like a fawn's. Freecloud had called it a *she*, but Tam could see nothing that made her obviously female. Two of her arms were rolling a sheet of stripped bark. A third hand made a curious, open-handed gesture beneath her chin, and then repeated it (or something like it) while her fourth hand was couched in the crook of her arm.

These aren't gestures, Tam swiftly realized. *They're language.* "Uh, thank you," she said.

The yethik repeated her first sign and then shuffled off, walking on the knuckles of her lower hands. The cave was open on one side, accessed by a gently sloping ramp. The space beyond was illuminated by rays of diffuse light that streamed through fractures in the cavern roof. Stalagmites and stalactites bigger than most of Ardburg's towers pillared the gloom, each of them dotted with darkened alcoves and glowing nooks. She could see shaggy silhouettes in some, sitting or conversing with one another using elaborate hand signals.

"Can they speak?" Tam wondered aloud.

"They sign," answered Freecloud. "And grunt occasionally. Also, for some reason, they laugh at almost everything Farager does. Aside from that they make no sound at all."

"I didn't know that about yethiks," she said.

It was hard to make out his expression in the low light of glowing embers, but the druin's voice was especially sombre. "Neither did I."

"Where are the others?"

"Farager took them to see if they could salvage anything from the skyship. They'll be returning shortly—I can hear them now."

Tam had sometimes wondered if Freecloud's long ears meant he could hear better than humans, and since she heard nothing but the hiss of sizzling logs and Cura's slow breathing, she concluded that yes, he obviously could.

"Will Rose be okay?" she asked hesitantly.

"She'll recover, yes." Freecloud motioned to the bowl beside her head. "But she won't linger here. The moment she can walk she'll insist on heading south. If we're lucky, the yethiks will know a way through the mountains, but if not"—he swiped a strand of sweat-matted hair from Rose's forehead—"she will try and go over them. I will follow her, of course. I suppose Cura and Brune will as well."

"And me."

"And you," he said, smiling sadly. "We are moths, you and I. And Rose, the flame." When Tam blinked she saw Cura's newest inkling in her mind's eye. *Bloody Rose*, wreathed in fire. She doubted he'd had the chance to see it while battling the Simurg, but this *was* Freecloud, and there was very little the swordsman missed.

"I don't like our chances of surviving a trek over the Rimeshields in winter. Brune, perhaps, could make it."

"We could wait for spring?" Tam suggested.

"Do you think Rose will wait for the snow to thaw while the Brumal Horde threatens our daughter's life?"

Tam shrugged. "Why would she care about Wren's safety now? We knew weeks ago that the Horde was headed for Agria. She could have rushed home then, right? She could have gone to Coldfire Pass in the first place instead of—"

"I know," Freecloud snapped. The druin's ears were stiff, his eyes so dark they held nothing but the reflected red glow of the fire within. There was an embittered edge to his voice she'd never heard before.

"I'm sorry," she said, swallowing. "I'm just the bard. It's not my place to—"

"No," he cut her off again. "You're right. We should never have gone to Diremarch. We should have refused the Widow's contract and headed for Coldfire Pass along with everyone else. We should have faced down the Horde instead of chasing after the Simurg, except..."

"Except," Tam prompted, when the druin's silence lingered.

A cynical twist tugged at his lips. "I'm a moth, remember? Where she goes, I follow. The tours, the contracts... All of it, I do for her. To be near her. To protect her, if I can. I'd rather be a father than a mercenary, but Rose..." His ears canted sideways. "Well, motherhood isn't really her style."

No shit, Tam thought. She tried to imagine Fable's front-woman nursing a babe, or spooning peas into an infant's mouth, and failed miserably.

Freecloud gazed down at Rose, studying her face as though intending to paint it from memory. "I don't blame her, of course. We are what we are. I fell in love with a tigress. How could I ask her to be anything else?"

At last, Tam heard a commotion in the cavern below. Thumps and grunts and growls heralded the return of Farager and his fellow hunters. Cura stirred restlessly on her pallet, threw an arm across her eyes, and fell back asleep.

"How did you and Rose meet?" Tam asked.

"Violently," said the druin, though his expression was wry. "I was sent into the Heartwyld to parley with Lastleaf, who was preparing to attack Castia and wanted my father's help in doing so. Unfortunately for the so-called Duke of Endland, my father is a stubborn ass who refused to send even a single golem. Unfortunately for me, Lastleaf was a vindictive lunatic who didn't deal well with rejection. He imprisoned me, and might have ordered me killed had a brave young satyr not set me free."

It took Tam a moment to clue in. "Roderick?"

"Roderick," he confirmed, smiling wistfully. "The two of us fled. Lastleaf sent his sylfs after us, but they found Rose instead."

"Wait, sylfs?" Tam said. "Like Wren?"

The druin's ears nodded affirmation. "Sylfs are often outcasts, but Lastleaf was nothing if not inclusive. He employed them as scouts and assassins. They ambushed Rose and her band, which, as you might imagine, did not go well for them at all."

"She killed them?"

"Most of them, yes. But one of her bandmates was gravely injured, and since I felt responsible for having led the sylfs to them, I offered to escort them to the edge of the forest. Rose was hopelessly lost by then, and far too close to the Infernal Shire."

Tam had never heard of the Infernal Shire, but it didn't sound like a wise place to wander into accidentally.

A log in the fire split, belching a flurry of red sparks.

Freecloud looked toward the tunnel mouth, and Tam could hear the satyr's voice echoing from the passage.

"The edge of the forest came and went," Freecloud said. "We crossed the mountains and found the Republic's army preparing to repel the Heartwyld Horde. Every day I promised Roderick we'd get out of there and go home, but every night I . . . decided otherwise."

Where's Brune to wink conspiratorially when you need him, Tam wondered.

"And then Lastleaf came storming from the forest with a hundred thousand wyld things in tow. He destroyed Castia's army and laid siege to the city. I could have escaped on my own and abandoned Rose to her fate, but by then it was too late."

"You were in love," Tam said.

"And always will be," uttered Freecloud, a moment before Roderick sauntered into the cave.

"We're back," announced the booker. He was bundled head to toe in mismatched furs, arm in arm (or *arms*, rather) with one of the yethiks, a black-furred one with a spear clasped in both right hands. Brune was with them, laughing and talking excitedly with Farager. They were all of them dusted with snow; Tam could feel the cold clinging to them like a jilted lover's scent.

Cura blinked awake and rolled over on her blanket. "Find anything useful?"

"Nope," said Roderick.

"We found Doshi," Brune said. He was carrying the *Spindrift*'s unconscious pilot in his arms, and now lowered him onto a vacant pelt. "The daft bugger was clinging to one of those whirly engines. He begged us to leave him be and let him die. We barely peeled him off before the whole thing went into the lake."

"Should have let the cur sink," Rod muttered, dusting snow off his hat.

"We rescued this as well," said Farager. He knelt and offered something to Tam.

"Oh," she said, recognizing *Hiraeth*'s sealskin case. Her stomach clenched as if steeling itself for a punch. "Is it...?" She fell silent, afraid to ask.

"Smashed to bits, I'm afraid."

Tam closed her eyes.

"Just kidding!" Farager laughed and set the case down at her knees. He unlaced the toggles so she could confirm that the instrument's whitewood face and slender neck were undamaged. "See? It's totally fine. The back half of your boat was mostly intact. We found this wedged under your cot, safe and sound. I had you going there, didn't I?"

"You..." *stupid fucking asshole*, Tam almost said, but instead she smiled. "You really did."

Chapter Thirty-seven

Sharing Smoke

The yethiks had salvaged quite a lot from the *Spindrift* before it sloughed through the ice and was lost to the lake. They were sorting through it all in the cavern below. Most of it belonged to Daon Doshi, since his quarters had been in the stern, but the man didn't seem to care that their hosts were already dividing the spoils among themselves.

The captain woke for long enough to bemoan the loss of his beloved skyship and launch a feeble attack on Roderick, who punched Doshi out of panicked reflex and knocked him out cold.

"I don't think he likes you very much," Brune remarked.

The booker cradled the offending fist and shrugged. "Yeah, well, he's not exactly the cat's pyjamas either."

Tam's heart went out to the captain. The man had cherished his freedom more than anything, and might still have it had Roderick not pushed him overboard. Left sprawled by the booker's retaliatory punch, he looked sad and small. His colourful attire, which had previously lent him an air of eccentric worldliness, now made him look like a mummer who'd gone rooting through a brothel's laundry for his latest costume.

He made his choice, she reminded herself, *when he obeyed Hawkshaw and refused to let us warn the others.*

Had Doshi suspected his employer's motive for wanting the Simurg dead? Tam didn't think so. The captain had spoken optimistically about the future—about a time *after* his tenure with the Widow—which didn't make sense if he'd known his mistress planned to make war on his entire species. The man had been chasing his freedom, she concluded, and nothing more.

"Come," Farager said. "Let me introduce you to the band."

Cura looked hopeful. "The band?"

"You mean the Raincrows?" Brune tugged his scarf loose. "I thought they—"

"Died?" The axeman shook his head. "Nope! Terrik, Robin, Annie—they're all here, safe and sound."

"Really?" Tam asked. There were many dozens of yethiks milling around the salvage below; she tried to spy Terrik's shock of red hair among them.

"No, not really!" Farager cackled and slapped his knee with a sackcloth hand. "They're dead! The Simurg made bloody icicles out of them! Except Annie, who I'm pretty sure got ate." He frowned. "Eaten? Ate? Whichever it is, she's as dead as the rest of 'em."

Brune shouldered up to Tam as Farager set off down the ramp. "Was he always this warped?" the shaman asked.

Tam pursed her lips, recalling a night at the Cornerstone when Farager had insisted on setting his drinks on fire before consuming them. He'd lost his beard, both eyebrows, and most of his hair by the time Tera kicked him out. "Pretty much, yeah."

Everyone but Doshi, Rose, and Freecloud (who refused to leave Rose's side) followed Farager below. Tam's gaze was drawn to the spires of rock in which the yethiks made their homes. Only the lowest rooms could be entered on foot, while those higher up required one to climb using painted handholds affixed to the rock face. The colour of the handholds seemed to designate where each path led, and Tam found herself following a bright yellow path up and around the soaring column.

"Band," Farager was saying, "is the yethik word for family." He signed as he said this, touching the thumb and forefinger of each hand and overlapping them. "And family means the whole tribe."

Brune dragged wet hair from his eyes and made a topknot of it. "So do they have names?"

"Of course," said Farager. "They choose their names based on their favourite things." He indicated a pair of yethiks rooting through a flame-eaten chest. "That black-furred one is Smell Of Wet Stone, and the other is First Snowfall."

Cura grinned. "First Snowfall, huh? I like that. What—hey, that's my stuff!" She shooed off the yethiks, grabbing a book entitled *Skeletons in the Closet: A Necromancer's Guide to Coming Out* from the hands of Smell Of Wet Stone.

They left the Inkwitch organizing her clothes into two piles: one for surviving garments and another for those too damaged to wear. But since most of Cura's outfits could be described as "flimsy black rags," it was hard to tell which mound was which.

Farager pointed out a few other yethiks with names like Berries Frozen On The Branch and Stars Reflecting On Ice. "Oh, and see these two?" The creatures he indicated were both huge and white-furred, with puckered scars crisscrossing their chest and arms. "They're brothers," he said. "The big one is Bashing In A Deer's Skull With A Rock, and the smaller is Pushing My Thumbs Into My Enemies' Eyes. Great guys," he added. "Maybe the best hunters in the band. Aside from me, obviously."

Another gaggle of yethiks were rummaging through Roderick's clothes, most of which were utterly destroyed. The booker went to join them, lamenting the loss of his wardrobe with the same theatrical despair as Doshi mourning his ship. The satyr wailed over fire-ravaged scarves, wept over scorched silk blouses, and nearly tore his beard out over the remains of something he referred to as an ascot, except the thing in his hands looked to Tam like a charred squirrel.

The influx of so much new bounty brought the "band" out in droves. They shuffled from their nooks bearing possessions they'd grown tired of, or curiosities they'd found while exploring. They bartered by using their top two hands to haggle in their silent language, while the bottom two proffered the wares they'd brought to trade. Items on display included glowing crystal shards, simple jewellery, a variety of painted hide armbands, and an assortment of figurines carved out of stone and horn. A few brave souls brought armour and weapons they'd looted from the Dragoneater's lair in the adjoining crevasse.

The bard spotted two yethiks in the midst of an apparently heated negotiation. One was offering a basket of hard white potatoes, while the other held a blade with three edges that Tam suspected was *Quarterflash*, the legendary longsword of Fillia Finn. She watched, dumbstruck, as the potato farmer took possession of his new weapon and began swinging it wildly.

"So how did you end up here?" Brune asked Farager as they toured the bizarre bazaar. "Doshi said you guys...uh, didn't last very long against the Simurg."

"Seventeen seconds," Tam said, drawing sidelong glances from the others. "Or something like that."

Farager grimaced. "Yeah, well, it felt more like *seven* seconds. Maiden's Mercy, it was over quick. We didn't stand a chance against that thing. We should never have taken that Wyld-spawned contract to begin with."

"Why did you?" asked Roderick. "I mean, no offence, but the Raincrows weren't exactly known for being the best of the best."

The man's lower arms bobbed when he shrugged. "That's exactly why we did it. Well, that and the gold, obviously. Five thousand courtmarks is a lot of money."

Tam shared a glance with the booker and Brune, neither of whom seemed eager to tell their guide that Fable had been offered ten times that amount.

"We'd been treading water in the arena circuit," said the ex-Raincrow, "but one night in Bastien an ogre got the jump on us and our reputation went to shit."

The satyr stroked his beard. "I heard about that. The thing turned out to be a mage, right?"

Farager signed a greeting to a doddering old yethik using four canes at once. She *clack-clack-clack-clack*ed by, smiling toothily as she did. "The wrangler—may he freeze in hell—claims he had no idea, but I suspect he wanted to give the crowd a show. The second the fight started the ogre threw a fuckin' lightning bolt at Robin. Fried him in his boots. The poor bastard had an awful stutter ever since, and he'd piss himself whenever something startled him. And believe me: *Everything* startled him. Anyway, things went downhill fast after that. We put our name in for the Megathon's grand opening but didn't make the cut. After that, we got desperate. We knew we needed something big to get ourselves back in the game."

"So you took on the Dragoneater," said Brune.

"Aye, and got our asses kicked. It hit us with its breath straightaway—stopped three of us in our tracks. Annie got an arrow off, I think, but you'd might as well hit a mountain with a mace for all the good it did." Farager sighed and shook his head. "Hubris, man. It's killed more heroes than monsters ever did."

That, Tam thought, *is a damn good line*. She would try to remember it for later, maybe use it in a song . . .

They came across a yethik pawning more of Daon Doshi's belongings, including the chest of alchemical grenades, which would have obliterated the back half of the skyship had the fire touched it. The creature traded one of the explosive clay balls for a frozen fish, and another for an anatomically embellished minotaur statue. At least Tam assumed it was embellished, or she doubted minotaur women would survive copulation.

"I think we should probably confiscate these," she said. "They're really dangerous."

Farager signed back and forth with the one trafficking the firebombs. "You'll need to trade for them, I'm afraid. She wants your scarf," he said to Tam. "And Roderick's hat."

The satyr crossed his arms. "Out of the question."

Brune made a grumbling noise. "Rod..."

"They might kill themselves!" Tam pressed.

Roderick snorted. "They can blow themselves to smithereens for all I care, I'm not giving—" He froze. His jaw dropped so low he could have swallowed a watermelon whole, and he swiped the hat off his head. "Here." He handed it over, motioning frantically for Tam to do the same. "Give her the scarf. Go on!"

The bard did as she was ordered. Once the transaction was complete, the yethik sauntered off to flaunt her flashy new attire, while Tam and Roderick found themselves the proud owners of a chest full of explosives.

But not *only* explosives, she realized, when Rod snatched up something from inside. It was spherical, but unlike the grenades, which were wrapped in wool sleeves, it was shrouded in black velvet.

Farager looked from Rod, to Brune, to Tam, all of whom were grinning from ear to ear. "What is it?" he asked.

Rod pulled the cloth from the glassy black scrying orb with a deliberate flourish. "This," he announced, "is how we're getting home."

The band kept mostly to themselves over the following days. They didn't reminisce about their fight with the Simurg or discuss the implications of the Widow's deception. Tam couldn't know for sure, but she suspected each of them (excluding Rose, who was grappling with the fallout of her overdose) were combating their fear and uncertainty however they knew best.

Cura read, or slept, or wandered off alone for hours at a time, while Brune, embracing his newfound *fain*, accompanied the yethik hunters on their forays into the Brumal Wastes. All but one of these excursions proved relatively uneventful, with the exception being the day Brune sniffed out a clan of rasks waiting in ambush. The ice trolls were killed or driven off, and the shaman was hailed as a hero. The hunters urged him to choose a proper yethik name, so he was known to them afterward as A Pint of Ale And A Hot Bacon Sandwich.

Rose grew stronger by the hour. After two days spent vomiting black sludge, she appeared to make a full recovery. That evening, however, she succumbed once again to the fever's clammy clutches. She begged Freecloud to find her more Lion's Leaf—or a drink, at least, to take the edge off her craving. He offered neither, and suffered a split lip while keeping her confined to their niche. Fable's frontwoman threw up one last bellyfull of bile before the fever broke.

Tam spent her free time exploring the cavern. She climbed as high as she dared up one of the pointed spires. She considered going higher the day after, but then her monthly cramps arrived and made the idea of scaling a sheer rock face as appealing as swallowing a handful of nails.

Instead, she asked Farager to teach her some of the hand signals the yethiks used to communicate. He began with the basics—*hello*, *good-bye*, *thank you*—before moving on to the most crucial aspect of learning a new language: the swear-words. Within hours she was calling Roderick a *shit-brained asshole* to his face while the satyr clapped appreciatively.

"What did you just say?" he asked.

"I said your hair looks nice."

"Really?"

"Sure."

He raked a self-conscious hand through his straw-coloured mop. Tam wondered how long it had been since the satyr had gone undisguised for days at a time, without a hat to hide his horns. "Thanks," he said.

On the morning of the third day she ventured into the Dragoneater's lair. It wasn't overly impressive. There were no heaps of glittering gold or chests overflowing with gemstones. There were plenty of bones, however, and lots of snow, as well as the occasional discarded weapon or scrap of rusted armour. She did stumble upon the hull of an old ship but couldn't discern whether it had plied the skies or the seas before it ended up here.

Shouldering her bow and grazing her fingers over the fletching of the arrows at her waist, Tam wandered out of the defile and onto the shelf of rock overlooking Mirrormere.

It was snowing lightly. The breeze off the lake went rifling through her clothes with freezing hands. The hole made by the Simurg was already glazed over by a pane of ice and blanketed by drifts of snow.

She found Rose standing alone on the bluff, her crimson cloak and wind-whipped hair stark against the endless white of the Wastes. Rose turned at the crunch of footsteps, clearly relieved to find Tam there and not Freecloud, who'd probably have ordered her back inside before she caught a chill. There was a halfpipe in her teeth and a spent match in her fingers.

Rose beckoned the bard with a tilt of her head. "Come stand here, would you?"

Tam shuffled over and put her back to the wind as Rose struck a second match. This close, she noticed for the first time that she was taller than the mercenary by at least an inch.

"Thanks." Rose blew a plume from one side of her mouth, then offered the pipe to Tam.

"I'm fine, thanks."

"I'll get a headache if I smoke it all," Rose said, though her grin suggested she might be lying. "C'mon," she urged. "All the cool kids are doing it."

Tam relented. She sucked down a lungful of smoke and coughed most of it back out before handing the pipe back to Rose.

"Not bad, right?"

"Not bad," Tam lied. Her mouth tasted like the ashes of a pissed-on fire.

Rose winked, took another puff, and squinted up at the sky. "They'll be here soon," she said, sounding considerably less enthusiastic than someone awaiting rescue from a wintry wasteland ought to have been. They'd contacted Rose's father immediately after finding the scrying orb. Even by skyship the journey north from Coverdale should have taken several days, since flying by night over mountains was potentially hazardous, so if their rescuers did arrive today it would mean they had flown day and night to reach them.

"Do you know who he sent?" she asked.

"Sent?" Rose coughed a cloud of smoke herself before passing the pipe to Tam. "My father didn't *send* anyone. He's coming himself. Him and Uncle Moog."

"Uncle Moog?"

"Arcandius Moog. The man who—"

"He cured the rot," Tam cut her off. "I know who he is."

"Then why ask?"

"I just—never mind." Tam decided to take a long drag of smoke instead of explaining that she'd been caught off guard. She was already thrilled by the prospect of meeting Golden Gabe face-to-face—and now she learned there were actually *two* members of Saga on their way? "The Kings of the Wyld," she murmured.

Rose rolled her eyes. "Gods, I'm sick of people calling them that. Kings of Sheer Dumb Luck is more like it. You wouldn't believe half the stories I've heard. It's a wonder they didn't die on their first tour of the Heartwyld, and a miracle they made it across the last time." She stole the pipe from the bard's hands. "Anyway, my father never killed a Simurg."

He might still get the chance, Tam thought, *thanks to us*. "So, what's next?" she asked, though the answer seemed obvious.

Rose tapped a clump of ash from the halfpipe's tip. "Nothing," she said. "We're done."

"What? What do you mean, *done*?"

"We killed the Dragoneater," Rose said. "This"—she waved a hand to indicate the lake below—"is the top of the mountain. As good as it gets. The Simurg was the biggest, baddest monster in the world, and we killed it. Not the Raincrows, or the so-called Kings of the Wyld. *Fable*." She drew on the pipe and breathed a stream of white smoke over one shoulder. "That's our story. And this is where it ends."

"What about the Brumal Horde?" Tam asked. "The Winter Queen?"

"The Winter Queen? You mean Astra, the Archon's wife?" Rose scoffed. "What about her?"

"She tricked us! She used you to kill the Simurg so she could take control of it. Freecloud thinks she's in league with the Brumal Horde."

"She might be," Rose admitted. "But the Brumal Horde's not our problem."

The wind picked up, tousling their hair and dragging at the bottom of Tam's longcoat. "What if Freecloud's right?" she pressed. "What if Astra and Brontide are working together? Do you expect people will thank us for what we've done? Will we be heroes, do you think? Or the fools who offered up the world on a silver platter?"

Rose took another drag and spent a moment examining the halfpipe's glowing tip. "It doesn't matter," she said eventually, though Tam could tell she was lying. "I made a promise, and I intend to keep it."

"A promise to Freecloud?"

"To myself," Rose said. She passed the pipe over and drew her hood against the chill. "I probably should have quit after Castia. I'd dragged my friends across the Heartwyld and got them killed. I would have died there if not for Cloud, and we'd *both* be dead if my dad hadn't arrived with every merc in Grandual at his back. But I couldn't quit. I didn't want to. I was raised on my father's stories, spoon-fed glory until I *hungered* for it—until I thought I'd starve without it."

Tam nodded. She, too, had been the daughter of a mercenary; they had that in common, if little else.

"Growing up," Rose continued, "I wanted more than anything to outshine my father, to be remembered as something other than *Gabriel's Girl*. But even after the cyclops, and *especially* after Castia, nothing changed. Instead, I'd become the catalyst for my father's greatest adventure. He was the hero, and I was his happily ever after. Just another damsel in distress," she said sourly. "I knew then that if I didn't do something *truly* remarkable, then that's how the world would remember me. If they remembered me at all. And then Wren came along."

For once Tam managed to exhale fumes instead of coughing them out. She said nothing, for fear of putting Rose off the topic of her daughter.

"I didn't want to be a mother," Rose confessed. "I wasn't at all ready, and if she was anyone but Cloud's . . . Well, there are teas . . . potions I could have swallowed . . . and *poof*—crisis averted." She was silent for a few seconds, gazing with her mind's eye down a path she might have taken. "But I could tell it was important to Freecloud. Children are a blessing to his kind. The sylfs, he says, are proof that our people and his need not be enemies. That we're capable of something better. Coexistence."

Tam raised an eyebrow. "A little late for that, isn't it?"

"Maybe," Rose admitted. "But anyway, a part of me hoped

that becoming a mother would change my mind. That having a kid would make me want to settle down. That it would be ... enough." She shook her head fractionally. "But it wasn't. If anything, it was worse. I—gods, this sounds awful—I actually *resented* my daughter, and Freecloud, because they needed me to be someone I wasn't. Because they *deserved* that, and I couldn't give it to them."

Tam blew another puff of smoke. She was getting the hang of this halfpipe, finally. "And now you can?" she asked.

"Now the Simurg is dead," Rose said. "Now I've done something my father can never do, and I'm ready to try again." A smile crept across her lips, thin and bright as the first glow of sunrise. "I was a hell of a mercenary, right? Maybe I'll make a decent mother, if it's not too late. I sure as hell can't be any worse at it than my old man."

Tam chuckled. "He was that bad?"

Before Rose could answer, a sound like crashing waves drifted down from above. Within moments, a skyship came plunging from the haze. It was the size of a fishing dhow, wreathed in streaming cloud, and though it was too distant still to read the name stamped on its hull, Tam knew the *Old Glory* the moment she saw it.

Rose reached over and plucked the halfpipe from Tam's gaping mouth. "He wasn't great," she said, stealing one last drag before flicking the ashen stub into the snow. "But he has his moments."

Chapter Thirty-eight

Old Glory

They bid farewell to their yethik hosts and were escorted by Farager's hunting party to the lip of ice overlooking Mirrormere.

"You're sure you want to stay?" Freecloud asked the ex-Raincrow before they parted.

"I'm sure," said Farager, signing his words as he spoke them. "There's nothing left for me south of the Shields. I've got no family left. My bandmates are all gone. But *this* lot . . ." Farager motioned to the warriors behind him. "They *get* me, you know? Besides, I'm going to be a father!"

"*What!?*" Freecloud's ears shot straight up.

"Are you kidding?" Roderick asked. "You're kidding, right?"

"Of course I'm kidding, ya dumb shits!" Farager cackled, and the yethiks at his back laughed hysterically. "See what I mean? I belong here." He waved, and his sackcloth arms flailed like a puppet drowning. "Good-bye and good luck!" he called out as they started across the ice. "Have fun fighting the Horde!"

A man whose resplendent robes marked him as either a wizard or a dreadfully eccentric librarian leapt up from the pilot's chair as Tam and the others climbed aboard Vanguard's old skyship. The bald crown of his head cracked against one of the clouded glass candle-jars suspended from the skyship's rigging.

"Snakes and bloody lions, who put that there?" He threw a glare at the offending jar. The old man's fringe of long hair was the same stark white as his beard, both of which shimmered like silk in the swaying candlelight as he sprang forward to greet Tam. "Welcome aboard!" he said, shaking her hand like a man trying to wrest his wedding ring from a snake's gullet. "I'm—"

"Arcandius Moog," she finished for him. "You were in Saga."

"I was!" The wizard beamed proudly.

"You cured the rot."

"True. Though a troll did most of the work."

"You burnt down the Riot House ..."

"That was purely by accident," the wizard insisted.

"... and killed Akatung the Dread."

"I only sent him through a portal to the bottom of the ocean, so *technically* the ocean killed him. Wait"—he frowned—"who are you and how do you know everything I've ever done?"

Gabriel, who she'd been introduced to when he first arrived, put a hand on her shoulder. Rose's father was everything she'd imagined he would be: charming and charismatic, attractive despite the silver streaking his fabled blond hair. "Moog, this is Tuck and Lily Hashford's girl."

"Ah!" The wizard's face brightened in recognition, then darkened at the memory of her mother's fate. "Ah." His sadness passed swiftly, vanishing into the wrinkles creasing his face. The wizard didn't seem the sort to dwell on sorrow for very long. "It's a pleasure to meet you ..."

"Tam."

"Tam!" He sized her up, frowning at her coat as though trying to remember which despotic druin warlord had been wearing it when he'd seen it last. "Gods of Goblinkind, you mercs are getting younger every year!"

"I'm just the bard," she told him.

"The bard? And you're still alive? Good for you!"

She was about to ask why he sounded so surprised when the wizard's gaze slipped past her. "Roderick, you irredeemable scamp! Get that flea-ridden arse of yours over here for a hug!"

Moog received each newcomer with the same relentless enthusiasm. He greeted Cura with a kiss on either cheek and a raised eyebrow for the new ink on her left arm. As Brune climbed over the rail he spread his hands. "The Big ol' Bear himself!"

The shaman's smile was pained. "The Wolf, now."

"Wolf?" The wizard studied him a moment. "I see it now, yes. It looks good on you, boy."

Brune straightened, smiling. "I think so, too."

"Uncle Moog!" Rose seemed happier to see the old wizard than her own father, who she'd met with a curt nod, a stiff embrace, and a muttered "Thank you" when he'd crossed the ice to meet her earlier.

"Rosie!" Moog threw his spindly arms around her. "And Freecloud! Tits on a treant, man, could you *be* any handsomer? No offence, Brune."

The shaman shrugged. "I'm used to it."

"And who is this sombre chap?" Moog asked of Daon Doshi. "You look like a baragoon ate your lunch!" Doshi offered a mumbled explanation of who he was and what "that idiot satyr" had done to his beloved skyship. "Doshi, is it?" The wizard looked surprised. "Any relation to—"

"Yes," said Doshi, without elaborating further.

Moog clapped his hands. "Excellent! Would you care to fly us home, then?"

The captain's face lit up like curtains on fire. "Really?"

"Of course! Frankly, I'm surprised I got us here in one piece! Got a little dicey coming over those mountains, eh Gabe?"

Gabriel's grimace suggested that *dicey* was something of an understatement.

"Your engine was probably freezing," Doshi pointed out. "You should have landed, smashed up the ice, and run it backward for a bit."

"See? Gabe? Didn't I say the engine was freezing?"

"You said *you* were freezing."

"I was! But we're in warmer hands now!" Moog slapped the worn leather headrest of the pilot's chair. "Take us to Coverdale, my good man! Assuming it's still there."

"Why wouldn't it be?" Tam asked.

Moog's mirth withered briefly. "Because the Horde was twenty miles north of it when we left."

Sometime later, when Rose had finished calling her father every foul word Tam had ever heard and many more she hadn't, they set out for Coverdale through a darkening sky.

The dhow's slanting sail, which was peaked like a tent above the flat-bottomed hull, flashed now and then as it raked static energy from the passing clouds. A single tidal engine whirred at the stern, wrapped in a halo of icy mist.

The *Old Glory*'s deck was furnished with time-worn sofas. Tam sat alone on one, Rose and Freecloud on another. Arcandius Moog lay stretched out on a third, fast asleep. Tam guessed the journey north had taxed the old man's endurance. There was a modest bar at the stern, behind which Brune was pouring and re-pouring drinks for Rod and Cura, who were seated on stools out front.

Gabriel was standing at the skyship's starboard rail, gazing out at the shadowed scarps of passing mountains. He and Moog had flown above the snowcapped peaks, but Doshi took them between.

"It's warmer in the canyons," the captain explained, "and we can use the wind at our backs to make up time. It took you three days to reach us?" He smirked, and Tam caught a glimpse of his old charm returning. "I'll have us back in two."

Gabe's sword, the legendary *Vellichor*, was slung sideways across his back. Even sheathed, Tam could feel a sense of pre-ternatural tranquility radiating from the Archon's ancient blade. Occasionally, as the cold night breeze swept over the deck, she could *smell* it—except it didn't smell like metal, or oil, or anything like a sword was supposed to. It smelled like lilacs and lush green grass, the fading scents of an unreclaimable spring.

In the end, Rose's anger was doused by two simple words: the name of the man with whom Gabe had left her daughter while he and the wizard raced north.

"Clay Cooper?" she said warily.

"She's at his place south of town," Gabe said. "And the Horde's been camped in Grey Vale for weeks."

"Camped?" Freecloud's ears twitched inquisitively.

"Waiting, it seems," piped Moog, who apparently wasn't sleeping after all. "Though it's anyone's guess what for. Brontide could be stomping through horse-turds in Cartea by now, but instead, the Carteans came to Coverdale. A few thousand of them arrived on the morning we left, and twice as many Agrians showed up the day before that."

"So many?" asked Brune, choosing a bottle of orange brandy from the cabinet beside him.

"It's not only them," Moog said, sitting up. "Half the mercs from Conthas to the Great Green Deep are in Coverdale by now. Every day Brontide tarries in Grey Vale he loses the advantage his numbers give him."

Since no one else dared to ask, Tam did. "How big is the Horde?"

Gabriel pushed himself from the rail. He slipped *Vellichor* off his back and set the blade at his feet as he sat down beside Tam. "The host that overran Cragmoor was no more than sixty thousand strong, but by the time it reached Cold-fire Pass there were thousands more."

"Everyone loves a winner," said Brune, using his teeth to pull the stopper from the brandy's neck.

Gabe looked grim. "After Coldfire it got even bigger. I'd guess Brontide has more than a hundred thousand with him by now."

"How did they make it through the pass?" Tam wondered out loud. "Didn't Saga hold it for three days against a thousand walking dead?"

That drew a smirk from Gabe. "You can't believe every story you hear, Tam."

"It was a thousand and one," said Moog with an exaggerated wink.

Cura waited until Brune splashed brandy into a copper mug before stealing it for herself. "I have a theory," she said, swirling her cup. "Most of these brand-new bands can't fight for shit. They wouldn't know an honest battle if it spat in their face. They prance around in face-paint and pretty armour, fighting basement-bred monsters that are either starved to death or drugged senseless. I mean, we've done our share of touring, sure, but most of these brats've never taken on a real contract, or stepped foot in the Heartwyld, or gone up against anything with a real chance of killing them."

Doshi steered around a looming rock outcropping. The candle-jars swayed and set their shadows dancing.

"I fear you're right," Gabe conceded. "Although half the bands who fought at Castia were just as green."

"Green as the god of orcs," said Moog.

"It may not be the mercenaries' fault," suggested Free-cloud, drawing eyes from all over the ship.

Rose, who was lying against him, craned her neck. "How do you mean?"

"The Heartwyld Horde was an army fuelled by hate,"

he said. "The Heathen promised them the chance to avenge themselves for the suffering they'd endured at the hands of the Republic. Lastleaf may have intended to establish an empire, but his Horde was out for blood."

Tam hadn't known the Heartwyld Horde had anything to avenge, or that monsters had suffered under the heel of Castia's Republic. There were no songs about that—not that she knew of, anyway.

"But the Brumal Horde is different," said Freecloud. "They're angry, yes, but they're desperate, too. Some will be survivors of Castia. Others will have fled from Grandual, forced to live on the margins of a world they once called their own. Brontide isn't offering vengeance—he's leading them in a fight against annihilation. If this Horde is destroyed, there may never be another one. Humans will hunt them to extinction— or take them captive, sell them off, and breed them for sport in the arenas." The druin looked pointedly at Gabriel. "The Horde, I believe, is fighting for its very existence. It's winning because it can't afford not to."

Tam spared a glance for Moog, who was sitting crosslegged on his couch. The wizard's expression was conflicted— hopeful but hurt, like a merchant who'd learned a bitter rival had come to ruin and was saddened to hear it.

Rose struck a match that guttered in the night breeze. "And you think Astra has something to do with this?" she asked Freecloud.

Moog's bushy brow's furrowed. "Astra? Why is that name familiar? Ah!" He tapped the shiny crown of his head. "Right! I had a cat named Astra. Spiteful creature! And *vicious*." He whistled. "I swear, it once killed a bird and left it on my doorstep in the morning."

Brune shrugged. "So what? Lots of cats—"

"It was an *eagle*," Moog finished.

The shaman nodded appreciatively and poured himself a drink.

Gabriel, meanwhile, had gone pale as birch skin. "You mean Vespian's wife? The Winter Queen?"

"The Winter Queen is a myth," said Rose. "You told me so yourself."

Her father shook his head. "Not a myth. A moniker. A made-up name for a very real and very dangerous woman, who..." He trailed off. Something unspoken passed between him and the wizard. "You've seen her, then? She's alive?"

"Alive is a relative term," Cura said.

Moog's knees cracked as he craned forward. "Where? When? What did she look like? Did she still have her, you know—" He wiggled two fingers above his head in mimicry of rabbit ears.

"We've seen her," Rose confirmed. "She...Well, it's a long story."

Gabe settled into his seat. "It's a long way home."

For a while no one spoke. The only sounds were the engine's sloshing whir, the creak of old boards, and the hum of hidden currents coursing through the sail's metal struts. It wasn't until Freecloud gently cleared his throat that Tam realized who it was they expected to tell the story.

"Oh," said Fable's bard. "Right."

Chapter Thirty-nine

Cold Clouds

By the time Tam finished recounting their journey with Hawkshaw, their brief stay at Ruangoth, their flight to Mirrormere, and, finally, their battle against the Simurg on the frozen lake, Gabe looked as though he might be sick.

"I just..." He rubbed despairingly at his face. "Why do I even bother rescuing you? Seriously? You fought the bloody *Dragoneater*? On purpose?" He glared at her from between splayed fingers. "You know I refused that gig, right?"

Rose shrugged, her pauldrons clanking.

"Not just because I thought the Warden was lying, or that his mistress was orc-shit crazy, but because if he *wasn't* lying, and she *wasn't* orc-shit crazy, then I'd be up against the *fucking Simurg*! It was a suicide mission!"

"Apparently not," said his daughter dryly.

Gabe's jaw clenched the way Rose's did when she was angry. "I heard about that stunt you pulled in Highpool, by the way. Taking on a whole tribe of orcs... fighting a marilith by yourself. Your uncle Moog and I crossed the Heartwyld to save you, remember? The *least* you could do to thank us is to not try to get yourself killed."

"How could I forget?" Rose's own anger flared like windblown embers. "Half the songs in the world paint me as a useless twit, waiting in Castia for her gallant father to come rescue her!"

"Is that what this was about?" Gabe asked, on the edge of his seat now. "Is that why you dragged your friends into the Brumal Wastes? Why you put their lives at risk? So you could get your name in a song?"

"She didn't drag us anywhere," Cura snarled.

"That's right." Brune's voice was gruff.

"We knew the stakes," said Freecloud. "We didn't follow her because she told us to."

"And why did *you* start a band, Dad?" Rose's smile was cool as a cadaver's feet. "Did you have some noble purpose in mind? Or were you just trying to fuck every farmer's daughter in Grandual?"

Moog snorted at that, but quickly masked his mirth behind a thoughtful frown.

Gabe didn't even blink. "I started a band because the centaur clans were stealing children who strayed too close to the forest. Because ghoul-spiders sucked the blood from our horses and left them hanging dead from the trees. Because, when I was sixteen years old, a wyvern swooped out of the night and flew off with a farmer's daughter I was madly in love with, while I cowered in the grass like a mouse." Gabriel straightened in his seat. "It took Clay and me two weeks to track that fucker down—but we did, and we killed it, and I can't say for sure if the bones I buried belonged to the girl I was looking for, but I wept over them just the same."

The skyship groaned as it climbed, passing through wisps of cold cloud. Lightning arced across the roofing sail, scoring Gabe's ire with a sizzling crack.

"Things were different back then," he went on. "The world was a dangerous place. The roads weren't safe. Monsters were *everywhere*, and if you heard something go bump in the night it probably meant that something was coming to kill you. But when was the last time a giant stormed through a city? Or a slag drake turned a whole forest to ash? Or the trees themselves came marching from the Heartwyld? Even the *rot* is nothing more than a nuisance nowadays, thanks to Moog."

The wizard wore a sheepish smile. "I only—" he started, but Gabriel went on raving.

"Yeah, we got famous along the way. And yeah, we enjoyed the hell out of it. But we didn't *crave* it. We got rich, too—but not by selling seats or splitting the overhead with some miserly wrangler. And you know what? You're right: I *did* fuck a lot of farmers' daughters."

"And blacksmiths' daughters," Moog added obligingly. "And innkeepers' daughters, jewellers' daughters, millers' daughters, stonemasons' daughters, stonemasons' wives, innkeepers' wives, grocer's wives—"

"Moog . . ."

"—that cobbler's mother, once—

"She gets it," Gabe told him.

"I got it," Rose agreed.

"But at some point," said her father, "things changed. We're not afraid to walk in the woods, or swim in a lake, or take shelter in a cave only to find out it's a dragon's lair. We toppled the giants, brought the ogres to their knees, burned the trolls and scattered their ashes to the wind. And now?" A laugh, bitter as black chocolate. "Now we're hunting down fairy tales, apparently."

"We are the ones going bump in the night," Freecloud murmured.

The cloud through which they passed seeped into Tam's skin and chilled her blood. She'd spent most of her life tormented by what monsters had done to her family. How many nights had she woken up screaming, sweating, sobbing for fear of some dread creature knocking down her door? It hadn't occurred to her that the "dread creatures" of the world might be doing the same.

She thought of the sinu murdered by Hawkshaw at the

temple in Diremarch, and the orcs Fable had slaughtered back in Highpool. She remembered them scrambling to escape the wrath of Rose and her bandmates, clawing at the stone walls, desperately trying to protect the weakest among them. She recalled the anguished wail of the cyclops set loose in the Ravine. Its flesh had been scarred by years of abuse, its spirit tortured by captivity into something hopelessly wicked.

Tam peered around the skyship's deck, seeing the same dawning awareness in the eyes of her companions. They'd have considered all this before, she was certain, but to hear it from the mouth of Golden Gabe—the most revered mercenary in all five courts—would lodge the truth of it like a dagger in their hearts. Roderick, hatless and horned, stared morosely into his lap.

"I wish you hadn't gone west," Gabriel told his daughter. "I wish, sometimes, that we hadn't saved Castia from the Heart-wyld Horde. We might have avoided this war altogether."

Rose said nothing. Her expression was a mask of cool restraint, but her eyes betrayed a hurt that Tam suspected her father alone was capable of inflicting. In a roundabout way, Gabriel was blaming *her* for the return of the Winter Queen and the emergence of the Brumal Horde, burdening Rose with the death of everyone who had lost their lives at Castia, and Cragmoor, and Coldfire Pass.

"We might have reasoned with Lastleaf," Gabriel said, helping himself to a share of the blame. "But instead we routed his army, shattered his dream of a new Dominion. We left him no choice but vengeance, and now..."

He left the rest unspoken, but the implication was clear to all.

Now, thought Tam, *his vengeance is upon us.*

Gabriel stirred, blinked, and wet his lips. "Which brings us back to Astra." He looked to Freecloud. "You think she's allied herself with the Brumal Horde?"

"I suspect so, yes," said Freecloud.

"Why?" Gabe wondered. "Lastleaf wanted to destroy the Republic and restore the Old Dominion. So what's his mother after?"

"You," said Tam. Her cheeks flushed under the sudden scrutiny of everyone on board. "At the lake...She said you killed her son."

The old hero shook his head. "I didn't, though—not really. I had my hand in it, sure, but so did everyone who resisted him at Castia, and every merc who fought alongside us."

"Lastleaf's own army deserted him in the end," Moog pointed out. "He took his own life in despair and was trampled in death by those he'd sworn to set free."

"So basically she has a reason to hate pretty much everybody," drawled Cura. "And now, thanks to us, she has a pet Dragoneater at her disposal."

"And probably an entire Horde," said Brune.

Tam shifted uncomfortably, wary of speaking again, but Gabriel turned to regard her. "Yes?" he asked.

"What if we didn't fight the Horde?" she proposed. "What if we made a deal with Brontide? We could find someplace for his army to settle, and maybe he would help us fight the Winter Queen?"

The idea sounded foolish the moment she'd said it, yet everyone—including Golden Gabe—looked as though they were giving it due consideration.

"I'm afraid it's too late for that," Moog said glumly. "It's a good plan, Tam. It really is. But there's too much blood between us and the, uh, them," he concluded, likely having stumbled over the word *monster*. "And besides, assuming Brontide and Astra are allies, it's likely they have a similar arrangement in place already."

"So we're back where we started," mused Brune. The shaman went to pour himself another brandy, but then nudged his glass aside and drank straight from the bottle. When he'd finished guzzling he wiped his mouth with the back of one hand.

"How do we go about fighting a rampaging Horde, a vengeful giant, a ruthless druin sorceress, and her undead Simurg?"

Rose looked from Brune to Cura, from Cura to Roderick, and from Roderick to Freecloud, nestled behind her. The druin nodded, tight-lipped, and took her hand in his own.

"*We* don't," she said, matching gazes with Gabriel, *daring* him to challenge her. "We're done."

By morning they were clear of the mountains, swooping over a dense pine forest that stretched out of sight in every direction. Brune and Tam stood together at the portside rail, gazing out over the sea of snowcapped trees. The sun was shining, the air winter-crisp, and the wind was...Well, the wind was bloody freezing, but the shaman's bulk was cutting most of it, so that helped a bit.

"The Hagswood," Brune announced, then pointed east. "Ardburg is just a few hundred miles that way. It's too bad we're in such a hurry, or we could ask them to drop us off."

Tam pulled a strand of wind-whipped hair from her eyes. "Will you go home after this?"

"I don't really know," he admitted. "My village has changed so much since I left. I have, too, I suppose. I'm not sure I belong there anymore. I wouldn't call it home."

"So where's home?" Tam asked.

The shaman spared a glance for his bandmates: Rose and Freecloud were asleep on one couch; Cura was out cold on another with a book splayed on her chest. "Here," he said. "With them."

Tam smiled. "They're your pack."

"Exactly." Brune grinned as well, gap-toothed and ruddy-cheeked behind the tangled curtain of his hair. "Pack, family, band—it's all the same to me. I don't know where I'd be without Fable," he mused. "Or what I'll be without them. I keep thinking about something Roderick said."

"That he could eat fifty socks without throwing up?"

"Oh, he'd throw up all right. He tried it once before, you know. Barely made it to forty—puked all over the place. But no. Back in Woodford, remember? You asked him if all ragas were monsters."

She *did* remember. "Only if they choose to be," she supplied.

The shaman nodded, scratching absently at a scar below his eye. "Only if they choose to be," he repeated. "But some of us—most of us, I think—don't have a choice. Not really. Rose didn't decide what the rest of the world named her. She didn't get to pick who her father was. None of us do. Rose was born to the sword, destined to be a mercenary the way a farmer's kid is destined to push a plough."

Tam thought of the farmer's daughter they'd met east of Highpool—the one who'd gone up against Rose with a rusty sword—and wondered if the girl would manage to change her fate.

And me? she wondered. *Did I escape Ardburg, or was I destined to be a bard, as my mother before me?*

"There's a reason my kind put so much stock in finding our *fain*," Brune went on. "When a shaman shams, they risk losing themself to the instincts of whatever it is they become, unless what they become is something so close to their nature it's like being in their own skin. And even then ... Well, you saw what happened in my village." He sighed, and blinked as though trying to shake the memory of a nightmare. "I spent most of my life trying to be something I'm not, thinking I was on the right path without knowing how lost I was—if that makes any sense. If it wasn't for Rose, and Cloud, and Cura, I'd probably be dead. Or worse: I'd be a monster, through and through."

The shaman put his back to the rail. He gazed at his sleeping bandmates with the open adoration of a father admiring his children. "I love them," he said, and then chuckled quietly. "Even Cura. I'd follow them anywhere. I'd fight until my last breath to keep them safe. And you, too. Tam. You're family now, like it or not."

Tam opened her mouth, decided she didn't trust herself to speak, and shut it. She gazed out over the endless expanse of forest instead, and so did Brune.

"Will you fight against the Horde?" she asked eventually. "Even if the rest of them don't?"

Brune shrugged. "I'm not sure it matters. I doubt one man will make a difference."

But one band could, Tam thought.

When Rose and Freecloud woke, Tam crashed on the couch they'd been occupying. She dreamt of Astra and the Brumal Horde, except in her dream the Winter Queen bore Rose's face and the Horde was nothing but yethiks. After that she was lost in a winter forest where the trees were blowing away like ash. In her dream she was running east, always east, as Hawkshaw dogged her heels. All at once he stepped out ahead of her, his crossbow levelled at her chest . . .

They veered west the next morning, skirting a range of mountains less daunting than the sort Tam had looked up to her entire life. Moog, who'd been glued to the rail since dawn, cried out suddenly. "There it is! Oddsford! Home to Grandual's greatest minds, and arguably the most beautiful city in all five courts!"

Tam was inclined to believe him, since her breath caught at the sight of it. From above, the city famed for its grand university resembled a maze of red-brick buildings and lush green parks, the trees of which were strung with lamps that twinkled blue and gold in the mist rolling off the slopes above. A tower so tall it rivalled the mountains reared over the city. Sparrows flocked at its crown. Crooked turrets branched from it like stunted arms, and Tam could have sworn the entire structure was leaning dangerously off-kilter.

"The Dreaming Spire," Moog said. "It's filled top to bottom with dusty old people and dusty old books." He cupped his hands and shouted at a woman watering plants on one of the tower's many balconies. "Oi, Helen! You old chewed boot!"

Helen—assuming the woman was who Moog thought she was—had barely looked up before the *Old Glory* blew past, trailed by its vapour stream and a cloud of bewildered sparrows.

By afternoon they were approaching Grey Vale, a hardwood forest nestled between encircling ranges. According to Gabriel, the Brumal Horde had been camped here for several weeks. The sky ahead was shadowed, piled with clouds so dark it seemed that night itself lingered over the valley.

A speck appeared before them, and soon materialised into a bird that was much larger than any bird ought to be, with slick black feathers and talons that could have torn a bull in half. A plague hawk, Tam guessed, noting the grey-green miasma steaming off it. It banked from the *Old Glory*'s path, beating north on poison wings.

"Is that a storm?" wondered Rose, peering westward.

If Daon Doshi had slept since being asked to pilot them home, Tam hadn't seen it happen. The captain stood and pulled his goggles down over his eyes. "Not a storm," he said. "It's smoke. The forest is burning."

Chapter Forty

Mercs in the Murk

Brontide was dead.

His body lay heaped like a hillock on the plain south of Grey Vale. Dead, too, were the trolls, the wargs, the firbolgs, and the wild orcs. Dead were the murlogs of the Western Wyld, the drakes of Wyrmloft, the fang spiders of Widow's Vale; dead were the spotted gnolls, the snaking basilisks, the lion-maned manticores, and every other fey and foul thing that had joined the giant's Horde. Bloodeater princes lay gutted amidst piles of pale-skinned thralls. Bone-hags sprawled under pestilent cloaks, their bony fingers still clutching their futile talismans. Whole clans of ogres were scattered in pieces around their fallen chieftains.

Dead. All of them, dead.

The Brumal Horde was defeated, vanquished, utterly destroyed. Corpses, both monster and mercenary, littered the earth to the very limit of Tam's sight. Smoke from the burning forest obscured most of the battlefield, and soon became so thick the band was forced to close their eyes and cover their mouths to avoid choking on the oily fumes.

Tam heard Gabriel swear under his breath. "Doshi," he growled, "take us down. We can't fly in this, and I'd like to know what the hell happened here."

Once they'd landed, Gabe and Moog went in search of answers. "Don't go far," Gabe warned them before he left. "Once this smoke clears we'll head for Slowhand's." He offered Rose a wan smile. "No need to keep Wren waiting longer than she already has."

Doshi and Roderick remained with the ship, while Tam shouldered her bow and set out after her bandmates, who picked a slow path through the carnage.

Woodsmoke prowled the battlefield. It stung her eyes and scoured her nostrils, but she much preferred it to the sword-metal tang of blood layered beneath. Sounds echoed from all around them: harsh laughter, snatches of song, dying groans, and the wailing cries of the mortally wounded. Somewhere near (or far—it was impossible to tell), a man was calling out in search of missing comrades.

There were mercenaries roaming the murk. Some were alone, gibbering quietly to themselves or their gods, but most were celebrating. They staggered among the littered corpses, pointing out goblins they'd hacked to pieces, urskin they'd slain, kobolds they'd bashed brainless with their shields.

A column of Agrian regulars with long spears and square shields tramped past, followed shortly after by a file of whooping Carteans on sturdy steppe ponies. Their leader, a man with raven's wings tattooed across his chest, dragged a shackled saurian on a chain leash behind him.

The battlefield was already swarming with those who preyed on the dead. Alchemists came to harvest organs, priests to gather souls. Thieves crept from corpse to corpse, rifling pockets and looting weapons, cloaks, belts, boots, and anything else they could pawn back in town. Claw-brokers, on the other hand, sought prizes of a different sort. They sawed at horns, snapped off claws, pried away scales, and claimed every exotic pelt they could find.

The scale-merchants had arrived as well. Tam saw trains of captive monsters being led through the smoke. Any creature fortunate enough to survive the day would be taken south to Conthas and sold off to wranglers in search of arena fodder.

And, of course, there were crows. Everywhere Tam looked were bloodied beaks and glassy eyes, black feathers mired in pooling blood. Her uncle had once likened the battlefield scavengers to distant relatives showing up at a funeral: *There'll be more of 'em than you can count*, he'd told her. *Nothing draws a crowd like a free lunch.*

And what a feast, Tam thought, picking up the pace so as not to lose the others in the gloom. She nearly tripped over a hydrake's severed neck. The beast was surrounded by scores of dead warriors, their bodies scarred by the thing's corrosive bile. Three of its seven heads had been cut off, while a fourth hissed fitfully, not quite ready to believe it was doomed.

Rose led them through a forest of felled treants whose limbs were scattered like brush after an autumn storm, then over the strewn rubble of shattered gargoyles. Harpies and mangled wolfbats lay where they'd fallen from the sky above. A rot sylph was moaning in the mud; the venomous sack of her abdomen had burst and was oozing noxious fumes.

"This way," Rose said, steering them clear.

The band found themselves meandering through a herd of slaughtered centaurs. In their midst lay the bodies of trampled mercenaries, and Tam gasped when she recognized the Halfhelm twins, Milly and Lilly, among the dead.

What if Bran is here somewhere?

The thought terrified her so much that she resolved not to glance at the pale-faced corpses any longer, lest she find her dear, dead uncle gazing back at her.

What looked like a hump of foothills up ahead resolved into the mountainous body of the giant, Brontide. The ruddy bronze flesh of his arms and legs was scored by hundreds of stabs, slashes, and bleeding cuts. Even still, the champion of the Brumal Horde wasn't quite dead yet. He groaned piteously and clawed at the blood-soaked earth by his sides. His

weapon—a ram's-headed maul the size of a toppled tower—
had fallen beyond his reach.

This battle, Tam concluded, would have been a sight
to behold—as epic in scale as the one in Endland six years
earlier—but she was not so foolish as to wish she'd been here
to see it. Bard or not, she'd have been hard-pressed to find the
grandeur in this, to siphon a few scant nuggets of glory from
the blood-soaked mire of such wasteful devastation.

"Bloody Friggin Rose, is that you?"

A man detached himself from a gaggle of mercs standing
around the corpse of a brumal mammoth. As he drew near,
Tam recognized Sam "the Slayer" Roth from the road to Highpool. The man's plate armour was scuffed and dented, stained
across the chest by something green. The bottom half of his
beard had melted away, and he was limping, using his fabled
greatsword as a crutch.

"Sam Roth." Rose halted, dragging fingers through the
scarlet tangle of her hair. "Still breathing, I see?"

"Ha! Just barely!" The big merc rapped an iron-shod fist
on his breastplate. "A blightbulb threw up on me! Would've
turned me to slop if I hadn't been wearing this. I'm sorry to
say my horse didn't fare so well, the poor wretch."

Poor wretch is right, thought Tam, recalling how the animal had struggled so mightily beneath Roth's considerable
bulk. *Imagine carrying this fat fuck all the way here just to get
puked on by whatever the heck a blightbulb is...*

"What happened here?" asked Freecloud.

Roth frowned. "You don't know?"

"We just got here," Rose said.

"Just got here?" The man's bushy eyebrows nearly leapt
from his face in disbelief. "Gods of Grandual, woman, you've
missed the greatest battle since the Reclamation Wars! A bloody
massacre is what happened here!" The Slayer spread his arms
to encompass the ruin surrounding them. "It was beautiful!"

"Did you see the Simurg?" asked Freecloud.

"The Simurg? Frosted fucking hells, are you still on about that?"

"We killed it," Rose said. Her tone was matter-of-fact, without the barest hint of conceit. "And the Widow of Ruangoth brought it back from the dead."

Roth looked skeptical, like a man who'd been told drinking a goblet of urine was the secret to eternal life. "I ... er—didn't see the Simurg, no," he muttered eventually. "Too busy running down real monsters, I guess."

"It looks like you slaughtered them," Brune said.

"We did!" said the Slayer. "The forest caught fire. Not sure how, or who got it started, but I'll buy 'em a keg of Kaskar's finest if I ever find out! The whole of Grey Vale went up in flames just before dawn. The Carteans had scouts in the hills thereabouts, but the Han claims it wasn't his boys who started it. By sunrise half the Horde was running wild on the plain, while the other half were busy finding their way clear of the trees. When they did, the buggers were burnt up and half-dead already! There was infighting, some said. Monsters killing monsters ..." The merc fingered the frayed edge of his acid-eaten beard. "As I said: It was beautiful."

Behind him, one of the mercenaries used an axe to hack off one of the mammoth's tusks.

"How bout a druin?" Rose asked. "Did you see a druin?"

The Slayer's eyes flickered to Freecloud's ears. "Nope. Though there was an Infernal!"

"Seriously?" asked Cura. "What did it look like?"

Roth drew himself up, as if impersonating the demon itself. "Big flaming bastard with spikes all over and a tail like a morningstar fixed to a chain. Fought with a burning net and a hammer made of molten rock. I figure the fucker killed half a hundred mercs before Ironclad brought him down."

"Ironclad?" Relief and disbelief laid claim to the divided halves of Tam's heart. Her uncle was alive! Or *had* been, anyway. "Did Bran Hashford survive, do you know?"

The man's armour clanked when he shrugged. "Didn't see, I'm afraid. But Branigan's a tough old bugger—I'd wager he's around here somewhere. Listen." He clapped Rose on the shoulder. "I could swap tales till I'm blue in the face, but we'd best leave a few for the bards, eh? We're bound for Coverdale and a cold pint, then on toward Conthas in the morning. I'll see you 'round?"

"See you 'round," said Rose, though her reply was drowned out by a sudden outburst of Brontide's whimpering.

"Maiden's Mercy!" shouted Roth as he limped back toward his men. "Would someone put that whining shit out of his misery?"

Rose squinted through the ash-flecked breeze at the injured behemoth. "We've seen enough," she snapped. "Let's get back."

The rest of them followed. Tam spotted the remains of a massive golem. The stone construct had been reduced to a pile of rubble. Freecloud paused to kneel by its head, reaching out to graze fingers over the weathered rock. The sigils carved into the pits of its eyes were dark and lifeless.

"Is it one of Contha's?" asked Cura.

"It used to be," said the druin. "But it was runebroken. Masterless. No longer under my father's control." He said nothing more, only stood and hurried off after Rose.

The band picked their way through the wreckage of a crashed skyship. Its mangled sail snapped and sparked, while the duramantium rings of its tidal engine spun in lazy circles, humming and sloshing; another broken thing with an aching song to sing.

Soon after, they came across a woman kneeling in the sludge. She was sobbing over a corpse wearing a veiled purple cowl. Tam immediately recognized the Prince of Ut, who had refused to take on the marilith after Fable's fight in Highpool.

Rose came to a halt, lowering her head in deference. The warrior's gold crown was askew, his famous green steel falchion resting in the mud near his hand. His chest armour was caved in, a crimson footprint left behind on the enamelled gold plate.

A dozen other mercs were dead nearby. Tam recognized Lucky Star among them, and the body of a creature that looked a bit like an owl but mostly like a bear lay in their midst, wheezing quietly through a chipped beak.

Tam returned her gaze to the fallen Prince. Here was one of Grandual's most celebrated mercenaries, now dead and cold in gathering dusk. Just a few miles south, his peers would be toasting their victory in taverns or around crackling bonfires. Would they remember him tonight? Would the bards sing of how nobly he'd fought? How grandly he'd died? Or would his death be nothing more than a sombre note in a thousand glorious songs?

At least he has someone to mourn him, she thought, glancing briefly at the woman weeping over him.

The others had begun trickling away when something tickled Tam's awareness. "Not weeping," she murmured.

Brune looked over his shoulder. "What's that?"

"She's laughing." Tam pointed at the woman on her knees in the muck, who was just now rising, and turning, and grinning with the hollow humour of a leering skull.

"Hello, Rose," said the Winter Queen.

Chapter Forty-one

Black Magic Woman

Tam hadn't even blinked before Rose had *Thistle* from its sheath and flung it, spinning, at the woman's head. Astra moved even before Rose let go of the blade, stepping casually from its path.

"Don't bother," said Freecloud, before Rose could try again with *Thorn*. "She's a druin. Or she was, once. You won't hit her if she knows it's coming."

Rose glared sullenly. She lowered her weapon, but Tam had no doubt she'd try again if her adversary was fool enough to let her guard down.

Astra was dressed more regally than she'd been at the lake, prompting Tam to wonder where an undead sorceress stopped off for a change of clothes. A Narmeeri crypt, by the look of it, since her body was bound in black cloth stitched with arcane red script. Strips of black silk draped from scalloped pauldrons on either shoulder, stirring languidly on the fetid breeze. Her jet hair climbed through a wrought-metal crown whose tines twisted like flames above her brow, and her pale ears hung limp to her shoulders. At the druin's hip was a long blade in a lacquered black scabbard that looked like the evil twin of Freecloud's *Madrigal*.

Her eyes were the bruised violet of grapes gone sour, and fixed solely on Rose. "You should be dead," she remarked.

"Says the woman who spent the last thousand years in a tomb," Rose drawled. She cast a cautious glance into the gloom around them. "Where's your pet?"

"You mean Hawkshaw? I sent him on an errand. Oh," she said breezily, when Rose's expression soured, "you mean *this* pet."

A flick of her wrist summoned a gale that slashed through the curtain of smoke and ash. Golden twilight flooded the plain, gleaming on blood-slick scales and glinting along the edges of shattered arms. But then a shadow blotted out the sky, and the Dragoneater touched down like a cyclone, dead feathers raining from its wings.

Tam stood rooted by its white-fire gaze, helpless to do anything but wait to be devoured, but then a moan from Brontide drew the Simurg's attention. It skulked over for a closer look, dragging its dusky plumage like chains in its wake. Every step it took caused a tremor beneath Tam's boots.

When Brontide caught sight of the Simurg, he froze. His hands—so huge they could have slapped castles to rubble—began trembling, and he drew a rasping breath.

"Please," he managed, before the Simurg's lion-lizard jaws closed around his throat. Tam heard the wet crunch of cartilage breaking, saw blood foam between the monster's teeth, then looked away as it pulled Brontide's throat apart in grisly strands.

Someone, somewhere, was yelling. Many someones, actually. Through the haze of falling ash, Tam saw mercenaries running for their lives toward Coverdale.

As if Coverdale is far enough, she thought morosely. *As if anywhere is*.

Astra's voice brought her back to the battlefield. "They still get hungry, you know. The dead, I mean. I have no idea why."

"What do you mean *they*?" asked Cura. "You were dead as a boiled egg until six years ago, remember?"

The druin's head tilted a fraction. "No, I do not remember being dead. I was murdered by slaves as the Dominion burned around me, and I woke to find the ancestors of those slaves floundering in the empire's ashes. My *husband*"—she spoke the word with disgust—"who'd promised that he and I would live as gods forever, was dead."

"He had it coming," Rose said in an obvious effort to goad her. According to Tiamax, Golden Gabe was famous for doing the same to his enemies—which was probably why he had a reputation as an arrogant asshole.

"I agree," said Astra. "Although Vespian, not unlike my more recent husband, had his uses. I did love him, once."

"Before he sacrificed your daughter?" Rose asked ruthlessly. "Before he robbed you of the death you so obviously craved? Before he committed genocide against his own kind to keep that awful sword a secret?"

Astra flinched, and when she did some spell of glamour faded for just an instant, showing Tam a glimpse of the Winter Queen's *true* face: withered eyes and sickly flesh that peeled like birch bark from a yellowing skull.

"The Archon was a fool," hissed the druin. "He summoned a power beyond his comprehension. *Tamarat* isn't merely a sword. It's a *sliver*. A living fragment of the Goddess herself. And he *bound it to me*. Fed me to her like tinder to the flame. I did not ask—"

Rose threw her other sword.

This time, Astra moved a fraction too late. But she *did* move, so the blade only scored the side of her head instead of slicing it into halves. She hissed in pain, and one of her white-furred ears landed in the mud near her feet.

Though she tried to stifle it, an incongruous giggle slipped past Tam's lips. Cura shot a dark look her way, while Freecloud winced (out of empathy, perhaps) and looked to Rose.

"Nice try," he said.

She grimaced. "Not nice enough."

Astra seemed not to have noticed her missing ear, but was outraged nonetheless. Her hands spasmed into claws at her side. She dragged them up—slowly, as if through water—and the corpses around her lurched to life.

Up came the Prince of Ut in his wine-dark cowl. Up came Lucky Star, wielding half a spear in one hand and half a shield in the other. A shirtless northerner with a blue stripe across his eyes staggered upright, and a red-haired woman bearing a spiked flail but missing most of her jaw stood next to him.

Cura drew a pair of wicked knives. Brune gripped his twinglaive with both hands. "How is she doing this?" he asked.

"Necromancy," said Freecloud.

"You don't say?" Brune snapped. He waved a hand at the woman's new bodyguards. "I meant how's she doing *this*. Most necros can barely make a skeleton dance. The best can turn a crowd of corpses into mindless zombies. They don't use people like puppets, and don't bring something the size of a fucking *village* back from the dead!"

"It must have something to do with the Goddess," Freecloud guessed.

"You mean the Winter Queen?" asked Cura.

The druin's ears signalled *no*, but he said nothing more.

"Were you leading the Horde, then?" Rose asked the sorceress. "If so, you did a piss-poor job of it."

Astra shook her head, a gesture made somewhat ridiculous by the bobbing stump of her absent ear. "I was more of a patron, really. I offered Brontide a safe haven in which to gather his strength. Once he had, I urged him to attack Cragmoor. I assured him of victory, and promised eternal life to those who fell in battle."

"There is no life," said Freecloud, "without free will."

For some reason, Tam's thoughts strayed to the golem they'd come across earlier. *Runebroken*, Freecloud had called it. *Masterless*. Did that mean every other golem was a slave, with no more agency than one of Astra's undead thralls?

"I don't understand," said Rose to the Winter Queen. "If you wanted the Horde to succeed, then why abandon them here? You had to know the courts would get their shit together eventually. Was the Simurg so important? You bartered one life in exchange for tens of thousands. You *doomed* them."

Astra sneered. "What do I care? They were beasts. Monsters. Born to be slaves and bred to be weapons. Yet they rebelled against the Dominion, and betrayed my son when—"

"Oh, fuck off," Rose swore.

"—when they abandoned him on the field at Castia." Astra's right hand strayed toward the hilt of her sword. Her voice was thick as ice over shallow water. A poison-black tear crawled like a fly down her porcelain cheek. "My poor child," she whispered. "My sweet autumn son. He was trying to help them, you know. He meant to offer them sanctuary—a realm where the fell creatures of this world could live beyond the depredations of humankind—and he'd have succeeded if not for one man."

Rose stiffened. "Don't you dare say it."

"Gabriel."

"What the *fuck* did I just tell you?" Rose snarled.

"Then again," Astra reasoned, "Gabriel would never have gone to Castia if it weren't for you. Which is why it will please me to kill you here, to know your father will share my pain— if only until I kill him as well."

"You'll need more than the Dragoneater to do that," Rose said, though even Tam could sense the insincerity in her words. Gabe might have been formidable once, but he was older now, and wasn't what he used to be. He wasn't even what he'd been at Castia, which (according to Rose) wasn't very much at all. "You had a whole army at your disposal," Rose said, gesturing at the corpse-littered plain around them. "Why let them die?"

Astra's laugh was eerily grating, a sound like a raven's beak scratching on a child's skull. "Let them die? My dear, I *killed them myself.*"

Brune, blinking, dragged a hand over his mouth. "This is..."

"Mad," Cura finished the thought for him.

"Mad," the shaman agreed.

"They would have failed me," said Astra, "as they failed the Dominion. They would have betrayed me, as they betrayed my son. Instead, they will serve me in death. As will you. And so, in time, will every creature in this world."

"Well that's ... typical," Rose said. She looked thoroughly unimpressed—or else was doing a magnificent job of pretending to be. "And then what? What's the point? Let's suppose you win—which you won't. Let's say you somehow manage to kill us all—which will never, ever happen, I assure you. Are you so desperate to rule the world that you don't care if your subjects are dead?"

"You mistake me," said Astra. "I have no intention of *ruling* the world. I am going to *end* it."

It felt to Tam as if the ash in the air had become a swarm of buzzing insects, scrabbling against her skin, burrowing into her flesh. Her blood was cold as ice. A frantic, animal fear curled its claws around her heart, and *squeezed*.

Freecloud spoke, obviously shaken: "You will bind every life to yours ..."

"And then free myself"—Astra sighed—"from this immortal coil."

Tam couldn't believe what she was hearing. *She's not that powerful. She can't be.* So far as Tam knew, all magic—from Cura's summoning to Brune's shamming—came at a cost. Power *always* had a price, and she imagined necromancy was no different.

But what if Astra had already paid that price? Or what if the purse belonged to someone ... or *something* else entirely?

A word wriggled in her mind like a maggot: *Tamarat*.

Despite her rising panic, Tam was about to reach for an arrow and try (however futile the attempt might be) to kill this mad, sad woman before she could make good on that terrible promise.

But then Rose pointed toward the woman's feet. "You dropped your ear," she said.

And Astra—who'd been an empress, then a goddess, and whose dark sorcery now threatened to snuff out every soul in Grandual—looked down.

Like an idiot.

Chapter Forty-two

The White-Feather Bolt

Rose lunged at the Winter Queen, arms outflung, summoning her swords to hand. They came spiralling from the muck—except Lucky Star knocked one aside with her shield, and the blue-striped mercenary stepped fearlessly in front of the other. Unexpectedly weaponless, Rose managed to stop short as the jawless woman swiped her spiked flail in an arc before her. The Prince of Ut darted forward, falchion in hand. Rose stumbled backward, twisting to get away.

Madrigal sang from its scabbard, carving smoke into shreds as it deflected the Narmeeri blade. Freecloud kicked the Prince in the chest and launched him backward.

Brune stepped up to cover Rose's retreat. He wrenched *Ktulu* into halves, using one to foul the flail's next strike and plunging the other through Half-jaw's neck, effectively severing her head.

Tam moved without thinking. She shrugged *Duchess* free, tore an arrow from her quiver, and—

Astra drew her sword, and the sound it made—the piercing shriek of a madwoman howling beneath a torturer's knife—startled Tam into fumbling her arrow. The druin plunged the sword's point into the ground, and the bard could see...*something*...in the lurid green surface of the blade:

hands scrabbling, a face twisted in anguish—but then Astra's voice steamed from the earth all around them.

"*Rise*," she commanded the corpses at their feet.

And they did.

All of them did.

Things that had been men and women; things that had been orcs, and urskin, and steel-masked gibberlings; things that wore the grey flesh of ogres, the long manes of ixil, the mangy fur of savage gnolls—everywhere Tam looked monsters and mercenaries were clambering to their feet, limbs askew, wounds weeping, crow-pecked eyes burning white.

The air thrummed with the flap of beating wings as the birds feasting on the dead took flight, a cloud as black as the smoke itself.

"We need to run," warned Cura.

"I have to kill her," Rose growled, gauntlets blazing. *Thistle* slammed into her open palm, but *Thorn* was hilt-deep in the blue-striped northerner. He was gripping the weapon with both hands, pitting his own strength against whatever ancient druin magic imbued the blade—which proved unwise, since ancient druin magic dragged his dead ass several feet through the air, put *Thorn*'s hilt into Rose's hand, and left him at her mercy.

And so, mercifully, she cut his head off.

Rose hefted her scimitars. "If we kill her—"

"We can't," Cura shouted. "We'll never reach her."

Already the Winter Queen was screened behind dozens of shambling thralls. The Simurg raised its gore-smeared maw as the giant beneath it began to stir.

"I hate to say it," Brune hollered, "but Cura's right."

Rose threw a pleading glance at Freecloud, who'd just hacked not-so-Lucky Star into several gory pieces. The druin looked from Rose to where Astra stood hidden behind a wall of walking dead. "We should go. Now."

Rose cast a despairing glance behind her before closing

ranks with her bandmates. "Brune and Freecloud have our flanks," she yelled, leading them away at a jog. "I'll take point. Tam, put an arrow in whatever comes at us from above."

"Will do," Tam said, without bothering to point out that she was only the bard.

"Cura?"

"Yo."

"Think you can you keep them off our ass?"

"With pleasure." Cura spun on her heel. The Prince of Ut had recovered and was leading a small host of mercs and monsters after them. The Inkwitch pushed up her sleeve, clenched her fist, and shouted, "*YOMINA!*"

The cloaked figure came swirling from her arm, long neck bowed beneath his wide-brimmed hat. He drew two swords from his chest and turned to face their pursuers.

Cura stood and staggered after Tam, who kept her bow taut and her eyes up as they ran. The sky was deafening with the screech of birds, dark with roiling smoke, though she caught a glimpse here and there of twilight blue. Cinders from the burning forest blew past, stinging like mites wherever they touched. From somewhere—from *everywhere*—came the keening wail of Astra's phantom sword.

Something resolved from the murk before them: large and lanky, with six arms, two jutting horns, and a mouth full of squirming tentacles. Rose's swords were spinning in her hands; she reversed her grip and leapt without slowing, plunging both blades to the hilt in its chest and tumbling over its falling corpse. One of its squirming tongues reached for Tam's ankle as she passed. She stamped down hard and it burst like a worm beneath her boot.

On they ran. Brune, wielding one half of *Ktulu* in either hand, smashed his way through a pair of grasping skeletons. *Madrigal* hummed like a harp-string as Freecloud cut the legs from a warg with an axe wedged into its head. Rose fought like a berserker up front, her blades a blur of blue and green as she dismembered a pair of spear-wielding lizardmen.

All around them was chaos. Living mercenaries grappled with dead mercenaries, claw-brokers ran for their lives, corpse-pickers became corpses themselves as their prey lurched awake beneath them.

Tam could feel the ground quaking, and a hurried glance over one shoulder confirmed the worst of her fears: The Simurg was on the prowl. It slunk across the smoke-screened battlefield like a hunting cat, devouring the Winter Queen's enemies wherever it found them.

Now and again Tam caught sight of *Yomina* stalking through the gloom nearby, hewing and hacking through clots of Astra's thralls.

Cura plucked at her sleeve. "Tam! Heads-up!"

The bard aimed her bow at the sky and found a harpy bearing down on them. The bird-woman's body was riddled with arrows, so Tam tried putting one through her face instead. That did the trick; she dropped like a stone and landed in a heap behind them.

"Good girl," said Cura, and something in Tam's belly blazed like a windblown ember at the summoner's praise.

Before long they had outrun the rising dead. Tam didn't know if there were limits to Astra's power, but apparently she wasn't capable of raising the entire Horde at once. *Or else we'd be dead*, she thought. *Well, maybe not dead . . . but definitely not alive.*

Rose stopped so suddenly the rest of them nearly bowled her over. "Fuck," she swore.

Brune swiped hair from his eyes. "Fuck what?"

"Fuck me," Cura hissed.

Gabe and Moog were just ahead. The wizard was tending to Roderick, who was using a white silk scarf to stanch a wound on his head. One of his curling horns had snapped off in the middle.

And the *Old Glory* was gone.

"Doshi stole our ship," said Gabriel.

"The salt-spawned shit-eater kicked me overboard!" Rod exclaimed. "I'll kill him! I'll wring his thieving neck!"

Brune pointed at the booker's head. "You're down a horn there, brother."

"What?" Roderick fumbled at his missing horn and his jaw dropped almost to his knees. "Vail's Bloody Cock, I am!"

Freecloud went to kneel beside Roderick, while Gabriel rushed to his daughter's side, scanning her for any sign of injury. "Rose, are you—"

"I'm fine," she said.

"What's happening here?" Gabriel asked her. "Did you find Astra?"

"We did," Rose told him. "I'll explain later. We need to get out of here *right now*."

Gabriel chewed his lip. He glanced worriedly at Moog, who was panting heavily, clearly exhausted. "Clay's place is halfway to Conthas. We should try—" He broke off suddenly as something split the air between him and Rose.

Tam turned, aghast, to see Hawkshaw striding toward them. The smoke fled his approach like shadows from a burning brand. The Warden tripped the firing mechanism on his crossbow and levelled it once again at Rose.

The sound of that bolt releasing was the loudest thing Tam had ever heard. Every one of Rose's bandmates moved to put themselves in its path, though none of them—not even Freecloud—was near enough to do so.

Only Gabriel was, and a heartbeat later he sagged to the mud with a white-feathered bolt buried to the fletching in his chest. His daughter went to her knees beside him, her swords falling from senseless hands.

Freecloud was on his feet, sprinting toward Hawkshaw. *Madrigal*'s music split the air behind him.

The Warden pushed aside his black straw cape. He drew the crude bone sword from the loop at his waist and gripped it with both hands as the druin came on. "I'm...sorry," he croaked. "I can't..."

"Shut up and die," Cloud snarled.

So charged was the moment, so fraught with dread and dire malice, that no one (not Freecloud, and certainly not Hawkshaw) saw the claw-broker's wagon come barrelling into their midst until it ran the Warden down. His body tumbled like a scarecrow beneath the threshing hooves and heavy wooden wheels.

The cart skidded to a halt and its driver stood to survey the ruin he'd left behind. Hawkshaw's body was reduced to a sodden heap of broken bones, bloodied flesh, and blackened straw. His bone sword was snapped in half. The black leather snowmask he'd worn to disguise his face had peeled off to reveal the blood-slick skull beneath.

The driver was horrified. "Gods, I'm so sorry! There's something...I don't know...something *big* back there. I wasn't looking where I was going."

Tam blinked. "Bran?"

The man stared at her blankly.

Can it be? she wondered. His hair was longer, his beard unkempt, and his face so filthy as to be almost unrecognizable, but Tam was sure of it now. It was her uncle Branigan. He was *alive*.

"Listen," he said, "if I owe you money we can discuss it later. We don't—"

"Uncle Bran, it's me."

"Tam?" Her uncle leapt from his perch, floundered through the mud, and pulled Tam into a hug that left her gasping for breath. Afterward, he gripped her shoulders and studied her face as though it were a map of everything she'd seen and done since he'd seen her last. A slow smile crept across his lips. "Maiden's Mercy, girl, what are you doing here?" His eyes flitted toward the mess he'd made of Hawkshaw. "Was he . . . ?"

"Our enemy," Tam assured him. "I'll tell you later. Gabe is—"

"Alive!" Moog shouted. The wizard was cradling Gabriel's head on his knees. "Well, he's breathing, anyway."

Branigan groaned when he recognized the man in Moog's lap. "Is that really . . . ?"

"It is, yeah."

Rose reached with trembling fingers to brush sweat-matted hair from her father's face. His eyelids fluttered weakly at her touch. "Can you help him?" she asked Moog.

Tears flooded the old man's eyes. "I'm not a healer, dear. And I fear he needs one." The wizard eyed the bolt in Gabriel's chest as though it were a serpent rising from his stewpot. "I think it may have pierced his heart."

"The heart is on this side," Rose pointed out.

"Is it?" The wizard frowned and placed a hand on his own breast. "Gods, you might be right."

Freecloud spoke up. "Rose—"

"Help me get him in the cart," she ordered.

"Rose." The druin put a hand on her shoulder and nodded gravely at the white-feathered bolt. "Look at the wound. It's putrid, already. I think . . ."

"What?" she asked.

"I think the arrow was poisoned," he said quietly. "I'm sorry."

Anger chased the hope from Rose's eyes, followed by a sorrow that threatened to crumple her face like parchment fed to a flame. "We'll take him to Coverdale," she mumbled.

Freecloud pushed his hair between his ears. "Coverdale isn't safe," he said, gazing north across the plain.

Grey Vale was still burning. The forest was an orange smear on the horizon, a glowing band against which the shape of uncountable horrors could be seen shambling across the darkening plain.

Bran coughed. "Conthas is too far..."

Gabriel stirred in Moog's arms, muttering words Tam couldn't make out. The wizard leaned in, listening, but it was Rose who deciphered her father's words.

"We're taking him to Clay Cooper," she said.

Chapter Forty-three

Slowhand

They bypassed Coverdale, which was swarming like a hive on fire as the townsfolk rushed to evacuate, and followed the rutted track that passed for a road through a forest of stark white birch. There were no stars, no moon by which to see, and so Branigan could only trust the horses to remain on course. No one slept; there wasn't room to do so anyway. Rose hovered over her father and mopped sweat from his brow while Moog offered soothing words, snatches of quiet song, and an hour-long joke that turned out not to have a punch line.

Gabriel died at dawn the next morning.

He didn't shudder, or scream, or utter any poignant last words, the way heroes were supposed to do. He only closed his eyes and squeezed his daughter's hand as hard as his fading strength allowed, until, at last, his grip went slack and he released a breath without bothering to take another.

"Stop"—the word fell like a stone from Rose's mouth. When Bran drew the cart to a halt she hopped over the side and disappeared into trees beside the road.

It was snowing lightly. Tam craned her neck and squinted against the skirling flakes. One caught in her eyelash, and when she blinked it stuck to her cheek, melting swiftly, and trickled to her chin.

Brune looked down at the body with puzzlement, as though he'd closed his fist on a gold coin and opened it to find a lump of coal. Cura clamped a hand over her mouth and stared blankly at the man stretched out at her knees. Freecloud, his ears sagging, watched the forest beside the road with eyes the colour of dull iron.

Moog slumped down beside Gabriel's body. He took his friend's head in withered hands and kissed him lightly on the forehead. "You bastard," he slurred through a rising sob. "You brave, stupid, beautiful bastard. How could you? How could you go on without us?" The wizard laid his cheek on Gabe's chest and sobbed until his tears dried up, then he straightened, sniffed, and choked on a phlegmy chuckle. "Clay's gonna kill you when he finds out. He won't—"

In the forest, a woman screamed. Not in fright, but in fury—a rage so powerful and painfully violent Tam wondered that the trees themselves didn't splinter at the sound of it. Freecloud started like a hound beckoned to its master's side, but Branigan clasped his shoulder and shook his head.

Freecloud settled onto his seat, and minutes later Rose emerged from the woods, climbed into the wagon, and ordered Bran to go on.

And so they went.

Clay Cooper owned a modest two-storey inn on the road between Coverdale and the Free City of Conthas. There was a stable out back, a bare-branched maple out front, and a shield-shaped sign above the door upon which the word *Slowhand's* had been spelled out in blocky script.

They rolled up sometime around midday. The road running past the inn was thick with refugees fleeing Coverdale, and the yard swarmed with mercs swapping stories and arguing over what to do next. Roderick offered to look after the horses. The satyr had been glancing skyward all morning, as

if expecting Doshi to return at any moment with the stolen
skyship.

*That, or he fears the Simurg might come swooping down on
us.* Unfortunately, the latter was a far more likely prospect.

Branigan stepped off the board and offered Tam a hand
down. Cura, Brune, and Freecloud followed. None of them
said a word, even when their names were called by mercenaries watching from the yard.

Rose didn't move. She was kneeling at her father's side, as
she had since she'd returned from the forest. She'd shed no
tears, and might have been watching paint dry for the lack
of expression on her face, but the sound of her scream still
echoed in Tam's memory.

The mood on the lawn was changing perceptively, from
generally chaotic to genuinely curious. Traffic on the road
congested further as passersby slowed for a look. Tam heard a
hundred voices whisper Rose's name in the sudden hush.

And another name, too.

The inn's door opened, and a man stepped out from inside.
He was big—taller than Freecloud, broader than Brune—but
aside from his size (and a vicious-looking scar slanting across
a punched-up nose) he was otherwise unremarkable: brown
hair, brown eyes, a brown beard shot through with flecks of
steely grey.

Clay Cooper, Tam assumed, whom the songs called Slowhand (when they called him anything at all). Gabe's faithful
friend was Saga's least notorious member, barely a footnote
in every story Tam had heard featuring Grandual's greatest
band. He struck an imposing figure now, she thought, glowering beneath a granite brow.

Moog drew a shuddering breath. "I'll go," he said. "I'll
tell him." The wizard climbed down from the wagon and ran a
trembling hand over the bald crown of his head, then tottered
up the beaten lane toward the step where Slowhand waited.

A serious-looking woman—Clay's wife, Tam supposed—
emerged from inside, followed closely by two girls. One of
them was very obviously their daughter. She looked to be a
few years younger than Tam, but was just as tall, and sturdily
built. Her face was broad and sun-browned, her hair bound
into a thick braid she tugged on absently as she surveyed the
yard. The other girl was much younger, with hair like a bolt
of pale green silk and bright eyes that grew wide when she
caught sight of her parents.

"Mommy!" She squirmed from the older girl's grip,
slipped the grasp of Slowhand's wife, and came running barefoot across the snowy yard. Freecloud moved to intercept her.
He scooped his daughter up and whispered something into
her ear before carrying her off, away from the wagon and the
woman grieving within.

Moog finally reached the inn's step. Whatever he said
rocked Slowhand like a punch and left the big man swaying
like an ox with an axe in its skull.

The bard heard whispers ripple out from where the two of
them stood, a low murmur of dread and disbelief. The wizard
was weeping openly now, and Clay Cooper's wife reached out
to graze her husband's arm as he looked toward the cart. Her
touch appeared to ground him. He said something Tam couldn't
hear from so far away, then laid a hand on Moog's shoulder as
he brushed by and started down the track toward the road.

By now the yard had grown deathly quiet. Several hundred mercenaries stood in rapt attention, and but for a few
desperate travellers, the torrent going past had come to a
standstill as well.

The silence startled Rose. She blinked, glanced over her
shoulder to see Slowhand coming. Tam was near enough to
see some new pain rise in the dark pools of her eyes. With
an effort that seemed titanic, Rose dragged herself from the
wagon and stood waiting for Clay as he approached.

"My father wanted——" was as far as she got before the giant embraced her, pulling the freezing plates of her armour against him, cradling her head in the palm of one massive hand. Neither spoke for a long while, and neither—unbelievably—cried. Rose, Tam suspected, had closed her heart off like a valve, and Slowhand, perhaps, had endured too much or had watched too many friends die for one more to matter.

More likely, Tam figured, *he's doing this for Rose, knowing that if he breaks, she'll break—no matter how tightly she's turned that wheel.*

At last, Slowhand set her free. And then, like a man resigned to stare into the sun even as it burned his eyes to ash, the grizzled merc turned his gaze upon his dear departed friend. Tam saw his barrel-wide chest rise and fall once, and again, and then, when he trusted himself to speak, he said to Rose, "May I?"

She nodded tersely. "Of course."

Slowhand leaned into the wagon and lifted Gabriel out. He did so gently, with deliberate slowness, as though his fallen bandmate were a child who'd fallen asleep by the fire and was only being carried off to bed. Rose's father, who'd appeared larger than life when Tam had met him just days ago, looked diminished in the other man's arms. His charisma, his easy charm, the assured grace with which he'd moved, and listened, and spoke...all of it was gone. Whatever gold remained in his hair seemed to grey before her eyes.

Clay Cooper bore Gabriel across the yard by the most direct route. Rose went after him, wordlessly bidding her bandmates to follow. Tam and Branigan trailed some distance behind, a pair of far-removed cousins bringing up the rear of a mourning procession.

The mercenaries crowding the yard shuffled to make a path. Helms were removed, chain coifs pushed back from lowered heads. Some of the warriors placed a hand over their heart, others offered prayers to the Spring Maiden. A few of the older ones brushed tears from their eyes, and even the youngest stared in open reverence.

There wasn't a merc in the world who didn't know Golden Gabe, though in truth not everyone thought kindly of him. Tam had heard some newer fighters claim he was overrated, that he'd come up in a simpler time and didn't have the stomach for fighting in the arena. Many who'd known him during Saga's touring days called him arrogant, brash, more concerned with exploiting his fame than earning it. Such sentiments, Tam imagined, were most often born of envy, but since the dead didn't warrant envy, what happened next was no great surprise.

Not to Tam, anyway.

Moog went to his knees, though whether anguish or admiration drove him there, she couldn't know. A pair of greybeards followed suit, bending a knee and bowing their heads. Beside them, a woman Tam identified as Clare Cassiber—better known as the Silver Shadow—stooped as well. A platinum-haired youth in black leathers, who she thought might be the frontman of the Screaming Eagles, knelt in the snow, then hissed at his bandmates to do the same. And suddenly, in a chorus of clanking mail and creaking leather, every single merc in the yard was kneeling.

They might have been stalks of grass for the attention Clay Cooper paid them, but Rose slowed and stared around, clearly amazed. The bard saw more than a few men and women offer Gabe's daughter a solemn nod, and Tam, to keep herself from gaping like a fool at every famous face she recognized, fixed her eyes on the door of the inn ahead.

It took forever to reach it, but eventually Slowhand and his burden disappeared inside. Rose went after him, flanked by Cura and Brune. Moog and Clay's daughter slipped in behind them. His wife held the door open for Tam, but the bard paused with one foot on the stoop, unsure whether or not she belonged inside.

"Go on," Bran urged. "I'll wait here." When she didn't move, her uncle nudged her with an elbow. "You're their bard, Tam. Whatever happens inside, you should be there."

He was right, of course. A bard's duty was to watch, to witness. For Tam to turn an eye when glory faded, when heroes were forced to endure heartbreak and hardship no strength of arms could overcome, was to betray that duty.

Tam stepped through the door.

She never sang about what happened beyond that threshold, nor spoke of it to anyone who wasn't present themself. What was obvious, though, to those who knew her before and after that morning, was that the woman who emerged was distinctly changed from the girl who'd entered.

Her smiles were shorter. Her laugh was louder. She became distracted at times, and would stare at nothing with a look of shattered sorrow that passed like a cloud the moment someone spoke her name.

She loved less quickly, but more fiercely, and made certain that those she cared for knew it well.

Sometimes she wept when it snowed.

Chapter Forty-four

Ashes on the Wind

Tam was asked to look after Wren while the others built Gabe a pyre. The young sylf, who was so chatty it was a wonder she found time to breathe, led the bard into the stable out back.

"All these were full yesterday." Wren indicated the dozens of empty stalls nearest the door. "But Auntie Ginny is a horse trader and she traded them all for money. Except, um, some people didn't have any money, but she gave them a horse anyway and told me not to tell Uncle Clay." She whirled on the bard. "So don't tell Uncle Clay, okay?"

"Uncle Clay?" Tam pretended to ponder something. "Is he the great big one with a long scar on his face?"

"That's him. He got that scar from falling down some stairs."

I bet he did, Tam thought with a wry grin.

The girl scampered over to a black stallion whose mane and tail were dyed a deep red. "This is Mommy's horse. His name is Heartbreaker and he only lets girls pet him. See?" She stroked the stallion's nose in demonstration, then pointed at a snow-white mare in the stall next door. "And this is Greensea. She's Daddy's horse, but Ginny lets me ride her sometimes because she's very gentle."

Tam's smile widened in the dim lantern light.

"Here is Tally's horse." Wren patted the nose of a speck-led brown-and-white palfrey. "She calls him Bert. And this big brown one belongs to Grandpa. She's really mean, though, and she bites everyone, and she doesn't like Grandpa very much at all."

Sadness slipped like a blade between Tam's ribs, but she kept her smile intact for the girl's sake. "What's her name?"

"Valery. Oh, and look over here!"

Moog had left the inn a while earlier (to decompress, he'd said, whatever that meant), and now Tam picked out his white fringe and beard in the gloom at the rear of the stable. The wizard was vigorously scratching the head of something in one of the larger pens.

"These are Uncle Moog's owlbears!" Wren announced.

Before Tam could ask what the hell an owlbear was, she saw for herself—and realized she'd seen one dying on the battlefield north of Coverdale. True to their name, they resem-bled nothing so much as brown-feathered bears with sharp black beaks and round yellow eyes. One of them squawked as Tam approached. The other purred like a cat beneath the wizard's scratching fingers.

"The big one is Gregor," Wren told her, "and the little one is Dane."

Tam wouldn't have called either creature *little*, seeing as though both of them were taller at the shoulder than she was, though one wasn't quite so massive as the other. "Are they your . . . pets?" she asked Moog.

"My dear companions," the wizard replied, with nothing but a sniffle to show for his earlier grief. "I wouldn't normally coop them up like this, but every mile between here and Con-thas is swarming with mercenaries who might mistake them for enemies." He withdrew a cluster of badly bruised bananas from the gods knew where and dangled them in front of Wren. "Would you like to feed them?"

She nodded enthusiastically. "Please!"

Tam scowled. "They eat bananas?"

Moog shrugged his bony shoulders. "Everything eats bananas."

While Wren and the wizard lobbed unpeeled bananas into the owlbears' gaping beaks, Tam moved into the grey light by the stable door. The day was growing colder; her breath steamed white in the frigid air. They were done building Gabriel's pyre, she saw—a pile of splintered chairs beneath a heavy oak table—and mercenaries were beginning to gather in clumps nearby.

She saw Lady Jain standing at the edge of the crowd, and recalled her admitting to robbing Gabe once upon a time. They'd become friends since, Tam guessed, since she'd rarely seen someone look so lost while standing still. The Silk Arrows, rainbow-bright in their garish attire, were gathered around her, but their numbers were diminished since Tam had seen them last.

Tam heard the scuff of a boot on the stable floor. Turning, she found Clay's daughter standing at her shoulder, gazing north. The sky above them was partitioned into halves: the pale gold of morning and the lavender wash of dawn. To the north, dark clouds—*snow clouds*—piled the horizon. Wind-blown ribbons of black smoke reached southward like the fingers of some spectral hand.

Tally had hold of her braid and was tugging it idly. The girl's knuckles were scabbed, and her nose, in profile, bore the telltale kink of having been broken at least once. Despite her size and sturdy frame, she didn't strike Tam as the aggressive sort, and her parents, from what little Tam knew of them, seemed incapable of raising a bully. She assumed, then, that Tally had come by her injuries honestly—perhaps in the course of standing up for someone incapable of looking out for themselves.

We all have a bit of our fathers in us, Tam thought, admiring the girl in silence.

"What?" Tally asked, when she caught the bard staring.

"Nothing." Tam returned her attention to the sky up north, fearing to see the first harbingers of Astra's undead Horde winging toward them. "How far is it to Conthas?"

Tally shrugged. "A few days. Less, if we ride hard."

Oh, we'll ride hard. "Do you think they know what's coming?" Tam wondered.

The girl's brow furrowed. Her knuckles went white on the braid in her hand. "What *is* coming?"

The bard considered the question as she peered at the distant storm. She didn't want to scare the girl, but it wouldn't do to sugarcoat it either. "Hell," she said finally.

To Gabriel's credit (and despite the looming threat of an undead Horde shambling south to kill them all), close to a thousand mercs, bards, bookers, and teary-eyed admirers were on hand to watch him burn. Cremation, of course, was a necessary precaution, since burying dead heroes seemed inadvisable when a necromancer-queen was on the loose.

Tam stood shoulder to shoulder with Cura, whose penchant for dressing all in black was, for once, appropriate to the occasion. Roderick joined them, hatless and bootless among his peers for the first time ever, so far as the bard was aware. The satyr collected an assortment of curious looks as he clopped his way across the snowy yard, from astonishment to outright scorn. One dour-faced merc amassed a noisy mouthful of phlegm, but a deadly glare from Rose forced him to swallow it with an audible gulp.

Slowhand pulled the cork on a green glass bottle of Longmourn Whiskey. The distillery had been destroyed by the Horde as they came south, which meant every remaining dram was a thing to be cherished.

"Matty sent me this when the inn finally opened last fall," Tam overheard him say to Moog, as if their old bandmate—now the emperor of Castia—was a kindly neighbour who dropped off a meat loaf from time to time. "It's been aged forty years in treant casks, apparently. I'd planned on hanging on to it until the next time we were all together." He shrugged, took a swig, sucked his teeth, and passed it to the wizard.

"Treant casks?" Moog sounded genuinely intrigued. "What does treant taste like?"

Another shrug. "Vanilla."

The wizard took a tentative sip. One of his eyelids twitched rapidly, and he heaved like a cat retching up a hairball before passing the bottle on to Rose. "*Vanilla*?" Moog hissed under his breath. "It tastes like an ogre's loincloth! And don't ask me how I know that!"

Rose drank deeper than either of them, then stepped forward and splashed the bottle's contents over the makeshift pyre. Afterward, she stood by her father's side and spoke as if the two of them were alone.

"You were a shit father," she told him. "Selfish and arrogant. Wholly unfit to be a parent." She looked toward the stable, where Wren could be heard telling Slowhand's daughter how many colours of horses there were in the world. "Runs in the family, I guess." She waited for a spatter of laughter before going on. "You told some good stories, though. You used to go on for hours about your endless adventures, your grand tours of the Heartwyld. You made it seem as if your life was a lot more exciting before I came along. And you never stopped talking about getting your band back together. Until, finally, you did."

There was a swell of excited chatter. Tam saw a smile slip on and off Slowhand's face like sunlight spearing through spring clouds.

"I used to wonder why you cared so much about those bandmates of yours. You *loved* them like you never loved me. These washed-up warriors, these haggard old men with limp wands and rusted swords."

"Hey," said Moog, pretending to bristle. "I resemble that remark!"

"But I know better now," Rose continued. Her dark eyes roamed the encircling mercenaries, and she pitched her voice to carry over their heads. "We all have our reasons for doing what we do. It might be the money, or the fame, or maybe, like me, you were just trying to piss off your parents." She paused until another bout of laughter subsided. "So we went and joined a band. We left our homes, abandoned our families, and hit the road. We spent every day and night with our bandmates. We ate with them, drank with them, argued over whether or not a hydrake counts as one kill or seven."

"One," said Brune.

"Seven," Cura said.

"We slept beside them, fought beside them, bled beside them. We trusted them to watch our backs and save our asses—which they did, time and time again. And somewhere out there, between one gig and the next, something changed. We woke up one day and realized that home was no longer behind us. That our families were with us all along. We looked around at these miscreants, these motley crews, and knew in our hearts there was nowhere we'd rather be than by their side."

Rose returned her attention to Gabriel's pyre, reaching to smooth the hair on his head. "Glory fades. Gold slips through our fingers like water, or sand. Love is the only thing worth fighting for. My father knew this. He loved his bandmates. He lived for them. He would have died for them if they asked him to, without question. Instead, he died for me." A breath. "So I guess he must have loved me, after all."

Tam had never known a silence so complete. She could hear the snowflakes whisper as Rose stepped away from the pyre and signalled Moog with a nod.

The wizard withdrew a small figurine from his sleeve: a bird carved out of dull black stone. A whistle brought it blazing to life—an open flame in the palm of his hand—and an exhalation sent it swooping toward the kindling piled beneath the oak table. The fire spread quickly, devouring the whiskey-soaked wood. Within moments it was blackening the boards beneath Gabriel, curling like talons around the table's edge.

Slowhand nudged the wizard with an elbow. "Show-off."

Moog opened his mouth to reply, but a shriek chopped his voice into silence. The sound of it—the sheer *volume* of it—was unmistakable, even before something obscured the sun and threw the world into shade.

Mercenaries craned their necks, bewildered. Tam, squinting against a flurry of snow, caught sight of feathered wings scything through the clouds above. She heard the word *dragon* on half a hundred lips, and figured it was probably best they hadn't yet grasped the danger they were in, lest pandemonium ensue.

And then Roderick screamed, "Fuck me, it's the Dragoneater!" as he hoofed it across the yard.

Pandemonium ensued. The crowd scattered like a nest of mice beneath the raptor's shadow. A few brave souls bared their swords. A few idiots drew bows and sent arrows arcing skyward. Tam heard a sucking *whoosh* and watched a wizard's fireball rise like a second sun. It burst in the clouds like spring fireworks, pointlessly pretty.

Wait until it lands, you fools! And in the meantime, she thought, *pray it doesn't land*.

Rose was running full tilt toward the stable.

"Your father's ashes!" Moog cried.

"Leave them for the wind," she yelled over her shoulder.

Freecloud took off after her, Brune and Cura hot on his heels. Tam followed, and Branigan caught up to her outside the stable. Her uncle's hair was slicked to his forehead as he peered skyward. "Is it true?" he asked. "Is that really the Simurg up there?"

It seemed the fear in her eyes was answer enough.

"Fuck me with a rusty dirk," he muttered.

Moog barrelled past them with his robes hiked above knobby knees. "Gregor! Dane!" he hollered to his owlbears. "Daddy's coming!"

Ginny hurried into the stable after him, which left her husband standing alone by Gabriel's pyre. Tam watched Slowhand's silhouette waver against the flames a moment longer, before finally he turned and stalked away, disappearing through the back door of his inn. He emerged a few moments later carrying an ugly slab of wood she belatedly recognized as a shield.

"*Blackheart*," she whispered.

Bran stirred beside her. "What?"

Before she could point it out, the wagon they'd brought from the battlefield came slewing into the yard. Roderick slid across the baseboard as it rounded the inn. He brought it skidding to a stop in the slush before them. "Get in!"

"Where are we going?" Tam asked, helping Bran into the wagon's bed.

Freecloud's mare bolted from the stable. Wren, looking remarkably calm, was seated in front of the druin, her fingers curled tightly in Greensea's white mane. Rose came after them, Heartbreaker thrashing like a branded mule between her legs. She yanked hard on the stallion's reins and nosed him south. "Conthas," she shouted, and went galloping off.

Chapter Forty-five

The Free City

The Free City of Conthas was many things to many people. It was a hub of trade for claw-brokers and scale-merchants, a base of operations to the huntsmen who supplied Grandual's arenas with fodder. Its proximity to the Heartwyld made it a natural staging point for bands brave enough to venture into the forest, and a haven for those who returned alive from that awful place.

As its name implied, the Free City lay beyond the borders of any court—but a city without rule is a city without rules. Anarchy reigned instead of kings. Chaos governed in place of ministers. Lawlessness and mayhem prowled the streets like wolves, preying on the innocent, devouring the weak. Criminals from all five courts made pilgrimage to Conthas as though it were some holy terminus, a refuge for villainous scum the world over.

Despite its sordid state, the city boasted a glorious past. It was here, some five hundred years prior, that the Company of Kings swept away the remnants of the Hordes that had overrun the Dominion. In the centuries since, Conthas (formally known as Contha's, and before that, Contha's Camp) had endured numerous attempts by eastern kings and southern hans to take the city by force. Even the notoriously aggressive centaur tribes gave the city a wide berth, preferring instead to raid towns and villages that weren't, as the horsemen put it, *Ict ish offendal putze*—which, roughly translated, meant "full of shitty assholes."

It was surrounded by two walls (both in disrepair), an encircling moat (which served double duty as a communal latrine and a convenient place to dispose of corpses), and was overlooked by a fortress so totally impregnable that no one had the slightest clue how to get inside.

Rose and Freecloud led the way toward the city. Roderick and Bran had taken turns driving the claw-broker's wagon, while Brune, Cura, and Tam sat hunched and wet in the creaking bed. Clay Cooper and his family rode just behind them, trailed by a crowd of weary refugees and a few hundred mercs who'd fled with them in the aftermath of Gabriel's funeral.

Lady Jain and the Silk Arrows were among those Tam could see, and the bard spotted Sam "the Slayer" Roth using *Fang* as a crutch as he hobbled along in his heavy plate armour. The warrior had been mounted on one of Ginny's horses when they set out from Slowhand's two nights earlier, but either his poor mount had died of exhaustion, or it had wised up and run off while the fat bastard got off to piss.

Either way, Tam thought, *it's in a better place now.*

"There." Freecloud pointed the citadel out to his daughter as they approached the city. "That's where your grandfather lives."

The sylf looked confused. "But Mommy said he was with the Summer Lord now. She said he could drink wine all day without getting in trouble, and that his hair was yellow again instead of grey."

"Your *other* grandfather," Freecloud said. "I told you about him yesterday, remember? He's a druin, like me."

"Does he have ears like a bunny, too?"

"He does, yes." For once the druin didn't bridle at the association. "But his are droopy, because he is very old."

Cura found a smirk and slapped it on. "You know what else droops when it gets old?"

"What?" Wren chirped.

"Yes, please," said Freecloud dryly. "Tell my five-year-old daughter what else droops when it gets old."

"Oh...um..." Cura wilted under the druin's glare. "Flowers?"

"I thought Contha was a recluse?" Tam wondered aloud. "Why does he live in the middle of the city?"

"He lives below it," Freecloud told her. "Lamneth is sealed. I am the only one to have entered or left it in almost a millennium."

Tam eyed the ancient druin citadel, its shadow stark against the morning sky. "Your father sent you to treat with Lastleaf, right? He must think you're dead."

The druin's smile was sickle-sharp. "I'd be surprised if he knows I'm gone, or even remembers he sent me away in the first place. My father was never especially considerate of others, and nine centuries of isolation has made him even less so." Freecloud returned his gaze to the hilltop fortress. He didn't look especially happy to be going home. "Solitude can do troubling things to a mind."

There were two armies camped outside Conthas. To the east lay the green-and-gold tents of Agrian regulars, arranged in ordered rows that reminded Tam of the vineyards she'd seen in the hills west of Highpool. To the west, scattered like the ashes of a kicked fire, were the yurts of Cartean clansman. Brune pointed out the wind-whipped pennant of the High Han himself.

"The Han fights alongside his army?" Tam asked.

"The Carteans are more like a mounted mob than an army," replied the shaman, "but yeah. The plainsmen value strength and prowess above all else. If a han doesn't fight his enemies, he'll end up fighting his friends."

Tam shifted on her seat. Her rump ached after a night of rutted road and Roderick's careless driving. She would have sworn the satyr *aimed* for the potholes. "Can a han be a her?" she inquired.

Brune blew into his hands to warm them. "Of course. Ever heard of Augera?" Tam shook her head. "They called her the Howling Han. She was among the most feared warlords of all time. She conquered the bottom half of Agria and the northern half of Narmeer before she died."

"How did she die?"

The shaman frowned. "Recklessness. Greed. The usual suspects. She set her sights on the Narmeeri capital and had the bright idea to march directly across the Crystal Flats. Took thirty thousand riders with her, and just...disappeared. To this day, the Carteans call the east wind Augera, and say it carries the cries of the Howling Han's thirst-crazed warriors."

"How do you know all this?" Tam asked.

Brune shrugged. "Drunk Carteans tell stories," he said.

By now they had come to the city's outer-east gate, called the Courtside Gate, which was thronged with refugees seeking safety behind the walls and mercs eager to slake their thirst at the local dives. Rose wielded Heartbreaker like a bludgeon, using the stallion's head to force a path through the press of parked argosies and overburdened wagons. Rough-looking men wearing soiled red tabards over rusted chain hauberks stood on either side of the entrance, collecting a toll on behalf of someone called Tabano.

"Most likely some jumped-up Gutter-Boss," growled Cura. "Fucking shit-eating rats," she added, in case it was unclear what she thought of those who extorted desperate people with nowhere else to turn.

One of Tabano's thugs sneered at Freecloud as they approached. "Rabbits are extra, chap. That's a full crown for you, and two coppers for—" He paused as he caught sight of Wren's face beneath her hooded cloak. "What have we here?"

"A half-breed runt!" said one of his cohorts, sauntering up. "And a girl, no less?" He withdrew a courtmark coin from the purse at his waist and offered it to the druin. "Tell you what—take this and leave the little one with us. We'll make sure she gets a roof over her head."

Rose slipped from her stallion's back and held her hand out to him. "Your helmet."

The thug regarded her warily. "Huh?"

"Give me your helmet," she demanded. "Now."

Either too scared or too stupid to refuse, he unhurriedly removed the dented iron pan from his head and handed it over. As he did, recognition bloomed on his pockmarked face. "Hey, aren't you Bloody R—"

The helm cracked across the side of his jaw. His eyes took a look at the back of his skull and he swayed like a tree deciding which way to fall. Rose pushed him over as she advanced on his friend, grabbing a fistful of the thug's tabard and pinning him against the stone wall.

"Take his purse." She pointed at the one she'd laid out. "And yours. Give a crown to every man, woman, and child without a weapon who comes through this gate until you're broke, then run back to your shithead boss—Tabo, was it?"

"T-Tabano," he stuttered. "The Baron of Saltkettle."

"Tell him Bloody Rose is in town, and the Winter Queen is on her way. Tell him the Brumal Horde is coming, and that every knife on his payroll—every thief, thug, and halfpenny assassin—had better be waving from this wall when they get here, or else he won't have anyone to steal from, rough up, or assassinate, because we'll all be fucking dead. Got it?" The man's jowls quivered as he nodded. "Go."

He scampered off. Rose remained on foot, leading Heartbreaker by the bridle through the outer city. They followed a muddy road littered with so many stone bricks Tam suspected someone had once tried to pave it and gave up partway through. The way was hedged by stables, smithies, stinking tanneries, and snoring mills. Conthas reminded her of a bruise: a ring of soured earth that grew darker the closer they got to the centre.

They passed through the city's Monster Market, a menagerie so vast and varied it made the one in Ardburg look like a pet shop by comparison. Tiers of stacked cages made a maze of the cluttered square, their occupants raging, pacing, or sitting sullenly in the shadowed corners of their prisons.

Tam caught sight of talons and beaks, wings and horns, glistening scales and blood-matted fur. Slick green tentacles curled around the bars of one cage, and those passing near gave it a cautious berth. A circle of massive wains surrounded the forum, their iron-barred windows offering glimpses of Heartwyld horrors bound for the arenas of Grandual. Many of them, Tam figured, had been taken as captives after the battle up north. They likely thought captivity was a fate worse than death.

But there were fates, she knew, even worse than both.

They passed a pen of rangy centaurs packed so tight they could barely move, their hands and hooves bound by heavy manacles. Tam peered into a roped-off pit filled with goblins, yowling like a thousand feral cats fighting over the crust of a sardine sandwich. A bowlegged fomorian—its face so hideously deformed even its mother would recoil at the sight of it—was being ushered into a stockade by a cordon of barking dogs and huntsmen armed with barbed polearms. Elsewhere, a pair of vibrantly striped gorilliaths were forced to pummel one another for the amusement of a jeering crowd. The whole square stank of soiled hay, stale urine, and callous neglect. The noise—a buzzing cacophony of squawks, roars, hisses, and growls—made Tam squirm uncomfortably on her seat.

She'd been fascinated by the market back in Ardburg. The monsters had seemed exotic at the time, inherently dangerous—as if cramped cages and filthy pens were exactly where such wild things belonged. Now, however, they felt to

Tam like victims, casualties of being born with scales instead
of skin, claws instead of fingers, or (in the case of a giant spider trussed by corded rope) eight bulbous eyes and poison-
laced mandibles instead of a proper face.

The bard saw a red-maned gnoll chained by her throat
to a stake. The hyena-headed creature was nursing a litter of
spotted pups and staring dazedly at the middle distance. Her
children, Tam supposed, would be taken from her once they'd
been weaned, and she would be bred again with another of
her kind—a specimen chosen for his size and ferocity. Her
offspring would be raised in captivity beneath some distant
arena, beaten and lashed by pitiless wranglers until they
became the savage monsters mankind required them to be.

Tam found herself scowling at the thought of so many
desperate thousands rallying to Brontide's cause. Their aim
hadn't been to destroy humanity—merely to *survive* it.

Clustered like crows around the next gate were goons of
a different sort: pale-skinned priests with shorn heads and
soiled white robes. When their leader turned her way, Tam
nearly leapt out of her seat. His mouth was sewn not quite
closed by a grille of polished bone piercings that stretched his
lips into a gruesome, lunatic smile.

"The Frost Mother has returned!" he slurred. "Let the
fires die, the candles burn to stubs. Let nothing remain but
ash and smoke to mark their passing!"

"Ash and smoke," groaned a woman at his side.

"Fuck your ash and smoke!" Cura swore, and the man's
hollowed eyes snapped in her direction.

"Rejoice!" he howled, his lips taut behind the bone cage.
"Our queen is coming."

"She will be here soon," crowed the woman. She lifted her
face and reached out to catch snowflakes in skeletal hands. "I
can feel her touch. I can taste her on my lips."

Tam was thankful when the priests were out of earshot.

"Behold," Roderick announced from his perch on the

baseboard, "the glory of Conthas. The one and only free city this side of the Wyld."

"What about Freeport?" she asked.

The booker scowled. "Just shut the fuck up and behold, all right? This here's the strip, though most folks call it the Gutter." He indicated the broad avenue ahead of them. "Little bit road, little bit river—it depends on the weather, really. Don't step in the puddles," he warned. "In fact, stay away from the water in general while we're here. Beer is fine. Wine is good. Rum is best."

"The coffee is shit," Cura muttered, and considering the stench coming off the so-called road, Tam wondered if the Inkwitch wasn't being literal.

Tam heard someone yelp behind them. She looked back in time to see Clay Cooper shove the grille-faced priest into a pool of yellow-brown water.

Moog laughed. Ginny scowled. Slowhand shrugged and nudged his mount onward.

Rose stopped walking and wheeled on them. "We didn't come here to drink," she said. Heartbreaker stamped a hoof in the mud and swished his bright red tail. "Brune, I want you to scour the fighting pits. Try to convince whoever's handy it's worth their time to join us." She tossed the shaman a clinking sack. "Bribe them if you need to."

"I'll need to," he assured her. "Wait, join *us*? Does that mean we're really doing this? Going up against the Frost Mother? I'm down for it, obviously, I just...I thought you said the Dragoneater was our last gig."

"That was before Astra used us to do her dirty work," Rose told him. "Before she...made it personal."

Brune nodded, his eyes flitting to Freecloud and back. "Fair enough."

Rose said to Cura, "Do you remember where Sinkwell is?"

The Inkwitch grinned. "Does a drunk know her way to the bar?"

"Find me alchemists, stormers, summoners—whoever you can scrounge up. Promise them enough reagents to last a lifetime, but if that fails—"

"Punch them until they come around?" said Cura.

"Exactly. Uncle Moog—"

"Say no more!" The wizard sidled up next to Cura. "I shall accompany the young lady to Sinkwell. I've got a few old friends hiding out there. And an enemy or two, I'd imagine. Ah, but we'll have the boys along to discourage violence." He motioned to the massive owlbears shuffling along behind him. Passersby gave Gregor and Dane a wide berth and even wider stares.

Rose looked to Clay as the old merc dismounted and stretched a kink out of his back. "Can you convince the Agrians and Carteans to stick around?"

Slowhand looked imploringly at his wife. "Can I?"

Ginny's expression was grim. Her jaw bunched like she was chewing through a stone, but she nodded.

Clay shrugged. "I'll try. Gabe usually did the talking, though."

"I know," said Rose. "Thank you." Tam wasn't sure whether she was thanking Slowhand for trying or his wife for allowing him to do so.

Branigan was chatting amiably with Lady Jain, and now the two of them looked to Rose. "What can we do?" her uncle asked.

Rose eyed the colourfully clad Silk Arrows as she considered her answer. "I don't know how long it will take Astra to get that Horde up and moving, but it's a good bet she'll be here within the next few days. We can't have her turning our dead against us. Cemeteries, family tombs, mass graves—everything needs to be dug up and burned."

"Great." Bran looked decidedly unenthused. "Sounds fun."

"And what'll you be doing while we're diggin' up the dead?" Jain asked.

"Freecloud and I are taking Wren someplace safe."

"To Grandpa's house?" the girl asked. Rose nodded, and the sylf tugged on her father's cloak. "Can Tam come with us? Please, Daddy?"

"Of course," said the druin, "if she wants to."

Wren's face brightened. "She wants to! Don't you, Tam?"

The bard squinted at the ruin of Contha's keep, looming stark against the glare of the setting sun. "You bet I do."

Chapter Forty-six

The Forest of Broken Things

They waited until nightfall to approach the fortress. The snow receded as they went up, giving way to bare stone and sparse yellow grass. Once, when her footing slipped on a patch of shale, Tam put a hand down to catch herself.

"It's warm," she marvelled at the stone beneath her fingers.

"It'll cool soon," said Freecloud. He was carrying Wren in the crook of one arm. The sylf was fast asleep and drooling on her father's shoulder. "The spire traps sunlight during the day, refracts it through a sequence of lenses, and focuses it into a beam hot enough to melt duramantium."

"Really?" she asked. "Is that how—"

"Less talking, more walking." Rose's voice lashed at their heels like a wrangler's whip.

"You'll see what I mean," murmured Freecloud.

They went the rest of the way in silence, but for the scuff of boot on stone and the labouring wheeze of Tam's breath as they neared the summit. She used *Duchess* as a crutch, leaning heavily on the unstrung ashwood bow. Neither Freecloud nor Rose (burdened by a sleeping child and a suit of plate armour, respectively) appeared wearied by the climb.

"This way." The druin led them through the ring of ruined arches circling the citadel's base, then down a worn stairwell into a darkness so complete Tam couldn't make out her hand when she waved it in front of her face.

Tam heard someone rifling their pockets, then a gently blown breath, before a soft light picked out the hard planes of Rose's face. She was holding a spiny pink seashell—the source of the illumination—which grew brighter when she blew into it a second time.

The bard chuckled. "I wouldn't have pegged you for a shell collector."

Rose examined the artifact in her hand. "I used to be. Uncle Moog gave me this when I was about Wren's age. He claimed to have found it on the beach near Askatar, and told me there's a fire sprite living inside."

The bard sniffed. "How does it actually work?"

"When it comes to Moog's magic," Rose told her, "sometimes it's better not to ask."

They proceeded underground, their footsteps echoing as they followed the druin down a gently sloping passage. There were no time-ravaged furnishings inside the citadel, no faded tapestries decorating the walls. There weren't even rooms— only a long, curving corridor that went on and on. The light of Rose's shell gleamed from sheer black stone overhead and underfoot. The air grew warmer, and soon Tam's shirt was clinging to the small of her back.

"We're here," said Freecloud eventually. "Watch your step."

The hallway opened onto an empty black void. A ray of light hung like a silver thread in the darkness. Tam saw a cloud of bats wing through it, dancing like dust motes in the slender beam.

She looked over at Freecloud. "It doesn't burn them?"

"It's only starlight," he replied. "During the day it would reduce them to ash in an instant. It turns this whole place into an oven."

Rose stepped as close as she dared to the edge of the chasm. "So how do we get down?"

The druin produced the moonstone coin he was always fiddling with. He stepped to the wall and inserted it into a small recess, then pressed it with a finger and turned it counterclockwise. The air to Tam's left shimmered like spilled lamp oil. By the time she turned to look, the void and its string of starlight had vanished, replaced by an enormous hall.

What she first mistook for buttressing pillars were in fact huge metal golems carved to resemble figures encased in plate armour, each of which rested their hands on the pommel of an upturned warhammer. Their eyes were dull green spirals within the shadows of sculpted helms. There was a throne shaped like a tipping basin at the far end of the hall, backdropped by the starlight column.

"Hmm." Freecloud turned the coin again, clockwise this time. The throne room *rippled* like a stone-struck pond and became some kind of foundry instead. The starlight shaft was directly before them now, shining down into a gigantic bowl of faceted black stone. Six moulding stations surrounded the bowl, each attended by constructs that moved with the deliberate efficiency of a waterwheel or a windmill—machines designed for a simple, singular purpose.

"Seriously?" Rose sounded incredulous. "Your father has his own Threshold?"

The druin didn't quite smirk, but he didn't *not* smirk either. "Who do you think made them in the first place?" he said, before retrieving the coin and stepping through.

Rose followed, and Tam brought up the rear. She tried not to think about the fact that, were it not for some trick of druin sorcery, she'd be stepping over a sheer drop that would leave her plenty of time to perfect her panicked scream before she hit the ground. She was so intent on blanking her thoughts that she didn't see the sentinel standing next to her until Freecloud addressed it.

"Orbison! Hello!"

The golem was tall and wiry, made of something that

looked like copper. Pipes coiled around his limbs, feeding into a single tube that ran up his chest and into his chin, giving the construct a stiff, almost erudite posture. His head reminded Tam of a teapot, since a small tube jutted like a horn from the front. The latticed squares that served him as eyes pulsed a vibrant green upon seeing Freecloud, but where his mouth should have been was a smear of corroded iron stamped with studded bolts. In lieu of answering, he waved instead.

"Orbison, what happened to you? Your mouth..." The druin's ears sagged. "Did my father do this?"

The construct, of course, said nothing, but a puff of steam and a short whistle came from the spout on his forehead. His eyes flared again, and with a long-fingered hand he pointed at the sylf sleeping in Freecloud's arms.

"This is my daughter. Our daughter," he said, no doubt warned by the prescience that Rose had been about to correct him. "Her name is Wren."

The girl stirred at the sound of her name. Her eyes fluttered open. "Am I dreaming?" she murmured.

Another puff escaped Orbison's spout as he admired her, along with a whistle perceptively softer than the first.

"Wren, this is Orbison. He was my friend when I was little. He'll be your friend now, too."

"Hi, Orbison," she said groggily. Her eyes drooped shut. She smacked her lips a few times and fell back asleep on her father's shoulder.

Freecloud made quiet introductions of Rose and Tam. The golem whistled cheerily at Tam, while the one he reserved for Rose sounded decidedly lewd.

"Okay, okay." The druin laughed. "Easy there, pal." His eyes strayed again to the golem's mangled mouth, and his smile trickled away. "Is my father in the workshop?"

Orbison nodded, pointing toward a corridor behind him.

"Take us to him. Please."

*   *   *

"My father was miserable for years after the Dominion fell," Freecloud said as they followed the construct deeper into Lamneth. Orbison had thrown open a hatch on his chest, bathing the way ahead in ghostly green light. "He'd been dragged into a war he didn't believe in, betrayed by his allies, and forced to watch as his precious army was smashed to rubble."

"Who betrayed him?" Tam asked.

"According to him? Everyone. The Exarchs were attacking one another, each trying to claim the biggest piece of the pie. My father only wished for order. He wanted the Dominion restored and Vespian returned to power."

"He didn't care that the Archon was killing his own kind to resurrect his wife?" Rose asked.

"All he cares about are his machines." The bard detected a trace of bitterness in Freecloud's voice. "The constructs, the Thresholds, the tidal engines—"

"Contha made the tidal engines, too?"

"He did," said the druin. "Anyhow, when war broke out he tried to act as a mediator, to make the Exarchs see the folly in fighting among themselves, but diplomacy failed, and he was forced to put his golems in the field."

"How did that work out for him?" Tam asked.

"Great, at first. He wiped out the Horde of Arioch and drove Coramant's legions back into the Heartwyld. Eventually, he was summoned by the southern Exarchs to treat for peace at what remained of Kaladar."

"Obviously a trap," Rose said.

"Obviously," Freecloud agreed. "But my father, though brilliant, was ever a slave to hubris. He believed his army was indestructible, and it's possible—though he would never admit it—that he hoped to become Archon himself. In any event, he was ambushed, his army utterly destroyed. He returned to Lamneth and sealed himself inside, then languished in darkness for the better part of two centuries, while the Dominion burned and the Hordes overran Grandual. He built nothing, did nothing—except curse those who'd brought the empire to ruin. I grew up alone, with nothing but constructs for company."

A whistle chirped up ahead of them.

"And Orbison, of course," he amended. "Then one day a bird—a finch, I think it was—found its way into the citadel. My father, for whatever reason, became fascinated with it, and eventually he went back to work and made a simulacrum of it."

Tam blew a stray hair from her eyes. "A simawhat?"

"A replica," Freecloud explained. "A tiny, metal bird. Except it couldn't fly. So my father killed the finch. He pulled it apart to see how it worked, and then he made one that *did* fly."

The bard winced. "Brutal."

"Indeed." The druin sighed. "He started sending me to gather specimens. Foxes, snakes, insects—anything he could dissect and replicate. He even had me hunting monsters. And then, eventually . . ." Freecloud fell silent.

Rose, frowning in the light of her magicked shell, glanced over. "Eventually . . . ?"

"He asked me to bring him a human."

Rose stopped walking. Her frown exchanged places with a full-blown scowl. "Tell me you refused."

"I refused," he assured her. Their daughter rubbed at one eye and muttered something in her sleep. "Of course I did."

"And you want to leave our *daughter* with him? I thought you said—"

"She'll be safe here. Safer than she will be with us. Unless we stay here with her." He was probing, Tam gleaned, hoping to find weakness in the armour of Rose's newfound resolve to defend the city above against Astra's Horde. When she didn't bother to reply, he went on. "Wren has nothing to fear from my father, I promise. He's not a monster."

Rose chewed on that like a rabid dog who'd been tossed a pork chop as a peace offering. "There are worse things in the world than monsters," she said, before turning and stalking off after their guide.

They turned a corner, descended a broad, curving stair, and traversed a bridge bordered on each side by waterfalls so sheer as to resemble panes of glass. Orbison traced an arc in one with a finger as they crossed, whistling quietly to himself. Before long they arrived at a pair of huge doors, half ajar. The construct rapped twice on one of them and waited.

They waited for so long that Tam was about to suggest the golem try knocking again when a reedy voice called out from within. "Enter."

The chamber beyond was (unsurprisingly) huge. Like the rest of Lamneth, it seemed designed to accommodate the stature of Contha's massive constructs. It was dark but for thousands of glowing green runes that gleamed in the dark like the script of an invisible book. By their light Tam could see that the ceiling above was thick with looping vines. Roots clawed like fingers through fissures in the walls, which were mottled grey rock instead of the glassy black stone from which the rest of the citadel was carved. The floor under their boots was snarled with snaking boughs, piled here and there with leafy outcroppings. Crooked white columns jutted from the growth underfoot, sprouting twisted limbs that reached to strangle one another, forming arches that dripped with scarlet creepers.

"Caddabra." Freecloud's voice was muted by reverence, or fear, or something between the two. "The Upside-Down Forest."

Tam blinked in the gloom. "Caddabra?"

"Its heart lies somewhere to the west, but it grows by the year, spreading like roots through the deep places of the world."

"I thought Caddabra was—"

"A fairy tale?" The druin's voice was wry. "Like the Dragoneater, perhaps?"

"Well ... yeah."

Freecloud's ears skewed to one side. "Few have cause to enter the forest, and few that do manage to find their way out again."

"Did you come to tell stories to children?" snapped a voice from somewhere ahead. "Or perhaps to confess why you've been gone for most of a decade on an errand that should have taken months? Orbison, bring them—or I'll have your arms off and you can knock with your head next time."

The golem whistled sullenly and set out through the upended trees. As they went after him, the runes populating the gloom began to shift, bounding from the path, or floating through the dark like so many fireflies. Tam gasped, but Rose gave voice to her astonishment before the bard found the breath to speak.

"Eyes," she uttered. "Cloud, what are these things?"

"Constructs," he whispered. "Replicas of the specimens I used to gather."

Tam's eyes were adjusting to the gloom. She saw what looked like a wrought-iron raccoon skulking along a bough near her feet. Its neck was skewed sideways, a seam of green light visible where its head didn't quite fit its body. A pair of squirrels leapt from their path. One of them, she noted, had a corkscrew tail and hovered for a moment each time it left the ground. Elsewhere, a steel-plated bear lay on its side, unable to rise. Its legs were mangled stumps that looked to have been crushed by its own bulk. Emerald light spilled from its open mouth, but no sound at all, since it hadn't been granted the means by which to roar.

She saw numerous other animals lurking among Caddabra's inverted eaves: a deer with tusks, a snake that slithered in circles. Every creature was misshapen in some way, some more than others. Many were hybrids, part of one creature spliced with part of another, and none of them quite as they should be.

They're experiments, she grasped. *Botched replicas of whatever their maker had on hand.* She wondered what happened to those he'd perfected—or if he'd perfected any at all.

There was a turtle whose neck was as long as her leg, and a snub-tailed mountain cat with two heads. Birds flocked among the foliage as well. Tam spotted a pink-bellied thrush with glass wings like that of a dragonfly, and a trio of ravens hanging from a branch on segmented silver tails.

Atop one arch was a round-faced owl with spiral eyes that tracked them as they passed. Tam recognized it immediately. She'd seen it twice before: once in the Silverwood, and again on the night she'd gone to throw stones at a farmgirl's window.

Had Contha been spying on them, watching his son in secret all this time?

She couldn't voice her concerns to Freecloud, however, since they'd arrived at a henge made of monolithic stone slabs that gave off a faint, pearlescent light. Metal scrap lay everywhere, rough lumps of a violet mineral Tam didn't recognize.

Kneeling amidst the circle of stones was something that might once have been a druin, but was something *other* now, as aberrant from the norm as the malformed creatures lurking in the forest around him. His face was gaunt and narrow, his eyes black as moon-shaped holes cut in the fabric of night. Pale pink fur sheathed ears gone limp as plucked daisies, and his almost translucent hair was so long it pooled like melted platinum around his knees. The figure wore a suit of close-fitting armour made of overlapping scale plates, each marked with a softly glowing rune. His limbs were long and bone-thin, near invisible for the dozens of inscribed duramantium bangles he wore on each. The ones around his neck chimed softly as he raised his head.

"Son," said Contha, the last living Exarch of the Old Dominion. "Welcome home."

Chapter Forty-seven

Four Words

"Orbison, tea." The ancient druin gestured absently, and a crosshatched rune on one of his bangles pulsed a vibrant green. The contruct moved to obey, clomping up the path behind them.

The bangles control the golems, Tam realized, and figured the runes on his armour served a similar purpose. *How many can he control at once? Hundreds, maybe? Or thousands, if whole legions were bound by a single rune . . .*

"Those bracers," said Contha, admiring Rose's armour. "They pair with the blades, yes? Where did she get them?"

"I stole them," Rose said, though the Exarch had directed his question at Freecloud.

"You recognize them, Father?"

Contha shook his head slightly, since his ears were too limp to convey expression. "No. They are simple weapons. Uninspired, and unworthy of my time. I prefer to kill more"—he indicated the construct upon which he was working now—"creatively, when I must. Violence should be a last resort. *True* power is a deterrent to such vulgar ends."

The Exarch's current project was lying on its back before him. It bore a tortoise's concave shell, but its six legs were long and jointed like that of a spider. They jerked spastically as the druin tampered with its insides. Contha was wearing a pair of gauntlets himself, each cuffed at the wrist by a spinning ring that looked like part of a tidal engine. They whirled as he worked, while lances of blue fire burned at his fingertips. The spider-thing's metal frame warped beneath his touch.

He's shaping it, Tam marvelled. *Working metal like it was clay, using nothing but his hands.*

If the Exarch passed on this knowledge—if he returned to the world above and shared the secret of such innovation with humankind—who knows what wonders they might fashion?

Or horrors, she was quick to remind herself, as a metal-work jackal limped past on three legs. Its leering eyes, shaped like the point of an arrowhead, were fixed on the child in Freecloud's arms. The thing emitted a rattling growl that distracted Contha from his work. A rune matching the shape of its eyes flickered on one of his bangles, and the jackal scampered off.

"Here we are." The Exarch turned over his creation. A sigil scored each facet of its shell: a circle bisected by a single line. He evoked a band around his emaciated bicep that bore an identical symbol, and the beetle-like construct surged to its feet. It scuttled in a slow half circle, then retraced its steps. Contha grunted. His eyes narrowed, and the rune on his arm blinked again. The spider-turtle took four jaunty steps sideways and then collapsed.

"By the Black Fronds of Nibenay!" Contha swore. "I've gone wrong, somewhere. Miscalculated. It should run like a spider, jump like a spider. I don't understand." His cuffs began spinning and his fingers flared alight.

"It needs more legs," Tam pointed out.

"It has enough!" Contha spat.

"Well, fine, but not if it's supposed to move like a spider. Spiders have eight legs."

"What?" The Exarch tore his gaze from the capsized construct. "Is that true?"

She opened her mouth to reply, but suddenly she wasn't so sure. "I, uh—"

"It's true," said Freecloud.

"*Kaksara*!" Contha cursed in druic this time. "Do you see, boy? This is why I need you here! To gather specimens! To fetch me real, live spiders so I don't waste my time with this"—he sliced one of the spurtle's legs off with a swipe of his hand—"this disastrous cock-up!"

"I can't stay, Father." Freecloud reached to take Rose's hand. "I'm in a band, now. I have a family."

Contha stared at their clasped hands with the morbid curiosity of someone peering into the depths of an outhouse. "A *family*? Son, you can't possibly—"

A cheery whistle signalled Orbison's return. The golem carried a tray bearing four cups of unblemished glass—each with a scatter of red leaves in the bottom—along with a perfectly spherical teapot that somehow didn't roll off onto the floor.

The golem had brought food as well: hollowed mushroom caps filled with a tart purple jelly that tasted nothing at all like grapes.

They roused Wren, who smiled when she saw Orbison and laughed when Freecloud introduced her to Contha. "You look funny," she informed him, without malice. Her grandfather ignored her. "How did your hair get so long?" she asked, but the Exarch went on eating, using his fingers to scoop the jelly from his mushroom bowl.

He won't even look at her, thought Tam. Could Contha hate humans so much? More likely, she reasoned, he was angry that a mortal woman had lured his son away, appalled that Freecloud would risk eternity to remain by her side.

"What happened to Orbison?" said Freecloud between sips of steaming crimson tea.

"Nothing." Contha gestured to the construct. "He's right there."

"I mean his mouth."

"Oh. I closed it."

The bard saw Freecloud's teacup tremble in his hand. "Why?"

"As punishment," said his father, and since the prescience told him Freecloud would press the issue, the Exarch was obliged to elaborate. "He tried to follow you. When you didn't return, Orbison feared some monster had got the better of you, or that Lastleaf had taken my refusal to join him personally and killed you to spite me."

"Orbison came after me?"

Contha licked jelly from his fingers and then slurped from his own cup. "He did. And by the time I'd realized what he'd done, the bolt-brained fool had reached the Heartwyld and was too far away for me to compel him home. I sent a bird to track him—I'm rather good at those, you know."

"I know," murmured his son.

Tam shuddered. She tried to imagine returning home one day to discover Threnody pinned and peeled open on the kitchen table while her father examined her insides.

"He had a run-in with an ogre," Contha said. "He defeated it—Orbison is quite handy in a fight, believe it or not—but his, unfortunately, is a gentle soul. He spared the ogre, who alerted his tribe, and by the time my reinforcements arrived he'd been rather badly mauled."

Tam glanced up at Orbison. *A gentle soul?* Could a construct show courage, she wondered? Could it know worry, or friendship, or fear? Apparently yes, since concern for Freecloud's well-being had compelled the copper giant to risk its well-being in the Heartwyld.

The Exarch went on. "My knights returned him to Lamneth, where I could see to his repairs. I'll confess I was tempted to scrap him. I might have, too, except none of the others can brew a decent cup of tea. So I made him whole again. And how did he repay me? Begging! Incessant chatter! He pleaded to be set free, so he could find you and bring you home." The Exarch regarded the golem with an ugly sneer. "Except you didn't really want to bring him home, did you, Orbison? You only wanted to join him in exile. To be rid of me, your master. To be *runebroken*." Contha spat that final word like bile from his mouth.

Freecloud was repulsed. "So you disfigured him?"

"*Defaced* is a more suitable term, wouldn't you agree?"

"Father—"

"Now he is quiet, and obedient, and the tea"—the Exarch closed his eyes and raised his cup—"is just as it should be."

Rose stood, yanking Wren to her feet. "We're leaving."

"We're not," said Freecloud. "Not with Wren. It's too dangerous in the city, and too late now to flee."

"You're right," said the Exarch. "Astra will arrive very soon. You cannot hope to outrun her now."

Freecloud's ears angled suspiciously. "You know about Astra? How?"

"He's been spying on you," said Tam.

The Exarch's eyes snapped to her, lips curling to reveal a glimpse of razor teeth.

"Is this true, Father?"

"Of course it's true," said Contha. "You're my son, are you not? When you failed to return I feared the worst." His gaze flickered to Rose as he said this, and his deepening scowl made it clear he considered *her* the worst.

"Astra has gone mad," Freecloud stated.

"She went mad long ago. Now she seeks revenge for the death of her son." The Exarch sighed, tapping a taloned finger against the rim of his glass. "That boy should never have been born. And his mother . . . Well, Vespian made a grave mistake in bringing her back. Assuming it *is* her he brought back."

"She leads an army of the dead," said Freecloud, "and intends to kill every man, woman, and child in Grandual."

Contha looked mildly amused. "Does she, now? How . . .

ambitious. Alas, so much for the brief and inglorious reign of humankind, eh? One could almost pity them, as one pities insects, or the grass that dies beneath the winter snow." His black-moon eyes drifted to Freecloud. "It is good you are home, son. You are safe here. We will wait out this storm together, you and I."

He made no mention of Rose, or of the child standing beside her.

"Orbison." The golem whistled when Freecloud spoke his name. "Will you please take Wren for a walk?"

The girl clutched her mother's arm with both hands, looking warily at the surrounding forest. "But there's scary-looking things out there," she said meekly.

Freecloud knelt. "They won't hurt you, Wren. I know some of them look frightening. Especially that one." He pointed to a metallic fox with a scorpion's tail prowling just beyond the stone circle. "But what did I tell you when you first met Brune?"

The sylf rubbed her eye, thinking. "That just because something is ugly doesn't mean it's bad."

"Exactly. And besides, you'll have Orbison to protect you. Did you know"—he leaned in to whisper in his daughter's ear—"that he has a light where his heart should be?"

"Really?" Wren looked up at the lanky golem.

Freecloud wore a wistful smile. "Show her, Orbison. Please."

The construct made a cooing noise and pulled open the hatch on his chest. Emerald light flooded the circle, and Wren's face brightened along with it. The golem lowered his arm and the girl tentatively took hold of it. When she was secure, he lifted her up and set her on his weathered green shoulder.

"I can see everything from here," she announced as they left the henge and plodded up the path.

"Go ahead," said Contha once the four of them were alone. "Ask. You think I don't know why you've come? It wasn't out of filial piety, that much is obvious."

"We need—" Rose began, but the Exarch cut her off.

"My son can ask for himself."

Freecloud's ears betrayed annoyance at his father's dismissiveness. Had *anyone* else in the world spoken to Rose that way, they'd be collecting their teeth off the floor right about now. The younger druin made a noticeable effort to calm himself before speaking. "We'd like to leave Wren here with you while we deal with Astra."

The Exarch's reply was immediate. "No."

"Father, please. We have no other choice. It's too late to run—you said so yourself."

"Then remain here. I will not force you to leave." Metal bands clattered as the Exarch waved a steel-shod hand. "The humans can stay if it pleases you. And the child, at least until it is reasonably safe for them to return to the surface."

"We can't stay," said Freecloud.

The Exarch seemed genuinely confused. "Can't? Why not? Do you care so much about the fate of..." He scowled. "What do they call that vile cesspit of a city above us?"

She saw Freecloud hesitate, so Tam decided to draw the druin's ire herself. "Conthas," she said. "They call the cesspit Conthas."

The Exarch looked to his son for confirmation. "They named it after *me*?" When Freecloud nodded, the old druin stood. His back was bent, his neck craned like a vulture considering a corpse, and Tam was shocked to see that, even standing, his hair draped all the way to his feet.

"*Let them die*," he snarled. "Let Astra scour that abscess clean so it can finally heal. Why throw your life away? There must be other warriors to stand in its defense. They need only kill a single druin sorceress and her Horde will crumble. They did so once before, remember."

Sure, thought Tam. *Kill the Queen, kill the Horde. Easy, right?* But they would have to reach her first.

The bard tried to imagine a typical mercenary fighting

through an undead legion of mercs and monsters (not to mention the Simurg, or Brontide himself) and getting close enough to put a blade through Astra's heart. They would fail, of course, and in death would become yet another soulless soldier in the Winter Queen's host.

In fact, if Tam was being completely honest with herself, she couldn't imagine Rose doing so either.

"I'll stay," said Freecloud.

"*What*?" Rose wheeled on him. "No. Absolutely not. You're kidding, right? Tell me you're kidding."

Freecloud kept his eyes nailed to his father. "I'll stay," he repeated. "But on one condition: Wren stays here with me. When she leaves—*if* she leaves—it will be my decision, not yours."

"Fine," said Contha grudgingly.

"*Not fine.*" Rose was almost shouting now. She tugged roughly on Freecloud's arm, forcing him to look at her. "What are you thinking? We can't stay here, Cloud. You know we can't."

"Rose..."

"Don't fucking Rose me," she snapped. "*We can't stay here.*"

Freecloud's smile was hopelessly sad. "We can. I am."

"What about Fable? What about Brune, and Cura, and Rod?"

"What about them?"

"You'd let them die?"

"I'd let them go!" The druin's ears flicked in irritation. "I'd send them away. This isn't their fight, Rose. It sure as spring isn't mine, and it doesn't have to be yours."

"Those people up there need our help," Rose said, and Tam could virtually hear Gabriel's voice underscoring every word. "If we don't stop her, Astra will kill everyone in Conthas."

"There's fifty thousand mercs in the city," said Freecloud. "Half the Agrian army is camped outside the walls, and half as many Carteans. They defeated the Horde once already. They can do so again, without us."

Rose wasn't convinced. "The Horde lost because Astra *wanted* it to lose," she told him. "You know that. And this time around they'll have the Winter Queen to back them up. And the Dragoneater, thanks to us."

"Thanks to *you*," said Freecloud, causing Rose to reel as if he'd slapped her. "You dragged us to Diremarch, remember? You took the Widow's deal. You put your career as a mercenary before our family, like you always have. And that's okay," he said, when she appeared on the verge of interrupting him. "It's what we both wanted. It's what we agreed on. But you promised, Rose... You *promised* the Dragoneater would be our last gig."

"But—"

"But what?" the druin cried. His fists were clenched, his ears a pair of pointed knives. "The city needs us? The people? The whole fucking world?" A mirthless chuckle. "There's always someone who needs saving, Rose."

"Cloud..."

"But it doesn't have to be you who saves them. It doesn't have to be Fable." Tam could see it was killing him to tell her this—but it was obvious, too, that he'd wanted to say all of it before tonight. She saw the druin's body tense as though he were readying himself for a blow. "Please," he begged her. "This one time... Choose *us* instead of them. Choose *me*."

Silence.

Something scratched in the darkness. Something rustled. Tam could hear her heart pounding in her ears. Or was it Rose's, a prisoner forever trapped within the black iron carapace of that armour?

Freecloud, being druin, knew her reply before the words left her mouth. Tam saw his eyes go dark.

"She killed my father," Rose said.

With those four words, any hope Freecloud had harboured that she might stay evaporated in an instant.

The druin's mouth was a hard line, his eyes evergreen. "I

know," he said. And then his expression softened, and he said again, as if in reply to another revelation altogether, "I know."

Contha (the vile little rat) wore a smirk that bordered on perverse, like a man who'd bet on both dogs in a fight and took joy in watching them tear one another apart. "You've made a wise choice, son. You and your daughter will be safe here. I will have Orbison show the woman out."

Freecloud's ears slanted sharply as he turned on the old man. "For fuck's sake, Dad, *her name is Rose.*"

The Exarch's smiled withered. He blinked several times. "Rose," he said at last, without deigning to look at her. "I will not forget it."

Chapter Forty-eight

The Exhumation of Conthas

Tam waited with Freecloud while Rose said good-bye to Wren. Mother and daughter walked hand in hand into the forest beyond the henge. The sylf was chatting happily about the things Orbison had shown her—flowers made of silver glass, birds that could fly backward—while Rose listened and laughed as if this wasn't in all likelihood the very last time they would ever see or speak with one another.

It was, all things considered, the most heroic thing Tam had ever seen Rose do.

The golem stood at the circle's edge and watched Freecloud with crosshatched eyes. Contha resumed work on his six-legged spider-turtle, muttering quietly to himself as his fingers sliced and soldered its innards. Tam watched the construct's legs thrash and told herself it couldn't feel, it wasn't real, it was just a mindless *thing*.

"You must think I'm an asshole," Freecloud said under his breath.

She glanced up at him. "I don't think you're an asshole."

He sighed, staring in the direction Rose and Wren had gone. "I feel like an asshole." They stood in silence a while longer, until the druin spoke again. "You have a choice ahead of you, Tam."

"I'm going with Rose," she told him.

"Of course you are," he said. "I mean up there. Tomorrow, or whenever it starts."

"It?" she asked, surprised she had the wit to be wry under the circumstances. "You mean the battle to decide the fate of every living thing in the world? *That* it?"

"Yes, that. But what part will you play, I wonder?"

She glanced over, dragging a strand of silver hair behind her ear. "I'm just the—"

"No," he cut her off. "You're not just the bard, Tam. Unless that's all you want to be."

Freecloud crossed his arms and leaned against one of the standing stones. Tam pondered the druin's words, absently rubbing a thumb against the weather-worn grip of her longbow. They waited side by side until a warbling toot from Orbison's spout heralded the return of Rose and Wren. The sylf had been crying, her cheeks still raw from having rubbed away tears.

Freecloud pushed himself upright. "I'll take you up," he said. "There's another way out, a Threshold that opens outside Lamneth's walls."

"The golem can do it," Rose said. Her voice was cold, her face impassive. She passed her daughter off and looked to Tam, who nodded in reply to the question in her eyes.

The bard half-expected Contha to gloat, but the Exarch didn't even bother glancing up from his work as Rose turned to leave.

Before she could, Freecloud took her hand. Rose started to pull away, but didn't, and as the moment stretched, Tam could see her trembling, as if the druin's touch were a scalding flame—and yet she couldn't force herself to let go, no matter how badly it hurt to hold on.

Finally, she did, and Tam imagined Rose's heart tearing into halves as the two of them followed Orbison up the winding path and away. They crossed the bridge and climbed the spiral stair, but instead of returning to the foundry the golem took them by a different route. They came to another bridge, and were halfway across when Orbison paused and peered over the edge.

"What is it?" Rose asked, sounding annoyed.

The construct whistled and pointed down. Tam and Rose joined him at the brink, squinting into the gloom. As they did, Orbison's ghostly green heartlight brightened so they could see a portion, at least, of what lay beneath them.

"Gods," Tam whispered, and heard Rose swear quietly beside her. "There must be hundreds of them."

"Thousands," said Rose.

"Do you think Freecloud knows about this?"

"He'd better fucking not," Rose grated, and then spat over the side of the bridge. "Let's go."

They stepped out of the Threshold onto the darkened hilltop. Glancing over her shoulder, Tam saw Orbison wave good-bye before the air beneath the stone arch shimmered and left her looking through it at a flurry of falling snow. The city sloped away below them, dotted here and there with guttering torchlight, gleaming windows, and several rampant fires.

Conthas, she recalled Bran telling her once, was a city of mercenaries: *Even the fire brigade won't lift a finger unless you pay them up front!*

On the hill south of Lamneth was a lofty chapel surrounded by a high wall. Light glowed behind coloured glass windows, and mirrored lamps threw broadening beams across the arc of a great golden dome.

"I wonder who lives there," Tam mused, gazing across at the fortified compound.

"My mother used to," Rose answered. "But she moved to Fivecourt last year and sold the place to Uncle Moog. He calls it the Sanctuary." She started at the sound of someone approaching, but relaxed as a shaggy, scarf-wearing wolf materialized from the shadows.

Brune was carrying his clothes in his mouth, and once he'd shammed he began hurriedly dressing himself. "Jain sent me to find you," he panted. "She—"

"Did you speak to the pit bosses?"

"Yeah, but—"

"Will they help?"

"Reluctantly, yes."

"What about the Agrians?"

"Leaving in the morning, apparently." The shaman was struggling to keep his socks dry as he pulled on his boots. "Their commander is a real asshole, by the way."

"Frigid Hells," Rose swore. "What about the Carteans?"

Brune rolled his shoulders. "Dunno. Slowhand's called a meeting at the Starwood. The local barons are there, and some of the senior mercs, along with a few weirdos Moog and Cura scrounged up in Sinkwell." Rose started downhill, but the shaman blocked her path. "Jain needs to see you first."

"Why?"

"Because . . . she wants to speak with you."

"Then tell her to meet me at the Starwood."

"Not Jain," Brune clarified, before Rose could push past him again. "Astra."

Conthas was going crazy around them. It reminded Tam of Fighter's Camp on a city-wide scale. Everywhere she looked were drunk people, dancing people, naked people; bards were singing, mercs were fighting, priests were shouting, "It's the end of the world!" to a chorus of raucous cheers.

Tam spotted argosies belonging to the Screaming Eagles, Flashbang, the Time Wizards, and countless bands she'd never heard of. There were a trio of skyships moored above a tavern called World's Away. All three boats were packed to the rails with revellers.

Brune led them through the veil of raining mist, skirting a stone fountain into which a line of industrious mercs were emptying kegs of frothing beer.

"What's wrong with these people?" Tam hollered to be heard above the noise. "They know what's coming, right? Why are they still celebrating?"

"Why not?" Rose countered. "If you thought you'd die tomorrow, would you waste the night weeping about it?"

Tam didn't bother responding—in part because she didn't feel like shouting, but also because yes, she probably would. She quickened her pace to keep up with Brune, who brought them up to speed as they walked.

As per Rose's request, Branigan and Lady Jain had organized the exhumation of Conthas. Every crypt and tomb was being ransacked, their contents smashed to dust. The moat was dredged, revealing several hundred corpses in various states of decay, a hoard's worth of mouldy courtmark coins, and a cantankerous merman who identified himself as Oscar and berated his captors until they set him free.

The graveyards were likewise pillaged: Skeletons were stomped apart, while the corpses were taken by cart to the square beyond the West Gutter Gate. When Rose remarked on how efficient Jain had been at coercing the citizens of Conthas to help out, the shaman snorted.

"That's because she promised they could keep whatever fortune they find, so long as they disposed of the bodies. These people aren't really helping," Brune informed them. "They're looting."

As they neared their destination there were more people standing than walking. Someone they passed called out to Rose, but when Tam turned to see who'd spoken she saw nothing but a shabby man draped in fine jewellery pushing a corpse in a wheelbarrow behind them.

Jain was waiting at the gate. The woman looked as shaken as Tam had ever seen her, which the bard took for a very bad sign.

"This had better be good," Rose told her.

"It ain't good," said Jain, and led them on.

Rose. Tam heard it again, from up ahead this time.

Rose. And again, except it sounded as though a dozen people were saying her name at once.

As they entered the square, a cannibal's kitchen of horrible smells assaulted Tam's nose: the rot-flower reek of spoiled guts, the sour-apple stench of putrefied flesh, and the underlying scent of an outhouse overflowing with curdled eggs.

The source of the stink was obvious: There was a pit here like the one across town in the Monster Market, but instead of yammering goblins it was filled nearly to the top with dead bodies. A dozen of Jain's Silk Arrows stood around it with buckets of lamp oil and guttering torches, the light of which picked out the tangled limbs and bloodless faces of those heaped below.

The source of the whispers, however, was less apparent—at least until Tam forced herself to look directly into the pit.

"Rose"—from gaping jaws, from mouths that should have been too broken to form the words.

"Rose"—from blistered lips, from tongues that writhed like maggots out of open throats.

"Rose"—from a thousand piled corpses, every one of them gazing up with white-fire eyes.

"Rose. Rose. Rose," said the Winter Queen in a chorus of disparate voices, and when the mercenary finally stepped to the pit's edge, the dead spoke as one.

"Rose."

"What the fuck do you want?" she asked.

A hundred slit-throat grins greeted her words. *"Tell me how he died,"* they asked.

"How who died?" Rose's voice was flat, but pain and anger flashed behind her eyes.

Papery laughter floated up from the pit. *"Gabriel,"* they said, and a frightened murmur erupted around the square. If anyone in Conthas was unaware that Grandual had lost its greatest champion, they would know before long.

A priest with crow-pecked eyes lurched upright in a nearby wheelbarrow. *"Was he in pain? Did he weep?"*

"Did he scream?" asked a woman below, fish-bitten and bloated. *"Did he curse my name with his dying breath?"*

"TELL ME," the dead commanded.

Tam had never been so scared in her entire life—not even when they'd faced the Simurg. Her fear then had been a fiery thing, burning through her limbs, fuel for a courage she hadn't known she'd possessed. But this was a cold, creeping, fathomless dread. It fuelled nothing, only *drained*.

It was all she could do not to flee from the pit, the square, the whole fucking city. She could tell Rose was unsettled, too, despite her brave face. Of everyone, Jain was the least bothered by the horror below. The mercenary stood with her hands on her hips and was glowering into the hole like a farmer finding out a fox had spent the night in her henhouse. She had wads of something—mint leaves, it looked like—stuffed up her nose.

"It doesn't matter how he died," Rose said. "My father is gone. Beyond your reach," she added, drawing an enraged hiss from below. "He's not your concern anymore. I am."

The corpse of a young girl in a soiled blue dress rolled her head to an impossible angle. *"I should have killed you by the lake,"* she said sweetly, *"but I wanted you to suffer. You will suffer, Rose. I'll make sure of it."*

"And when you are dead," said a man elsewhere in the pile, who must've been rich since someone had gone out of their way to steal his clothes, *"you are mine. I will wear your soul like a glove."*

"You will be my tool," the eyeless priest informed her. *"My puppet-general. With you to lead them, my armies will scour every corner of the world."*

A woman with half her head caved in wheezed up at her, "*Your meddling cost my son his life. And now you, Rose, will be the instrument of my revenge.*"

"Your son?" Jain's brow knit in confusion.

"*Lastleaf,*" said Tam and Rose at once.

"Ah." The southerner chewed on that for a moment before deciding she didn't much care for how it tasted. She hawked and spat a mouthful of phlegm down onto the pile. "That's for your son," she said.

The pit writhed in fury. Tam heard another bout of muttering from those gathered to watch, and a few tittering laughs as well.

The bard recalled Astra's grief on the battlefield south of Grey Vale. She tried to conjure sympathy for the woman whose so-called life had been bought and paid for with the blood of her children—the daughter first, and now the son. But then Tam's eyes returned to the dead girl in the blue dress with her head on backward, and sympathy threw open the window, waved from the ledge, and leapt to its death.

Fuck her, Tam thought. *Everyone suffers. We've all lost people we love, and it's not always—or ever—fair. But only a monster paints everyone with the same bloody brush. And only a madwoman wants the world to suffer with her.*

"You shouldn't have come here," Rose said. "You should have gone to Ardburg first. Or Fivecourt. Anywhere but here."

The squirming pile groaned. "*Why?*" they asked.

"Because this is Conthas," Rose answered, as if needing to explain that water was wet. "The Free City. They don't take kindly to queens here, or conquering armies."

"Damn right," Jain said through a grin.

Rose dragged a hand through her hair. "Listen, Astra, what happened to your son . . . It wasn't right. My father told me how the Republic treated him."

"*Like a beast,*" said the stripped nobleman.

"*Like an animal,*" said the fish-bitten woman.

"*Like a monster,*" said the girl in the blue dress.

"Yes," Rose admitted. "Like a monster. But Lastleaf wasn't evil. Not really. He wanted to *change* things, not destroy them entirely. He was fighting to make the world a better place for those like him. But—"

"*YOU DO NOT KNOW,*" the pit howled up at her. "*THE AGONY. THE ANGUISH. THE VOID A CHILD LEAVES BEHIND WHEN IT IS GONE.*"

"*But you will,*" said the priest in the wheelbarrow.

"*You will very soon,*" said the little girl.

Rose cocked her head. "What do you mean?"

"*Do you think I can't see her?*" the Winter Queen asked with the ashen lips of the potbellied nobleman. "*Do you think I don't know what you're hiding?*"

Tam's heart stopped beating. Her next breath was an involuntary gasp. She glanced toward Rose and found her parchment-pale, still as stone.

The woman with half a head grinned toothlessly. "*Contha thinks himself clever. He thinks himself safe. But I have eyes in the dark, and I can see him now. I can see his son. And I can see . . .*"

"Oh, please, no," Tam whispered.

"*. . . your daughter,*" said the girl in the dress, her words jarring like violence on a sunny day. "*I will kill her, Rose.*"

"Burn them," Rose said to Jain. "Burn them, now."

"*And I will use your hands to do it.*"

"Burn them!" Rose screamed.

At a frantic gesture from Jain, the Silk Arrows she'd stationed around the pit tossed buckets of oil over the heaped corpses. Others lobbed torches onto the pile, and the fire caught quickly—chewing up flesh, blackening bone, turning wisps of tattered hair into blazing filaments.

And all the while the corpses laughed, a sound like a thousand dying breaths drifting up on oily smoke. They laughed in the wagons still rumbling toward the square, in the carts delayed by the traffic entering the city. The priest in his barrow cackled, one bony finger pointed at Rose, who was standing over the pit as though she meant to dive in and kill every one of Astra's thralls before the fire consumed them.

"I will end you!" Rose howled. "Do you hear me, you cold-lipped cunt? If you come here—if come anywhere near my daughter—I will find you on the battlefield and I *will cut you the fuck down*!"

She turned and stalked back toward the gate, pushing aside those too slow to clear a path. Brune and Jain went after her, but as Tam made to follow, the priest's wheeze tickled her ear like a pestering fly.

The bard whirled and walked over to the wheelbarrow. The thing's flickering gaze settled on her. Its grin fell away, and Tam could sense something—*Astra*—looking out through its eyes. The feeling was eerily sinister, like seeing the shape of someone watching you from a darkened window.

"*You*," it said.

"Me," she replied, and drove her knife down into its skull.

Chapter Forty-nine

Here and Now

In a tavern called the Starwood they found Slowhand and Moog sharing a long oak table with a handful of city delegates, while an audience of mercenaries, soldiers, rogues, and restless thugs looked on. Cura and Roderick were just inside, and had cornered someone the bard couldn't see until Rod saw Rose coming and pushed their quarry toward her.

"Look who I found!" he announced.

"You didn't *find* me," said Daon Doshi. "I returned of my own volition. I couldn't in good conscience—" He stopped there, evidently finding it hard to speak with Rose's knuckles buried in his gut. "I deserved that," he groaned, and when Rose's other fist caught him hard across the jaw he stumbled, touching fingers to his bloodied lip. "I deserved that, too. Wait!" The pilot raised a hand before Rose could throw another punch. "Listen, please! I panicked, okay? You saw what was happening on that battlefield! Heathen help me, the dead were coming back to life! What did you expect me to do?"

"I expected to drag your corpse off that ship and fly away," Rose grated. "My father—" She stopped herself short, closed her eyes, and waited until her fury drained away. "Why did you really come back?"

"I told you. My profound sense of honour forbade me—"

"Try again," Rose told him. "One more lie and you go swimming in the goblin pit."

The captain swallowed nervously. "Fine," he huffed. "We're surrounded! The sky around the city is swarming with fiends. I couldn't escape if I wanted to. And believe me, I wanted to."

Lady Jain barged up beside Rose. "So why aren't they attacking?"

Doshi looked twice at Jain, then self-consciously adjusted the goggles on his forehead. "I, ah . . . Who are you?"

"You were saying," Rose prompted, before Jain could introduce herself.

The captain cleared his throat. "Well, my guess is that the Widow—or the Winter-whatever-the-fuck-it-is-we're-calling-her-now—is setting a trap."

Rose scowled. "A trap for who?"

"You," said Tam. "Obviously."

Fable's leader flashed her an irritated glare, but Brune leapt to Tam's defense.

"She holds you partly responsible for Lastleaf's death," the shaman reminded her.

"And you killed the Dragoneater once already," said Cura. "She's afraid of you, Rose."

"She'd better be." Rose turned back to Doshi. "Where's the *Old Glory* now?"

The captain pointed up. "The roof. I may or may not have crash-landed in the pool up there." The others stared at him a moment. "Okay, yes, I crash-landed in the pool. And listen"—Doshi cleared his throat—"Roderick told me about what happened to your father. I'm sorry, Rose. Truly. If I hadn't left . . ."

"It doesn't matter," Rose told him. "If you hadn't left, you might be dead. Hawkshaw would've still been waiting for us, and my father would have died just the same."

"Where's Freecloud?" Cura wondered aloud, more to change the subject than out of genuine curiosity.

"He's staying with Wren."

The Inkwitch and Brune shared a troubled glance, but tactfully opted to lay off questions for the time being.

Roderick, however, possessed the tact of a battering ram to the groin. "What, like forever? Why? Doesn't he——"

"Forget your godsdamned Queen!" bellowed Slowhand from across the room. He slammed the table before him with both hands. Cups toppled like drunks, vomiting whiskey, wine, and beer onto the weathered oak. "Lilith isn't here, Lokan. You are. This is your call to make."

"And I've made it," said a handsome, hook-nosed northerner who, judging by his lavish armour and general haughtiness, must have been the Agrian commander. "Which is why I'm taking the army back to Brycliffe. If my queen orders us to return and lift the siege, so be it——but I'm not risking ten thousand soldiers——"

"There won't *be* a siege!" roared Slowhand. "This isn't Castia! We don't have warded walls or lightning turrets. Unless we stop them, the Horde will roll over this place like..." He paused, groping for a suitable metaphor. "Moog, help me out here."

"Purple!" shouted the wizard. "Wait, no, fishcakes!"

Clay scowled. "You weren't listening."

"I wasn't listening," Moog admitted. "Sorry."

"Piss on Agria," said a Cartean with raven's wings tattooed across his broad chest. "And fuck its queen. My han has no wish to fight alongside these craven bushlanders anyway!"

The Agrian commander drew his sword. "Insult my queen again, horsefucker."

"I fucked *one horse*," said the Cartean. "And who even told you that? Nazreth?" he turned an accusing eye on a fellow clansman, who shook his head emphatically.

A profoundly uncomfortable silence followed, broken by a dull scrape as Rose dragged a chair to the table and settled into it.

The northerner returned his sword to its scabbard and fixed her with a haughty stare. "And you are?"

"You know who I am," said Rose. Her voice was calm, commanding, cool as a sword sheathed in a snowdrift. Her eyes roamed the table. "Who are you?"

One by one Conthas's would-be defenders introduced themselves, beginning with Lokan—the northerner in charge of Agria's army—and Kurin, First Feather of the High Han's personal bodyguard.

There were a dozen or so bands in the room, most of which had a representative at the table. They didn't bother introducing themselves to Rose, but the bard recognized more than a few. Mad Mackie led a band called Flashbang, who were famous for hunting ghosts, wights, wraiths, and any other incorporeal thing with a bad attitude. Jeramyn Cain, who she'd seen in the yard outside Slowhand's, was the frontman for the Screaming Eagles.

A few of Kaskar's favoured sons were present as well, including Garland (of Garland and the Bats) and Alkain Tor. The frontman for Giantsbane, who'd slain hundreds of monsters during his long and illustrious careeer, wore a leather patch over the eye he'd lost to the chicken back in Ardburg's arena.

Next to present themselves were the self-styled Robber Barons of Conthas. Tain Starkwood, the Baron of Rockbottom, was built like Brune—except Brune had a neck, whereas Tain had a pile of muscles that appeared to be cutting off circulation to his head. He was missing most of his teeth and half of every finger on his left hand.

The Baron of Knight's Landing was an arachnian named K'tuo who only spoke Narmeeri and offered Rose (through a translator) a marriage proposal along with his name.

"No thanks," she said dryly, already turning her attention to the man beside him, an obese Phantran wearing enough silk to make tents for a whole army of foppish noblemen.

"Tabano, the Baron of Saltkettle," the man introduced himself with an accent thicker than Doshi's but half as charming. He made a flourish that sent a wave of sickly sweet perfume billowing across the table. "I believe my associates had the pleasure of meeting you at the city gate."

Tam recalled with a smile the sight of Rose bashing a man's face in with his own helmet.

Next up were the twin baronesses, Ios and Alektra. The former was wearing black fighting leathers and ruled a part of the city called Telltale, while the latter dressed like a high-born lady and governed a ward known as the Paper Court. The sisters very obviously hated one another, and while Alektra pledged five hundred swords to Rose's cause, Ios promised fifty assassins who were worth, by her own estimation, twice what her sister could supply.

Moog introduced a pair of curiosities he and Cura had dug up in Sinkwell. The first was a garishly clad summoner named Roga who was carrying a statuette of something round and pink in the crook of one arm.

"Is that a . . . pig?" Tam asked under her breath.

"Elephant," said Cura. "Don't look at me—they're Moog's friends. Sinkwell is full of nuts like these two."

Moog's other "friend" was Kaliax Kur, a rough-looking woman with a shorn skull and a mess of vicious scars marring a face that probably hadn't been all that pretty to begin with. She wore a suit of scorched wood armour inlaid with metal plates. What appeared to be the ring of a tidal engine was strapped to her back, attached by looping copper wire to a lance she leaned on like a staff.

"What's her deal?" Tam asked.

"I'm guessing 'orc-shit crazy' is her deal," Cura muttered.

The last member of Slowhand's council was, without a doubt, the most beautiful woman Tam had ever seen, and the only one who needed no introduction.

Larkspur, the world's most notorious bounty hunter, had

straight black hair, eyes like starlit pools, and beestung lips that seemed fixed in a permanent snarl. She wore a black steel breastplate and taloned gauntlets—one of which was curled round the haft of a wicked-looking scythe. Her most remarkable feature, however, was a pair of black-feathered wings draped over her shoulders.

There was a boy standing beside her. He was tall for his age, which Tam supposed was a year or two older than Wren. His almond-shaped eyes, arched nose, and fierce scowl marked him as the woman's son, but his skin was several shades darker, suggesting his father was a southerner.

And a damn big one, she guessed, assessing the boy's broad shoulders.

With Larkspur present, the bard was feeling decidedly better about the city's chances of surviving the battle to come, at least until the bounty hunter opened her mouth.

"I'm leaving, too," she said.

Slowhand deflated visibly. "What? Why?"

"You know why. If you don't stop Astra here—"

"We *will* stop her here. We have to. Besides, you'll never make it back in time."

"I know that," she said. "But if Conthas falls... Well, then the rest of the world will need him, Clay. More than it ever has."

"Him?" Tam whispered, but Cura only shook her head.

Slowhand and Larkspur locked eyes for a long moment. "Good luck," he said finally.

The Agrian commander wore a satisfied smirk. "Perhaps you should consider abandoning the city as well," he said to Clay.

"We're not abandoning the city," Rose told him. "Every person Astra kills becomes another foot soldier in her army. Assuming she can raise most of the Brumal Horde, she has maybe eighty thousand monsters under her command, along with every merc they managed to kill at Grey Vale."

"We beat the Horde once," boasted Kurin, crossing his arms over the wings inked on his chest. "We will beat it again."

Didn't Freecloud say the same thing? Tam mused. The difference was, this horse-fucking fool actually believed it.

"They were panicked," Rose argued. "Confused. Desperate to escape a burning forest, and more than likely being attacked by their own dead. This time they'll be relentless, bound to obey Astra's commands. She won't let them run. She won't even let them *die*. We beat the Horde at Castia because we broke their will, but the Winter Queen's army has no will to break."

"She can't control all of them at once," said the summoner with the elephant in her arm. He looked at Moog. "Can she?"

The old wizard smoothed his white beard against the front of his robe. "I, uh...maybe?" he said. "Necromancers draw on their own life force to animate the dead. That is, most of them do. But the Winter Queen...well, she's dead herself, or something like it. However it is she's doing what it is she's doing, Astra believes herself capable of enslaving every soul in Grandual." Moog wrung his bony fingers. "I don't see that we have any choice but to take her at her word, or risk the consequences."

"And those consequences..." mused the Baron of Saltkettle.

"Well, death," said the wizard, as though the answer was evident. "The utter annihilation of every living creature in the world."

Tam saw Clay Cooper's keg-sized chest rise and fall in a long sigh. "This again," he grumbled.

Rose stood, addressing the room. "We have to stop her. We need to do it here and now, before it's too late. And we can only do that if we work together." She looked from face to face around the table. "Carteans, Agrians, mercenaries, soldiers, sorcerers, thugs—it doesn't matter what you are, so long as you're willing to fight. The rest of Grandual may not know it—hell, they probably won't believe us if we live to tell them—but we may be all that stands between them and oblivion." She levelled a pointed stare at the Agrian commander. "If we fight this war separately, we die. So either stand with us now, or flee and face us on the battlefield once we're dead."

An ominous silence followed, and then the Baron of Saltkettle cleared his throat. "I don't suppose you have a plan, then? Some miraculous scheme to kill the Winter Queen and dispel her Horde in one fell swoop?"

Rose's teeth flashed like a naked blade in the lamplight. "As a matter of fact, I do."

Chapter Fifty

Eve of Annihilation

The Agrians left in the night. Tam and the others saw them go from the Starwood's rooftop patio. The band was loitering around a sizzling oil brazier, alone but for a dozen iced-over tables, a few frozen hedgerows, and Moog, who was scavenging some items from the *Old Glory* before relinquishing it to Doshi in the morning. The skyship was half-submerged in the shallow pool behind them, but the captain had assured Rose he'd have it battle-ready by the time Astra and her Horde showed up.

"Fucking cowards," Rose muttered. She drew a lungful of smoke from the pipe in her mouth as she watched the Agrians depart.

"It's better that cowards flee before a battle than during one," said Brune.

Cura passed him the bottle of cheap red wine they were sharing between them. "That's insightful. I'm impressed."

"Thanks," said the shaman. "I read it on a beermat at the Shattered Shield."

"You can read?" She grinned. "Now I'm *really* impressed."

"He's right, though," said Roderick. The satyr was sitting with his hooves dangling over the side of the building. "Fleeing soldiers are notoriously bad for morale."

Tam had retrieved *Hiraeth* from the skyship earlier and braced the sealskin case against her side as she peered over the ledge. "I don't think morale is going to be a problem."

The street below was a strip of pure bedlam, a riotous river teeming with two sorts of people: those far too drunk to worry about the Winter Queen, and those hell-bent on catching up to the former. The air was filled with shouting and laughter; a hundred bards played a hundred songs on everything from drums and mandolins to reedy pipes and chiming brass bells. It was hard to tell the dance circles from the fighting rings, and difficult to discern either from the orgies springing up despite the cold.

Tam had lost count of counterfeit Roses roaming the crowd. There were hucknell-red heads everywhere, and a few of them looked more like Rose than Rose, since Fable's frontwoman hadn't died her hair since the end of the tour and her golden roots (along with Tam's plain brown ones) were growing out.

Tam was also surprised to see Oscar the merman, who'd been dredged from the city's moat, bobbing along on a sea of hands. His foul mood had given way to wine-fuelled glee, as evidenced by the bottle clutched in his webbed fingers.

One of the skyships that Tam had seen earlier—a pot-bellied carrack called the *Barracuda*—was drifting over the thoroughfare. Revellers on board were pouring streams of sloshing booze into the open mouths and raised cups of the thirsty masses. The ship's captain was nowhere in sight; instead, a queue of scantily clad women were taking turns at the steering console.

Speaking of captains... Tam spotted Daon Doshi's yellow robe and striped skullcap outside a tavern across the street. He was sucking face with a woman Tam couldn't make out until the two of them finally decided that breathing was more important than swapping saliva.

Cura had been watching the pair as well. "Wait, is that...?"

"Jain," Tam finished. "Those two . . . makes a lot of sense, actually."

The summoner laughed. "They kind of do."

"They can wear each other's clothes," Tam suggested.

"And rob people blind."

"Gods," the bard said through a smile, "they're made for each other."

"Agreed." Cura's mirth melted away. "It's too bad . . ." She left the rest unsaid, but the implication was tacit nonetheless.

"You should go, too," Rose said, eventually.

All of them glanced at one another.

"Who?" asked Roderick.

Rose put her pipe out on the snow-mantled ledge. "All of you. Astra may have us surrounded, but I'm sure a small party could slip the noose. Go east. Or wherever."

"You mean *run*?" Brune sounded incredulous.

"Run. Live. For a little while longer, anyway."

Cura said, "You're joking, right? You just called what's-his-nuts a coward for leaving."

"Lokan," Rose supplied.

"Whatever. And now you want us to follow him? To abandon you here so we can die a few weeks after you?"

"It could take years—" Rose began.

"Fuck that," Cura cut her off. "And fuck you for suggesting it."

Rose laughed, a sound Tam hadn't ever expected to hear again, considering what she'd lost, and what she stood to lose in the days to come. "I had to try," she said.

The Inkwitch regarded her warily, like a startled cat summoned back to its master's lap. "No you didn't. You've got a family to defend, yeah? People you love that need protecting? Well, so do I."

"So do I," Brune echoed.

"Me too," Tam said.

Rose was about to reply when someone called out from the stairwell behind them.

"Rosie! Love! I've been looking everywhere for you!" The voice belonged to a scrawny man with a patchy beard and a black smile. He was wearing a longcoat several sizes too big for him that dragged in the snow as he sauntered forward.

Tam didn't know the man, but Cura and Brune were less than enthused to see him, so she decided on a whim that she hated his guts.

Rose eyed him narrowly. "What do you want, Pryne?"

The man spread his hands, which, Tam noted, were stained the same dark colour as his teeth. "I heard you'd come to play hero, so I came to help."

"Go away."

"Now, now," said Pryne, "is that any way to speak to an old friend? Let alone one who comes bearing gifts..." He withdrew a cloth from his coat pocket and unfolded it, careful to keep the contents sheltered from the snow.

Tam couldn't see what it was, but between the man's smarmy demeanor and the way Rose recoiled from his offering, she could hazard a guess. Pryne was a dealer.

"Look at these beauties," he cooed. "There's enough Leaf here to take on a dozen Hordes!"

"Not interested," Rose told him.

"Sure you are," he said. His voice was slimy and sibilant. He struck Tam as a man well practiced at convincing addicts they wanted what they didn't need.

Tam saw Cura fingering one of several knives strapped to her frame. Brune was pondering the wine bottle in his hand, likely debating whether to drink from it or to smash it over the dealer's head.

"I'll even give you a discount," Pryne said. "You know, considering you're saving the world and all that."

Rose gazed at the dealer's offering. Some mute distress flashed behind her eyes, as though she found herself confronted by the ghost of a long-dead nemesis. But then her expression slackened. "Give it here," she said with a sigh.

A sound like a whimper came from Roderick. The booker said nothing, however. Nor did Brune, or Cura, or—to her own surprise—Tam, who was wise enough to know that some battles needed to be fought alone, even if it meant you lost them.

"Atta girl," said Pryne, handing over the cloth. "I brought you the best, of course. Made it fresh this morning, so it'll be less bitter than you're used to. You've got an even dozen there, which..." He faltered as Rose drew them out of the cloth. His chuckle was palpably disingenuous. "Now be careful, Rosie, or—"

Rose crushed the brittle leaves in her fist. When she opened her hand they were nothing but dust, which the wind carried off into the cold Conthas night.

The dealer's eyes bulged. "What the hell? Are you out of your fucking mind? You just *threw away* sixty bloody courtmarks! I expect to be paid for those!"

"Sure thing." Rose grinned. "How's the end of the week sound?"

Pryne's hand twitched toward the knife on his belt, but for all his apparent faults he wasn't *that* stupid. He relaxed, and his slimy grin gradually returned. "I'll see you before then, I think. We both know what's coming, Rosie. The moment that Horde shows up you'll come crawling to me, and you'd better have a full purse and a bloody convincing apology when you do."

"Can I throw him off the roof?" Brune pleaded.

"Can I cut his balls off first?" asked Cura.

Pryne bolted for the downstairs door. "Rot take the lot of you," he called over his shoulder.

No one spoke for a while after he left. Roderick kicked his feet and watched the crowd below. Rose stared at the black stain on her hands—wondering, perhaps, if she really did possess the courage to face the Horde on her own. Brune drank and tried catching snowflakes on his tongue. Cura hummed quietly to herself. The tune was familiar, and it was a moment before Tam recognized it as the song she'd composed for Brune.

She unlaced the toggles on the sealskin case and eased the heart-shaped lute from inside. She sat next to Roderick and nestled *Hiraeth* in her lap. When she plucked a few exploratory notes the others glanced her way.

Cura smiled, which made the effort of playing worthwhile before she'd even started.

"Sing with me?" Tam asked.

An arched brow, a quirk at the corner of the summoner's lips. "Why not?"

Tam played. They sang. The satyr swayed beside her, tapping out the beat on his thighs. Rose and Brune listened intently. The shaman began nodding almost as soon as the song began, and by the end he was bobbing along, blinking to forestall the threat of tears.

Moog emerged from inside the *Old Glory*. He sidled up next to Rose, who put an arm around the old man's slim shoulders.

Tam sang the last verse herself, since she hadn't yet written the words when she and Cura performed the song together in a Diremarch hovel.

A mother's cry, a father's crime
We cannot leave the past behind
Only in the end we find
The missing piece, the borrowed time

We bear the weight of stolen thrones
With broken hearts and broken bones
The saddest song I've ever known
Is the howling of the wolf

"Blood of the fucking gods," Brune said when she'd finished. "I love it. I love it, Tam. Thank you." She managed to lower her lute before the shaman's huge arms enveloped her. He squeezed her once and then kissed the top of her head before stepping away.

"She's a bard, after all!" jeered Roderick. His tone was playful, but the words rankled for some reason Tam couldn't quite put her finger on.

"Could I make a request?" asked Rose.

Tam blew on her fingers to warm them. "Anything but *Castia*."

Cura chuckled. Brune, still smiling, looked to Rose like a boy expecting his mom to slap a sibling.

"I think you know the one," Rose said. And then added, quite unnecessarily, "Please."

She did, as it happened, know which song Rose had in mind.

As it began, she thought, *so it ends*.

The bard was a few chords into *Together* when Moog interrupted. "Ah, wait! Just a moment, sorry!" The wizard rummaged through the many pockets of his robe for an awkward length of time before finally withdrawing a small leather satchel. He drew a pinch of blue powder from inside and sprinkled it over the flames in the brazier. It sparked, and left a smell like cinnamon in the air. He said nothing afterward, only gave her an exaggerated wink and a double thumbs-up.

When she once again plucked the first note of the song Tam nearly jumped out of her skin. The sound echoed back to her from everywhere at once, and it wasn't until she pulled another few notes that she realized where it was coming from. Whatever enchantment Moog had cast over the brazier, the music she played was emanating from every torch and bonfire within earshot.

The noise in the Gutter faltered as the celebrants looked around, bewildered. Up and down the strip instruments fell silent and conversations died. Windows were thrown open and curious faces peered out, no doubt wondering why their fireplaces and candles were playing music.

Cura offered Tam an assuring nod. "Go on," she whispered.

Go on, said the night around them.

The bard took a breath, aware that the whole city might hear it, and then she sang.

The bards say the Winter Queen herself led the Horde against Conthas. They say the city's defenders were outnumbered three to one, and that monsters fought shoulder to shoulder with men and women against the unrelenting army of the dead. They tell us that Clay Cooper slew the giant Brontide in single combat, or that Bloody Rose did, or that a girl with silver hair killed him with a single arrow—when in fact none of these three are true.

Bards, you see, are full of shit. They'll say just about anything if it means a free drink or another copper coin in their hat.

But of all the stories told about the days before and after the destruction of Conthas, none is more absurd, more categorically far-fetched, than the tale of Tam Hashford and the Singing City.

According to the bards, she performed on a rooftop, and her voice, amplified by sorcery, was heard in every corner of Conthas. It's said she played her mother's now-legendary song on her mother's then-legendary lute, and that she sang the first verse all by herself, timid and tremulous, until a second voice—lower, but also female—joined in. During the chorus, we're told, she was accompanied by her remaining bandmates, including none other than Bloody Rose herself.

The stories would have us believe that war-weary mercs

wept at the sound of Rose's voice. She might have made a magnificent bard, some claimed, had the world not made her a killer instead.

Hundreds more joined in for the next verse. Most people know that song by heart, and there's not a drunk in the world who doesn't consider themself an exceptionally gifted singer. When the chorus rolled around once again, it's said that even the soberest citizen of Conthas shrugged off their inhibition and sang along.

On every street, in every square; in brothels, and taverns, and scratch dens; in brawling pits, and dice-houses, and candlelit temples—anywhere a lamp sputtered or a fire roared, they sang. Thieves crooned it while they rifled pockets, harlots hummed it in their lover's ears; wranglers serenaded the monsters in their pens, and pits, and cages.

Mercenaries, for all their pomp and pageantry, are a sentimental lot, and so the thousands crowding the streets of Conthas clung to one another and bellowed at the top of their lungs, because they might be dead tomorrow, and *un*dead the day after, but they were *alive tonight*. Even the musicians chimed in: drumming and strumming and plucking along, each one adding their own flavour to the stewpot of simmering melody.

The most fanciful accounts of the night tell of a druin standing on a dark hillside, gazing with an immortal's bone-deep melancholy on the spectacle below. Others float the outlandish notion that the singing city could be heard even by the approaching Horde. They imagine a host of shuffling corpses cocking their heads and listening to that distant, defiant song, the flames in their eyes guttering as some lingering spark of their humanity drew breath.

You will know, of course, that Lily Hashford's masterpiece ends unaccompanied by music. During its final verse, the city-wide chorus faded as well, shedding voice after voice as an oak sheds its leaves at the onset of winter, until the only one singing was the girl who'd started it all.

Her voice—bolstered by the courage of sixty thousand souls—was no longer the timorous thing of minutes earlier. Now it was strident, steady, clear as a starry summer night. In fact, there are some who swear it was Lily Hashford herself who sang that final verse.

And when she, too, fell silent, it was several heartbeats before the applause began in earnest.

At which point, the bards unanimously agree, the strangest thing occurred.

Tam Hashford stood. She grazed her fingers over the whitewood face of her mother's lute and whispered some secret message into the instrument's heart-shaped bowl. And then she gripped its slender neck with both hands and smashed it to splinters on the ledge before her.

Chapter Fifty-one

Friends and Foes

Tam stared at the ruin of her mother's lute.

She waited for remorse to storm in, throw its hands in the air and yell, *Fool girl! What have you done?*

In the space of a few heartbeats she'd managed to wreck a beautiful instrument, destroy her livelihood as a bard, and break the last material bond she shared with her mother. This last, she knew, should have gutted her. It would have, mere months ago.

She'd been a very different person mere months ago.

While smashing *Hiraeth*, Tam had felt a profound sense of *rightness*. In doing so, she had set free a sorrow she'd been holding on to since childhood. Her mother's memory remained inside her: an unforgettable fire. But where once it had scalded to touch, it was now a comfort—a soul-suffusing warmth that could, if nurtured, heal a great deal more than it hurt.

And what was more: She'd finally made the choice Free-cloud had warned her was coming. As a bard, it had been her duty to watch, to distance herself from the men and women whose stories she was supposed to tell. Only it turned out she was ill-suited for watching, incapable of standing by while others put their lives at risk.

And distance? she mocked herself. *Distance went out the window when you jumped in bed with a bandmate...*

Tam became gradually aware that the others were watching her: Roderick with openmouthed shock, Brune and Cura with a mix of startled surprise and genuine concern. Moog was too busy wiping his red-rimmed eyes to look at anything but the sleeves of his robe.

Rose, however, was smiling. "You were a terrible bard," she said.

"I know."

"You're fired."

"Fair enough."

"So, what's next?"

Tam blew a strand of silver hair from her eyes. "I thought I might try joining a band."

"Hmm." Rose pretended to consider that. "Got any experience?"

"A little," she confessed. "I once killed a cyclops with a single arrow."

"Is that so?"

Tam nodded. "Ask anyone."

Rose's smirk grew wider still. "In that case"—she spread her hands—"welcome to Fable."

Despite its double walls, an encircling moat, and two very advantageous hills, Conthas was ill-suited to withstand a siege. Of the four gates, the only one that still functioned was the Wyldside portcullis in the outer curtain wall. In fact, the city had never once repelled an invading army, preferring instead to welcome its would-be conquerors with open arms.

Roderick likened this tactic to the business practice of a seedy brothel. "First you lure them in," he explained. "Then you get them drunk, fuck them silly, rob them blind, and dump them in the alley out back."

"I don't think that's going to work this time," Tam pointed out.

In response, the satyr shared a sly smile with Rose. "We'll see about that," he said.

Fortunately for Conthas, both Rose and Slowhand were veterans of siege warfare. Rose had been trapped in Castia for months while the Heartwyld Horde festered beyond its walls. When plague decimated the Republic's commanding officers, she had assumed control of the city's defenses, and had personally led its remaining soldiers out of the gate during the Battle of the Bands.

As for Slowhand . . . Well, everyone and their dog's barber knew what Saga had endured at Hollow Hill. Clay's shield, *Blackheart*, was testament to what became of those who attempted to kill him. Tam doubted the Winter Queen's hide would make for a very stout shield, but a pair of supple leather gloves probably wasn't out of the question.

If anyone could save Conthas (and, quite honestly, Tam wasn't sure anyone *could*) it was these two.

Come morning, Slowhand turned the Starwood into an improvised command centre. From here, he plotted the city's defense and hosted an endless stream of mercenaries, gangsters, and alchemist types he hoped could help implement Rose's plan—a plan even Moog referred to as "orc-shit insane."

"Don't get me wrong," he was quick to clarify. "I love it. But it's crazy as socks on a centipede!"

Rose took to the streets, overseeing the effort to turn Conthas into a killing ground. Avenues were cleared, or cluttered, or barricaded in order to create blind alleys and funnel Astra's horde toward defensible choke points. Buildings were burned or demolished as Rose saw fit. Argosies were retrofitted, or disassembled, or turned into bombs and towed up the sloping hillsides.

The Sanctuary on the southern heights (known to the locals

as Chapel Hill) was designated as both a field hospital and the inevitable site of a "last stand" should things go sideways.

"Hills," her uncle Bran had pointed out with characteristic cheer, "make excellent places to die."

Along with Alkain Tor and Mad Mackie (the leaders of Giantsbane and Flashbang, respectively), Branigan was put in charge of organizing the mercenary bands into three companies that could move and operate independently of one another. One would lie in ambush, while the others made it look like they were putting up a fight and losing.

Bran's company was comprised almost entirely of old campaigners, veterans of the Heartwyld who jokingly dubbed themselves "The Rusted Blades."

Brune was entrusted with making sure every pit-fighter and street tough was armoured and equipped for war, while Cura set up shop in a low-ceilinged pub called the Cavern and began the long, tedious process of executing the most critical part of Rose's plan. At one point, the queue of women waiting outside the pub was more than a mile long.

Oscar the merman (suffering from a hangover that made him even grumpier than he'd been the day before) was appointed "Lord Commander of the Moat" and presented with a ceremonial silver trident. He saluted Rose and swam away, vowing to kill, as he put it, "every dead-eyed bugger who swims on my turf!"

Tam and Roderick accompanied Rose on a tour of the city's various wards, from the sordid squalor of Rockbottom and the smog-ridden streets of Saltkettle, to the decadent dens of the Paper Court, whose Baroness Alektra offered them iced cakes and white tea from the Phantran coast—which Rose quaffed like it was a shot of strong whiskey.

"Where are these five hundred swords you promised me?" she asked of Alektra.

The baroness smiled. "Running an errand," she said cryptically, and then waved over a servant. "More tea?"

Alektra's *errand* turned out to be a full-scale assault on her twin sister's neighbouring territory. Hoping to catch Ios unprepared, the baroness's men raided the warrens of Telltale shortly before noon. They met no resistance whatsoever, though, since Ios, anticipating her sister's treachery, had arranged an attack of her own. While Alektra's men were looting Telltale, Ios and her assassins stormed the Paper Court. When next Tam saw the Baroness of Telltale, she was leading her sister around on a silver leash.

Rose met briefly with Kurin, the High Han's bodyguard, whose scouts reported that the Horde was moving more slowly than anticipated and wouldn't arrive until the following day. Before they parted, Rose told Kurin to pay Cura a visit at the Cavern. "Skip the line," she said, "and tell her I sent you."

The Ravenguard warrior looked confused, but nodded anyway and trotted off.

Their next stop was the Monster Market, where Rose gathered the hunters and wranglers together and explained their part in her plan. One of them—a swarthy wrangler wearing a hat decorated with griffin feathers—refused to comply with her demands, and a few of his associates rallied behind him. Since she didn't have time to negotiate (and wasn't very good at it anyway), Rose dangled him over the goblin pit until he saw the wisdom in her plan.

In the meantime, Roderick (who *was*, in fact, a brilliant negotiator) made a circuit of the forum. Fable's booker talked to trolls, bargained with bugbears, conferred with kobold chieftains, offering every single prisoner in the square a simple choice: freedom or death.

Those who chose freedom were informed of their role in the battle to come, while the few who refused were granted something the wranglers begrudged immensely: a quick and merciful end. The bodies were beheaded and burned immediately after.

When Tam asked Roderick why some would prefer to

die instead of fight, the satyr struck a match on his remaining horn and used it to light his pipe. "All sorts of reasons," he said. "Could be they hate humans. Could be they fear the dead, or don't want to become one of Astra's thralls if shit goes south tomorrow. And some of them... Well, they're monsters, Tam—and I mean that literally. The Heartwyld is an evil place. Warped and twisted. Live there long enough, and it gets to you. Infects you. I've seen it happen."

"And if we win?" Tam wondered. "What'll happen to the ones who fight with us?"

The booker sucked a long drag off his pipe. "They'll have to try and get along with humans, same as I did." He exhaled smoke through a sardonic smile. "You're not all assholes, you know."

"Just most of us?"

"Just most of you," he said amiably, then nodded to the corpse of a firbolg before them. "Now let's burn this prick and get back to the pub."

The mood that night was sombre. The weather took a turn for the worse, and Rose had mercenaries working in shifts to shovel snow and keep the streets clear. While she and Slowhand pored over an expansive map of the city, Tam and her bandmates returned to the Monster Market and doled out bowls of hot stew to the creatures captive there.

The gesture was, for the most part, greatly appreciated—except by a minotaur who stared at his helping in open disgust. "What is this, beef? I can't eat this! Have you got a salad or something?"

"No, I haven't got a fucking salad," said Roderick.

The minotaur stared flatly between the bars of his cage. "Be a lot cooler if you did."

When they returned to the Starwood, Rose ordered them to their rooms. "Get some rest," she said. "Or try to." Before

Cura took off, Rose stopped her and jutted her chin at the summoner's latest tattoo. "Do we need to talk about that?"

The Inkwitch matched gazes with Rose. "Do *you* need to talk about it?"

"Nope."

"Then we're good," said Cura.

"Good."

Upstairs, Tam and the Inkwitch found themselves once again relegated to the same room. There was a bed against either wall, so Tam stood by the door and waited for the other woman to pick which of them belonged to her.

Cura promptly chose the one on the right. She dragged the blankets and the sheets off and bundled them all together, then crossed to the room's only window, pushed open the casement, and hurled the whole bundle into the alley outside.

She turned to face Tam, her black hair tossing in the cold breeze, and stared down Fable's former bard as if daring her to speak.

"I guess we'll have to share a bed," Tam said.

Cura replied with an impish smile, "I guess so."

Tam awoke before dawn to find Cura sitting on the edge of the bed. Torchlight beyond the frosted window picked out the treant tattooed on her back, the flaming wreath of *Agani* traced in scar tissue and shadowed ink. Tam reached out to touch it and the summoner flinched, but didn't move away.

"Did I wake you?" asked Cura.

"No. Did you sleep at all?"

"A little. Not much." She looked over her shoulder. "Listen, Tam, this was..."

"Oh, gods," Tam groaned, "you're not going to give me another knife, are you?"

Cura laughed quietly. "Not this time, sorry." She turned and traced the line of Tam's cheek with her fingers. "This was perfect. Thank you. I couldn't have asked for a better last night."

The word *last* barged into Tam's mind before *perfect* had a chance to settle in. "You don't think we'll survive this?" she asked.

"You might."

"All of us might."

Cura withdrew her hand. "Battles don't work like that, Tam. Especially not with the odds we're facing. Some of us— most of us, probably—will need to sacrifice everything so the rest have a chance to survive."

"I know that," said Tam. "That doesn't mean it has to be you."

Cura's voice was pained. "If not me, who?"

There were voices in the street. Frantic shouting outside their window. The sound of doors banging open, footsteps pounding down the hall. Light, at last, crept through the window and painted the ceiling in shades of muted fire.

Dawn had arrived. And with it, the Horde.

Chapter Fifty-two

The Beginning of the End

Tam was standing with Cura, Brune, and Roderick outside the Sanctuary on the city's southern hill. From here she could see more than she might have wished of the land surrounding Conthas. Astra's Horde was ranged northeast of the city: a teeming, crawling, shuffling eyesore of awful shit.

Her mind unhelpfully picked out a few recognizable monsters among the masses. Brontide was easy enough to spot, since he was leading the way and carrying the ram's-head maul she'd overheard the other mercenaries refer to as *WHAM*. The giant's flesh had turned a pallid blue, while his long hair and beard had gone the yellow-white of curdled milk. His head sagged sideways because the Simurg had savaged his throat so terribly.

According to Moog, killing the undead required burning them, decapitating them, or destroying the rotten organ that passed for their brain.

If only the Dragoneater had bit a little harder, Tam mused, *we wouldn't have a rampaging giant to deal with*.

"What about skeletons?" Cura had pressed the wizard. "They don't have brains."

"Raising skeletons isn't necromancy," the wizard insisted.

"It's puppetry. And I'd suggest avoiding those who practice either."

The Horde also boasted a great many things that resembled giants but weren't, like two-headed ettins, humpbacked fomorians, and rock hulks whose long, stone-riddled arms dragged furrows in the mud. Tam even recognized a cyclops here and there, though none as monstrous as the one Fable had fought back in the Ravine.

Other obvious horrors included giant spiders, slithering drakes, furless firewolves, and shaggy mammoths whose tusks were stained black with gore. She saw a gelatinous blob covered with bloodshot eyes, an impossibly huge tortoise with what looked like a small castle teetering on its back, and the four-headed hydrake she'd stepped over on the battlefield just days ago.

Around these, in numbers beyond counting, were what Roderick blithely referred to as the "meat and potatoes" of the Horde: orcs, imps, goblins, trolls, ogres, ixil, and rat-faced kobolds. There were packs of loping wargs, herds of limping centaurs, knots of hooded snake-men, and scuttling colonies of horse-sized insects—alongside hundreds of other creatures she didn't know and couldn't name.

What made Astra's host *truly* frightening (aside from their burning eyes, putrid flesh, and their eclectic variety of grievous injuries) was their silence. In life, they would have snarled, screeched, roared, and hissed as they closed on the city. But in death they were voiceless, vacuous husks— a dreadful reminder of what awaited every soul in Conthas should they fail to stop the Horde here and now.

"Gee," said Cura dryly. "I wonder where Astra's hiding out."

Further study of the approaching host revealed that Astra wasn't hiding at all, unless the tented palanquin borne by a half a dozen gargantuan firbolgs (each of which looked like a miniature Brontide with a horn instead of a proper nose) belonged to someone *other* than the Winter Queen—but Tam guessed probably not.

"Oh shit," Roderick swore. Tam followed the booker's bleak gaze and saw *another* army approaching from the west. This one, so far as she could see through the haze of blowing snow, was made up entirely of humans. These were the mercenaries who had died during the battle at Grey Vale, or been caught by surprise when Astra had raised the dead in its aftermath. And out front, garbed in the green-and-gold panoply of Queen Lilith of Brycliffe, were—

"The fucking Agrians," Brune growled.

Tam's heart, already quaking in fear, went in search of a corner to cry in. *Not only did Lokan rob us of ten thousand soldiers*, she thought miserably, *he handed them to the Winter Queen on a silver platter.*

Astra's fliers weren't here yet, but Tam assumed they would arrive soon, cinching around the city like a hangman's noose. The Simurg, thankfully, was nowhere in sight.

Rose came striding from the compound gate with Branigan, Jain, Slowhand, and Moog in tow. Fable's leader had traded her battered scrap armour for a black leather cuirass and sleek steel sabatons. She wore a bright scarlet cloak over one shoulder with the cowl drawn to hide her face.

Jain sauntered up to Tam and offered her a pair of gloves made of rough grey wool with worn leather pads sewn onto the palms. Two fingers on the right-handed glove—the ones she would use to draw an arrow—were cut away. "Here," she said. "I made these for you."

Tam looked up, amazed. "You *made* these?"

The older woman tossed a loose-knit braid over one shoulder. "Basically, yeah."

"So you stole them..."

"It ain't stealin' if they're dead," Jain said matter-of-factly. "Anyway, I did the snipping myself."

Tam decided to pretend Jain was kidding about the gloves belonging to a corpse. She resisted the urge to smell one and instead pulled them on, wriggling her bare fingers. "Thank you."

Beside them, Roderick was swimming in an oversized chainmail coat and holding a spear upside down. He used the butt end to draw Rose's attention to the crawling wall of green-and-gold shields out west. "Astra's got us over a pickle barrel now," he informed her. "How is this plan supposed to work if we're fighting on two fronts?"

"It doesn't," said Rose. "We'll need to deal with them quickly. Or at least hold them off until we can lure Astra into the city."

Tam's uncle cleared his throat. "I hate to be the voice of reason here—hell, I'm not sure I've ever *been* the voice of reason before—but there's gotta be twenty thousand of them over there."

"Thirty," said Jain. "Check your eyes, old man."

"Thirty, then. Either way, dealing with them quickly probably isn't an option."

"But holding them off is," said Slowhand. "How many mercs are in your company?"

"The Rusted Blades?" Bran shrugged. "Fifteen thousand, give or take."

Clay turned to Rose. "Can you spare them?"

"I'll have to," she said. "But can you hold them off with so few?"

Slowhand's eyes flickered to his daughter, Tally, who was leading Heartbreaker through the chapel gate. "I'll hold them," he promised.

"*We'll* hold them," said Moog.

Satisfied, Rose turned to Jain. "I need you to get a message to the Han: Once his riders are done harassing the Horde, they're to circle the city and help relieve the Rusted Blades at the Wyldside Gate."

"The Han's a stubborn old sot," said Jain. "What if he says no?"

Rose took her stallion's reins with a nod for Slowhand's daughter. "You think a Cartean han will pass up the chance to kill ten thousand Agrians without diplomatic repercussions?"

The other woman laughed. "Fair enough. I'll get Daon to give me a lift."

Roderick spat on the ground. "You mean Doshi? Assuming he hasn't made a run for it, that is."

"Run?" Jain grinned. "That man's lucky he can walk after what I did to him last night."

"Just make sure you deliver the message," Rose said.

"Will do." Jain waved and jogged off downhill.

Finally, Rose turned to her bandmates. "All set?"

"Ready to roll," Brune said.

Cura cracked her knuckles. "Let's do this."

Tam only nodded, wishing she'd thought of something suitably cool to say.

"Listen," muttered Roderick, "if things don't . . . I mean, if you guys—" He clamped his teeth shut on something close to a sob. "It's been an honour, truly. Thanks for letting this old goat tag along, eh? And for"—he reached to thumb the stub of his broken horn—"for letting me be me."

Rose pulled the satyr into a hard embrace. Cura hugged them both, so Tam hugged Cura, and Brune threw his great big arms around all of them at once.

Someone sniffed. Someone chuckled. Tam closed her eyes, overcome by the sense of having woken in the grey watch before sunrise and wishing each second could last an eternity. But it doesn't. It can't, of course. The sun always rises.

They were halfway down the hill when the battle that would decide the fate of every soul in Grandual began in earnest.

The Carteans had divided their riders into units of five

hundred, called Wings, the first of which hit the Horde in a wedge of bristling lances and threshing hooves. While the first Wing retreated, the second arrived, followed by the third, the fourth, and so on, until finally Astra was forced to commit her swiftest thralls to pursue them.

The Carteans peeled off, trailed by a funnelling mob of centaurs, wargs, trollhounds, and countless other loping atrocities. As they did, Tam saw one of the riders pull off their helmet to reveal a shock of bright red hair. She guessed by the figure's armour and their piebald pony that it was actually Kurin, but the Winter Queen couldn't know that—not unless one of her minions was close enough that she could see through its eyes.

Astra had known Rose by reputation before hiring her to kill the Dragoneater, and she'd seen that reputation earned at Mirrormere, when Rose had slain the Simurg almost single-handedly. She would know by now that Gabriel's daughter was in charge of defending Conthas, and would seize any opportunity she could to deliver a mortal blow to the city's already tenuous morale.

Rose's plan hinged on Astra being as determined to kill Rose as she was to kill Astra. With half the Horde chasing down a decoy, the Winter Queen would have no choice but to commit herself to a direct attack on the city.

And so far, it appeared to be working. Tens of thousands took off after the Han's horsemen, who were showering their pursuers with bowfire as they skirted the north half of the curtain wall.

Rose, guiding Heartbreaker at a trot, led her band east along the Gutter. The city's broad thoroughfare was empty now but for a few watchful urchins (agents of the local barons), and Tam couldn't help but think how much nicer the city seemed without an excess of people selling shit, stealing shit, or stomping through shit on their way from one tavern to the next.

Despite its name, the East Gutter Gate wasn't *technically* a gate—just a great big hole in the city's inner wall. Broken hinges suggested there had once been a pair of massive doors, but they had long since rotted away.

They came to the Monster Market, where the creatures who'd volunteered to fight were being kept under guard. Their cages were arranged in a half circle facing east and would be opened shortly after the Horde breached the outer wall, buying time for the fleeing mercenaries to retreat and rally beyond the second wall. It wasn't an ideal scenario for the captive monsters, but she supposed a fighting chance was better than dying in cages when Astra took the city.

"There goes Mackie," Cura shouted, as another Rose revealed herself on a postern tower to the south. Flashbang's frontwoman drew back her hood to reveal newly cropped and freshly dyed red hair. She usually fought with a whip named *Darkest Hour* that could (according to the songs) turn a wraith's heart to ice, or reduce a skeleton to powder with a single snap, but just now she raised two scimitars in open defiance of the approaching host.

But would Astra fall for it? She'd already sent her swiftest thralls after Kurin and his riders—would she strike out at this second false Rose as well?

Apparently yes, since Brontide kicked the postern apart like it was made of sand. Through the snow and the showering dust, Tam saw Mackie sprinting south along the curtain wall. Her own company of fifteen thousand were stationed among the mills and warehouses of the outer city. Their task was to lure a portion of Astra's forces away from the centre and delay them as long as possible.

Rose was gazing east. Heartbreaker snorted restlessly beneath her, a symptom of his rider's anxious energy. "We could end it now," she murmured.

Brune and Cura exchanged nervous glances.

"Say what?" asked the shaman.

"We could try and kill Astra before the Horde destroys the city. Before her fliers arrive, or the Simurg . . ." She blinked to dispel the devastation in her mind's eye. "We could spare so many lives."

Cura scoffed. "By throwing away our own, you mean? We lure her in and spring the ambush, Rose. That's the plan. Going out there is suicide."

"I know that," said Rose. "But so does Astra. She'll expect us to hide behind our walls."

"That's what walls are for!" Cura pointed out. "Hiding behind!"

Brune tugged at his scarf. "Just so we're clear, are you proposing we toss our meticulously devised strategy out the window?"

"I am, yes."

"And suggesting instead that we attempt a blatantly foolish, totally reckless charge into the heart of the Winter Queen's army?"

"That's right."

"Sort of a 'cut the snake's head off before it swallows us whole' sort of deal?"

"Exactly."

Brune shrugged. "I like it."

Cura bit back a probably scathing rebuke of Rose's ridiculous amendment to an already feeble plan and threw her hands up. "Fuck it, I'm in."

All three of them looked to Tam, who'd been waiting for this moment since flubbing her response on the hilltop earlier. "Who wants to live forever?" she asked.

Rose's answering grin was beautiful in the way an assassin's dagger was beautiful.

"Are we taking one of the companies with us, at least?" Cura asked. "I mean, I know we're good—but we're not *that* good."

Rose shook her head. "If we fuck this up, the others still have a chance of pulling this off."

The summoner's derisive snort suggested she didn't think much of the city's chances of winning this contest once Fable was playing for the other team.

Rose nudged her mount in the ribs and cantered over to the man in charge of setting the monsters loose. "Let them out!" she ordered.

The man—a Heartwyld huntsmen, Tam guessed—took a long drag from his pipe before answering. "I'm not to open the cages till Bloody Rose tells me to."

Rose kept her hood drawn, but pushed back her cloak to reveal the scimitars strapped to her hip. "I *am* Bloody Rose," she said. "And I'm telling you to."

The huntsman squinted into the shadows of her cowl, as though reluctant to believe her without a glimpse of her namesake red hair, but the steel in her eyes convinced him just as well. "Y-yes, of course." He tapped out his pipe and went to relay her command to his fellow guards.

Rose urged her mount toward the half circle of cages. There were some three thousand prisoners in total, including the pint-sized cave dwellers chittering excitedly in the pits to either side.

"I've been fighting monsters my whole life!" Rose shouted at them. "If you and I had met on an arena floor, I'd have killed you. And if you'd managed to catch me alone in the Wyld? Well, I'd have killed you then, too."

A pair of hyena-faced gnolls in one of the cages laughed hysterically at that, but none of the others found it particularly funny.

"I never hated your kind," Rose went on, as the guards pulled the keys off their belts and set out for the cages, "but I was taught to believe we were enemies—just as you were raised to believe I was yours. I thought that killing monsters made the world a better place. I was wrong."

Her stallion shifted nervously as Brontide laid waste to another section of wall.

"I can't erase the past. And I can't promise you a future. Because now, too late, we find ourselves threatened by a common enemy: one whose aim is to exterminate every single one of us." Rose drew *Thorn* and aimed its tip at the Courtside Gate. "And *she is right there.*"

There was a chorus of angry snarls from the cages. The goblins and kobolds and gibberlings yowled in their pits. Tam saw a hunched gorilliath grip the bars of her cell and shriek in fury, while a copse of chain-linked treants shook so violently that their leaves rained down.

"The Winter Queen lied to you!" Rose told her captive audience. "She fed you empty hope and left you starving. She used you! And when she had no more use for you, she betrayed you! And *she is right there.*"

The men approaching the cages balked as their charges growled and hissed.

"Because of her, Brontide is nothing more than a mindless slave! Because of her, your army was destroyed—your friends and family raised from death and used as fodder! And she *is right there*!"

The monsters howled and screamed as the guards fumbled keys into locks.

"I promised you freedom!" Rose shouted. "And now you are free!"

Cells and cages clattered open. Planks were lowered into pits. Manacles were broken, discarded in the snow.

"*I promised you vengeance!*" Rose cried, lifting *Thorn* overhead. "*Come with me now, and take it!*"

Heartbreaker turned and took off like the edge of the world was crumbling behind him.

The monsters went roaring after.

Cura nudged Brune with an elbow. "Go," she said. "And try not to kill Astra before Tam and I catch up."

The shaman snorted. "You'd better hurry, then." His leathers shredded as he bounded away.

Tam and Cura found themselves in the midst of the mob by the time they reached the Courtside Gate. All around them were bellowing orcs, barking gnolls, horse-headed ixil tossing their braided manes. Tam nearly tripped over the tail of a saurian screeching like a bat come sunrise.

Behind them, sprinting on stubby legs, were hundreds of gremlins, goblins, kobolds, and scrawny gibberlings in their sealed iron helms. Ahead were the faster creatures: the galloping centaurs, the lumbering ogres, the treants taking one giant stride for every five of Tam's. The rushing throng tapered to a point tipped by Rose herself, who was charging toward the heart of the Horde with a sword in the air and her red cloak snapping in the gale behind her.

Shame there isn't a bard here to see this, Tam thought, *because it would make for one hell of a song.*

Chapter Fifty-three

Birdsong on the Battlefield

What Tam found most revolting about Astra's host wasn't their ghoulish appearance. It wasn't their bloodless pallor, their slackened mouths, or the sorcerous fire blazing in the crow-pecked hollows of their eyes. It wasn't the axes lodged in cloven skulls, the arrows studding gore-soaked chests, the spear shafts jutting from oozing abdomens. It wasn't their breathless silence, though this was even more unnerving up close than it had been from her vantage on Chapel Hill.

What *really* repulsed her, above and beyond any of these vile virtues, was the *smell*.

She'd experienced something like it on the plain south of Grey Vale, but it had been masked at the time by woodsmoke and the sour tang of fresh blood. Since then, however, the Horde had ripened considerably. Their myriad mortal wounds had festered from neglect. Their flesh had putrefied, so that it sloughed like thick cream when struck, and their clot-strangled limbs bloated like wineskins heavy with septic pus.

The stink, as they closed with the rancid ranks of the Winter Queen's Horde, turned Tam's stomach and threatened to buckle her knees. She was grateful for the cold, which went some way toward quelling the reek, and was glad she'd had nothing but a heel of hard bread and a swig of water for breakfast.

Astra's monsters, it turned out, weren't quite a match for their living counterparts. They fought without guile, driven only by a senseless desire to kill, while Rose's rampaging thousands attacked with a ferocity rivalling the mercenary herself. They ripped and tore and slashed their way through the ranks of white-eyed dead, piercing Astra's depleted centre like a spear, driving straight for the tented palanquin ahead.

Tam fought side by side with Cura, who hadn't yet summoned one of her inklings to help. The Inkwitch fought with a pair of serrated knives, occasionally clenching one in her teeth so she could hurl a dagger into something's eye.

Though Tam managed to get a few arrows off before the fighting got thick, it soon seemed a bad idea to press on with nothing but a spar of ashwood to protect herself. Tam was wearing armour—a suit of sleek gorgon-scale—beneath her red leather longcoat, and Moog had furnished her with a sword called *Nightbird* from the chapel's armoury, which the wizard claimed was home to all sorts of ancient relics.

Reaching across, she drew the weapon from its scabbard, then swore loudly.

Glass? That daft old bugger gave me a glass fucking sword!?

The blade looked sharp, certainly, and was so light it felt as though she were holding nothing at all, but Tam could see right through its clouded, blue-black blade. She doubted it could survive a fall to the ground, much less a strike against an enemy's armour. Had Moog even bothered to examine it first? Or had he simply grabbed the first scabbard he saw?

"Tam!" Cura snapped, and she looked up to see a boggart bearing down on her. It resembled a naked fat man with tufts of mould and fungal scales growing all over its body. Someone had opened a gash in its belly from which its innards dangled in shrivelled ropes.

Here goes nothing, she thought, ducking the boggart's pudgy grasp and chopping at its head with her stupid glass sword.

Her stupid glass sword went right through its skull.

The blow barely jarred her arm, and Tam wondered if this was what it felt like to wield *Madrigal*. Needless to say, by the time she'd cut a rask in half and sheared through the neck of a zombified sinu, Tam found it in her heart to forgive Moog for giving her what looked like a mantelpiece ornament to fight with.

Later, as she and Cura fought back-to-back amidst a crowd of greasy frogmen, the Inkwitch shot her a wry but weary grin. "Guess those lessons with Rose paid off, huh?"

Tam ducked an incoming tongue-punch and fed *Nightbird* to the urskin's open mouth. "I've got some moves," she admitted, and was rewarded with a clipped laugh.

They saw Rose's red cowl just ahead. Fable's leader was still on horseback, urging her stallion on as though charging headlong into ocean surf. *Thistle* and *Thorn* blazed blue and green as she hacked her way through. When something like a spine-covered stork loomed ahead of her, Rose sent *Thistle* spinning sideways to hew through one spindly leg. The huge bird fell awkwardly and Heartbreaker threshed it beneath his hooves.

Cura got shouldered by an orc impaled by the haft of a spear. The summoner crashed into Tam, and both of them went down in the slush. From her back, Tam swung the bow in her left hand. *Duchess* cracked across the orc's jaw and snapped one of the yellowed tusks jutting from his bottom lip.

"Summon something," she hissed at Cura.

The Inkwitch threw a dagger instead. It opened a gash in the brute's throat but didn't kill him. He carried a tooth-studded club in his remaining hand and raised it to strike.

"Fuck," Cura swore. She pawed at her sleeve, took a breath with which to scream an inkling's name.

Brune leapt over them both and slammed into the thrall. Orc and wolf went tumbling through the muck. The shaman recovered first, but one of Rose's recently liberated treants saved him the trouble of killing the orc by stomping its skull with a gnarled foot.

Tam offered the treant a grateful wave.

It waved back, but then shrieked in panic as a wyvern seized its branches and hauled it into the air.

Looking up, Tam found the sky swarming with fliers, from bare-breasted harpies and bloodshot eyewings to whole packs of wolfbats and flying monkeys (which she hadn't believed were really a thing until just now). Falling gargoyles pummelled through head and helm, blowing skulls apart like hammer-struck melons. Swooping plague hawks left corrosive clouds in their wake that reminded Tam of the spray thrown off by tidal engines, except an engine's mist didn't rust your armour and melt your goddamn face off.

Tam and Cura crouched low as they ran. Brune barged a path ahead of them. With her bandmates to protect her, Tam sheathed her sword and resumed shooting arrows at any target she could find, including the bulging venom sac of a rot sylph. The sac burst, showering a cluster of thralls with a sizzling green ooze that disintegrated them almost instantly.

By the time they caught up to Rose she was almost to the Winter Queen's litter. The horn-nosed goliaths bearing it set their burden down and started forward. Tam forced herself to look past them, to the figure seated behind the windblown veils of diaphanous black silk.

Can you see us, Astra? Have you realized yet who's coming for you?

Tam considered launching an arrow at the Winter Queen right now but decided against it. Even if her aim was true—if the wind didn't blow it astray or a firbolg didn't lurch into its path—Astra was still a druin, and the prescience would warn her it was coming anyway.

Rose charged the litter bearers without slowing, flanked by Tam, Cura, Brune, and a handful of hearty monsters. A lion-maned raga was among that lot, as was the minotaur who'd refused beef stew last night. His horns were strung with gore, and he howled a colourful litany of obscenities as he trundled alongside them. The pair of gnolls who'd found Rose so amusing back in the square were present as well. Their identical stripes gave Tam the impression they were brothers. One was laying about with a battle-axe, while the other had appropriated something's femur and was wielding it like a club.

Three of Astra's firbolgs were down, then four. Tam tried to put an arrow between one's eyes, but the shaft glanced off its nose-horn. Cura planted a knife in the back of another's knee. When it dropped, the raga put a fist through its eye and withdrew an apparently necessary part of its brain, since it died almost immediately.

The Winter Queen stood as the last of her bodyguards fell. She stepped to the front of the gilded platform, lifting some bulky apparatus in one hand.

It's not her, Tam realized, even as the figure—stoop-shouldered beneath a tattered black straw cape—tore the curtain aside and levelled his double-decked crossbow at Rose's chest.

Hawkshaw wasn't wearing his snowmask, and though Astra had resurrected him, she'd done nothing to repair his face—which, thanks to being run over by the claw-broker's wagon, was an obscene mess of torn flesh and fractured bone. His eyes, unlike her lesser thralls, were dull black voids, and his shattered teeth were clenched in a tortured rictus as he pulled the trigger.

The bolt splintered against the gauntlet Rose raised to shield her face.

Tam sent an arrow at the Warden's head, but the curtain fouled its flight. One of Cura's knives scraped off his shoulder but didn't stop him from resetting the deck on his crossbow and taking aim once again. Rose yanked hard on Heartbreaker's reins, trying to turn him, but the stallion reared instead, and the white-feathered bolt split the barding on his chest. He toppled, throwing her clear.

Cura and Brune rushed the platform, but Rose's shout brought them both up short.

"He's mine!"

The Inkwitch swore under her breath, and the wolf snarled, but neither defied her. Hawkshaw (puppet or not) had been responsible for Gabriel's death, and standing between Rose and revenge was as wise as diving for pearls in plate armour.

Hawkshaw let the crossbow fall and drew the bone sword at his hip. The top third of it had snapped off, but its jagged point looked no less threatening for it.

"If I kill you," he slurred, "she'll let me go. I can finally be with Sara."

Blood sluiced from Rose's blades as she summoned them to hand. "I don't know who Sara is," she remarked, "but if she's dead, then I promise you'll see her soon."

Tam glanced behind them. More and more of Astra's minions were giving up their pursuit of the Han's horsemen. "We should get back to the city," she warned.

"This won't take long," Rose promised.

"It doesn't matter," Tam argued. "The Queen's not here! Killing Hawkshaw means nothing!"

"He murdered my father."

"He's just a *tool*! Astra murdered your father. And she'll do the same to Wren—and everyone else—if we don't stop her. We need to go, Rose. *Now*, before it's too late."

"It's already too late," said Cura. "Look."

The Inkwitch was right. They were surrounded. Astra's thralls had returned like the evening tide to envelop Rose's dwindling company. And worse: Every companion they'd lost between here and Conthas was now an enemy. Tam could barely make out the city for the blowing snow, though she could see Brontide marauding through the outer wards, a malevolent child stomping on frogs in shallow water.

They had gambled their lives on being able to reach the Winter Queen and kill her quickly.

Gambled and lost.

Astra played us for fools, Tam thought bleakly. *She tricked us, trapped us, and now we're dead.*

Something snagged her eye as it emerged from the Court-side Gate. *Many* somethings, actually, led by two towering figures swinging massive hammers in devastating arcs. Her mind floundered in confusion. Were they monsters? Had one of Sinkwell's wizards conjured a clump of earth elementals to help fight?

Her ears picked out a sound amidst the savage noise: a lilting, lyrical hum—as incongruous as birdsong on a battlefield, or bright laughter echoing through the halls of a crypt.

It sounded, to Tam's beleaguered heart, like hope.

Chapter Fifty-four

The Scabbard and the Sword

Freecloud hadn't forsaken the people of Conthas. He hadn't abandoned his bandmates or succumbed to his father's intractable will. And, most importantly, he hadn't given up on Rose.

He'd only pretended to, Tam realized. He'd played his part, bided his time, let his father think he was content to remain below while his friends perished and Conthas burned.

But he wasn't. He was *here*, and he'd brought a legion of stone sentinels to back him up. Each golem was twice the height of a man, with glowing green eyes and cuffed fists they used to pummel and punch through the hapless dead. Leading them was a pair of giant duramantium knights—great big bastards who waded knee-deep through the Winter Queen's army. Tam could barely make out the druin in their midst, a speck of sky blue in the grainy grey chaos.

"My hero," Rose murmured.

Tam glanced over. "You knew?"

"Of course I knew," she said. "The poor fool loves me."

"Come!" bellowed Hawkshaw, beckoning Rose toward the palanquin stage. "Fight me! Kill me, if you can!"

Rose ignored him, addressing her bandmates instead. "We're going back!"

Heartbreaker lurched to his feet. For a moment Tam feared

he might be dead, and that Rose would be forced to fight her own horse, but the stallion simply didn't know Hawkshaw's poison would kill him, and wasn't about to let a single arrow stop him now.

Rose vaulted onto his back and began rallying the monsters around her, shouting and pointing toward the city behind them.

Astra wasn't going to make it easy. Every eye in the Horde turned upon Rose. Her name gusted from a thousand breathless lips. The fighting on all sides grew more frantic than ever as the Winter Queen's minions hurled themselves at Fable and their allies.

Hawkshaw's screams hounded them as well. *"Kill me!"* he howled at Rose's back. *"KILL ME!"*

Tam tried to oblige him, shooting on the run as they started west, but her arrow thudded into the Warden's shoulder instead. He broke the shaft with his fist, hurled it away, then leapt off the litter and set out after them.

With Astra's will focused on Rose, Freecloud's golems were hewing through her army like a battle-axe through sodden wood. His knights, especially, were wreaking havoc among the Winter Queen's ranks. Their hammers cleared dozens at a time, or crushed condensed enemies to bloody pulp. While mortal foes might have fled from their path, Astra's thralls attacked without regard for their life, queueing to be slaughtered like bulls at a butcher's door.

Fable, on the other hand, was forced to fight for every inch of ground. The Horde seethed around them. Rose's dwindling force was beset on every side, an island of living souls amidst a storm-wracked sea of shambling dead. Everywhere Tam looked were grasping claws, raking talons, gnashing teeth, snapping mandibles, coiling tentacles, and ghastly, ghostfire eyes.

Brune had a snake-woman's tail in his teeth, while Cura—who *still* hadn't summoned a fucking thing for some reason—pulled a hatchet from a saurian's head and then put it back in, with feeling this time. A gorilliath striped red and gold was wrestling with a skeletal wyvern. The great ape cracked the creature's neck apart and used its spine to beat one of Astra's hobgoblins to death.

Others among Rose's company weren't faring so well. An orc went down when a harpy tore his throat out, then lurched back to life a moment later and attacked the bloody-fisted raga who'd been defending his flank. One of the gnoll brothers had died earlier and was harassing his sibling, who was holding his brother at bay with an axe. The minotaur charged a knot of Astra's kobolds. A few of the critters were trampled, but the rest quickly overwhelmed him.

One of Cura's knives got snagged under the helmet of a scrawny gibberling. The bugger didn't have the courtesy to die, and instead got its long fingers around the summoner's throat. Tam lashed out with *Nightbird*, severing its arm, and pulled Cura from its reach.

"My knife!"

"I owe you one anyway," Tam yelled, dragging her on.

Heartbreaker went down again, pierced through the neck by a barbed javelin. The stallion tried to stand but was bleeding out and couldn't find the strength to rise. Brune hovered over Rose as she straddled the dying animal and pushed both swords into his neck. When she'd put an end to his misery, she wrenched the weapons in opposite directions, making damn sure Astra couldn't bring him back from the dead.

The delay allowed Hawkshaw to gain on them. He was shouting at Rose, demanding she turn and face him. The Warden was so determined to catch up that he all but ignored the monsters around them. The gorilliath seized him with both hands and hurled him into a crowd of dead gremlins.

Tam could see Freecloud clearly now. The druin moved like a spectre across the battlefield, evading clubs and swords and sailing arrows with such ease as to seem incorporeal. He dodged blows before his opponents thought to deal them, retaliating with ruthless efficiency. *Madrigal* sang in his hands, and a rune-etched torc on his arm glowed the emerald green of a golem's eyes.

Where Freecloud fought with cool precision, Rose attacked with wild abandon. She assailed each new enemy like she bore it some personal vendetta. What she couldn't hack, slash, or stab, she elbowed, kicked, or shouldered aside. Tam had seen Kaskar berserkers fight with more careful consideration than Bloody Rose in the heat of battle.

Step by brutal step, she and Freecloud carved a path toward one another. In a moment of uncanny clarity between dodging a plant-monster's swiping vine and cutting through its pulsing stem, Tam found herself wondering why Astra even bothered trying to keep the two of them apart.

Didn't she know? Couldn't she see? This was *Rose and fucking Freecloud*! The Winter Queen could have placed a mountain between them, or a sea, or the whole black ocean of night—it didn't matter. They would scale it, or swim it; they would scour every star until they found one another.

Freecloud had once compared Rose to a flame to which he was inescapably drawn, but in truth they were both of them burning: he with a candle's slow and steady light, she like a flaring match. Rose was attracted to the druin just as he was to her, and might have extinguished herself a thousand times were it not for his guiding light.

He's the scabbard, mused the part of Tam's mind that still thought itself a bard, *and she's the sword. They belong together, and they're so close now . . .*

Freecloud sliced through a half-eaten ogre.

Rose chopped down a white-eyed werewolf.

Freecloud split a galloping centaur down the middle.

Rose cut a troll's head into halves.

He thrust his sword through a scuttling rust-eater and left it there.

She buried hers in a soaring plague hawk and didn't bother watching it fall.

They lunged at one another next, crashing into an embrace that became an epically perilous kiss considering they were in the midst of a raging battlefield. Rose's hands clawed at Freecloud's hair, and the druin swept her into a dip—which Tam felt was a bit grandiose until she saw the dead minotaur charging her. The bull-headed brute tripped over Rose's boots and ran down Hawkshaw instead. Its horns punched through the Warden's chest and the beast's momentum carried them both into the frenzied crowd.

"Our daughter?" Rose asked.

"Safe," Freecloud told her. "She's with Orbison. Somewhere deep in Caddabra by now."

"Orbison? Won't your father just order him back?"

The druin's long ears signalled no. "I fixed him. Or broke him, rather. He'll meet us at Turnstone when we're finished here. Anyway, I think my father will be too preoccupied with his missing golems to worry about the two of them. And speaking of Contha"—Freecloud's hand strayed to a rune-inscribed rod tucked into the sash at his waist—"we should get back to the city before he overrides my control."

The stone sentinels had formed a circling cordon around them. The towering knights stood on opposite sides of the protective ring, using their hammers to deter Astra's Horde from overrunning them.

Rose frowned. "Your father can do that?"

"He can."

"But would he?" said Cura. "Is he really that callous?"

Freecloud paused before answering, but Tam and Rose said, "*Yes*," as one.

The Inkwitch arched an eyebrow at the druin. "Your dad sounds like a dick."

"He really is," said Freecloud, then turned to Rose. "I

assume you had a plan in place before you cast it aside in favour of charging recklessly into certain death?"

Rose and Brune shared a look. The wolf gave a small whine, and Rose shrugged. "That's right," she said.

"Would I have disapproved of it had I been there at the time?"

"Probably," she admitted.

"Does it involve luring Astra into a trap using yourself as bait?

"Basically, yeah."

"Well, then"—Freecloud wrenched *Madrigal* from the rust-eater's carapace—"let's go bait the trap."

They battled their way to the Courtside Gate.

Desperate to keep her quarry from getting away, Astra's thralls attacked with renewed ferocity. If not for Contha's golems, Fable and their monstrous allies would have been overrun long before they reached the city. There were several hundred of the hulking sentinels (scarcely a fraction of the army she and Rose had discovered on their way out of the Exarch's citadel), each with an S-shaped sigil engraved in the sockets of its eyes. The duramantium knights weren't linked to the band on Freecloud's arm, but were instead controlled by the rod secured at his waist.

The golems, though hardy, were not invincible. Now and then one of the Winter Queen's minions—one of the bigger ones, usually—would tear the head or arms off one or knock it over and shatter it to rubble. Each sentinel had a glowing grilled vent where its mouth might have been, and Tam saw a mob of dead kobolds climb one of the constructs, pry off the grate, then ram a barbed spear into the socket until the golem's eyes flickered and it collapsed in a heap.

A wyvern came plummeting down with its wings and

talons outstretched. Tam raised her bow, but one of the knights caught the creature dead-on with a hammerblow that sent it soaring out of sight. Tam briefly imagined some grizzled Brycliffe farmer a hundred miles away braving the snow to feed his cows and finding a twice-dead wyvern lying broken in his yard.

Astra—wherever the hell she was hiding—threw everything she had at them, overwhelming the sentinels with sheer numbers. As Fable passed beneath the Courtside Gate every one of the defenders who'd been killed by the Winter Queen's thralls or by Brontide's rampage came to life and converged upon them.

Brune yowled as a stray arrow thudded into his flank. Freecloud narrowly missed being dive-bombed by a gargoyle. The surviving gnoll (who'd managed to dispatch his undead brother) got his leg lashed by a coiling tentacle. Tam leapt to his defense, whipping *Nightbird* from its scabbard and slicing through the leafy limb before it could drag him away.

He cuffed her shoulder and muttered, "*K'yish*," which she assumed was hyena for *thank you*.

And now, to Tam's horror, Brontide himself came plodding toward them. His maul dragged through the outer city, ploughing through shabby tenements and grinding unlucky fighters into bloody smears.

But reinforcements were coming from Conthas as well: The trio of battle-ready skyships were flying to their aid, though one was barely airborne when a hail of wolfbats blew across its deck like a tempest. The vessel tipped sideways, spilling its crew overboard, and went spiralling into the Gutter. The bats took a run at the *Barracuda* next but were skewered by a broadside of spear-length crossbow bolts.

Freecloud grazed the rod at his waist, directing the duramantium knights to head off Brontide. Tam felt the tremor of the giant's footsteps through the soles of her boots, and a sudden pang of fear threatened to choke her. Up close, the colossus seemed *unreal*, as indomitable as the Dragoneater itself. If Tam had been alone—or among strangers, even—she might have fled, or fallen to her knees, helpless in the grip of sheer terror.

It was Rose's courage—and Cura's, and Cloud's, and Brune's—that kept her moving forward, and she understood, now more than ever, the strength that came from being in a band.

When you fought by yourself, you looked after yourself. When your life was in danger, you did whatever you could to preserve it. If you fought for the glory of some noble lord, you were apt to flee the battlefield behind him when the tide turned against you. And when things looked truly hopeless, even bravery pinned to the loftiest ideal was inclined to point out some distant oddity and beat it while your back was turned.

But a bond between bandmates was different. It was, as Rose had declared over her father's pyre, something familial. When you fought alongside those whose lives meant more to you than your own, succumbing to fear simply wasn't an option, because *nothing*—not a lifeless Horde, or a vengeful queen, or even a staggeringly huge, zombified giant—was as scary as the prospect of losing them.

Tam's fear evaporated in a flush of swelling pride as she considered—*really* considered, for the first time since smashing her mother's lute—what being a part of Fable meant to her. A new home. A second family. Friends she loved, who loved her in return.

They hadn't said so. They didn't need to. They were here beside her, drawing the same inexhaustible courage from her as she was from them. And that was enough.

Even when the shadow of the colossus fell upon them, it was enough.

Chapter Fifty-five

Sacrifice

As if in mockery of Tam's burgeoning confidence, the haze of cloud and smoke above Conthas billowed as something incomprehensibly vast surged through it. The Simurg's bulk sheared the veil like the hull of some titanic ship. Dusky feathers rained from its wings as it descended toward them.

Its talons closed on one of the knights, hoisting the construct off its feet and tearing it apart as though it were nothing more than a straw-stuffed doll. The raptor discarded the duramantium limbs and turned a ponderous half circle above the boiling multitudes of the Brumal Horde.

Hurricane winds raked over the band as it landed on the gate behind them, crushing it, and dragging down a whole section of the curtain wall.

In death, the Dragoneater was degrading rapidly. Its tail-feathers were gone, its fanning crest was depleted as well. As it bowed its head, Tam saw a lone figure perched between two of its twilight quills.

Say one thing for the Winter Queen, she thought sardonically, *the woman knows how to make an entrance.*

All at once the feverish assault of Astra's thralls relented. They scattered like fish from a grasping hand, dispersing into the ruins north and south. Their mistress had no need for them now, having pincered Rose and her bandmates between her two most potent weapons. Glancing bleakly in either direction, Tam couldn't help but wonder if there was a technical term for when a blacksmith replaced his anvil with a second hammer and just pounded the shit out of some poor tool.

Freecloud winced, apparently pondering something similar. "I don't suppose you have a plan for killing the Dragoneater a second time?"

Rose shook her head. "I don't."

"I do," said Cura. She dragged the black-feather shawl from her shoulders, pulled loose the sash belting her tunic, and shrugged it off despite the cold.

"What are you doing?" Tam asked.

"What I must," said the Inkwitch. She sounded distant, disconnected, like a sleepwalker insisting she answer a knock at the door.

Rose put a hand on the summoner's bare shoulder. "Cura..."

"I can do this," Cura insisted.

"Not alone, you can't."

She looked back. Her lip curled, not quite a smile. "I'm not alone."

Rose swallowed. Nodded. Let her hand fall away.

"*KURAGEN!*"

Brune growled his concern, and Freecloud's ears made his disquiet obvious as he took a step toward the Inkwitch. "Cura, you don't—"

"*YOMINA!*"

"Stay back," Rose snapped, as the vulture-necked swordsman and the sea goddess leapt to engage the Simurg.

"*MANGU! HARRADIL! NANSHA!*" Cura screamed as though stretched on a torturer's rack. One by one her nightmares took shape: a pale serpent with feathered wings; a hammer-wielding giant wearing a blood-soaked blindfold; an old woman made of soiled junk holding a pair of squirming white goats...

"*ABRAXAS*!" Cura stumbled as the winged steed kicked free of her arm. Her voice was hoarse. Blood streamed from her nose, trickled from her ears.

Rose barred Tam with an arm as she started forward. "Don't."

"She's killing herself!"

"She's not," Rose told her. "She's killing *them*."

Them? Before she could ask, Tam noticed that Cura's tattoos weren't only fading as she called their names—they were *disappearing*, peeling themselves from her flesh so that not even the scars that defined them remained.

Cura wasn't only using her power—she was relinquishing it entirely.

"*MELEAGANT*!" A spider made entirely of bones scuttled from her abdomen. "*RAN*!" A cloaked figure swirled into being—three pairs of long-nailed hands emerged from either sleeve, and six more held its garment closed. "*KINKALI*!" The silver-scaled women linked by chains slithered from her calf.

What terrors had this woman witnessed? Tam wondered as the inklings took shape. What trauma had she endured and internalized—and then evoked time and time again in service to her band?

From her knees, Cura sobbed, "*AGANI*!" The monstrous tree clawed from her back, howling as its crown caught fire. The summoner went to all fours and vomited into the muddied snow. Brune groaned in empathy, and Freecloud looked ready to rush to her aid regardless of the fact that Rose had warned him not to.

The inklings converged on the Simurg. It managed to snag the winged snake in its teeth and swat the garbage-woman so hard she went sprawling, spilling her armful of goats, but it could only defend itself against a few adversaries at once. *Abraxas* struck it with a bolt of blue lightning. The giant, *Harradil*, cracked his hammer across the Dragoneater's skull. Tam saw the Winter Queen slide from her perch and out of sight.

The bone spider, *Maleagant*, began spewing strands of razorwire webbing at the Simurg's hind legs. *Kuragen* grappled its head, burrowing her salt-slick tentacles into its nostrils and through the burning sockets of its eyes. *Yomina* went to work on its forelegs, hacking through flesh and bone like a lumberjack on a Lion's Leaf bender.

The scales on the Simurg's belly had begun to flake off. Its remaining feathers were withered and grey, no longer sheathed in armouring ice. Whatever complex biology had granted the Dragoneater its coldfire breath had been shredded to uselessness by Rose's blades.

Even diminished, though, it was hardly a pushover.

Its powerful jaws sheared through the winged snake. It caught and crushed the cloak-of-hands called *Ran*, then stomped the hag, *Nansha*, into a pile of scattered trash. Her goats screamed and puffed into wisps of black cloud.

It's not enough, Tam dreaded. *One by one, it will kill them—and then us, unless Brontide reaches us first.*

Except Cura wasn't finished yet. She raised a trembling arm, like a sacrifice opening her veins above some wicked altar. There was blood on her lips, blood trickling from her nose. Droplets of deep red stained her pale skin, which was otherwise *pristine*. For the first time since a girl's grief had compelled her to press an edge to her flesh and drive away pain with pain, she was *free*.

Or almost free.

"*BLOODY ROSE!*" she cried.

The apparition of Fable's frontwoman blazed to life, its molten boots steaming in the snow. Tam half-expected it to confront Rose, for the two of them to acknowledge one another the way sisters separated at birth might recognize their long-lost twin, but it sprang into the sky without looking back.

Cura collapsed into the slush. Rose rushed to her side. Freecloud peered with narrowed eyes at the embattled Dragoneater, probably searching for sign of the Winter Queen.

To the west, the skyships were closing in on Brontide. The *Barracuda* circled beyond his reach, launching another volley of missiles from its portside rail. The bolts stuck and shivered in the giant's head but couldn't punch through his thick skull. The other ship, a sleek frigate called the *Atom Heart*, went straight for him, veering sharply aside when Brontide brought his maul swinging in a lazy arc. Someone on board—either a wizard or some madman with a wand— sent a barrage of sizzling magic bolts at the titan's face. They missed, and forced the deep-bellied *Barracuda* to swerve from their errant path.

A flock of foul things tailed both vessels, so Tam *almost* didn't notice the smaller skyship bringing up the rear. The *Old Glory* had been drastically retrofitted since she saw it last. The hull had been nailed over with battered steel plates, and a ridge of spikes bristled down its prow. Faster than either the carrack or the frigate, it soared straight past the giant's nose. Brontide swiped at it with one huge hand, but Doshi cinched the rigging; the cutter dropped steeply, and had almost hit the ground before, with the boom of a faraway thunderclap, its sails fanned open.

The giant raised his ram's-head maul, and might have smashed the *Old Glory* to kindling had the remaining knight not swung its hammer hard against Brontide's kneecap, shattering it. The juggernaut went down like a bottle-struck drunk, demolishing a dozen neighbourhoods as he crashed to the ground.

Looking back to the Simurg, Tam found Astra's precious pet monster in equally dire straits. It closed its jaws on *Agani*, who willingly offered up its burning branches. As Tam had seen it do once before in Ardburg, the tortured treant released its fiery leaves all at once. They went spiralling down the monster's gullet (she could see the glowing torrent through patches in its plumage) and destroyed whatever desiccated organs remained inside the Simurg's body.

Kuragen, her slick tentacles straining with effort, tore most of the monster's lower jaw away. *Harradil* collapsed its eye socket with a violent hammerblow. The silver-scaled twins called *Kinkali* looped their chains around the Simurg's neck and began a spirited tug'o'war that threatened to saw its head off. *Yomina* withdrew his seventh sword—the one sheathed in his heart—and thrust it to the hilt in the monster's breast.

The Dragoneater shuddered, sagging beneath the inklings' onslaught. It tried to rise, but the bone spider's webbing snared its legs. The Winter Queen—who was out of sight, but obviously still alive—gave vent to her frustration, shrieking through the Simurg's shattered jaw. As she did, the flame-enshrouded figure of *Bloody Rose* came streaking like a comet from on high, so hot that every snowflake in the city became a hissing droplet.

It plunged straight into the Dragoneater's open mouth, down its throat, into the charred cavern of its stomach.

And exploded.

Consumed from within by a mushrooming cloud of indigo fire, the once-mighty Simurg was obliterated in a mile-wide blast of burnt flesh, blackened bones, and burning feathers.

Tam, standing half a block away, was blown from her feet and sent tumbling across the ground. She rolled groggily to her knees, reclaiming her bow and fumbling to collect what few arrows remained to her. By the time she returned her attention to the smoking remains of the Simurg, Cura's inklings were dissolving one by one into wisps of black cloud.

The apparition of her uncle *Yomina* was the last to go. The vulture-necked swordsman turned to face his niece. His straw hat tilted—a gesture of farewell, perhaps, or of gratitude—and then he vanished.

By now a keening wail was rising all around them as the Winter Queen raged. The sound was drawing closer, growing louder, circling like a cyclone around a flimsy farmhouse.

"We need to move," said Rose, looking up from Cura's ashen face.

"That could be a problem," said Freecloud. He eyed the torc on his arm. The runes had stopped glowing, and the rod at his waist was no longer giving off light.

Looks like Contha doesn't like others playing with his toys.

A moment's glance confirmed Tam's fears: The golems protecting them were standing still, slack-limbed. The sigils in their eyes had gone dormant. Beyond the sprawl of slouching tenements, she saw that a similar fate had befallen the duramantium knight. It stood frozen in the midst of a hammerblow that might have ended Brontide's unlife once and for all. Instead, the giant grasped it in two hands and wrenched the knight's head from its body. Though its armour was impenetrable, whatever comprised the golem's core was never intended to withstand the tantrum of a pissed-off giant.

"We'll have to run for it," Freecloud declared. And indeed, of the few dozen monsters remaining in their escort, most of them were already dashing for the gate to the inner city.

"I think..." Tam squinted west through the slanting snow and the dust thrown up by the giant's collapse. She was searching for the *Old Glory* but didn't see it anywhere.

"You think what?" asked the druin.

"I think Doshi is—"

Her words were drowned out as the skyship went roaring above them, hounded by a cluster of harpies screaming with Astra's voice. Tam's hand strayed to her quiver, but the winged women were dropping faster than moths at the mouth of a forge, riddled with arrows streaking from *inside* the ship. Doshi banked right, turned a slewing circle over the smoking remnants of the Simurg, and brought the *Old Glory* to a hovering halt beside them.

There was a snarling harpy impaled on one of its forward spikes, and an altogether friendlier face grinning over the rail.

"Y'all need a lift?" hollered Lady Jain.

*   *   *

Despite having tossed her whole plan out the window less than an hour before, Rose's ill-fated attack on the palanquin managed to serve her strategy perfectly. Incensed that her nemesis had slipped her grasp, and enraged by the Simurg's demise, the Winter Queen herself led the assault on Conthas.

Which wasn't to say Astra did so recklessly, cocooned as she was by an unbreachable maelstrom of monstrous dead. She'd seized absolute control of the sky by now. The *Barracuda* had ventured too close to the ground and was slapped to pieces by the crippled giant, while the *Atom Heart* was on fire, out of ammunition, and on the run from a clutch of wyverns.

Doshi dropped them off inside the East Gutter Gate. Cura was unconscious, still. Her breathing was shallow, her skin slick with cold sweat. Before leaving the ship, Brune crouched beside the summoner, wincing as the wounds he'd suffered as a wolf oozed blood down the muscled breadth of his back. He swept Cura's hair aside and kissed her brow. She stirred, grasping weakly at the shaman's wrist.

"I . . ." she murmured, ". . . fight."

Brune chuckled. Tam saw him sniff and drag the back of one soiled hand across his cheek. "You've done enough," he told her. "Rest, little sister. We'll take it from here."

Too exhausted to speak, Cura laid her fingers on the shaman's arm.

Brune didn't bother to wipe away the next tear to streak through the grime on his face. "If I don't see ya," he whispered, "I'll see ya."

"Make sure she gets to the Sanctuary," Rose called to Doshi.

"I will," the captain said gravely. "I swear it."

As the *Old Glory* went roaring toward Chapel Hill, Lady Jain sidled up between Rose and Tam. "Vail's Bloody Cock," she swore. "I reckon I'm in love with that man."

"Love?" Tam sputtered. "Doshi? You met him, what, yesterday?"

"The day *before* yesterday." Jain shrugged. "But the loins want what the loins want, as they say."

"Nobody says that," Tam assured her.

"Get ready," said Rose, eyes hooded by her crimson cowl. Her bracers flared as she squared herself to the eastern gate. "Here she comes."

Chapter Fifty-six

Fighting Dirty

They fought Astra in the mud-brick blocks of Knight's Landing, whose baron—the arachnian named K'tuo—went to war flanked by a pair of his six-armed kin. The trio wielded eight swords, seven axes, and three spears between them, and fought as if they were a single entity, a hunter's hive mind with three separate bodies.

Brune stood guard over Tam while she depleted her restocked quiver, putting shaft after shaft into every abomination in sight. When the shaman was set upon by a scorpion the size of a warhorse, Tam drew *Nightbird* and kept Astra's minions at bay until the wolf prevailed.

Rose pitted herself against an ogre encased head to toe in steel plate scrawled with vulgar words in yellow paint. The brute looked like one of Contha's golems, but though his armour made him almost invulnerable, his clumsy attacks made it obvious he couldn't see for shit. He didn't know Rose had climbed him until she put her swords through the slitted visor of his helm.

Their resistance lasted until the massive war-tortoise crashed through the wall beside the gate, burying the insectoid baron and his fellow arachnians beneath a landslide of stone bricks. The castle perched atop the tortoise's weathered shell—a precarious structure bristling with sharpened wood palisades—was inhabited by reptilian saigs armed with bolas, which the lizardmen used to hurl pointed, poison-tipped seashells with deadly accuracy.

Rose called the retreat, and the defenders of Knight's Landing melted westward.

As they withdrew, Tam saw Astra stride beneath the arch of the Gutter Gate. Her blackmetal crown glinted in the ashen light, and the silk strands affixed to her shoulders thrashed in the freezing gale. Straight-backed and imperious, she looked as though she were an empress gracing a hall of admiring courtiers, and not a death-obsessed necromancer bent on eradicating every soul in the city.

"*I'm coming for you, Rose,*" said her thralls in eerie unison.

"Go fuck yourself!" Rose shouted over her shoulder.

Papery laughter slithered into Tam's ear, making her squirm.

They fought Astra in the shabby streets of Rockbottom, where Baron Starkwood led a levy of ugly, musclebound thugs by proxy of being the ugliest, most muscular among them. They were reinforced by the city's stable of pit fighters, who ranged from bearded, battle-scarred northerners to wiry Narmeeri snake-wrestlers—called so not because they wrestled snakes, but because they wrestled *like* snakes, stunning their opponents with lightning strikes and then subduing them with grapples.

The combined forces ran roughshod over their enemy, and were on the verge of pushing them all the way back to Knight's Landing before the tables (as tables tend to do in pitched warfare) turned against them.

All the muscles in the world couldn't protect Tain Starkwood when a slag drake vomited a jet of scalding magma all over him. The baron disintegrated like a snowman under the Summer Lord's glare, leaving nothing behind but a duramantium belt buckle that read *Invincible* floating on a pool of gurgling lava.

The resistance crumbled entirely when Brontide, crawling on his elbows since his knee was destroyed, began pummelling the defenders with his fists.

"Back!" Rose bellowed, and the Winter Queen's susurrant laughter hounded their heels once again.

"*Surrender,*" said her hundred thousand mouths. "*Embrace oblivion.*"

Embrace oblivion? Tam scoffed under her breath. *Thanks, but no thanks.*

They fought Astra among the ramshackle hovels of Riverswell, trapping the dead in blind alleys and pelting them with whiskey-bottle firebombs from the rooftops above.

They fought on the snowy slopes of Blackbarrow, whose residents turned a collection of food carts and rangy mules into two dozen makeshift chariots. The resulting stampede was disastrous for everyone involved, but effective nonetheless.

They fought amidst the plundered crypts of Wightcliffe, baiting thralls into open graves filled with everything from sharpened spikes to a highly acidic slop co-engineered by the city's tanners and the alchemists' guild.

Even the Winter Queen's entourage fell prey to ambush. As it followed the broad boulevard of the Gutter into Saltkettle, a pair of explosive-laden argosies rolled down either side of the bisecting thoroughfare.

Astra's frustrated snarl tore through the city. She threw a hundred thralls into the path of one, which bounced and tipped sideways, detonating well before it reached the Gutter and setting several buildings on fire. The other rumbled on unhindered, and for a brief moment Tam allowed herself to believe they'd done it—that the sorceress and her puppet army would be undone in one fiery instant—before Brontide, compelled by Astra's panicked command, dragged himself into its path. The war wagon exploded against the giant's face. The resulting blast stripped the flesh from his bones. His hair and beard burned like a dry broom fed to a furnace.

He pushed himself up, arms flexing beneath the charred leer of his smouldering skull.

"You've gotta be kidding me," Tam heard Freecloud groan.

But then Brontide's brittle neck snapped beneath the weight of its burden. His head hit the ground, crushing dozens of risen dead, then rolled like a boulder into the Gutter. His body shuddered violently and went still.

A desultory cheer erupted from the city's defenders, but the howl of the storm drowned them out and the Horde surged like an ocean intent on drowning the world.

They gave up Saltkettle without a fight, retreating as swiftly as they could toward the base of Chapel Hill. A group of Rockbottom thugs, unfamiliar with the turf of a rival baron, fled down a blind alley and were cornered by the four-headed hydrake.

Tam ran, though the muscles in her legs were screaming for rest. The weather was getting worse by the minute. The snow through which they fled was ankle-deep and piling fast. The wind whipped her hair and tugged at the ragged hem of her longcoat as she hustled to keep up with Rose and Free-cloud. Brune loped off to scout the way ahead.

"*Vermin.*" Astra's voice haunted their retreat. "*You scuttle like rats in your warren. But I will root you out,*" she promised, "*and exterminate every one of you.*"

A dozen dead centaurs came charging from a sloping side street. Rose's scimitars cut the legs from one, fouling the momentum of those behind it. Freecloud slipped between them, his blade shearing through torsos and lopping off heads.

Tam, who had neither the martial prowess of Bloody Rose, nor the effortless poise of a druin swordmaster, saw one of the horsemen bearing down on her and did the first rational thing that came to mind: She tossed her bow in a snowbank and leapt through the open window of the house beside her.

She spent a moment flailing wildly, tangled in gauzy linen drapes that did their best to strangle her. She gained her feet and started for the door but tripped over a footstool she hadn't noticed in the gloom and went sprawling across the grimy rushes carpeting the floor.

Suddenly something was on her. It hissed in her face, scratched at the scales of her armour, and sunk fangs into her hand when she tried to push it off.

A kobold, she guessed. *Or an imp, maybe? Make that several imps*, she thought, as more of the creatures attacked her in the dark. Tam caught one with an elbow, flung another off her foot, and scrambled to her feet. She caught sight of a thrashing tail and hackled fur against the window's wan light before another of the devils leapt at her face, raking its talons across her cheek and drawing blood.

She raced for the exit, cursed when her hip caught the corner of a wooden table. One of the imps (or kobolds, or whatever the fuck these monsters were) leapt onto her back. Its claws caught in her hair as it struggled for purchase.

Finally, Tam reached the door. She yanked it wide, exposing her assailants to the light. Whirling, she saw them scurrying for cover...

... but not before she realized they were cats.

She clamped her jaw shut on a curse, resolved never to speak of this to anyone, and promptly left, slamming the door behind her. By the time she found the others, they'd cut the centaurs to pieces. It looked as though a whole regiment of cadaverous cavalry had been butchered in the street.

"You're bleeding," Rose pointed out.

Tam pressed fingers to her face, wincing as her touch found a searing claw mark beneath her right eye. "I'm fine," she insisted.

Madrigal hummed as Freecloud returned the blade to its sheath. "Find some trouble, did you?"

Tam patted *Nightbird*'s pommel. "Nothing I couldn't handle," she said, ignoring a muffled yowl from the house behind her.

Rose jogged off, while Freecloud reclaimed Tam's bow and offered it to her with a smirk. "Vicious things, cats," he said, then winked and set out after Rose.

Tam wiped blood from her face with the cuff of her coat before following.

They were forced to skirmish twice more before escaping the ward—first against a pack of decaying trollhounds, then with a gang of zombies Tam mistook for allies until they drew close enough for her to see the flames in their eyes. She stood her ground this time, and used *Nightbird*'s keen edge to cut through the neck of a pale-faced boy hardly older than herself.

The kid's half-severed head peered into the depths of Rose's hood. "*You disguise yourself?*" it asked with Astra's voice. "*You cannot hide from me, Rose. I will find you. I will make you suffer. My son's death will be aven—*"

Tam finished hacking the boy's head off, then kicked it down the slope behind them.

"Thanks," said Rose.

"Anytime," Tam replied.

Brune joined them at the boundary between Saltkettle and the Paper Court, which was very clearly demarcated by the quality of construction between one ward and the next, as the shabby tenements of Tabano's domain gave way to two- and three-storey buildings of mortared stone.

The shaman was panting heavily. Gore slathered his jaws and slicked his once-white fur. There were three black-fletched arrows studding his hide, one of which he snapped off with his teeth as they arrived.

"Are you okay?" Rose asked.

The wolf bowed his head, a nod. Tam grimaced as blood speckled the ground beneath his snout.

Rose took the shaman's face in both hands, speaking words Tam couldn't hear as Freecloud broke the fletching off the other two arrows. Whatever she said, Brune growled quietly in response.

"All right," she said. "Lead the way."

They hurried on, skirting the eastern flank of Chapel Hill, making their way north and west toward the main thoroughfare and another confrontation with Astra's main force. Stealing glances across the city, Tam could see that nearly all of Blackbarrow was on fire. The flames were spreading fast, already chewing at the blocks of its bordering wards.

The Winter Queen's Horde moved west through Conthas, threading the valley floor like a pestilent river overflowing its banks. Its vanguard—the roiling knot inside which Astra was ensconced—found itself embattled on two fronts. The sell-swords of the Paper Court (who had sold their swords to Ios in the wake of Alektra's downfall) charged down the wide avenues of their ward, while the assassins of Telltale struck from the shadowed alleys of theirs.

Fable reached the Gutter in time to see Ios herself take a very literal stab at the Winter Queen. The assassin fought her way through Astra's vortex of undead defenders, forcing the sorceress to draw her shrieking sword. It became immediately clear, however, that Telltale's baroness had never tried to kill a druin.

She doesn't know about the prescience, Tam gathered, as the woman's knife slashed nothing but empty air. *She can't know that Astra can anticipate her every move.*

Which meant, of course, that the assassin was doomed.

Ios threw a dagger that was dodged with ease. She lunged, but her opponent curled like smoke around her blade.

The Winter Queen's sword was in and out of the assassin's heart before Ios knew she was dead. The baroness gaped, stumbled, and would have fallen had the druin not uttered a word and poured her wine-dark soul into the decanted husk of the woman's corpse.

And just like that, Tam thought, watching Ios rise to take her place among the Winter Queen's thralls, *another loyal soldier joins the legion of the damned.*

Despite their succession of small victories—killing the Simurg, stopping Brontide, goading Astra into pursuing Rose—Tam couldn't shake the feeling of being trapped in a coffin as nail after nail after nail was hammered into the lid.

It wasn't long before Rose signalled the order to withdrawal yet again. She made a spectacle of herself, ensuring her crimson cowl was tantalizingly visible as they fled west around the base of Chapel Hill. Tam was relieved to find Lady Jain at the rear of the retreating crowd. She and her girls put a volley of arrows into the faces of their closest pursuers.

Another pair of bomb-laden argosies were cut loose to cover their withdrawal, barrelling down the hillside and decimating swathes of fetid foot soldiers. Elsewhere, whole blocks of buildings exploded as Astra's thrall stumbled over hidden tripwires. Bodies and burnt timber leapt skyward on blooms of fire.

As they followed the road into Sinkwell, Tam sighted a host of shambling dead clogging the street ahead. She'd already put an arrow to string before recognizing her uncle and Clay Cooper among them, weary but alive.

Slowhand, it seemed, was a man of his word: He and the Rusted Blades had managed to hold the Wyldside gate against overwhelming odds. As his haggard veterans merged with the exhausted defenders, Tam overheard Clay inform Rose they'd left the Han's horsemen to mop up what was left of the Agrians, and to make sure the dead stayed dead.

The survivors of Mad Mackie's company were trickling in as well. Many of them were wounded, and those unable to fight were taken by cart up the back side of Chapel Hill. Rose ordered Jain and the Silk Arrows to escort them.

Rose assigned Tam to the third-storey balcony of a

south-facing inn called the White Lion, which provided a clear vantage of the street below.

"Clay. Bran." Rose addressed the pair of old mercs as though they were common soldiers and not the heroes of a hundred tales (though, to be fair, Uncle Bran was the author of most of his). "Go with her. Watch her back."

Her uncle seemed relieved by the appointment, but Clay Cooper was less enthused.

"I should stay near you," he insisted.

"You should stay *alive*," Rose told him. "I'm less worried about Astra than I am about Ginny murdering me if I get you killed."

Slowhand frowned and fingered the scar angling across his nose. "Fair enough."

"Good." Rose nodded. "And I'm serious about needing Tam looked after. She's got an important role to play."

"Really?" Tam asked. "Because it feels like I'm being relegated to 'distant spectator.'"

"Not quite," Rose assured her. "You're going to kill the Winter Queen."

Astra's Horde spread across Conthas like rot, infecting its streets, polluting its squares, defiling the Free City as it had never been defiled—which was quite a feat considering what a muddy pisshole the place had been before they arrived. Like some insidious arterial poison worming its way toward the heart, the dead converged in their thousands upon the woman waiting for the Winter Queen to round the base of Chapel Hill.

Rose had left her father's fabled sword with Alkain Tor for safekeeping, but now she stood with both hands on its hilt and the point of its scabbard resting on the ground between her boots. She still wore her cowl, and glared over *Vellichor*'s pommel like a woman sentenced to death watching the sun rise on her final day.

Freecloud stood at her right shoulder, Brune her left. The shaman's breath gusted from between his jaws. Rose reached to lay a hand on his scruff, though whether she did it to comfort the wolf or herself Tam couldn't know.

Around them, crowding the boroughs of Sinkwell and the west-facing slope of Chapel Hill, were the last defenders of Conthas: the Rusted Blades and the remainder of Mad Mackie's company; the sorcerors of Sinkwell, and the battle-weary survivors of every ward they'd relinquished to their implacable foe. Alkain's mercenaries were the only ones yet unscathed, since they'd been ordered to wait here in ambush. Now they emerged from home and hovel into the streets, their heads and faces swaddled against the blustery cold.

The Horde, meanwhile, had ground to a halt. Things that had once been men and women stood slack-jawed, their heads canted as if listening for some quiet command. Monsters great and small ceased to skitter, scuttle, slither, or stomp, waiting mindlessly on their mistress's order. Plague hawks and wyverns wheeled slow circles in the grey sky, while rot sylphs and eyewings hung like gruesome baubles from the smoke-clouded canopy.

"Are you afraid?" asked the Winter Queen. Her voice was the rustle of dead leaves blowing across the face of a tombstone.

Rose considered the question. "Not of you," she said eventually.

A dry chuckle. *"You should be. Don't you know what I am?"*

"If I promise not to ask," Rose said, "will you promise not to tell me?"

The Winter Queen ignored her. *"I am a conduit. An unholy vessel. Within me is an essence greater than you can possibly imagine."*

"I can imagine quite a bit," Rose drawled, and Tam heard Clay Cooper chuckle quietly to himself.

"She thrives on my pain," confessed Astra, as though she and Rose were the only two souls in the city. *"She inhabits the void my children left behind, and she will do the same to you, Rose, when your daughter is dead."*

"Does this 'unimaginable essence' have a name?" Rose asked.

"She is Tamarat," said the knifing wind. *"Darkness incarnate. The Devourer of Worlds."*

Tam saw mercenaries exchange what she assumed were nervous glances, though their expressions were hidden by hood and helm. Even Freecloud looked shaken. His ears, pinned flat against the sides of his head, betrayed a terror the druin could barely suppress.

Only Rose seemed indifferent to the other woman's declaration. "The Devourer of Worlds?" She shook her head. "Not this time. Not my world. You've gone mad, Astra. You're a prisoner to your grief." Rose's fingers flexed on *Vellichor*'s hilt. "But I'll set you free. And for whatever it's worth: I'm sorry about your son. Truly, I am. Lastleaf deserved better. His people deserved better."

"His people?" The Winter Queen's scorn was accompanied by a flurry of snow. *"Those creatures were not his people. Their kind—and yours—are as chattel to us. Your existence is pointless, ephemeral, so fleeting as to seem unreal. And you, Rose, are nothing more than the smoke rising from your father's pyre."*

Rose turned and said something to Alkain Tor, who was standing behind her.

"You are the ashes of a—"

"Ashes?" Rose cut the sorceress off, her tone incredulous. "Smoke? I don't think so."

All over Sinkwell, mercenaries were pulling back their hoods, tearing off their helmets, uncoiling the scarves swaddling their heads.

"I'm the *fire.*"

Chapter Fifty-seven

The War of Roses

Red, red, everywhere. The brilliant red of spring flowers, the garish red of fresh blood, the blinding, bedazzling red of a setting sun. Tam gasped in amazement. Her eyes picked out innumerable hack-job haircuts and hucknell-bean hues, a whole *army* of counterfeit Roses filling the street below and blanketing the slopes of Chapel Hill. It wasn't just the women, either: Men, too, had chopped their hair and shaved their beards, or dyed them red in solidarity.

There were thousands of them.

Tens of thousands.

And now they charged, screaming defiance into the varied faces of death itself, roaring like a cleansing fire toward the septic stain of the Winter Queen's Horde.

And so the rout of Conthas ends, Tam thought, *and the War of Roses begins.*

Rose remained standing as her army surged forward, waiting until her crimson cowl was lost amidst the rush of vivid red. Only then did she unclasp the cloak at her shoulder, pull it free, and let it fall.

Tam blinked, and would have tripped over her jaw had she been running along with everyone else.

Rose's hair was *gone*.

Or most of it, anyway. She'd cut away all trace of the colour for which she was famous. Only a scrub of gold remained, bright as a sun-struck coin.

"She looks just like Gabriel," murmured Slowhand, who was leaning against the wall behind her.

Branigan swigged from a bottle he'd looted from the bar inside. "It's uncanny."

Tam stole the bottle from her uncle and took a swallow, then made a face like a yawning cat. Whiskey. Not her favourite. "Good thing she can't hear you," she told Bran. "She'd be furious."

Clay shrugged. "You sure about that?"

In fact, she wasn't. Not anymore.

Below, Rose barked an order to Brune. The huge wolf dipped his head and went bounding toward the battle raging farther down the street. Alone (or as alone as two people could be amidst the rush of redheaded thousands), Rose and Freecloud leaned in to one another. He put a hand on her neck. She laid a hand on his chest, and whatever words they shared were lost to the roar and clash of arms.

At last, they joined the flow of warriors running past, and Tam's breath caught as Rose pulled *Vellichor* from its scabbard. She'd heard bards refer to the Archon's blade as a doorway to another realm, but she hadn't expected the door to be *open*. Through the flat pane of its surface she caught a glimpse of blue sky and green grass blowing on a rising hill.

And now the denizens of Sinkwell—the witches, wizards, and weirdos Moog had convinced to join the fight—threw the Winter Queen a welcoming party of their own.

Roga, the summoner they'd met at the Starwood two nights earlier, dashed his pink stone elephant on the ground and brought it to life. The thing was enormous—three times the size of a Brumal mammoth—and painted all over with whorls of white and yellow despite looking to Tam like something used to awe children at a birthday party, it caused a fair bit of havoc as it stormed through the congested ranks of Astra's Horde.

Kaliax Kur, the scar-faced psychopath with a tidal engine strapped to her back, powered it on and aimed the lance to which it was attached in the enemy's general direction. Lightning sprayed like water from the weapon's tip. It leapt from foe to foe, leaving corpses blackened like a forest of charred stumps. The woman's wood armour was oozing smoke, and even from so far away she smelled like pork roasting over a campfire.

Hundreds of heroes were wading into the fray. Jeramyn Cain led the Screaming Eagles against the four-headed hydrake, while Clare Cassiber went toe-to-toe with a saig raider. The white-eyed reptile fought with a net and a hook-shaped jawbone. It managed to snare Claire in the net and sink its hook into her leg, but she lopped off its head, cast off the net, and limped back into battle.

Elsewhere, the men of Giantsbane scaled the war-tortoise's shell and began assaulting the fortress. Alkain Tor lobbed a torch over a palisade wall, and before long the whole thing went up in flames.

Scanning the battlefield, Tam thought she spied Hawkshaw's blood-slick skull gazing up at her, but when she blinked the Warden was gone, no doubt enduring another painful death his mistress wouldn't let him enjoy.

The Horde was in disarray. The Winter Queen was so intent on killing Rose that being confronted by *literally thousands* of her had left the sorceress flummoxed, unsure of where to commit her strength. She hadn't seen Rose draw back her hood, and so couldn't know that the one woman she was looking for was the only one she *wasn't* looking at. Astra's fliers

appeared paralyzed by indecision, flapping in frantic circles
as the sorceress sought to locate her nemesis below.

And here came the *Old Glory*, swooping from the hilltop
like a steel-plated sparrow in a sky full of hawks. Her spiked
prow punched through swarms of smaller monsters, while
those too big to take on directly were shredded by bowfire,
courtesy of Lady Jain and the Silk Arrows.

Doshi brought the skyship low over the corpse-choked
thoroughfare so the girls could hurl firebombs into the enemy
ranks. A series of *thwump*ing explosions bloomed along the
strip; bodies—and pieces of bodies—went cartwheeling over
the rooftops.

It looked to Tam as if the whole eastern half of Conthas
was on fire. Thousands of Astra's thralls would be caught in
the flames, with the rest forced to outrun the inferno devouring the city behind them.

Even the weather was turning in their favour. She wasn't
sure if the storm had been Astra's doing or not, but the wind
dropped off and the snow no longer slanted as it fell.

Tam began raining missiles into the press of pale bodies.
Slowhand had lugged a whole crate of ammunition to their
perch, and the old merc busied himself by handing her arrows
as fast as she could set them loose. Before long her arms were on
fire and her fingers were freezing. Her enemies were so densely
packed she could have killed them with her eyes closed, but
for every one she dropped another rose to take its place.

She wasn't the only one picking off targets from above.
Mercs thronged every rooftop and window along the Gutter,
and while most selected targets at random, some couldn't help
but take desperate shots at the Winter Queen—which was
futile, of course, since whatever her thralls failed to intercept,
Astra evaded with ease.

Tam yelped as something with ropy tentacles for arms
pulled itself over the balcony rail. The creature's head resem-
beld a budding flower, and split open to reveal five fanged

petals and a slick, prehensile tongue. There was a spear lodged
in its throat, which she guessed was what had killed it in the
first place. The creature had no eyes that Tam could see, but
its tongue probed the air like a snake hunting for prey outside
its burrow.

"I'll handle this," said Bran. He lobbed his bottle at the
creature to distract it while he hefted a steel buckler and
pulled his hammer, *Bullseye*, from the loop at his waist.

The creature's tongue snagged the hammer as Bran raised
it to swing, so her uncle pinned his weapon to the wall and
used the edge of his shield to chop through the coiling muscle.
The shield bit into the wall and the tongue snapped back into
the monster's mouth, whipping blood in an arc across Branigan's face. Sputtering and half blind, he left his shield stuck
in the wood and swung his hammer two-handed. Instead of
aiming for the monster's head, he pounded the butt end of the
spear already lodged in its throat, driving it deeper down the
creature's gullet. It split open down the centre, and Bran sent
it toppling over the rail with a kick.

Afterward, her uncle reclaimed his shield and spit out a
mouthful of the monster's blood. "Anyone know what the hell
that thing was?" he asked.

Slowhand only shrugged. "Ugly," he said.

Out in the street, Roga's pink elephant shattered and
faded away. Glancing to where she'd last seen the summoner,
Tam found him impaled on a wyvern's tail, limp as a flag of
surrender on a windless day.

Kaliax Kur went down a few seconds later. The lightning
streaming from her lance bounced off the reflective scales of
a basilisk, setting her armour on fire and frying the woman
in her own skin. To her credit, she managed to survive long
enough to ram her lance into the basilisk's mouth. The serpent convulsed as the current tore through its body. Its scales
cracked like a rotter's mirror, exploding into shards that tore
everything around it to shreds.

"Hey." Slowhand's voice dragged Tam's attention back to the balcony. "Did we win? Is the battle over?"

She eyed him skeptically. "What? No."

He pressed an arrow into her hand. "Then keep fucking shooting."

Tam rolled her eyes, but accepted his offering and buried it in a bugbear's skull. "Have you seen Moog?" she asked.

Clay pointed. "There."

She followed the gesture in time to see a poof of yellow smoke that left several hundred of Astra's thralls suddenly transformed into zombified chickens.

Tam spotted the old wizard standing on an overturned crate in an alley mouth. He was brandishing a gnarled wand and looked extraordinarily pleased with himself, at least until the chickens spooked him off his box and chased him down the alley.

The *Old Glory* made a run for Astra's inner circle, but a wyvern hurled itself against the skyship's armoured hull and sent it careening out of control. Tam lost sight of it as it spun overhead, but she could hear Jain and her girls screaming like a boatload of rafters going over the edge of a waterfall.

Scanning the hysteria below, Tam tried to determine if they were winning or losing, but the scene was too chaotic to make sense of. Everywhere she looked, red-haired warriors were killing, screaming, dying, flailing, hacking, or rising from the dead.

She saw one of Rose's doubles skewer a centaur on the tip of her spear, and another get her head bashed in by an ogre's club, and another hack through the neck of a saurian, and another torn apart by a spindly birch-bark treant.

A few of them managed to confront Astra herself, but fell quickly to the druin's phantom blade. Before long, the sorceress was surrounded by undead Roses. The sight made Tam's skin crawl, and probably wasn't doing the defenders' morale any favours.

The *real* Rose was almost through the Winter Queen's circling minions. She and Freecloud hadn't even bloodied their weapons, huddled as they were in the midst of a throng, escorted by a veritable who's who of Grandual's greatest mercenary bands: the Boomtown Rats, Overkill, the Vandals, and the Thunderers, who'd killed a wyvern in a chapel near Ardburg last spring.

Tam could see the Duran brothers fighting alongside Tash Bakkus, known throughout the five courts as the Iron Maiden. She picked out Warfire's flaming swords as they chopped their way through the white-eyed dead. Courtney and the Sparks were part of Rose's entourage as well. They'd been among the bands to defeat the Heartwyld Horde at Castia and were doubtless wondering how the hell they'd found themselves embroiled in yet another hopeless battle against overwhelming odds.

Brune was leading the way, snapping and snarling, using his body to bludgeon a path for those behind him. He was raked by talons, slashed by knives, pummelled by mauls and clubs and fists—but he endured, heedless of his mounting insurmountable injuries.

Tam remembered Cura warning her that some among them would need to sacrifice everything so that others might survive, and the summoner's words suddenly seemed like a premonition.

Brune wasn't concerned with survival, leastways not his own. He was fighting for his bandmates. His *pack*. He'd surrendered himself to the beast within—another sacrifice laid at Rose's feet—and Tam found herself *envying* him the chance to do so.

Neither she nor Brune saw the mammoth falling until it was too late. The beast had been wading through the crush beside the shaman when one of Rose's doppelgangers mounted its head and drove the spiked butt of her battle-axe into its skull. It toppled sideways, crushing Brune's hind legs and pinning him beneath it.

Tam cried out, supressing the urge to leap from her balcony and rush to his aid. Even Rose might have stopped to help had Freecloud not shouted something that spurred her on. They were *so close now*, hardly a stone's throw from the woman whose death would put an end to all of this.

Sunlight streamed from *Vellichor*'s blade as Rose raised it overhead.

Madrigal tolled like a temple bell as it slipped from its scabbard.

Slowhand was so intent on the battle below that he'd neglected to pass Tam another arrow, and Bran—

—was staring, dumbstruck, at the crude tip of the bone sword jutting from his stomach.

Tam turned slowly, as one entombed in freezing water, to see Hawkshaw's nightmare rictus grinning back at her.

"You should have killed me when you had the chance," he grated.

She'd been about to reply when something that looked like a fist but felt like a hammer caught her chin, and the dark came swirling down.

Chapter Fifty-eight

The Spark and the Snowflake

"*Tam.*" Her mother's voice called from beyond the door. Tam's eyelids twitched. Her mind roused itself from sleep, sluggish as a cat caught in the sun.

"*Tam, get up.*" Her father this time. Insistent. What time was it? Why was it so damn cold? Had she left the window open?

And speaking of cats, she wondered, *where is Threnody?* Tam turned her head, expecting to feel her pet's fur tickle her neck. Instead, she felt a sharp stab of pain. *Pain? That doesn't—*

"*Tam!*" The voice was more insistent this time, but it did not belong to her father. It was Uncle Bran.

"Tam! Get up!"

Her eyes fluttered open. Grey light. A roof, but not her own. A sound like ten thousand people screaming from the bottom of a well funnelled into her ears, growing louder, and louder, until it crashed over her like a bucket of ice water.

Tam bolted upright, wincing at the ache in her neck, the throbbing in her head, the stinging soreness in her jaw where Hawkshaw's fist had—

Hawkshaw!

She was looking through the open balcony doors, where

two figures were wrestling in the gloom of the White Lion's upper commons. The larger of the two hurled the other over a table before turning to face her.

"Are you okay?" asked Slowhand.

"I am," Tam said, without actually knowing whether she was or not. "Bran . . ."

"I'm here!" her uncle croaked. He was lying on his side, still impaled by the Warden's sword.

"You're alive!"

Bran grimaced. "For now. I swear on the Summer Lord's Beard, though, if that fucker's hurt my liver . . ."

"Tam!" Slowhand shouted over her uncle's rambling. "You're here to kill the Queen, yes?"

She nodded.

"So do it. I'll handle this—" He winced as a chair flung by Hawkshaw broke across his back. "I'll handle—" He flinched as a spinning bottle struck his shoulder, shattering on impact. "I'll—" A second bottle smashed against the back of his head. "Oh, for fuck's sake," he swore. "Go save the world, will you?"

"Right," she said. "And Slowhand . . ."

"Mm?"

She jutted her chin toward Hawkshaw. "He's the one who shot Gabe."

Something *hardened* in the old merc's face, and his huge hands curled into fists. He said in a voice freighted with quiet menace, "Did he now?"

Tam didn't bother watching what happened next. But if the Warden *could* be killed, she figured that Clay Cooper would find a way. She grabbed her bow and scrambled to Branigan's side. "Uncle, are you okay?"

The old man's eyes floated a moment before landing on her. "Why wouldn't I be?"

"There's a sword in you."

"Ah, well . . . there's a sword in all of us," he said, then winked as though he'd said something profound. Which, to be fair, he kind of had.

Doing her best to ignore the grunts and thuds behind her, Tam stood to assess the bedlam below. It was almost impossible to tell the living from the dead, since Astra was raising mercenaries as fast as they fell. There were ten thousand battles raging all at once, so it took Tam a few seconds to find the one she was looking for.

Rose and Freecloud were on their own now. The company escorting them had dissolved into separate bands, each of them fighting on the fringes to keep the Horde at bay. By now every thrall surrounding Astra was a fallen merc, forcing Rose to hack through several clones of herself as they closed on the sorceress.

Madrigal sang like a choir in Freecloud's hands. *Vellichor* seemed light as a feather in Rose's. She and the druin fought in perfect unison, slashing and spinning like dancers in the midst of a brawl.

They were untouchable, unstoppable, possessed of a savage grace that Tam, watching from on high, could define only as *elemental*. Like a landslide, or a tidal wave, or a wildfire raging unchecked, Rose and Freecloud crashed through Astra's thralls, gaining momentum with every step.

A loud crash yanked her from reverie. Tam glanced over her shoulder to see Hawkshaw rise unsteadily from behind the bar. Shards of glass clung to the Warden's skull, glinting like some grisly mosaic as he clambered over the countertop.

"Why do I always get the stubborn ones?" she heard Slowhand growl.

Beside her, Bran was lying with his eyes closed and his chin slumped on his chest.

"Uncle!"

"I'm just resting my eyes."

"You're not resting your eyes, Bran—you're dying!"

He blinked, suddenly alert. "Dying? I'm not dying! Why would you even say that?"

"Then talk to me," she insisted, blowing through her exposed fingers to try and warm them. "Sing me a song."

"Sing?" His agitation ushered in a fit of violent coughing. "Blood of the Gods, girl, can't you see I'm dying here!"

She chose an arrow from the crate, checked to make sure it was straight and sound. "Hum, then. I don't care." She nocked the arrow. Sighted down its length. "Just let me know you're still alive."

Tam watched in awe as Rose sheared through two of her undead doubles at once. She pivoted on her heel, plunging *Vellichor* through the chest of another. She let go of the hilt and activated her bracers; her scimitars leapt from their scabbards, and Rose sent them spinning away. *Thistle* sank into the chest of a red-bearded merc and carried him off his feet. *Thorn* cut the wing from a diving harpy—the bird-woman veered wildly and thumped off the roof above Tam.

Mere seconds after she put it there, Rose reclaimed *Vellichor* from the thrall in which she'd buried it and whirled away, hewing its head off on the backswing. She leapt to take on her next opponent, the dazzling glare of a sylvan sun flashing from her blade.

The light scythed across the face of the Winter Queen, drawing her eye. Tam saw the sorceress flinch as she recognized first the Archon's sword, and then, a split second later, the woman wielding it, whose golden hair gleamed like a new crown.

The entire Horde hitched on a stolen breath, and for a moment Astra's labyrinthine concentration faltered. Her fliers hovered in the sky, and a thousand listless corpses were stuck down as they froze in place, a mirror of their mistress's stupefaction.

The sound of splintering wood threatened to derail Tam's concentration. The muscles in her arms were complaining that she'd held her shot for too long, but she kept her eyes on Rose, waiting for the signal she knew was coming. Bran was humouring her, humming a weak, wavering rendition of the song that was his sister's lasting legacy.

Freecloud, inexplicably, ignored a thrall's clumsy chop at his ribs as he moved to close the distance between himself and Rose. The blade bit into his side, yet he charged past without bothering to retaliate.

What? Tam frowned. *What is he doing?*

The druin sliced through one enemy while blocking the incoming hammer of another with nothing but an upraised arm. The blow snapped his limb like a twig, but the druin bowled his opponent over and staggered on. He put *Madrigal* through the face of another thrall and leapt over its falling corpse without bothering to retrieve his sword.

Tam's eyes flickered to Rose, who was too busy fending off phantoms of her former self to see Ios, Telltale's undead baroness, lunge at her from behind.

Oh. Realization rocked Tam like a punch, except it hurt *so much more* than a fist. A part of her, she realized, had always known it would come to this.

Rose dispatched the last of her adversaries and turned, too late, to defend herself.

Freecloud leapt between them, his back square to the assassin's thrusting blade.

Bran's humming filtered through the sudden, soul-cleaving silence, a terribly appropriate underscore to the tragedy unfolding below.

Every battle has a cost, Freecloud had told her once. *Even the ones we win.*

By the time Tam blinked tears from her eyes it was over. For a heartbeat Rose and Freecloud stood frozen face-to-face, so close they might have shared a single breath between them, and then Freecloud was falling, dying, dead at her feet, and the assassin was headless, tipping backward as blood fountained from the stump of her neck.

Rose didn't stop to mourn, though her heart must be breaking.

She didn't scream, though her soul would be crying out loud.

She let grief and fury and love drive her onward, lifting her blue-sky blade like a pennant as she hurtled toward the Winter Queen.

Astra stepped to meet her, a sneer pulling at her lips. *"Now . . ."* she seethed.

Rose summoned *Thorn* to hand.

" . . . you . . ."

She hurled the scimitar at Astra's head.

" . . . are . . ."

It missed, of course. Because you couldn't kill a druin by attacking it directly.

" . . . mine!"

Their swords clashed. Sparks and snowflakes dissolved between them. Rose's impetus carried her through the space Astra had occupied a moment earlier. She skidded, spun, lashed out again.

The Winter Queen reeled under Rose's assault, and Tam, whose whole world was pinned to the point of an arrow, saw black smoke curl from Astra's lips as the dead began rising around them.

Rose attacked, and attacked, and attacked—unable to overcome the druin's prescience. A wild swipe knocked the blackmetal crown from Astra's head, but left Rose hopelessly exposed.

The Winter Queen turned an evasive step into a deadly counterstrike. Her banshee blade cut an inexorable arc toward Rose, who twisted, turned her face toward her bandmate on the balcony above, and nodded.

Bran's humming fell silent. The clamour of Slowhand's fight with Hawkshaw ceased to exist. Tam's muscles relaxed. Her heart constricted like an hourglass, until the space between one trickling heartbeat and the next stretched on forever. She'd been aiming the arrow already. All that remained was to let it go.

She drew a breath.

She let it go.

"Sorry?" Tam had asked a short while earlier.

Rose stepped closer, lowering her voice. "I said you're going to kill the Winter Queen."

"That's impossible."

"They said killing the Simurg was impossible." Rose grinned. "We did it twice."

"But she'll see it coming," Tam said. "If I shoot her, she'll just dodge it anyway."

Rose put a hand on her shoulder, leaning closer still. "Then shoot *me*."

Tam's aim was true. The arrow went streaking toward Rose, who *should* have used her sword to parry Astra's strike, but instead she raised it like a shield and angled the blade *just* so.

The steel-tipped shaft deflected off *Vellichor* and tore a ragged hole in the Winter Queen's throat. Astra tried to speak, but could only gasp around the black ichor boiling from her ravaged neck. And Rose, her side split open by the druin's sword, rammed *Vellichor* through the part of Astra's chest where her heart used to be. The sorceress died that instant. Her glamour faded, pale flesh succumbing to the wrath of centuries as she sagged to the ground.

Tam heard a heavy thump behind her, and assumed that Hawkshaw, whether or not he deserved it, was finally at peace.

The entire Horde was collapsing at once. Without Astra's magic to compel them, they slumped like puppets cut from their sorcerous strings. Wyverns and wolfbats spiralled from the sky as the fires in their eyes blew out.

Rose was still on her feet. The Winter Queen's sword was lodged in her side, and Tam (watching in grief and disbelief past the blurred arc of her bow) winced as Rose pried the blade free with bloodied fingers. She pitched forward, but turned her momentum into a lurching step, then another, stumbling around broken bodies and shattered arms until she stood over Freecloud, lying dead on a bed of bloody Roses.

The whole city seemed frozen but for snowflakes falling, and falling, and falling.

And Rose fell with them.

Epilogue

The Promise

The following is an excerpt from *The Wyld Heart*, the first memoir of Tam Hashford. Select passages can be found in the song titled *The Ballad of Bloody Rose*, widely believed to have been written by Tam Hashford as well. *The Wyld Heart* was later adapted for the stage by Kitagra the Undying and retitled *Fable: A Love Story*.

> *Conthas burned to the ground. Apparently, this is a regular occurrence. Every few decades or so a fire goes unchecked and razes the entire city to ash. The locals think of it as a time of renewal. A chance to start over, to sweep away the old and build something new.*
>
> *New taverns, for instance. New pubs, new scratch-dens; new gambling holes and fighting pits. New ale-houses, dice-houses, tap-houses, and whore-houses. From what I understand, Conthas is like some drug-addled, sex-crazed, booze-swilling phoenix that refuses to stay dead.*
>
> *But not this time. This time, it died for good.*
>
> *Everyone's got a theory as to why this is. Cura blames the weather. She says that everyone smart enough to skip town before the Horde arrived had*

settled in Brycliffe or Fivecourt by the time spring rolled around, and couldn't be bothered to return. Roderick thinks that since more monsters are being bred in captivity and less captured in the Heartwyld, it was inevitable that Conthas—for decades a staging point for bands brave enough to enter the forest—would eventually outlive its usefulness.

I've got a different theory: I think it's haunted.

Now, I'm not saying there are ghosts and ghouls kicking through the ashes every night (although there probably are), but something about it just feels . . . off. All told, nearly two hundred thousand men, women, and monsters died in that valley, and while the fire took care of their bodies, I suspect a part of them lingers still. There's an almost palpable sense of recrimination in the air. An eerie disquiet that begs the question, "How did it come to this?"

There is nothing, I think, so wasteful—or so pointlessly tragic—as a battle that should never have been fought in the first place. All of us lost something at Conthas. Some more than others. Some so much more than others.

We waited out the winter at Clay's inn, which the Horde had left untouched as it came south. Coverdale, too, was spared its wrath. Astra didn't care about destroying our homes. It was our souls she was after.

Both of Brune's legs were broken when that "damn dirty elephant" (as he puts it) fell on him, so he spent the following months recuperating by the fire and drinking Clay's whiskey while swapping stories with Roderick and Uncle Bran—whose liver had, in fact, fallen victim to Hawkshaw's blade. Luckily, Moog happened to know a surgeon who successfully replaced Bran's skewered organ with one belonging to a recently deceased orc.

If you're interested in the benefits associated with having the liver of an orc, feel free to find my uncle and ask him for yourself. Seriously—he won't shut up about it.

Cura wasn't much for company in the weeks after the battle. She would sleep for days, and sometimes stare at nothing for hours at a time. Often, I'd find her touching fingertips to her skin, tracing the scars that were no longer visible. Not to me, anyway. Her inklings—the memories, and the people they represented—were such an intimate part of Cura's past, and so deeply ingrained in her persona, that I wonder if she'll ever get used to living without them.

She and I... Well, it's complicated. I won't get into it here, mostly because I'm not sure how to explain it myself. She makes me happy. I try to do the same. We laugh together, cry together, and sleep together. Need we call it anything more?

She's my best friend. And yeah, I love her.

Don't tell her I said that.

Speaking of love, Lady Jain and Daon Doshi were married that spring in the yard behind Slowhand's inn. Roderick, of all people, stood witness for the captain, while Jain's bridesmaids totalled no less than all seventeen of the Silk Arrows.

I heard Rod say to Doshi as they filed down the aisle, "You're gonna need a bigger boat."

There was dancing, and drinking, and fireworks (courtesy of Arcandius Moog). At some point I stumbled off to pee and found Clay Cooper standing beneath the budding maple in his front yard. There was a newly installed headstone at his feet, and I could see crude letters etched in starlight across its face.

A grave for Gabriel, I realized. I asked him what it said.

He replied, "We were giants, once."

When Brune could walk without crutches, we made plans to go north. Cura and I were headed for the coast (I'd always wanted to visit Freeport, and she insisted I see an Aldean sunset), but I had a stop to make in Ardburg first.

On the morning we left Slowhand's, Tally begged her parents to let her come with us. She was almost fifteen, she insisted—practically a woman grown—and while it looked as if Clay might indulge her, Ginny was having none of it.

We were almost to Coverdale by the time she caught up. Moog, who was accompanying us as far as Oddsford, made the girl swear up and down she hadn't run away from home. As proof of her parents' blessing, she pointed out the familiar blackwood shield strapped to her back: a parting gift from her father.

I suspect Tally would have followed us regardless of whether or not she had permission to do so. I was her age, once. Hell, I'm practically her age now. And what can I say? The world is big, the young are restless, and girls just want to have fun.

On the way to Ardburg, Brune and Roderick began discussing their next venture—one that reflected the change of heart they'd had over the past several months. Starting in Ardburg, they would buy out the contracts of so-called monsters being sold or enslaved for sport in the arena. Those willing to give coexistence a whirl would be found gainful employment as crafters or labourers, while those too feral or embittered would be set free far from any human settlement.

There will be kinks, of course, but it's a noble ambition. If our war against the Winter Queen taught us anything, it's that evil thrives on division. It stokes the embers of pride and prejudice until they become an inferno that might one day devour us all.

As we journeyed north it became increasingly clear that although we may have saved the world, we sure as hell hadn't fixed it. Inspired by the successive victories of the Brumal Horde, creatures who hadn't yet learned of its fate were in open rebellion all over Grandual—which didn't do our hope of reconciliation any favours.

To make matters worse, Death Cults had begun springing up in each of the five courts. Adherents of the Winter Queen were taking up necromancy like it was knitting, which inevitably led to whole towns being sacked and plagues of undead roaming unchecked through the countryside.

Grandual needed heroes, but many of the bands it relied on for protection had been decimated by the Brumal Horde, and the rest were too busy touring arenas to lift a finger. You'll never guess who it was that came to the realm's aid. Go on, I'll wait.

Give up?

It was Contha.

As winter thawed, the Exarch's golems marched in their thousands from Lamneth's depths. He sent emissaries to every court in Grandual and agreed to send constructs to any town or city in need. The Sultana of Narmeer refused his aid, but others (Queen Lilith of Agria, for instance, whose standing army had been utterly destroyed by the Brumal Horde) accepted readily. By now, I'll bet, every hamlet in Agria boasts a golem defender, and I've heard that duramantium knights patrol the roads into Fivecourt.

What changed the Exarch's mind? Beats me. It's possible that meeting his granddaughter made him realize that druins and humans weren't so different after all. More likely, he feels guilty for having withheld his help when we needed it most, and is trying to honour Freecloud's sacrifice by serving those he died to protect.

Whatever Contha's reasons, the world is a safer place because of him. And yet I can't help but recall his unwillingness to acknowledge Wren in any meaningful way, or to look anyone but his trueborn son in the eye. I should cut him some slack, I suppose. As Freecloud once pointed out: His father spent centuries alone in the dark, so it makes sense he'd end up a reclusive weirdo.

We reached Ardburg late one evening and took rooms at the Cornerstone. Tera and Tiamax marvelled over how "grown up" I looked, while Edwick insisted on hearing the song I'd written for Brune. The next day I took Cura on a tour of the city. We visited the king's bathhouse and took a stroll through the Monster Market. I introduced her to Willow, who flashed me a conspiratorial wink as we went our way.

I ducked into a tailor's shop shortly after. Cura gave me one of her looks when I came out, but said nothing.

Eventually we arrived at the house I'd once called home. My father was away at the mill, but I figured he'd be back soon. I peered through the kitchen window, and was relieved to see the place wasn't covered in dust or littered with empty bottles. I'm not sure why, but it surprised me to see he'd left my chair at the table along with my mother's.

I ached to go inside, to show Cura my old room and introduce her to Tuck. When she asked why I couldn't, I told her about the promise I'd made to my father on the morning I left: to never return, and so never break his heart if one day I failed to show up.

I didn't like it, of course, but I could understand it. And yet . . .

I was sure he'd have heard about Conthas by now. He would know that Fable went toe-to-toe with the Winter Queen, and he would know how it ended. If he never saw me again, my father would almost certainly assume I was dead. He would blame Rose for having lured me away. And himself, of course, for letting me go.

I heard a meow, and looked down to find Threnody purring at my feet. I picked her up and gave her a snuggle before Cura and I hurried off. Thren followed us for half a block before doubling back.

In the days and nights since then I have often imagined my father arriving home that afternoon to find Thren waiting on the step. It's possible he unlocked the door and let the cat in without bothering to acknowledge her, but I think he probably picked her up to say hello.

At which point he would have noticed the slim yellow ribbon I'd tied around her neck.

I hope, in time, he'll forgive me for breaking my promise.

Occasionally, someone—usually a child—will ask me if Bloody Rose is dead.

She is, and she isn't.

The stories generally agree that Rose and the Winter Queen killed one another, but the truth (as is often the case) is more complicated than that.

To begin with, the woman we knew as Bloody Rose was a fiction all along. She was a guise assumed by Golden Gabe's rebellious teenage daughter, who was so desperate to ascend the pedestal upon which the world had placed her father that she sacrificed her whole identity to do so. Rose wasn't only a mercenary—she was an actress as well, and had inhabited her role so thoroughly even she had forgotten it wasn't real.

I would argue that Bloody Rose died in a forest south of Coverdale shortly after her father passed away. I can still hear her scream echoing in the trees, and when she'd emerged a short while later, there was something *different about her. If you'll permit me a none-too-subtle analogy: When you clip a rose at its stem, nothing about it changes immediately. Its thorns remain sharp. Its petals are beautiful, still. But little by little its majesty fades, and I believe that when Gabriel died, Bloody Rose was doomed as well.*

In any event, she did not survive the battle at Conthas. She died a hero, fighting on behalf of people she'd never met for a future she wouldn't be a part of. And because of that, I suspect, she will have finally attained the immortality she'd been after all her life.

The bards tell us that we live so long as there are those alive who remember us. In that case, I think it's safe to say that Bloody Rose will live forever.

It was growing dark by the time she spied the ruins through the trees ahead. She skirted the battlements until she found the breach where Clay Cooper was said to have stood against a hundred bloodthirsty cannibals. Clay used to joke that he'd only counted ninety-nine, but she guessed both numbers were largely inflated. Saga's bard hadn't survived the battle, so the band themselves were left to tell their tale.

The keep's gate was barred. That was good. This was the Heartwyld, after all. Fell things lurked in the forest, especially at night. She climbed the pitted stone wall and hauled herself between two mouldering crenellations, wincing as the stitches in her side threatened to tear. She took a running leap over a gap in the ramparts, then came to the crumbling stair that led into the fortress itself. It was dark inside, so she withdrew the spiny shell from her bag and blew into it until its pale pink glow was sufficient to light her way.

It had been years since she'd walked these halls, but she knew them well. Saga wasn't the only band that had withstood a siege in this place. While not exactly sure of her destination, she had some idea as to where to find what she was looking for. Or whom, rather.

She heard a sound—a voice—and straightaway her hands began to shake. Her mouth went dry, and her heart hammered like a sinner seeking refuge behind a chapel door. She saw light ahead, and when she turned the next corner she found two figures seated before a crackling fire. One of them was huge—a burnished bronze construct whose teakettle head was tilted as he listened intently to the excited chatter of his companion. The other was . . .

"Wren," she said.

The sylf turned. The fire's light silvered her hair and threw her face into shadow. For a breathless moment, she wondered if the girl would even recognize her.

"Mommy?"

She'd forgotten how to breathe—or speak, for that matter—so instead she went to her knees and spread her arms as her daughter hurtled toward her.

For so many years she had borne the burden of a name not quite her own. She'd been looking forward to living without it—to being *Rose* again, after all this time. But now, it seemed, she was destined to live by yet another alias.

Mommy. She smiled, breathing in the freshwater scent of her daughter's hair. *I like the sound of that.*

Acknowledgments

Writing a book as an aspiring author and writing as a published one are, I've recently come to learn, two very different journeys. You think you've got the lay of the land, but in fact the map has changed and you're wandering blind into a territory you thought you'd conquered.

Thankfully, there were a few guiding stars I used to keep myself on course, none more constant than my dear friend Eugene, who was endlessly supportive, helpfully critical, and always willing to talk me through a scene, a character, or the whole bloody book if necessary. I'd be hopelessly lost without him.

Heather Adams (my agent) and Lindsey Hall (my former editor) were both invaluable sources of wisdom. Lindsey pulled double duty as my therapist on several occasions, and I will be forever grateful for our relationship, both as professionals and friends.

Which brings me to Bradley (my new editor) and Emily (my UK editor). Working with them this time around was an absolute joy. Whether I was fanboying over video game references with Bradley or debating the true meaning of "smirk" with Emily, this book was made *so much better* because of them. They are both amazing at what they do, and I'm honoured to walk this road alongside them.

I'm thankful as well to everyone at Orbit who acts as champions for books they so clearly love, and to the artists—Richard

Anderson and Tim Paul—whose cover art and maps (respectively) inspire me daily.

Speaking of champions, I find myself indebted to literally thousands of readers, writers, bloggers, and book reviewers who read *Kings of the Wyld* and said nice things about it online, or to friends, or in their local bookstores. Special thanks to the members of the *Fantasy Faction* and *Grimdark Fiction Readers and Writers* groups on Facebook, and to the communities at r/fantasy and Goodreads. I am so deeply grateful to you all. Also, both Scott McCauley and Felix Ortiz have created some truly beautiful art based on my books, and I am humbled by them both.

If I listed by name every new friend I've made since getting published I'd have the highest daily word count of my life. Instead, I'll thank Mike, Petros, Petrik, Melanie, Ed, and RJ here, and promise to buy a beer for everyone else when I see them next.

A great many authors have been tremendously supportive as well (here's looking at you, Sykes), but Sebastien de Castell and Christian Cameron have each gone above and beyond to offer valuable advice and even-more-treasured friendship over the past year.

I owe the most, however, to my family, which includes Bryan Cheyne, Natasha McLeod, and the infinitely patient Hilary Cosgrove. My parents continue to be endlessly encouraging and have hand-sold my books like they were Bibles on the eve of Judgement Day. I will never be able to thank them enough for all they've done. Also deserving of gratitude are the newest members of my family: my stepsister Angela, my niece Morley, and my nephew Maclean. I love you all, and my life is so much richer for having you in it.

Lastly, Tyler.

There aren't enough words in the world to convey how proud I am of the man you've become, and how grateful I am to have been born your brother. I dedicated *Bloody Rose* to you, but in truth every word of every book, every triumph big and small, is ours to share. I love you, Ty.

extras

www.orbitbooks.net

about the author

Nicholas Eames was born to parents of infinite patience and unstinting support in Wingham, Ontario. Though he attended college for theatre arts, he gave up acting to pursue the much more attainable profession of "epic fantasy novelist." Kings of the Wyld was his first novel. Nicholas loves black coffee, neat whiskey, the month of October, and video games. He currently lives in Ontario, Canada, and is very probably writing at this moment.

Find out more about Nicholas Eames and other Orbit authors by registering for the free monthly newsletter at www.orbitbooks.net

if you enjoyed

BLOODY ROSE

look out for

AGE OF ASSASSINS

by

RJ Barker

TO CATCH AN ASSASSIN, USE AN ASSASSIN...

*Girton Club-Foot, apprentice to the land's best assassin, still has
much to learn about the art of taking lives. But his latest mission tasks
Girton and his master with a far more difficult challenge: to save a life.
Someone, or many someones, is trying to kill the heir to the throne, and
it is up to Girton and his master to uncover the traitor and
prevent the prince's murder.*

*In a kingdom on the brink of civil war and a castle thick with lies Girton
finds friends he never expected, responsibilities he never wanted, and a
conspiracy that could destroy an entire land.*

Prologue

Darik the smith was last among the desolate. The Landsman made him kneel with a kick to the back of his knees, forcing his head down so he knelt and stared at the line between the good green grass and the putrid yellow desert of the sourlands. Nothing grew in the sourlands. A sorcerer had taken the life of the land for his own magics many years ago, before Darik's parents were born, and only death was found there now. A foul-smelling wind blew his long brown hair into his face and, ten paces away, the first of the desolate was weeping as she waited for the blade – Kina the herdsgirl, no more than a child and the only other from his village. The voice of the Landsman, huge and strong in his grass-green armour, was surprisingly gentle as he spoke to her, a whisper no louder than the knife leaving its scabbard.

"Shh, child. Soonest done, soonest over," he said, and then the knife bit into her neck and her tears were stilled for ever. Darik glanced between the bars of his hair and saw Kina's body jerking as blood fountained from her neck and made dark, twisting, red patterns on the stinking yellow ground – silhouettes of death and life.

He had hoped to marry Kina when she came of age.

Darik was cold but it was not the wind that made him shiver;

he had been cold ever since the sorcerer hunters had come for him. It was the first time in fifteen years of life that the sweat on his skin wasn't because of the fierce heat of the forge. The moisture that had clung to him since was a different sweat, a new sweat, a cold frightened animal sweat that hadn't stopped since they locked the shackles on his wrists. It seemed so long ago now.

The weeks of marching across the Tired Lands had been like a dream but, looking back, the most dreamlike moment of all was that moment when they had called his name. He hadn't been surprised – it was as if he'd sold himself to a hedge spirit long ago and had been waiting for someone to come and collect on the debt his whole life.

"Shh, child. Soonest done, soonest over." The knife does its necessary work on another of the desolate, and a second set of bloody sigils spatters out on the filthy yellow ground. Is there meaning there? Is there some message for him? In this place between life and death, close to embracing the watery darkness that swallowed the dead gods, are they talking to him?

Or is it just blood?

And death.

And fear.

"Shh, child. Soonest done, soonest over." The next one begs for life in the moments before the blade bites. Darik doesn't know that one's name, never asked him, never saw the point because once you're one of the desolate you're dead. There is no way out, no point running. The brand on your forehead shows you for what they think you are – magic user, destroyer, abomination, sorcerer. You're only good for bleeding out on the dry dead earth, a sacrifice of blood to heal the land. No one will hide you, no one will pity you when magic has made the dirt so weak people can barely feed their children. There is the sound of choking, fighting, begging as the knife does its work and the thirsty ground drinks the life stolen from it.

Does Darik feel something in that moment of death? Is there a vibration? Is there a twinge that runs from Darik's knees, up his legs through his blood to squirm in his belly? Or is that only fear?

"Shh, child. Soonest done, soonest over."

The slice, the cough, blood on the ground, and this time it is unmistakable — a something that shoots up through his body. It sets his teeth on edge, it makes the roots of his hair hurt. Everything starts changing around him: the land is a lens and he is its focus, his mind a bright burning spot of light. What is this feeling? What is it? Were they right?

Are they right?

A hand on his forehead.

Dark worms moving through his flesh.

The hiss of the blade leaving the scabbard.

He sweats, hot as any day at the forge.

His head pulled back, his neck stretched.

Closing his eyes, he sees a world of silvered lines and shadows.

The cold touch of the blade against his neck.

A pause, like the hiss of hot metal in water, like the moment before the geyser of scorching steam hisses out around his hand and the blade is set.

The sting of a sharp edge against his skin.

And the grass is talking, and the land is talking, and the trees are talking, and all in a language he cannot understand but at the same time he knows exactly what is being said. Is this what a hedging lord sounds like?

The creak of leather armour.

"I will save you." Is it the voice of Fitchgrass of the fields?

"No!"

"Only listen . . . " This near the souring is it Coil the yellower?

"Shh, shh, child." The Landsman's voice, soothing, calming. "Soonest done, soonest over."

"I can save you." Too far from the rivers for Blue Watta.

"No." But Darik's word is a whisper drowned in fear of the approaching void. Time slows further as the knife slices though his skin, cutting through layer after layer in search of the black vessels of his life.

"Let me save you." Or is it the worst of all of them? Is it Dark Ungar speaking?

"No," he says. But the word is weak and the will to fight is gone.

"Let us?"

"Yes!"

An explosion of ... of?

Something.

Something he doesn't know or understand but he recognises it – it has always been within him. It is something he's fought, denied, run from. A familiar voice from his childhood, the imaginary friend that frightened his mother and she told him to forget so he pushed it away, far away. But now, when he needs it the most, it is there.

The blade is gone from his neck.

He opens his eyes.

The world is out of focus – a haze of yellows – and a high whine fills his ears the way it would when his father clouted him for "dangerous talk". The green grass beneath Darik's knees is gone, replaced by yellow fronds that flake away at his touch like morning ash in the forge. He stares at his hands. They are the same – the same scars, the same half-healed cuts and nicks, the same old burns and calluses.

Around him is perfect half-circle of dead grass, as if the sourlands have taken a bite out of the lush grasslands at their edge

His wrists are no longer bound in cold metal.

Is he lost, gone? Has he made a deal with something terrible? But it doesn't feel like that; it feels like this was something in him, something that has always been in him, just waiting for the right moment.

He can feel the souring like an ache.

There had been four Landsmen to guard the five desolate. Now the guards are blurry smears of torn, angular metal, red flesh and sharp white bone.

Darik rubbed his eyes and forced himself up, staggering like a man waking from too long a sleep. A movement in the corner of his eye pulled at his attention. One of the Landsmen was still alive, on his back and trying to scuttle away on his elbows as Darik approached. The smith knelt by the Landsman and placed his big hands on either side of his head. It would be easy to finish him, just a single twist of his big arms and the Landsman's neck would snap like a charcoaled stick. He willed his arms to move but instead found himself staring at the Landsman. Not much older than he was and scared, so scared. The Landsman's lips were moving and at first the only sound is the high whine of the world, then the words come like the approaching thunder of a mount's feet as it gallops towards him.

"I'msorryI'msorryI'msorryI'msorry . . . "

"It's wrong," Darik said, "this is all wrong," but the Landsman's eyes were far away, lost in fear and past understanding. His mouth moving.

". . . I'msorryI'msorryI'msorry . . . "

Darik stared a little longer, the killing muscles in his arms tensing. Now his vision had cleared he saw beyond the broken bodies of the other Landsmen to the shattered corpses of those who had died beside him. They had been picked up and tossed away on the winds of his fury.

Darik leaned in close to the Landsman.

"This has to stop," he said, and let go of the man's head. The words kept coming.

"... I'msorryI'msorryI'msorry."

He could see Kina's corpse, dead at the hand of the knights then shredded into a red mess by his magic.

"I forgive you," said Darik through tears. The Landsman slumped to the floor, eyes wide in shock as the smith walked away.

Inside the thick muscles of Darik's arms black veins are screaming.

Chapter 1

We were attempting to enter Castle Maniyadoc through the night soil gate and my master was in the sort of foul mood only an assassin forced to wade through a week's worth of shit can be. I was far more sanguine about our situation. As an assassin's apprentice you become inured to foulness. It is your lot.

"Girton," said Merela Karn. That is my master's true name, though if I were to refer to her as anything other than "Master" I would be swiftly and painfully reprimanded. "Girton," she said, "if one more king, queen or any other member of the blessed classes thinks a night soil gate is the best way to make an unseen entrance to their castle, you are to run them through."

"Really, Master?"

"No, not really," she whispered into the night, her breath a cloud in the cold air. "Of course not really. You are to politely suggest that walking in the main gate dressed as masked priests of the dead gods is less conspicuous. Show me a blessed who doesn't know that the night soil gate is an easy way in for an enemy and I will show you a corpse."

"You have shown me many corpses, Master."

"Be quiet, Girton."

My master is not a lover of humour. Not many assassins are; it is a profession that attracts the miserable and the melancholic. I would never put myself into either of those categories, but I was bought into the profession and did not join by choice.

"Dead gods in their watery graves!" hissed my master into the night. "They have not even opened the grate for us." She swung herself aside whispering, "Move, Girton!" I slipped and slid crabwise on the filthy grass of the slope running from the river below us up to the base of the towering castle walls. Foulness farted out of the grating to join the oozing stream that ran down the motte and joined the river.

A silvery smudge marred the riverbank in the distance; it looked like a giant paint-covered thumb had been placed over it. In the moonlight it was quite beautiful, but we had passed near as we sneaked in, and I knew it was the same livid yellow as the other sourings which scarred the Tired Lands. There was no telling how old this souring was, and I wondered how big it had been originally and how much blood had been spilled to shrink it to its present size. I glanced up at the keep. This side had few windows and I thought the small souring could be new, but that was a silly, childish thought. The blades of the Landsmen kept us safe from sorcerers and the magic which sucked the life from the land. There had been no significant magic used in the Tired Lands since the Black Sorcerer had risen, and he had died before I had been born. No, what I saw was simply one of many sores on the land – a place as dead as the ancient sorcerer who made it. I turned from the souring and did my best to imagine it wasn't there, though I was sure I could smell it, even over the high stink of the night soil drain.

"Someone will pay for arranging this, Girton, I swear," said my master. Her head vanished into the darkness as she bobbed down to examine the grate once more. "This is sealed with a simple five-lever lock." She did not even breathe heavily despite holding her entire weight on one arm and one leg jammed into stonework the black of old wounds. "You can open this, Girton. You need as much practice with locks as you can get."

"Thank you, Master," I said. I did not mean it. It was cold, and a lock is far harder to manipulate when it is cold.

And when it is covered in shit.

Unlike my master, I am no great acrobat. I am hampered by a clubbed foot, so I used my weight to hold me tight against the grating even though it meant getting covered in filth. On the stone columns either side of the grate the forlorn remains of minor gods had been almost chipped away. On my right only a pair of intricately carved antlers remained, and on my left a pair of horns and one solemn eye stared out at me. I turned from the eye and brought out my picks, sliding them into the lock with shaking fingers and feeling within using the slim metal rods.

"What if there are dogs, Master?"

"We kill them, Girton."

There is something rewarding in picking a lock. Something very satisfying about the click of the barrels and the pressure vanishing as the lock gives way to skill. It is not quite as rewarding done while a castle's toilets empty themselves over your body, but a happy life is one where you take your pleasures where you can.

"It is open, Master."

"Good. You took too long."

"Thank you, Master." It was difficult to tell in the darkness, but I was sure she smiled before she nodded me forward. I hesitated at the edge of the pitch-dark drain.

"It looks like the sort of place you'd find Dark Ungar, Master."

"The hedgings are just like the gods, Girton – stories to scare the weak-minded. There's nothing in there but stink and filth. You've been through worse. Go."

I slithered through the gate, managing to make sure no part

of my skin or clothing remained clean, and into the tunnel that led through the keep's curtain wall. Somewhere beyond I could hear the lumpy splashes of night soil being shovelled into the stream that ran over my feet. The living classes in the villages keep their piss and night soil and sell it to the tanneries and dye makers, but the blessed classes are far too grand for that, and their castles shovel their filth out into the rivers – as if to gift it to the populace. I have crawled through plenty of filth in my fifteen years, from the thankful, the living and the blessed; it all smells equally bad.

Once we had squeezed through the opening we were able to stand, and my master lit a glow-worm lamp, a small wick that burns with a dim light that can be amplified or shut off by a cleverly interlocking set of mirrors. Then she lifted a gloved hand and pointed at her ear.

I listened.

Above the happy gurgle of the stream running down the channel – water cares nothing for the medium it travels through – I heard the voices of men as they worked. We would have to wait for them to move before we could proceed into the castle proper, and whenever we have to wait I count out the seconds the way my master taught me – one, my master. Two, my master. Three, my master – ticking away in my mind like the balls of a water clock as I stand idle, filth swirling round my ankles and my heart beating out a nervous tattoo.

You get used to the smell. That is what people say.

It is not true.

Eight minutes and nineteen seconds passed before we finally heard the men laugh and move on. Another signal from my master and I started to count again. Five minutes this time. Human nature being the way it is you cannot guarantee someone will not leave something and come back for it.

When the five minutes had passed we made our way up the night soil passage until we could see dim light dancing on walls caked with centuries of filth. My own height plus a half above us was the shovelling room. Above us the door creaked and then we heard footsteps, followed by voices.

". . . so now we're done and Alsa's in the heir's guard. Fancy armour and more pay."

"It's a hedging's deal. I'd sooner poke out my own eyes and find magic in my hand than serve the fat bear, he's a right yellower."

"Service is mother though, aye?"

Laughter followed. My master glanced up through the hole, chewing on her lip. She held up two fingers before speaking in the Whisper-That-Flies-to-the-Ear so only I could hear her.

"Guards. You will have to take care of them," she said. I nodded and started to move. "Don't kill them unless you absolutely have to."

"It will be harder."

"I know," she said and leaned over, putting her hands together to make a stirrup. "But I will be here."

I breathe out.

I breathe in.

I placed my foot on her hands and, with a heave, she propelled me up and into the room. I came out of the hole landing with my back to the two men. *Seventeenth iteration: the Drunk's Reversal.* Rolling forward, twisting and coming up facing guards dressed in kilted skirts, leather helms and poorly kept-up boiled-leather chest pieces splashed with red paint. They stared at me dumbly, as if I were the hedging lord Blue Watta appearing from the deeps. Both of them held clubs, though they had stabswords at their sides. I wondered if they were here to guard against rats rather than people.

"Assassin?" said the guard on the left. He was smaller than his friend, though both were bigger than me.

"Aye," said the other, a huge man. "Assassin." His grip shifted on his club.

They should have gone for the door and reinforcements.

My hand was hovering over the throwing knives at my belt in case they did. Instead the smaller man grinned, showing missing teeth and black stumps.

"I imagine there's a good price on the head of an assassin, Joam, even if it's a crippled child." He started forward. The bigger man grinned and followed his friend's lead. They split up to avoid the hole in the centre of the room and I made my move. *Second iteration: the Quicksteps.* Darting forward, I chose the smaller of the two as my first target – the other had not drawn his blade. He swung at me with his club and I stepped backwards, feeling the draught of the hard wood through the air. He thrust with his dagger but was too far away to reach my flesh. When his swipe missed he jumped back, expecting me to counter-attack, but I remained unmoving. All I had wanted was to get an idea of his skill before I closed with him. He did not impress me, his friend impressed me even less; rather than joining the attack he was watching, slack-jawed, as if we put on a show for him.

"Joam," shouted my opponent, "don't be just standing there!" The bigger man trundled forward, though he was in no hurry. I didn't want to be fighting two at the same time if I could help it so decided to finish the smaller man quickly. *First iteration: the Precise Steps.* Forward into the range of his weapons. He thrust with his stabsword. *Ninth iteration: the Bow.* Middle of my body bowing backwards to avoid the blade. With his other hand he swung his club at my head. I ducked. As his arm came over my head I grabbed his elbow and pushed, making him lose his

nce, and as he struggled to right himself I found purchase on
the rim of his chest piece. *Tenth iteration: the Broom*. Sweeping my
leg round I knocked his feet from under him. With a push I sent
him flailing into the hole so he cracked his head on the edge of
it on his way down.

I turned to his friend, Joam.

Had the dead gods given Joam any sense he would have seen
his friend easily beaten and made for the door. Instead, Joam's
face had the same look on it I had seen on a bull as it smashed its
head against a wall in a useless attempt to get at a heifer beyond –
the look of something too stupid and angry to know it was in a
fight it couldn't win.

"I'm a kill you, assassin," he said and lumbered slowly forward, smacking his club against his hand. I had no time to wait
for him; the longer we fought the more likely it was that someone would hear us and bring more guards. I jumped over the
hole and landed behind Joam. He turned, swinging his club. *Fif-
teenth Iteration: the Oar*. Bending at the hip and bringing my body
down and round so it went under his swing. At the lowest point
I punched forward, landing a solid blow between Joam's legs.
He screeched, dropping his weapon and doubling over. With a
jerk I brought my body up so the back of my skull smashed into
his face, sending the big man staggering back, blood streaming
from a broken nose. It was a blow that would have felled most,
but Joam was a strong man. Though his eyes were bleary and
unfocused he still stood. *Eighteenth iteration: the Water Clock*. I ran
at him, grabbing his thick belt and using it as a fulcrum to swing
myself round and up so I could lock my legs around his throat.
Joam's hand grasped blindly for the blade at his hip. I drew it and
tossed it away before he reached it. His hands spidered down my
body searching for and locking around my throat, but Joam's
strength, though great, was fleeing as he choked.